Spire of Tavnir

THE TINDORIA CHRONICLES BOOK 2

Spire of Tavnir

Hannah Pennington

May It Happen Press

Praise for Spire of Tavnir

"*Spire of Tavnir* captures the essence of adventure, unfolding the fantasy world of Tindoria to engulf you in enthralling quests, and reveal prophecies and magical secrets! I love how the battle of light against darkness incorporates an aspect of Christian truths, and I'm intensely anticipating the third installment!"
- CHARITY A. LAND AUTHOR OF THE LEGACY OF CHEVOLTA series

"Whoa! I was not prepared for the ride *Spire of Tavnir* took me on! This book truly kicked things into high gear and had me on the edge of my seat! In the midst of heightened stakes, the story is grounded in truth and so relatable to the Christian walk. I didn't want to put it down!"
- ANGELA KNOTTS MORSE AUTHOR OF THE SON OF AVARIA TRILOGY

"Interesting and thrilling. Hannah Pennington never fails to enchant! Each chapter unfolds with pristine quests, stunning secrets, and mystical elements of Tindora. With battles of the past, betrayal and vengeance looming, and an intriguing prophecy, *Spire of Tavnir* is crafted as an engaging read. Can't wait to get my hands on the next book!"
- DAVID BAKER, AUTHOR OF THE CHRONICLES OF CANCATIA

For information contact:
Hannah Pennington
www.hannahpenningtonauthor.com

Paperback: 979-8-986-9831-3-4
Hardcover: 979-8-986-9831-5-8
Ebook: 979-8-986-9831-4-1

May It Happen Press

Second Edition

Developmental edits by Victoria Lynn, Glory Writers
Copyedit and line edit by Addison Horner, Avocado Tree Press
Proofread by Renee Dugan
Formatting by Hannah Pennington
Cover Art by Hannah Pennington © 2024
Cover Design by Hannah Pennington © 2024
Map by Hannah Pennington © 2024
Typefaces: *Aegean* by Matt Frost and *Luminari* by Philip Bouwsma

To all the amazing brothers out there, whether by blood or bond, who bring love and laughter—and maybe a little annoyance ;P—to our lives.

Pronunciation Guide

Characters
Arnis: ar-nis
Baraden: bear-uh-den
Bareth: bear-ith
Briefur: bree-fur
Brohd: brode
Caito: kay-toh
Cevian: seh-vee-in
Demina: deh-mi-nuh
Eldrain: el-drain
Elethýna: el-uh-thee-nuh
Elken: el-kin
Emmid: em-mid
Evinsor: ev-in-zor
Fallon: fal-lun
Feltzspar: feld-spar
Freign: frain
Helmir: hel-meer
Helnah: hel-nuh
Klarn: klarn
Laena: lay-nuh
Lingolm: ling-golm
Rake: rake
Rhowen: roe-win
Scalaed: skuh-laid
Tavnir: tav-neer
Telfath: tel-fath
Tessyn: teh-sin
Thendrell: then-jrull
Vytia: vi-tee-uh
Waldens: wall-dinz

Locations
Adamas: ah-duh-mass
Allendia: a-len-dee-uh
Anguill: ang-gwill
Arfire: ar-fire
Endlewood: en-dull-wood
Endrial: en-jree-yull
Flüm Allarway: floom a-lar-way
Flüm Thrae: floom thray
Hvitria: hvit-tree-uh
Lakéthion: la-kay-thee-on
Lethios: lee-thee-os
Rhydrah: rye-jruh
Tharretill: ther-i-till
Thornbrill: thorn-brill
Tildain's Chasm: till-dain
Tindoria: tin-dor-ee-uh
Yolderain: yole-duh-rain

Creatures & Races
Azeur: a-zuer
Froxil: frox-ill
Hündr: hŏon der
Kottran: Kot-ren
Trarewolf: trare-wolf
Varsie: var-see

Items
Abrielstone: ay-bree-ul-stone
Clavnir: klav-neer
Dacvir: dak-veer
Ilvir: ill-veer
Yelnight: yell-night

The Realm of
Tindoria
Endlewood
(Emerald Mou
Flüm Elster
Drian Forest
Greenfields Road
Flüm Aldeyin
Lakéthion
Sea of Starlight
The Deltas of Aldeyin
Great South Road
Flüm Lesta
Diamo P
Flüm Luster
The White Coasts
Sea of Starstone
Flüm Helfar
N
W
E
S
Miles
25
50
75
100

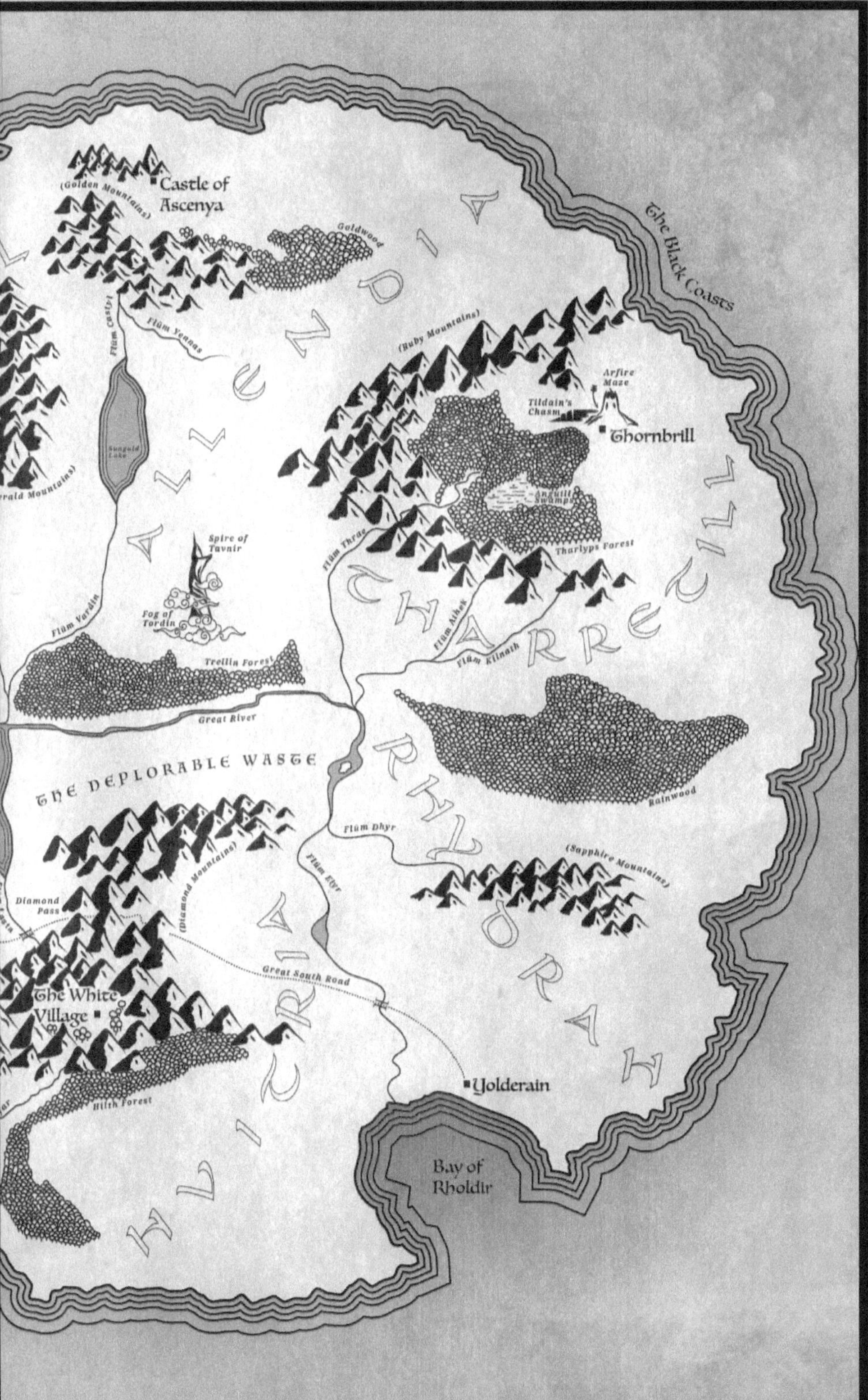

(Golden Mountains)
Castle of Ascenya
Goldwood
The Black Coasts
Flüm Castyl
Flüm Yennas
(Ruby Mountains)
Arfire Maze
Tildain's Chasm
Thornbrill
Sunguld Lake
Anguill Swamp
Emerald Mountains
Spire of Tavnir
Tharlyps Forest
Flüm Thrae
Fog of Tordin
Flüm Vardin
Flüm Athel
Flüm Kilnath
Treilia Forest
Great River
Rainwood
THE DEPLORABLE WASTE
Flüm Dhyr
Diamond Pass
(Diamond Mountains)
(Sapphire Mountains)
Flüm Klyr
Great South Road
The White Village
Yolderain
Hilth Forest
Bay of Rholdir

Contents

Prologue

Kyle couldn't scream as he plummeted from the sky—his dream wouldn't let him.

Wind howled past his ears, pulling his face and clothes. He shot through a cloud and the world opened below, a rippling ocean of green grass and hills. The wind stroked the land with a current that flowed down the emerald mountainside.

Before he could impact the earth with a fifteen-year-old-sized crater, his dream stopped him. Kyle now floated several feet in the air. The blue sky matched his wide eyes, and his dream guided him across the landscape, over hills and borders of plump shrubbery.

Kyle had always been a lucid dreamer, but something was different about this one. He flexed his hands, trying to bend the imagery to his will, but the world flexed back, rendering his efforts useless. He ruffled his auburn hair in frustration. Something else was in control here.

He flew over hills of green feathery waves, and the scent of wildflowers swirled around him. This surprised him; he could never smell in his dreams before. Over another hill, Kyle saw a small cottage with a yellow thatched roof. An aged fence, barely knee-high, framed the yards, some parts crumbled and missing. A cow, blonde like the roof and with full udders, munched away at the grass. She didn't sense Kyle, which came as no surprise; Kyle was invisible in his own dreams.

He didn't know what he had experienced to influence this imagery, but before he could find an answer, he was brought to the window of the cottage. *Whoever lives here,* Kyle guessed, *is pretty poor.*

Cracked cabinets hung open to reveal mostly bare shelves. The table, big enough for one person, sat in the corner with a single, equally rickety chair. A tiny vase of mini lilies decorated the tabletop. They matched the faded patterned quilt squarely tucked around the humble mattress at the other end of the room, which also held a small wood-burning stove.

Kyle amended his first impression: whoever lived here was poor, but very neat.

The front door opened with a musical creak, drawing his attention. A young woman swept through the doorway, smiling to herself as she placed her empty basket by her feet. Humming softly, she untied her headband, and a windswept curtain of wine-red hair spilled down her back. She dusted her patched, faded dress and slipped off her well-worn shoes.

Knowing this woman couldn't see him, Kyle moved himself into the house to watch. Her smile entranced him. She rolled up her sleeves, revealing sun-tanned arms that had clearly seen many years of labor. Pulling a ceramic jar of flour from the sparse shelves, she stopped as a distant neigh rang out from the hills. She and Kyle turned toward the door.

A shimmering unicorn bounded gracefully down the lush

hills, its long spiral horn sparkling like crystal. It carried a rider, Kyle realized, and when the magnificent steed drew to a stop in front of the humble home, Kyle was sure the rider had the wrong address.

A man clothed in golden armor that gleamed like the sun dismounted his unicorn, his chartreuse cape sliding off the saddle like a river of spring. A crown encircled his dark-blond hair, matching the sword that hung by his side. His eyes sparkled in a piercing green, and his immaculately trimmed beard framed his strong jawline. Keeping his eyes on the door, he smiled at the woman inside.

Kyle stood transfixed. This man's smile, which had not even been directed at him, flooded him with peace. *This dude's a protector or a guardian. And quite possibly a superhero.*

The woman took a tentative step onto her threshold and fell to her knees.

"Your Highness!" Her voice trembled in shock and wonder. "You have traveled far from your land, and I am at your service, humble though it may be." She dared to raise her head, her eyes wide. "Why have you come here?"

"I have been watching you for many years, Tavnir," he said kindly. "And I have decided to choose you as my apprentice."

Bewildered, Kyle looked between them during the exchange. Surely this woman couldn't even write her own name, much less have any kind of education. *How could she be a viable candidate?*

Tavnir bid her visitor inside, muttering to herself as she tried to remain composed. "The Golden Prince? In *my home?*

What in the world do I do?"

Raising an eyebrow, Kyle floated in behind them. The Golden Prince sat at Tavnir's table as she poured him a cup of water.

"What drives you to walk the many miles to Endlewood nearly every day?" the Prince asked.

Tavnir drummed her fingers on the clay pitcher and nervously replied, "Surely Your Highness knows if he's been watching me."

"I have seen you give nearly everything you have to the needy in the lower parts of the city," the Prince said. "I would like to know why, when you yourself were not born into much wealth."

Tavnir's tanned cheeks blushed. "Your Highness, what I *have* been given can still be shared. I have a garden, a cow, and a kitchen. This provides more than enough for me, so whatever remains I give to those who need it so they may feel the dignity and joy I experience every day when I wake up alive. If I have the chance to do good, I should do it. Isn't that why I am here?"

The Golden Prince smiled again, and Kyle felt a rush of power hit him. *Yeah, this Prince is definitely more than human.*

"Come with me, Tavnir, and I will teach you the histories of the world, give you sight beyond your abilities, and wisdom to share with all countries."

"Oh, I cannot say no to you, my Prince." Tavnir shuddered. "You are the son of the Celestial Empress!"

"You may say whatever you want," the Prince said. "This

invitation is free for you to accept or decline."

Tavnir searched his eyes, and her shoulders loosened. Her posture straightened as she said, "I accept."

The Prince held out his hand, and Kyle followed as he led her to his unicorn.

"This position will be the highest in the land," the Prince told her as he held her hands, "and many will lust after it and your life. Do you still accept?"

"I do." Tavnir did not hesitate, and her voice had gained a new boldness. "What of him?'

The Prince and Tavnir turned to Kyle, who felt like he had been struck by lightning. Their eyes penetrated him, searching for answers, and Kyle could only think one thing: *they shouldn't be able to see me.*

Then the world swirled into blackness.

CHAPTER 1

The Shadows are Watching

Something stirred in the shadows. Melanie could feel it.

She squeezed the cold stone railing, eyes closed and head tilted upward as she inhaled the night air from the palace terrace. Faint feathery tickles licked her fingertips. Distant lures tempted her to succumb to the darkness—a voiceless siren beyond the music and laughter in the ballroom behind her.

Fireworks screamed and whistled before exploding in the starry sky, and cheers and partying filled the streets. The lively music of Endlewood's citizens blew in front of Melanie, while the sophisticated arrangements of King Eldrain's party soared behind her. With Helnah defeated, the kingdoms were rejoicing.

A royal party would have been any twenty-year-old woman's dream, but Melanie couldn't enjoy it. The banished scribe Baraden had revealed she and Jason were part of a prophetic scroll, and they wouldn't be able to leave until they fulfilled it. Melanie refused to believe it. She wanted nothing more than to leave this palace and this realm. Surely there was a way to avoid being some sort of savior. Melanie dreaded adding such a weight to her already laden heart. Her throat closed as she tried to purge her mind from the memory of Elken—the man who had captured her heart—flipping through the air, tossed like a discarded doll into the black foggy abyss.

Melanie opened her eyes and caught the familiar black shape of Scalaed appearing in her peripheral. The dragon purred in concern.

"Not really," Melanie replied. "So much has happened." She slid her hands off the railing to wrap them around her arms. The whispering shadows vanished at the loss of her touch. "Elken is gone. So much for his Abrielstone."

Scalaed nodded understandingly. He pulled Melanie close with his tail, tucking her under his head. His warmth permeated Melanie like a comforting blanket. While she gently stroked his scales, Scalaed's mind began to wander, and the dark thoughts he often kept at bay crept in. With Elken gone, he could have Melanie to himself again. Besides, she had only known the guy for a few weeks. Scalaed had been with her his whole life. Elken couldn't have mattered that much.

With an aggravated snort, Scalaed shoved the thoughts away and buried his churning jealousy. Those thoughts were unkind.

"You alright?" Melanie lifted her head at his noise.

Scalaed nodded and ushered her back into his embrace. He wanted her to stay here forever. He never wanted to be separated from her again. She was safe as long as she was with him.

He gently shifted himself to shield her from the royal party behind them.

"I just want to go home." Melanie's voice broke, and she sank deeper into Scalaed's warm bulk.

Unlike his sister, Jason intended to enjoy the festivities, but he was swarmed by richly dressed guests who bombarded him with questions about Helnah's dragon army.

"How many dragons are there?"

"Where have they been all this time?"

Some guests even pressed coins in his hands as either a sign of thanks or incentive to return their children.

"Praise the Celestials we have you."

"Save my son, please!"

"I haven't seen my little girl in months!"

Jason tried his best to answer them, but the cacophony of voices drowned him out, cornering him, crushing him.

A hand slipped through the bodies and pulled him from the crowd, spinning him back onto the dance floor. Able to breathe again, Jason looked down at his small dance partner who skillfully led him away from the droves.

"You look like you needed a rescue." Fallon smiled. The young froxil's bright eyes matched the golden candlelight, and her fox tail swished playfully.

"Thanks, Fallon." Jason sighed and took control of the waltz, his attire stiffening his movements. He wore a gold-embroidered green jacket with double-breasted buttons, above which was tucked a ruffled collar of ivory lace. Two coattails behind him trailed down to his knees, and he wore burgundy trousers tucked into polished black boots.

"Are you alright?" Fallon asked, her orange dress twirling like a tiger lily. "All this must be so hard."

"It's been a crazy twenty-seven days, yeah."

"Do you need anything?"

"Right now, I'm just focusing on the next right thing."

"Which is?"

"Wait for General Lingolm to collect the Yelnight crystal. Then I return to the Arfire Maze to save the children."

Fallon nodded thoughtfully. "My cousin Briefur and I can cover the distance quickly. There's plenty of preparation to do with my people already there. We can go to Thornbrill and send you a message when he arrives."

"Will it be those birds again?" Jason asked with a wary smirk.

"Unfortunately yes," Fallon giggled. "Avis Messengers are the fastest in the realm. When a Hündr reaches adolescence— that is, thirteen years of age—one of the many lessons we learn is how to send Avis messages without mistranslation."

"How did you do?"

Fallon blushed. "Not very well. It was quite embarrassing, and it happened only two years ago, so I remember it vividly."

The song faded to an end, and Fallon bowed in respect to her partner, her fluffy tail swaying behind her. "I will take my leave now. I have far to travel tomorrow, and it would be wise to get some sleep."

Jason returned the bow. "Goodnight, Fallon, thanks for the dance."

As the fox girl vanished in the crowd, Jason searched for his sister. He instead met Baraden's sky-blue gaze. The scribe had been watching him from one of the long tables lining the walls, his only movement the steady stirring of his jeweled cup. Jason averted his gaze. He had no time for some scroll. He hadn't even read it. He had a much more important mission. He hoped if he ignored it long enough, the idea of the Spire's Scroll would fade, and he and Melanie could go home.

Jason turned toward the towering doors that led to an expansive terrace and found Briefur leaning against a pillar. The trarewolf held a goblet in one hand while he stared skeptically at the passing guests.

"You don't look to be much of a party person," Jason said, chuckling as he picked a glass off a nearby table display.

Briefur's icy eyes narrowed. "Oh, you'd be surprised." He straightened off the wall, giving one final glance at the guests. "Something smells off."

Jason stopped sipping. "What do you mean?"

Briefur shook his head, nose twitching. "Not sure."

"Enemy?" Jason rested one hand on his knife.

"Not a person." Briefur sniffed again. "A force, an omen, I don't know. I can't explain it. It smells of darkness."

"That's comforting," Jason deadpanned as he took another sip.

Briefur patted Jason on the shoulder. "Be wary, my friend.

The forces of evil can hide behind beauty and comfort."

"I'll keep an eye out."

"I better catch up to Fallon." Briefur returned his goblet. "The girl has slipped away again," he added with a knowing smirk.

"She's a quiet one," Jason agreed.

"Oh yes. I'll see you soon, Celestials willing." With a nod, Briefur slipped through the crowd, eyes vigilant.

Jason passed his empty glass to a servant and stepped outside onto the terrace. The warm interior stuffiness instantly vanished, and he was met instead with the open coolness of the fresh night. Ivy leaves crawled around the stone railing, and small flowers peeked out under the leaves. Hoping to funnel some of the refreshing air into his fancy clothes, he slipped off the collar and fanned himself with it. As his eyes adjusted to the night, Jason saw Melanie and Scalaed far down to his right.

"There you are," Jason called as he approached them.

"Hey," Melanie greeted softly.

"Man, if I stayed in there any longer, I might have stripped off more than this collar; I'm melting!"

"Where's Poison Ivy?"

"Wouldn't you know it, she's not really a party animal, so she's off in the woods doing who-knows-what. Probably sleeping, which honestly, you should do, too, Mel. You look miserable. Why don't we call it a night?"

"Where? We arrived in Endlewood only hours ago. We don't have an inn or anything."

"Melanie, we're guests of the palace; we're staying here. I'll go back inside and see which rooms they've given us." Remastering his collar, Jason returned to the party.

Melanie sighed. "I hate feeling this way," she finally said to Scalaed. "This grief is suffocating! Am I crazy to feel like this considering how short a time I've known Elken?" Melanie met Scalaed's eyes. Hers were brown pools swirling with confusion and tears.

Scalaed didn't know how to respond; he agreed with her, but somehow, saying so would not be what she wanted to hear. He faced them toward the city and warbled a tone, saying she and Elken had experienced danger every day, spent hours upon hours in each other's presence. Forming a tight bond had been inevitable.

Jealousy twanged the string of the heartlink, and Scalaed cursed it back into the depths of himself. He needed a filter or something, because he couldn't live if he muted the heartlink altogether. It had been torture when he'd had to do it in his prison in Helnah's volcano. The only way he'd kept Helnah's mind control at bay was by erecting a shield around his mind and heartlink, but this was different. He couldn't risk tainting the heartlink with his feelings.

Or could he?

Scalaed tilted his head in thought. If he could let Melanie feel what he did, she might get over Elken and be happy again. She would be his again.

No, that's wrong! Scalaed roared internally at the conflict. Why was he like this now?

Oblivious to her dragon's struggles, Melanie looked down at the street below. Twinkling lanterns lit up the walls in small circles of orange, ivy scrawled along the buildings, and the black shadows of night beckoned to her again.

Something pricked at the back of Melanie's mind. She had phased through walls twice now. But what if it wasn't the walls, but the shadows she used to walk through? Was that what the wisps of voices were telling her?

Melanie looked again at the darkness spilling like a curtain from under the terrace. Focusing, she closed her eyes. She felt her hands pressed on the railing and her feet planted on the tiled floor. She imagined the shadows pooling under her, forming a puddle—a doorway for her to escape. She imagined her feet melting into the darkness as it swallowed her like a heavy blanket, carrying her down the castle walls to the street below.

A wave of warmth and deafening silence descended upon her, and Melanie opened her eyes. A gasp ripped through her throat as she found herself descending weightlessly through a world of flickering gray. Forms of buildings and lampposts floated past her as she sank through their shadows. At last her feet touched the ground, and she touched the wall in front of her. Her hand disappeared into the cold beyond it. Melanie found herself wanting to stay in here, in the peaceful quiet, the private warmth, and with no one around.

But it was late, and she needed sleep.

As she stepped from the wall, the night bit her with a harsher cold than she remembered. She wished again for the velvety shadows. Wrapping her arms around herself, she craned her neck up to the castle terrace far above.

Jason had joined Scalaed on the terrace, and both looked at her with wide eyes and open mouths.

Melanie allowed herself to smile at their reactions.

"You could have told me you were going to show off your superpower!" Jason threw up his hand. "So you know how to control it now?"

"I think so."

"Great, can you get back up here? I know where we're staying."

Exhaustion flooded Melanie, and she shrugged weakly. "I can't. Scalaed?"

Without hesitation, Scalaed swooped down to her. He examined her posture in concern. She was like a wilting flower that had given up hope of seeing rain. Scalaed gave her a small lick on the cheek to comfort her, then gently nudged her onto his back. When Scalaed returned to the ballroom terrace, the two palace servants charged with escorting the siblings to their rooms gasped and skittered away from him. Paying them no heed, Jason helped Melanie dismount. Her orange ball gown scrunched in her arms as she slipped off rather inelegantly.

"So graceful," Jason teased as his sister straightened herself in his arms.

"Oh, I know, a real princess." Melanie managed a small smile. "Scalaed, you'll have to stay here until we get to our rooms. I'll get you in a bit."

The dragon nodded and sat on his haunches. His tail

wrapped around his claws, and he tucked his wings in close, attempting not to intrude in the public space too much.

The Verdant Suite sat on the fifth floor of the palace with green banners rippling from the clay-tiled rooftop. The servants, a man and a woman only a few years older than the siblings, led them down the marbled halls to a quiet common area furnished with cushioned sofas surrounding a brightly burning fireplace in the center. In the middle of each of the three walls stood a pair of doors made of green-stained wood, and the servants opened a pair for the siblings, their ornamental brass hinges giving the slightest squeak.

The male servant gave each sibling a small key with a ribbon. "The rooms are connected with two doors inside. Only when both are unlocked from their respective sides will the doorway open."

"See, I'll be right next door if you need anything, Mel." Jason patted her shoulder.

"Will you be needing a lady's maid, madam? Someone to help you dress or draw baths?" the female servant asked.

"No, thank you." Melanie shook her head politely. "I think I can manage."

"And you, sir?" the male servant directed his question to Jason. "Would you prefer a valet?"

Assuming the term referred to the male equivalent of lady's maid, Jason also declined.

The servants took their cue to leave and did so wordlessly with a synchronized bow.

"Well, goodnight, Jason." Melanie gave him a small smile, absently twirling the ribbon in her fingers.

Jason gave his sister one last encouraging nod, then vanished into his suite.

Melanie stepped into her room and took in the space. A large bed buried beneath pillows of assorted sizes greeted her first. A side table next to the bed held a lamp that burned in a comforting yellow. Across the room from her was a glass door flanked by towering windows that led out to a balcony big enough for Scalaed.

Melanie opened the door and signaled Scalaed with the heartlink. Looking to her left, she saw her private washroom with an eggshell-white tub and matching washbasin. She traded her ballgown for the soft cotton gown folded next to the washbasin. Without another word, she pushed a dozen pillows off the bed, flopped onto the mattress, and threw the layers of fluffy comforters over her face.

She heard the thump and shuffle of Scalaed landing on the balcony, but she didn't have the energy to acknowledge him. A repetitive scraping against the window demanded otherwise. Melanie threw off her covers and lay glaring at the woeful red eyes peering through the glass.

"I'm trying to sleep, buddy." Melanie sighed as she dragged herself to the balcony door and opened it a crack so he could hear her. "It's time for bed, Scalaed, what is it?"

Scalaed shrugged. He simply wanted to hug her goodnight.

Melanie softened and slipped under his warm neck, wrapping her arms around him. "Goodnight, Scalaed." She felt his deep rumble of a voice vibrate through her bones, and it comforted her. Perhaps she would sleep decently tonight.

Scalaed listened to her heartlink, wishing he could do something to ease her pain. He wished he himself could be enough. Yet here he was, contending with a dead man. Pulling back, he asked Melanie why she'd fallen in love.

Melanie knitted her brow as she met his quizzical gaze. His question may have been innocent, but his tone was subtly condemning. "I didn't intend to, Scalaed," she began. "It just happened. That's how falling in love works. You can't really plan it, and sometimes you don't even ask for or expect it."

Scalaed swatted at the thought that intruded into the heartlink, but it was too late.

"My fault?" Melanie backed away, hurt stinging her eyes. "My grief is my fault?"

Scalaed tried to recover the conversation from an argument, but Melanie had already set off.

"That is not fair, Scalaed. 'If I hadn't fallen in love in the first place, I wouldn't feel this way.' What kind of statement is that? You think I would only mourn the death of a companion if I loved him? If it had been Briefur, or Fallon, I would still grieve. I've never seen someone die before, okay?" Melanie's voice cracked around the lump forming in her throat.

Scalaed's nostrils flared in opposition, and the heartlink

burned from his jealous end. Melanie's eyes widened as she clutched her chest. "Ow! Stop it Scalaed!"

The dragon, seeing he had caused her pain, recoiled, and he instantly calmed.

Melanie shook her head. "I don't know what's gotten into you, but you need to grow up." She stepped back inside her room, one hand ready to close the door, and gestured flippantly at Scalaed. "Sleep off whatever jealous thing you've got going on, and then we'll talk. Goodnight."

The glass door shut. Even though Scalaed could see Melanie as she bundled herself in the green sheets, she felt miles away from him. Scalaed sank back on his haunches. He needed someplace to think. Someplace to cool the heartlink.

He launched himself off the balcony and ascended over Endlewood. The city, though sleepy, constricted him and his thoughts. The wild space of the hills and the fields beyond called to him.

The midnight air whooshed under his wings, cool and clear. The rolling grass whipped in a frenzy below him as he passed. Scalaed touched down by a copse of trees and paced around them. Anger swirled in him. Anger at Melanie and anger at himself. He needed to release it before hurting Melanie again. As it rose into his throat, Scalaed roared a blinding pillar of fire into the sky. Green hills lit up in gold and orange, and any nature song silenced at the echoing voice that flooded the fields. The thunderous crackle of fire faded, and Scalaed dropped on his stomach. The grass near his nostrils ruffled in his breath, and he watched the green blades dance until his blinking began to slow.

The ground shook next to Scalaed, and his eyes shot open as he whipped his neck around to face the noise. Poison Ivy pawed with disinterest at the grass, her long black claws tilling the soil like butter. Scalaed blinked tiredly. Had she had such claws before?

The green dragon met his gaze and cocked her head, as if to ask what he was looking at.

Scalaed shook his head dismissively, but Poison Ivy's fuchsia eyes drilled into him.

Scalaed hesitated. There was a new intelligence in her eyes he had never seen before. She also never expressed any desire to have a conversation with him. Could she even understand him? She had always been more dumb beast than he.

Finally, Scalaed growled inquisitively, asking what she wanted.

Poison Ivy's eyes glimmered, and she looked away.

Maybe Scalaed had been mistaken. He shook out his wings in preparation to fly back to Endlewood.

Soon.

The voice swept a chill through Scalaed like a windstorm, and he slowly turned to find Poison Ivy eyeing him with her glowing stare. Did she just speak to his mind?

Wide-eyed, Scalaed loosed a small squeak that meant *What?*

Poison Ivy shook her head, huffed, then took off into the night, her lean green form disappearing beyond the hills.

Alone in the silence once more, Scalaed turned his

thoughts over and over. Had he imagined it? Poison Ivy was Jason's dragon, and Melanie had told him about the green dragon's origin story. She was a poisoned horse. Is that why she smelled so peculiar? Scalaed sighed, knowing these questions would have to wait until morning when minds were rested. His own weighed him down and begged for sleep. With much effort, Scalaed leaped into the air to return to the castle.

As Jason readied himself for bed in the washroom, he feared what torment would besiege his dreams. He buried himself under the green blankets of his bed, regretting that sleep wasn't optional. *Why can't humans function without it?* The weight pressing at the back of his eyes reminded him it was around midnight, and sleep was crawling up to him whether he wanted it to or not. He tried to deflect it, but it was too late.

The distant screams of men grew louder. Jason stood before the Fortress of Thornbrill, battered and gore-streaked. The metallic smell of stagnant blood filled the air, and Jason wandered the carnage in shock. Men screamed as hungry dragons descended upon them. Jason saw severed limbs, and a flash of green drew his attention to a ravenous Poison Ivy, whose mind was under Helnah's control. She wheeled around toward the young Lakéthionic soldier Aleth and tore off his head with a sickening crunch.

Jason crumpled, trembling, his lungs too frozen to breathe. He couldn't close his eyes. Metal screeched behind him as armor was shorn from bodies. During the real fight, adrenaline had blinded him to the reality of battle, and now it came to haunt his dreams. Gripping his bloodied knives in crusted knuckles, he muttered, "I'm not here, I'm not here, it's not real."

Suddenly he was running blindly through the troops, dodging wyverns who began to cry in childlike voices.

"Don't leave us!"

"Help us, please!"

"Come back, Jason!"

Wren, the little dragon boy, screamed. The next time Jason blinked, he found his knife sunk into the wyvern boy's chest, his other hand pressed against the hilt. Terror fueled his desperate need to fix his grave error, and as he saw a faint glow under his hand, he looked back up. His blood ran cold. It was no longer Wren, but Helnah. The evil dragon leaned down, her joints popping, and she hissed with carrion breath, "You can't save them all. You'll never be strong enough. You are nothing!"

Jason launched upright, wide awake. His heart hammered against his ribcage, and he could see the faint thumping through his bare chest. Jason leaned forward on lifted knees, shaking, and he felt the cool air of the suite chill the sweat on his back.

Jason hadn't told Melanie about his nightmares. He

couldn't add more woes to her conscience. *What good would it do anyway?* Jason thought as he rubbed his face.

Taking steadying breaths, he tried to shake the images from his memory, but they had been burned in his mind forever.

CHAPTER 2

Missing Persons Report

The lazily spinning ceiling fan of Kyle's bedroom came into focus as his eyes shot open. He didn't move at first, instead compiling the images of his dream together. Kyle had had many crazy dreams, but this one was different. The colors, the details, the smells, they all felt real. Shaking his head, he flung off his pajamas onto one of his many mountains of books.

"Okay, Kyle, just breathe," he told himself as he pulled on jeans and white T-shirt. "Pull yourself together and get through this. There's too much going on as it is."

Getting a frantic call from his aunt and uncle had not been how Kyle wanted to start his week. When his cousin Jason failed to return home after visiting Melanie two days ago, and neither sibling answered their phone calls, Kyle's Aunt Lucy and Uncle Ian had dropped by his family ranch in Fredonia in hopes their children had wound up here. Kyle's family did what they could to help them through this nightmare, which amounted to making countless calls.

Kyle trudged down the stairs to an overlap of voices coming from the kitchen. The adults had been up for hours. Ian was yelling into his phone from the dining room, but Kyle didn't have the energy to eavesdrop.

"Morning, Mom," he greeted the women in the kitchen, "Aunt Lucy." He made sure to omit the word "good."

His mom, April, smiled sadly from her seat at the island, and Lucy clutched a mug of now-cold coffee through her blanket. Dark circles wreathed her blue eyes as she stared at the wall. Her blonde hair was lifeless and unkempt from restless nights.

Kyle gave them each a hug. No other words were said.

Ian scuffed back into the kitchen, the phone dead weight in his hand. Lucy stood up, scanning her husband for any sign of good news. Ian, weighed down with defeat, simply shook his head and held Lucy close as she cried. Unlike his wife, Ian maintained a clean appearance. His high-and-tight haircut was fresh, and his face was clean-shaven. His appearance was the one thing he could control amidst the chaos, and government habits were hard for him to break.

Kyle was the first to break the silence. "Who was that?"

"The police station." Ian's voice was hoarse. "They said we could file a report, but they can't send out search parties for another day."

"What? Why?" Lucy jerked her head up.

"Statistically, people around Melanie and Jason's age return within the first seventy-two hours. They won't green-light resources for an investigation until they suspect foul play and that they didn't voluntarily disappear."

"I'm sorry, but that's unacceptable!" April shook her head.

Kyle's dad, Conrad, entered the kitchen from outside through the sliding door. The polar opposite of his brother,

Conrad had chosen the country life. His long auburn hair, a color Kyle had inherited, stuck out under his cowboy hat. Conrad had never shaved his beard from the day he could grow one, and it was the focal point of his vanity; his wife April would claim he used more hair products than she did.

"The cops won't do a manhunt yet," Kyle whispered as his dad walked into the kitchen. Too stressed to eat much, Kyle munched on a slice of toast.

"Stupid." Conrad shook his head, dropping his hat on the counter. "Listen, I sent the stable hands home for the day to give your aunt and uncle privacy, so I'm gonna need you to feed and water the horses this morning, okay?"

"Sure, Dad." Kyle walked to the door and slipped on his boots.

"This can't be happening," Lucy sobbed, and Ian held her more tightly.

"We'll find them," he told her. "I'm gonna call some friends at the ranger station and see if they can help."

"In the meantime"—April stroked Lucy's hair—"let's start calling anyone else who might know Melanie and Jason."

Lucy nodded, sniffed, and slipped out of Ian's arms to reach for her phone on the marble countertop. She stared at the screen for a while, then quickly typed in a number.

"Thank you, have a nice day!" Edmund waved happily to the leaving customer. Whistling to himself, he walked along the displays. Mornings were slow at Bert's Butts & Cuts, and Edmund took the lull in customers to check for all the meat approaching its sell-by date. Some product had already been discounted, and at this rate, whatever hadn't been snatched up during the deal would be pulled.

"What time are you leaving, Ed?" Gus called from the back. "Got studying to do?"

"Forensic science test tomorrow. I'll probably leave an hour or two early, depending how busy we get," Edmund replied and looked out the window, reminded of the days Melanie would come to shop for off-cuts.

"What's wrong, son?" Gus asked, noticing Edmund still looking out the window.

"Nothing." Edmund shook his head and turned to the back of the store. While Gus meandered about the sandwich bar, checking for the fifth time that everything was clean, Edmund began storing meat to be turned into sausages. After he sealed fatty trimmings from chops and steaks into zipper storage bags, he paused. There was a time bags just like these would go to Melanie. He sighed, peeled off his gloves, and leaned against the wall, hand resting on his cell phone in his pocket. With still no customers, he contemplated calling Melanie to catch up on each other's lives, but he didn't know what he would say, or if she would even pick up. It had been a long time.

The store phone rang.

"Bert's Butts and Cuts Butchery," Gus answered as he stood up, "this is Gu—Lucy? …Uh, yeah, he's right here."

Gus held out the phone to Edmund, a mask of concern over his face, and Edmund's heart dropped at the implications of this call.

"Hello?" Edmund asked tentatively. "…No, I haven't. We haven't spoken in years." He put his phone on speaker.

"…know what to do, who else to call, I'm just trying everyone and…" Lucy's voice cracked with emotion, pitching higher as she held back cries.

"Lucy, Lucy, hey," Gus interrupted firmly but calmly. "Listen to me, darlin', I'm assuming you called the police, right?"

"Yes," came a sniffly reply.

"Have they checked her house?" Gus asked.

"No, we only filed the missing person's report this morning. Ian is going over to her place now. Melanie and Jason have been missing for two days!"

"Let me go, too," Edmund said. "I'm actually going into criminal justice, and I want to help."

"I'll take any help I can get," Lucy said. "What's your phone number so I can text you her address?"

Edmund told her his cell number, then the call ended. He exhaled, running his fingers through his hair as he started pacing. "You know, Melanie once told me we couldn't be together because 'it's too dangerous.' I never thought about what she meant, I just assumed it was a slip of the tongue."

"You think there might have been something of substance?"

"I don't know." Plopping down in the nearest chair, Edmund leaned on his clasped hands, his heart pounding. "She has to be okay," he mumbled. "She needs to be okay."

Edmund called Melanie's cell, hoping her number was the same, but as he feared, it went directly to voicemail. So he left a voice message. "Hey, Mellie. Um, it's me…Edmund. Are you okay? No one can seem to get a hold of you or Jason. Please, please, call me back as soon as you get this."

After hanging up, Edmund buried his head in his hands. His phone pinged with a GPS marker from Lucy. He shot up, digging his car keys from his pocket. "I'm going out there to find her."

"Edmund." Gus put a hand on his shoulder. "Be safe."

"I will," he said and closed the shop door behind him.

Edmund hopped in his sand-colored 4Runner and mounted his phone on the dashboard. The map told him Melanie's house was an hour and a half away, and he yanked his vehicle into drive. Tires squealed as he spun the 4Runner around and sped down the road.

"Go faster!" he yelled at the car in front of him.

With the radio turned off, Edmund was alone with his thoughts. After Melanie had turned him down, he had only seen her at school, but being in different classes kept their exchanges short and rare. Then she moved away, and he started college. He had no idea what she had been up to the last two years.

The entirety of the drive was a blur until he tore off the highway and barreled down Melanie's drive. Leaving the engine on, Edmund jumped out and looked her house up and down. Well, it wasn't a house. The aluminum hull of the camper sat under the mottled shadows of the trees.

She lived in this thing? Edmund lowered his brows as he approached. "No broken windows..." he noticed. "Door's fine."

He grabbed the doorknob and, seeing it was left unlocked, crept inside. Turning on his blacklight, something he carried on the daily since starting his forensic classes, he swept the purplish beam all over the camper, but nothing triggered suspicion. In fact, everything appeared to be normal inside. Investigating her car port, Edmund recognized Melanie's maroon sedan. A faded blue coupe was parked next to it. He deduced it was Jason's.

"Where did you go, Mel?" he wondered aloud.

The sound of crunching shrubbery drew Edmund around the back of the trailer. Two men emerged from the forest, and he recognized one of them as Melanie's dad, dressed in his park ranger's uniform.

"Lucy told me you would be here," Ian said, offering his hand.

"Hope you don't mind." Edmund returned the handshake. "I didn't see anything suspicious in her camper."

"We didn't either." Ian gestured to the man next to him. "This is my brother Conrad."

"Oh, hi." Edmund shook Conrad's hand. "Nice to finally put a face to the name. Melanie has mentioned you. I'm sorry about your dogs."

Conrad froze, his eyes narrowing. "What do you mean?"

Edmund looked at his hand, still in Conrad's, then backed up. "Melanie had told me they were put down."

Ian and Conrad exchanged looks, and Conrad released Edmund's hand and folded his arms. "Why would Melanie lie about something like that?"

"She didn't buy meat for them?" Edmund's stomach dropped. "She came to my dad's butcher shop every week for months until that point."

"Meat?" Ian took a step closer.

"The scraps, offcuts, things like that. Wait, so you don't have dogs?"

Conrad drummed his fingers on his arm. "I do, but they're alive and well."

Ian hadn't moved. The man was intensely stiff, scanning Edmund from head to toe. "Why was she shopping for meat?"

Edmund could only shrug helplessly, discomfort wiggling its way through his chest. "Well, now I don't know." *Why did she lie to me for so long?*

Conrad cautiously approached the camper and knelt down under the window. "Ian?" He looked back, a grim expression on his face. "Would you come over here and look at this, please?"

The park ranger dismissed Edmund and mirrored his brother's position.

"What is that?" Conrad asked.

Ian tensed his jaw and traced his hand over a massive claw print. One of many. With four talons measuring close to six inches long, the print was nearly the length of Ian's leg.

"Not a bear." Ian scanned, warily retrieving his hand.

Conrad shot him a look. "No kidding. I didn't ask what it wasn't."

Edmund peered over their shoulders and pointed into the shadows. "What's that shiny thing?"

Ian reached to where Edmund was pointing and pulled out a Pop-Tart wrapper. "'Frosted S'Mores.' Melanie's favorite, but she's not a litterbug."

Edmund gently received the trash and turned it around in his hands. As the older men murmured among themselves, discussing the frightfully large animal tracks, Edmund slipped away to the camper's front door.

Wrapper folded in his hand, he reentered Melanie's home to find the trash can. The space still smelled like her. Edmund began opening various cabinets and drawers until he found the one hiding the trash bin. Giving one last glance to the wrapper, he tossed it into the black plastic abyss, then dropped into the nearest seat.

A hollow thud met his weight, and he froze. Thoughts swirling as he immediately switched to detective mode, Edmund slipped off and knelt in front of the seat. His fingers expertly danced under the lip of the edge.

His heart skipped a beat.

A secret compartment, he realized.

With some convincing pressure to the hidden latch, the seat cushion opened with a startlingly loud click.

Wide-eyed and heart racing, Edmund lifted the hinged cushion back and pulled out the photo album that had been hidden inside. With shaky hands, he flipped through the pages. What he saw nearly made him drop the book.

"What the—?"

Kyle squinted in the midday sun as he walked to the stables. Metal fencing framed the dusty acreage that ten horses called home. The stables were housed in a yellow stucco building with a red-tiled roof. A galloping horse on the weathervane creaked as it barely moved.

The smell of horse manure and feed grew stronger as Kyle entered the open breezeway. Five spacious stalls lined each side of the stable, and Kyle's boots clopped down the stone floor as he made his way to the last stall on the right.

The ranch was a sanctuary for horses on the mend. Conrad was an equine surgeon, and April was an equine veterinarian. They had met in the same school. With a bubbling creek, trees for shade, and a variety of wild vegetation, their ranch was not a bad place for a horse to recover.

Darcy the pit bull scampered up to Kyle, licking his hands and panting happily. After scratching her ears, Kyle sent the dog on her way. Darcy's German Shepherd partner, Kuzco, lay fast asleep in his bed.

Making his way to the end of stables, Kyle visited his first patient: a gray Appaloosa named Babe. He smiled as he entered her stable.

"Hey, beautiful." Kyle stroked the pregnant mare's velvet muzzle. "How are we today?" He tucked himself under her neck and hugged her gently. The horse's breathing grounded him, and with her standing over him like a shield, he felt safe.

But Kyle had chores to do.

Grabbing a bucket of brushes, he let his thoughts run loose in conversation with the mare. As he worked the curry comb in circular scrubs into her gray and white spotted coat, he rambled, "…and on top of that new development, I had the strangest dream last night." He brushed Babe from neck to rump. "You know how when you come in from outside, you can feel you've been somewhere? Like…your body feels different, as if the place you've been is still stuck to you. That's what I felt like when I woke up."

Babe made no comment.

"You're a fantastic therapist, you know that?" Kyle chuckled. He cleared the shed hair and dirt from the comb and swapped it out for a stiff brush. He ran the brush through Babe's hair, removing everything brought up by the curry comb. "It felt like I had really been in my dream. Say, do I smell like wildflowers to you?"

Babe turned to face him as he approached her rear, gazing into him with her deep brown eyes. She gave him a gentle snort, and Kyle smiled faintly. "Of course. I *am* super stressed. That makes a lot of sense; my dreams are just going into overdrive."

Kyle cycled through the other grooming brushes in his kit, bringing Babe's coat to a shine. He brushed her mane and tail in silence until he reached her hooves. Sliding his grip down the back of her leg to her fetlock, Kyle squeezed softly, signaling the mare to lift her hoof. Digging the hoof pick into the buildup under and around her horseshoe, he chiseled away the dirt and muck. With a final sweep from the brush end, Kyle repeated the steps on her other hooves.

He plopped into the straw in the corner of Babe's stall. "Enough about me, how are you doing, girl?" He gestured from his slouched position. "Just a few more months till ya pop, huh?"

The mare swished her tail.

"What do you think, colt or filly?"

Babe tilted her head, then scuffed the floor.

"I think you're right," Kyle agreed, and with a slap to his knees, he rose to fetch water and feed. He scratched Babe's ears and kissed her muzzle before leaving.

He was walking to the back of the stables where the tack and food were stored when he heard loud chirping.

Spinning to find the source of the noise, Kyle saw a ruffled ball of feathers trembling in the corner.

"Well, what have we here?" Kyle quickly put down his bucket and knelt closer to the baby bird.

Kyle scanned the small chick, mentally filing through his countless books.

"You're a cactus wren. The state bird, according to my books. What are you doing here, little squirt?"

The bird chirped angrily, hopping from side to side, indecisive on which direction it wanted to flee.

"Lemme guess, you got evicted for a noise violation?"

Kyle cocked his head as the bird continued to cheep at him. "Filthy living conditions?"

Still, the bird ignored him.

"Oh, I see," Kyle said in understanding as he rose to his feet. "Your siblings accidentally kicked you out of your nest, where you were then chased by a hawk or bobcat or something."

The bird continued to sing its song of annoyance.

"Hey, your secret's safe with me," Kyle assured it as he put on work gloves. "I won't tell your mom, don't worry. Let's just get you back to her."

Kyle approached the baby wren and, with a swift, delicate swoop, clutched the bird in his gloves. Stunned, the bird sat in silence as they left the stables and walked toward the trees.

"My guess is you couldn't have come from far," Kyle told the bird. "You're just a little guy, after all. So something tells me…" He trailed off as he scanned the area. "…you came from that cholla cactus. Really, because it's the only one close by." He chuckled.

The bird did not acknowledge.

"Your mama is very smart, you know," Kyle said as he located the nest. "In the books I've read, she builds her nest in super thorny, prickly vegetation to keep you safe." He gently lifted the baby bird and opened his gloved hands. The baby hopped into the nest and tweeted shrilly. "But that only works if you stay put, you little goober, okay?" Kyle stroked the chick's head with his finger. "There you go. Be good! Or next time I'm telling your mom."

Kyle shook his head with a smile as he returned to the

stables. He froze when he thought he saw a person standing out of the corner of his eye, but when he looked, there was no one. Wildflower scent caught in his nose, but when he sniffed in shock, it was gone.

His thoughts immediately honed in on his dream, but he shook them from his head. He didn't have time for such foolishness. He had a busy day of work ahead, and he already had a late start.

The binder trembled in Edmund's hands as he stared into the eyes of the black dragon in every photo. He had only managed to look at the first six pages when he heard the Waldens brothers make their way around from the back of the camper. Slamming the album shut, Edmund hurried out of the camper to his vehicle's cargo hold, where he quickly stowed the evidence in an old Bert's Butts & Cuts bag.

He stared at his hands which gripped the bag shut, a torrent of thoughts barraging his brain. *Are the photos fake? Dragons aren't real, you idiot, of course they have to be fake. But the tracks we just saw...even Ian couldn't identify them. Dragons are* not real. *Keep this book away from everyone until you're sure; there's absolutely no sense in adding more insanity to this case.*

With a steadying breath restoring his common sense, Edmund shut the rear hatch of his 4Runner just as Conrad and Ian walked into view.

"Any guesses about those tracks?" Edmund asked, trying to stay level-headed.

"We found a line mark in between the prints that indicate the creature was dragging a tail." Ian rubbed his eyebrow. "But the *scale* of the thing..."

"Arizona is home to a lot of gila monsters," Edmund suggested.

"The biggest one ever recorded was still only barely over two feet." Conrad shook his head then pointed behind him. "What we saw is so much bigger."

"Aren't lizards indeterminate growers?" Edmund pressed. "The Grand Canyon is a protected park of nearly two thousand square miles, parts of which haven't been fully explored. Maybe there's a super lizard species that has managed to live hundreds of years in hiding and secretly just kept growing."

"You're starting to sound like one of those sasquatch people," Ian scoffed.

"Sasquatch?" Conrad knitted his brows, scoffing in nearly an identical way. "A lizard this size would be closer to a dragon or dinosaur. Speaking of sasquatch, animal tracks can easily be faked." Conrad turned grim. "This was probably a prank by whoever is behind Melanie and Jason's disappearance."

The sun slid across the sky as evening approached, and Kyle had finished tending to the last horse, a sassy black gelding named Pony Stark. Sweaty and hungry from running on a lunchtime snack, he trudged into his house's mudroom. He kicked off his boots, peeled off his jeans, damp socks, and smelly T-shirt, and promptly hopped into the shower in the adjacent bathroom.

The rushing water relaxed his muscles. Knots loosened in his back, and the steam curled around him, fogging all the glass and mirrors. He stood there, eyes closed and head bowed, deep in thought.

I hope Dad and Uncle Ian found some clues.

Once again, his mind wandered to last night's dream. Kyle's fingers began to itch, flexing restlessly. A small nagging voice begged for him in the back of his mind. Suddenly consumed with the need to write down his dream, Kyle rushed through the rest of his shower. He had made it a habit over the last few months so he could master lucid dreaming, but with the black dread of his cousins' disappearance, he had forgotten to do so that particular morning.

Hastily drying his hair with a towel, Kyle threw on his bathrobe and ran to his room where he pulled out his dream binder. His dream spilled through his fingers in startling detail, and his pen scribbled to keep up. By the time he finished, Kyle leafed through what he had written and noticed how it filled more pages than any of his previous dreams. His fingers had calmed, though, and the impatient restlessness had gone. His stomach growled, so Kyle shut the binder and made his way to the kitchen to find food.

There was no planned dinner, which Kyle understood. *Who would want to cook at a time like this?* So he microwaved a frozen calzone and ate alone. Aunt Lucy and his mom sat in the sunroom doing a puzzle with an audiobook playing faintly from one of their phones. Kyle knew puzzles were his aunt's favorite, and she had a fondness for fantasy novels, so his mom had probably suggested the distraction. There wasn't much else they could do. When Kyle finished eating, he put his plate in the dishwasher, adjusted his robe, and peeked into the sunroom. "I'm headed to bed now."

April left her seat to hug her son. "Thank you for being so helpful, baby." She pressed a kiss into his cheek, and Kyle squirmed with a smile.

"You're welcome."

"I'll be helping you tomorrow, okay?" April promised.

Kyle nodded and said his good nights as he headed up the stairs. He didn't remember brushing his teeth or changing into pajamas; he must have slipped into autopilot. The next thing he realized, he was staring at the ceiling. With no end to the stress in sight, Kyle braced himself for the same routine tomorrow. He prayed for answers, and for Melanie and Jason to come back.

Edmund grappled with his emotions during the drive back to the butcher shop. The photo album exuded foreboding into the vehicle's cab. He couldn't escape it and constantly shot looks through his rearview mirror, clenching his steering wheel until it squeaked.

The Bert's Butts & Cuts dinner rush was approaching by the time Edmund parked, and he would have to man the sandwich bar. Grabbing the album, still concealed in the plastic bag, he rushed inside. The bell above the door chimed as chaotically as his entrance, and he ran directly to the back of the shop.

He placed the album on the far end of a processing table and, leaving it in the bag, cracked it open to steal a few more glances at the photos. His stomach churned with uneasiness as he took in each one. *What does any of this mean? What happened to you, Mellie?*

"Oh, you're back!" Gus boomed as he exited the walk-in freezer.

Startled, Edmund quickly closed the bag and shoved it behind him.

"Yeah," he said with an awkward clearing of his throat.

"So, did you find anything?"

"Well—"

The front of the store echoed with multiple bell chimes.

"Oh, tell me later." Gus checked his watch. "Ought to prepare for the rush, son. I'll meet you out there."

Edmund gave the album a final nudge into the mound of matching bags, threw on his apron, and tried to mentally switch into sandwich-bar mode as he headed to the front of the shop.

Gus looked at the work tables and sighed. "He really needs to clean up better." He approached the mound of plastic bags and opened the two at the top. Inside he found old labels and plastic wrappings. With another sigh, Gus swiped his meaty arms along the table, sending everything into the overflowing trash bin next to it, which he promptly stuffed down, tied up, and tossed into the industrial dumpster out back.

CHAPTER 3

Pastries and Blue Jays

Dreams of horror and pain whipped around in Melanie's mind like the tattered wisps of a ghost. Helnah's blood-curdling screams and roars rattled her skull at her thunderous death—death by Melanie's hand. Melanie had killed someone. But not before Helnah had killed Elken. In a torturous replay, Melanie watched Helnah launch Elken through the air, and something glittered as it flew from his neck.

Melanie's legs turned to jelly. It was his Abrielstone. Elken's screams ceased as he vanished into Tildain's Chasm, and his Abrielstone landed with a soft *twink* at her knees.

When she awoke, it was like she hadn't slept at all. Melanie squeezed her eyes shut, trying to remember what was reality. *Did Elken's Abrielstone really fall off?* Melanie felt hot tears trickling out the corners of her eyes. *I can't remember!* Like an avalanche, despair crashed upon her. *He never came back because he's dead. His Abrielstone must have fallen off, and that's what my dream was trying to remind me.* Deep down, she had known as much.

With a stifled sob, Melanie detangled herself from the sheets and rolled out of bed, dragging her feet on the blond wood floor. She looked around the suite in despair. Her legs refused to move. They rooted her in place as if that would keep the day from moving on, but Melanie knew stewing in her sorrow would make her feel worse. Gritting her teeth, she forced one foot forward, then the other.

Grief swamped the air like tar, but Melanie fought it and the tears as she changed out of her clothes into something more versatile: a white, ruffled blouse under a violet jerkin, paired with a riding skirt which had been converted to flowing trousers. She wore a matching dark leather belt and boots. Melanie surmised Jason had requested the outfit since she had nothing else suitable for straddling a large flying reptile.

Her final touch was the ring Elken had given her. She hesitated before slipping it on her finger and stared at it in the morning light pouring from her floor-to-ceiling windows. The central ruby stone was flanked by two smaller diamonds and offset by complimenting bands that wrapped the top and bottom. The metal itself was unknown to her, heavy like gold but almost black with a purple translucence. With a thick band of filigree and accent stones, it was somewhat of a statement piece. Wrapping her hands together, she pressed them to her lips.

"Goodbye, Elken," Melanie whispered. Releasing those words into the world brought a fresh wave of sorrow. But the grief felt lighter, as if Melanie had let go of a piece of it. One by one, she would let go of the rest of the pieces in her own time.

She opened her eyes. Tears beaded on her lashes and cast the room in a misty haze. Blinking her vision into clarity,

Melanie steadied her breathing as she walked to a large, framed mirror above the washbasin. Her fingers autonomously combed her hair back into a ponytail as she blankly stared at her reflection.

The mirror rippled, and Melanie's hands froze. Her reflection had changed. Determined brown eyes with a sharp gaze pierced her soul beyond the silver glass. In the mirror, Melanie held her head high with confidence and fearlessness as she held *Ilvir* above her head in victory. Her hair gathered in a braided bunch at the nape of her neck, and she was donned in glistening black armor.

Melanie's fingers released her ponytail as her arms fell by her side.

"Do not be afraid of the unknown," said a tender male voice that sounded like it echoed from every particle of the room and permeated every cell of her being. "Ask for strength, and I will grant it. Ask for peace, and I will be with you. What you see will be yours. You need only make the choice to rise, for you are needed. You are valuable."

Her reflection smiled at her, untainted by pain but radiating with encouragement and fearless authority. Then the mirror rippled once more, and the vision faded. Melanie continued staring wide-eyed at her present self. Overcome with a longing for what future-Melanie had, she finished tying her hair back with resolve. Then she remembered she might be in the Spire's Scroll, and the grief and fear returned to knead her insides.

No, Melanie rejected. *I will not be a fearful, miserable mess. I want to be brave. I have to do the right thing.* Then her emotions rolled away to unveil the truth buried beneath. *I don't care about myself; I just can't bear losing anyone else!*

Her heartlink fluttered, which startled her—a good morning from Scalaed.

Melanie smiled sadly at the rhythm and opened the balcony door. The dragon cocked his head, snorting smoke into her face.

Melanie nodded her head. "Yes, I forgive you, Scalaed. I'm glad you're feeling better."

The dragon warbled inquisitively.

"Not really," Melanie confessed as she strapped *Ilvir* to her side, which almost brought her some comfort; at least she already had one thing from the vision. "Bad dreams. How about you?"

Scalaed tilted his head in a dismissive shrug, changing the subject with his next growl.

Melanie took a deep breath. "Breakfast does sound like a good start." It would distract her from Elken's death and the dread of the Scroll, so she gave Scalaed a determined smile.

Dreading the idea of returning to sleep, Jason dressed into the Tindorian clothes that had been dropped off sometime predawn by a servant. He washed his face and neck to help him wake up and clean off the sweat, then he threw on a flowy ivory blouse. It reminded him of something pirate-y. The look changed after he donned a green leather jerkin and closed the silver clasps at his front. To complete the ensemble, he wore simple beige trousers and laced up a pair of gray leather boots, somewhat reminiscent of a fairytale prince.

Without warning, the male servant from yesterday entered Jason's suite with barely a knock. Bright-eyed, he said, "Good morning, sir! I've just come to deliver your breakfast." He placed a large silver tray on a side table and examined Jason with clasped hands. "Are the clothes to your liking?"

"Yeah, they fit really well, thank you."

"Ah good. Enjoy your breakfast, sir." With a bow, the servant departed.

Jason was walking quickly toward the alluring tray of food when a knock sounded from the suite's adjoining doorway. *Melanie must be awake,* Jason thought as he opened the door on his side. Melanie, having already opened her door behind his, smiled in greeting. Balancing a tray of food identical to his on her hip, she asked, "Want some company?"

Jason smiled and stepped aside for her to enter.

Being a suite, the room was furnished with a small, espresso-colored wood dining table by the windows. The siblings set down their trays and sat in the two chairs opposite each other, discerning which breakfast item to eat first.

Jason decided on the large golden pastries wrapped in brown paper. "Ooh, these are warm." He held up one of the pillow-shaped pastries.

Melanie lifted hers. The sugary smell had restored her appetite, and she stared hungrily at the warm bread in her hands. Flaky dough wrapped around a speckled, sweet-and-tangy filling that oozed out the top. Melanie bit into it, quickly putting a hand under her chin as the pastry burst in her mouth.

"Oh, gosh," Melanie said, eyes twinkling and mouth full, "this is better than any cinnamon roll. I didn't even realize how hungry I was; I didn't eat much at the party last night."

"So glad we got two of these, then." Jason grinned and took another bite.

"Plus the scrambled eggs," Melanie added as she scanned the rest of her tray, "the reddest bacon I've ever seen, and a ramekin of some kind of oatmeal, I think." She took a sip from a stout crystal glass. "Ooh, this stuff is pink, but it tastes a lot like orange juice!"

The heartlink hummed, and Scalaed landed on Jason's balcony. Melanie leaned over to open one of the window panels, and the dragon puffed into her hair, blowing it over her head and into her face.

"Scalaed," Melanie snickered as she cleared her face.

Jason smiled. It was good to hear her laugh. He hooked a thumb over his shoulder. "I'm gonna try to ignore Baraden if he comes around today." Melanie listened with a raised eyebrow. Jason lowered his voice. "He was staring at me last night. I mean, how does Baraden know that scroll is even about *us* anyway?"

Melanie nodded as she unwrapped her second pastry. "How do we know it's not?" Scalaed leaned in for a sniff, and she ripped off a piece for him.

"We already did a whole bunch of stuff like fighting in a battle." Jason waved his hand. "Heck, I was literally in the front lines."

Melanie froze. It wasn't so much what Jason said that struck her, but how he said it so nonchalantly.

"Jason," she said softly, "I have been so caught up in my own mess, I never once thought to ask how you were doing."

Jason's demeanor changed. His hazel eyes darkened as he glanced downward, and his shoulders dropped an inch. "I'm okay."

"Jason—"

"I'm still in one piece, and that's all that matters if I want to rescue Helnah's prisoners who have had it far worse than me." Jason leveled his stare, and Melanie closed her mouth. "I'll never forgive her for what she's done to them."

"She's dead." Melanie's tongue felt like lead. "She doesn't need forgiveness anyway. She killed Elken."

Scalaed snorted, voicing his own distasteful opinions on the High Huntress. Jason pursed his lips and placed a gentle hand on Melanie's.

"It hurts," Melanie finally said, her voice a soft crackle. "Every time I say his name, it gets caught in my throat. From the first moment I met him, he only ever helped me. He never left my side, despite the danger I led us into, and I later discovered this..." Melanie furrowed her brows, searching for a word as she took in a stabilizing breath. "...this *peace* around him. He made me feel safe. I didn't have to hide myself from him. I guess when you do that, you can't help but fall for someone." Melanie sighed, the muscles in her face relaxing, then finished. "I'm beginning to let him go."

Jason nodded in understanding.

Fairest morning, O blessed recipient!

Jason flinched at the jarring interruption, nearly throwing his breakfast.

"What's wrong?" Melanie asked, eyebrows scrunched.

"Ugh, it's the bird."

"Excuse me?"

Jason straightened as he realized what this meant. "Must be from General Lingolm!"

A blue jay landed on the open windowpane between them.

Ah! Azeur squealed excitedly. *My dear Jason, what a gift it is to see you alive! Indeed, I had little faith an alien such as yourself would have risen victorious against Helnah, but clearly you have been blessed by the Celestials!*

"Uh-huh, thanks, Azeur," Jason said. "Tell me you have news of the Yelnight crystal."

Mercy's sake, boy, are you always so demanding? I have only ever served you, most selflessly I might add, and you have never treated me in kind!

Melanie narrowed her eyes. "Is he supposed to be saying something because he's not doing anything."

This message is for Jason alone, Azeur directed his telepathy to Melanie, who jumped at the mental intrusion. *You may be his sister, whom I am honored to finally meet, but the rules of Avis Messengry are clear: speak only to the recipient regardless of all else present.*

"Sorry," Melanie said softly, wide-eyed. "Should I leave then?" She was already scooting her chair back toward Scalaed, whose attention was now solely on Melanie's closeness. He brought her in even closer with his head.

Not at all! Azeur cried. *I will be silent to you, but you may still bear witness to my magnificence.*

The bird turned back to Jason, who continued, "Maybe if you weren't a scammy, pompous bag of feathers, I'd be nicer."

Azeur flung a wing over his chest, offended. *Good sir!* He cried in a tone Jason had never heard before. *I am not forced to bear messages. I do so out of the infinite goodness and love of my heart! You have no insight on the many thousands of miles I have flown, the energy I've spent to cross such distances, and to ask for something as simple as hafanut butter in return for my envious speed and telepathic security is an acceptable transaction!*

The Avis Messenger's outburst struck Jason dumb.

"I'm sorry, Azeur," he finally managed to say.

I don't believe you are. Azeur narrowed his eyes, beak turned upward. *I may be a bird. But I am not stupid.*

"I really am sorry!" Jason clenched his fists by his sides. "I just…really need to rescue those kids."

Azeur sighed. *Indeed. I apologize for speaking in such an unseemly fashion.* The bird blinked in confusion as he checked himself, his telepathy murmuring. *Maybe I am pompous.* Lifting his head back up to face Jason, he delivered the message. *Sweet Fallon conveyed the message on General Lingolm's behalf. The general is on his way to the Hündr relief camp at the base of the*

Fortress of Thornbrill with Yelnight crystal from Rhydrah. Fallon also wishes to inform you the amount of crystal is less than you hoped for. Human beings are capable of great selfishness, and most wouldn't part with what they had without demanding it be paid for in gold. The Yelnight crystal you do have was given freely by the parents of the poor victims. We all pray it is enough.

Jason's chest flared with heat. "How can people refuse to help these poor kids?" he cried. "Do they have any idea what they've suffered? That the crystal is the only thing that reverses the poison? What about other kingdoms?"

Azeur shook his head wearily. *My dear Jason, greed is a ravenous beast that blinds the selfish from the needs of others. Be not deceived by the fair company you keep, for not all are as noble. Yolderain is the crystal capital, and it would be time wasted to hunt the rare and coveted remnants elsewhere. Now, I must take my leave. I have…much to ponder.*

The blue jay fluttered upward, spiraling to the heights of the city before zipping away in a blue blur.

"Sounded like quite the conversation," Melanie said. "From the one side I could hear, that is."

"I'll feel much better once we get underway," Jason sighed. "We're going to Thornbrill. Scalaed, can you get Poison Ivy for me? She should be outside the city near the foothills."

Scalaed tossed a reminding look at Melanie, then fanned out his black wings and took to the sky.

"Thornbrill." Melanie grimaced at the taste it left in her mouth.

"You *are* coming, right?" Jason asked.

Melanie thought of her vision and knew warrior-Melanie hadn't gotten where she was by sulking in a room. "Yeah." She tried to smile. "I'll be much more useful there than sitting here doing who-knows-what."

"I think volunteering will be good for you."

The siblings finished their breakfasts in silence and scanned the skyline of green towers outside. They peered into the blue sky, waiting for their dragons.

"You know, Scalaed told me something interesting about your dragon." Melanie tilted her head. "Said she was evolving or something. He thought he heard her use telepathy."

Jason slowly turned to face his sister, who eyed him suspiciously.

"Do you happen to know anything about that?" she probed. "Something you'd like to share?"

Jason shook his head adamantly. "No, this is the first I'm hearing of it. But if I could start communicating with Pi, that would be a great thing."

Melanie gave an unconvinced hum.

"You don't think so? You and Scalaed have an intimate bond; what's wrong with me wanting one with my dragon, too?"

"It's not that, and I think you know it, Jason." Melanie leaned forward on her elbows and stared knowingly at her brother. "Helnah's poison courses through your dragon's veins. Who knows what kind of traits it could induce? I'm betting nothing good."

"She's my dragon, Mel," Jason retorted. "I've always had

her under control, so whatever happens can't be that bad."

The rhythmic whooshing of leathery wings grew louder, ending their conversation, and the siblings walked out onto the balcony. Poison Ivy landed gracefully in front of them, and Scalaed swooped down behind her, demanding a neck scratch from Melanie.

Jason met Melanie's critical gaze while he petted Poison Ivy. "She'll be fine. She probably spent her time hunting and keeping to herself, isn't that right, girl?" He scratched her behind her scaly ears. "Haven't been a menace to any farms or hamlets, have you?"

The green dragon snorted ambiguously.

"Anyway." Jason cleared his throat. "I want to be at Thornbrill when Lingolm arrives so I can start treatments ASAP. We could race there," he added slyly, swinging atop Poison Ivy, "but I already know we'd win."

Melanie and Scalaed opened their mouths, feigning offense.

"Pi flew from Thornbrill to Lakéthion in a mere two hours," Jason bragged, adjusting his dragon's reins in his grip. "No way you can beat that."

Poison Ivy tossed her head sassily, and Scalaed narrowed his eyes.

"Is that a challenge?" Melanie put her hands on her hips.

"Trust me," Jason said pityingly. "It won't be."

CHAPTER 4

Mission: Reversible

Jason's mind swirled with thoughts as he flew Poison Ivy over Tindoria. The children would be freed. The Hündr tribes were ready to receive them, the crystal was on its way, and kingdom carriages were en route to bring the children home.

A black thought dripped into his mind. *How do you know you can save that many?*

Jason tightened the reins. *Because I have to. I'm their only hope.*

Clouds veiled the sun, whiting out the sky. The Ruby Mountains and the nearing fortress looked even more gray in the overcast daylight.

Jason exchanged looks with his sister flying next to him and gave an encouraging nod.

Hündr meandered between the many round tents dotting the encampment below. Canid-tailed figures carried supplies throughout the grounds. Trarewolves were robed in furs of charcoal shades, the froxils in oranges and browns, and the acoyts wore the sandy blonds and beiges of coyotes. Other tents in various colors—unlike the neutral-colored leather shelters of the Hündr—blended among them. Volunteers from the kingdoms had joined the cause, offering clothes and food and medical equipment.

When the dragons landed, Jason was met with cries of recognition. People swarmed him as he dismounted, begging to know how long it would be before they were reunited with their children.

Scalaed carried Melanie far away from the ruckus, folding up his wings to shield her. No stranger would get close to her. Instead, he would take her to friends she knew: Briefur and Fallon. Locking onto a scent drifting from a cluster of Hvitrian tents, Scalaed followed it with purpose.

When the clamor grew too intense for Jason, Poison Ivy roared, silencing the people.

"I have to see General Lingolm, and I promise I'll get right to work," Jason said as he slipped from his dragon's back.

"I'll take you to him," came a lilting feminine voice from the crowd.

Jason's heart fluttered.

Laena emerged from the crowd and Jason caught himself staring. Her coral blonde hair was pulled back in messy waves and streaked with soot. The same went for her clothes, a plain, sleeveless blouse and fitted linen pants.

"Laena." Jason found himself at a loss for words. "Hi." He hadn't expected to see her here. He'd last seen her when returning her to Endlewood after curing her dragon poison and restoring her human form.

"Hi," Laena said with a bashful smile.

Jason's nervousness almost matched hers. "What are you

doing here?"

"I couldn't very well sit idly by." Her lilting brogue had returned more strongly since her rescue, and it entranced Jason. "I was given my life back, and it was high time I did something useful with it." Laena took his hand in hers. "Come with me."

As she led Jason and Poison Ivy deeper into the camp, he found his tongue. "What did you do before?" Jason asked. "Your life before Helnah?"

Laena sighed. "Embroidery, poetry, politics, music—the typical frivolousness expected of a noblewoman."

"Noblewoman?" Jason's heart skipped, and he scanned her up and down once more. *Surely a noblewoman wouldn't dress like that.*

"I am the second daughter of the Lord Evinsor, Baron of Edgestone," Laena explained. "My father has a place in the king's courts, though my mother died giving birth to me. My older sister is married to an officer in the royal army, and she lives on the far side of Endlewood."

"Oh," was all Jason could say. "And what exactly have you been up to *here?*"

Laena stopped when she caught him staring at her ash-riddled clothes. "I was in the Arfire Maze."

Jason's blood ran cold. "*Alone?*"

Laena straightened, her turquoise eyes glimmering like the ocean. "I was gathering the children, spreading the word of your coming, so all would be in the same place to better aid your mission."

"Laena," Jason lowered his voice and crossed his arms,

taking a step closer. "Something dangerous lives down there. You can't just go in with no protection!"

"I am aware of the Maze demon." Laena's expression darkened. "But the children are more important than my fear." She held his gaze with determined boldness, her posture erect, her words written in stone.

Jason felt his nose burning. *Am I blushing?*

Laena held his hand again, which sent another wave of heat to his face, and they approached a tent waving the Lakéthion flag.

General Lingolm appeared to have just arrived. Posted by the tent, he dismounted his horse, which captivated Jason. The horse's coat was a pale blonde, and it shook its lavender mane. Poison Ivy snorted, unimpressed. General Lingolm turned to face his visitors, holding a chest fastened with a large iron lock. While the filth of war had been cleaned from his appearance, dark bags sat under his eyes, and his posture held a weary slouch from the relentless riding. But his eyes sparkled with bright hope.

"I trust you got my message?" he asked.

"Yes." Jason's eyes locked onto the chest. "Is that it?"

"It's all we could get." Lingolm sighed. "That, and the generous loan of the Vhysper horse."

Jason looked back at the general's steed. "A what horse?"

"A Vhysper. Only the fastest horse breed in Tindoria," Lingolm answered. "They cost a fortune to own. You'll often find them in grand fairs and tournaments. But this mission deserves their speed, and we are fortunate to have found a

Vhysper owner accommodating." Lingolm unlocked the lid of the chest to open it. "I dearly hope this will be enough."

Jason's stomach dropped. The white glittery powder within only filled half the chest. "I'll make it work," he said, in assurance to himself as much as to the others, as Lingolm gave him the chest. "Thank you so much, General."

Lingolm bowed his head. "No, thank you. I can't wait to see my nephew Gavlin again."

With the chest hooked under one arm, Jason turned and stroked Poison Ivy's scaley forehead and said to Laena, "Let's go, then. We'll bring Pi for protection."

"Will you not bring anyone else?" Lingolm asked. "I assure you will have no trouble recruiting volunteers."

"I'm the only one who can heal them," Jason replied. "And with a crowd of people, we're bound to draw unwanted attention from whatever called the Maze home in the first place."

"I understand. May the Celestials be with you."

Nodding in appreciation, Jason mounted Poison Ivy and held out his hand for Laena to mount behind him. She took it without hesitation. Jason stiffened as her soft hand slipped from his grip to wrap around his chest. He hoped she didn't feel his nervously beating heart. Signaling Poison Ivy forward, Jason could only focus on his thrumming heartbeat against Laena's hands as each beat brought them to the edge of the compound.

There, Laena dismounted and entered one of the last tents to retrieve a cloth-woven basket filled with neutral-colored robes. "The children will be needing these," Laena strained as she hoisted a thick strap over Poison Ivy's shoulders. She attached the basket and continued, "Could you grab another pack? We may have to make several trips."

Without hesitation, Jason did as directed. Once loaded, they both mounted Poison Ivy and continued the trip to the open mouth of the Arfire Maze. Jason's fingers anxiously toyed with the reins as he scanned the slowly approaching black mountains. Deep within them, dragon children waited for him, and Jason could feel their longing for the impossible oozing from the mountains. The longer they waited for him, the more the suspense ate away at his nerves. As they neared the Iron Gateway, he stared at the fortress passing by.

"What is it?" Laena asked as she followed his gaze.

"There's a light in one of the windows," Jason said, still looking up at it.

"Where?"

"There, the lower window, just above the drawbridge."

Sure enough, a small orange light flickered in one of the windows. Then it moved, and Jason and Laena tracked it as it passed through different halls.

"That's Thendrell, most likely," Jason guessed. "As part of his surrender treaty, he asked if he could stay behind in the fortress alone, with no guards. I think that's kind of suspicious. Briefur said he was going to send his sister Bareth to spy."

"Are you sure he's completely alone?"

"He agreed to random checkups to make sure he is," Jason replied. "I don't know if he's had one yet, though." He looked back at the fortress. The light was gone.

"Huh…" Jason was slightly concerned that a Thornbrillian remained in his own fortress. No one knew what he could be doing behind those walls.

Melanie tried to swallow the anxiety swelling in her throat. The fortress, and all its memories of Helnah, the battle, and Elken, planted a sickening weight in her stomach. She forced her gaze down toward Scalaed's glistening red spikes as he walked through the camp to keep it off the glaring mountainside. To move past the grief, she would help the volunteers with whatever they needed. For the first time, she addressed the voice from her vision, hoping it could hear her. "Give me strength," she whispered, locking in on the image of her reflection.

The voice, faint and loving, said in her heart, "It is yours."

The nausea dissipated, and Melanie's lungs breathed uninhibited. Unable to stop the surprised smile that played on her lips, she set her shoulders with new resolve and dismounted Scalaed.

"Melanie!" Fallon waved from a tent. "Hello, Scalaed!" The young froxil ran up to them, fox tail flicking.

"Hi, Fallon." Melanie waved back, and Scalaed bobbed his head in greeting. "There are so many people here. How can I help?"

Fallon grabbed her hand. "This way."

Scalaed followed closely behind Melanie. Humans and Hündr erected tents, carried bedding, and started cooking fires. Anxious voices and the smell of soup filled the air.

"Aren't the children going straight home?" Melanie asked as she examined the system.

"They must wait for the carriages," Fallon explained. "After the battle, my people sent Avis Messengers to the other kingdoms with news of Thornbrill's fall and the truth of what happened to their children. Depending on their speed, the faster stagecoaches could arrive today, while slower carriages might not be here until tomorrow or the day after."

"I see."

They arrived at a stack of crates. Some held clothes, and others were filled with vegetables and fruit.

"Briefur and I have been delivering these to the proper tents. Grab one of these crates and follow me."

The froxil scooped up a crate of clothes half her size. She nearly dropped it, but Scalaed caught the crate in his jaws and placed it on his back, folding up his wings to hold it in place. He warbled for Melanie and Fallon to load him up and spare their weak arms.

"Oh, thanks so much, buddy," Melanie sighed gratefully.

The three wound through camp toward a yellow square tent. Briefur opened the flap to greet them.

"Good to see you again, Melanie! Let me take those." He unloaded the crates off Scalaed's back and stacked them with the others inside the tent. Briefur leaned back and sat on one with his knee raised.

"I saw Jason leave for the Maze," he said.

"Oh, good." Melanie meandered into the tent, Scalaed poking in his head after her. "Those poor children have waited long enough."

"How are you, Melanie?" Fallon asked. "Returning here… it must be hard."

"I'm managing." She gave a reassuring smile.

Fallon rocked on her feet. "I'm excited to hear what the Scroll reveals."

Melanie's heart twisted. She wanted to be brave like her reflection, but all she could say was, "We should focus on this mission first."

A flutter through the heartlink told her Scalaed hoped helping the kids would fulfill the Scroll and they might be sent home today.

Briefur's icy gaze drilled into her. "You *are* staying to read the Scroll, yes?"

"Yes…" Melanie began. "Listen—just curious—why does everyone think this Spire's Scroll is about us? I hardly feel qualified."

Briefur's mouth curved up on one side. "And what, pray tell, would be these qualifications?"

"I don't know, whatever the Scroll says, I guess." Melanie raised her shoulders defensively.

Briefur's mischievous smile spread and he stood to his feet. "So you dismiss your candidacy on the grounds of lacking qualifications you might actually have, but you refuse to read the Scroll to find out."

Melanie tilted her head with the ghost of a smirk and wagged a finger. "I didn't dismiss myself. I'm going to read the Scroll, I'm just..." She shifted her weight. "I'm afraid of what I'll find. That it really *is* about me."

Briefur crossed his arms, his face a mask of amusement. "Fallon and I will be by your side. But if it's not about you, well..." Briefur shrugged with a sigh. "At least say goodbye before you go home."

Heat engulfed Jason and Laena as she directed them to the center of the Maze. Having dwelled here for two weeks, Laena had memorized the way. Poison Ivy, not nearly as affected by the heat as the two humans, raised her wings to shield her riders from popping lava.

"Jason," Laena asked, eying his dragon, "I've been meaning to ask: why does your dragon look like a horse?"

"She was one before the lookout tower back there shot her during our escape. The arrow was poisoned with the same stuff you all got."

Laena's arms stiffened. "Why haven't you cured her like you did me?"

Jason straightened. "Honestly, it hasn't crossed my mind.

Having my own dragon has been super convenient, and I think she's fine with it; she hasn't told me otherwise. She seems happy. Animals might not care too much anyway."

"They're smarter than you give them credit for," Laena added seriously. "Especially when they're dragons." She slipped off and approached a gateway Jason had never seen. Beyond it was a dull red glow.

Laena turned back to him, her lips thinned in determination. "We're here." Then she disappeared into the darkness.

Jason urged Poison Ivy to follow. The first he noticed was the cooler temperature. It wasn't a drastic change—Jason guessed it was cooler by only a few degrees—but it would be more comfortable to work in. The next thing he noticed, as his eyes adjusted to the lighting, were the tiers of rock that spiraled in countless levels around the cylindrical chamber. Pockets dotted the tiers, alcoves that each housed a timid wyvern.

With the low orange-red light of the lava far below, Jason could only see the countless eyes tracking him woefully from the shadows.

After Jason's eyes adjusted to the darkness, he saw Laena standing at the first alcove, stroking the wyvern's nose. When she rose, she pressed her hands together. "Ready?"

Jason scanned the place once more, the daunting number of wyverns weighing on his chest. With a deep breath, he locked eyes with Laena and said, "Let's get started."

Dismounting, Jason carefully approached the green

wyvern, who tracked him with golden eyes. He knelt and spoke softly. "I'm here to help you." Jason held out his hand to touch the wyvern's diamond-shaped scar. "You can be human again, but you need to stay still for me, alright?"

The wyvern looked back and forth from Jason to Laena and nodded.

"I'm going to give you a tiny cut." Jason slowly unsheathed his knife. "I promise it's just a little prick so I can give you this medicine." He showed the wyvern the opened chest. "Can you be brave for me and be very still?"

The wyvern trembled but did her best to give a nod.

Jason smiled. "I knew you could. I'll be fast, I promise." He pressed the knife into the scar, and the wyvern squeezed her eyes shut, whimpering. Like an X-ray, Jason's vision saw the veins and arteries, and after cutting a sizable entrance, he quickly pressed a small handful of the powdered Yelnight crystal into the incision. He closed his eyes, and the familiar tingling in the back of his mind returned. When he honed in on it, the tingling rushed to his hands before spreading to the rest of his body. He felt the crystal bubbling into cool, clear jelly as it flooded the wyvern's veins. Enhanced with his help, it began soaking up the black poison at Jason's command.

Next came the heat. More intense than the Arfire Maze, Jason began to sweat as his whole body heated like a furnace. Every muscle throbbed, and when he opened his eyes, golden light from his hands faded as it seeped into the incision.

"You did it!" Jason said breathlessly as he patted the wyvern. Within a minute, Laena was giving a robe to the girl the dragon once had been.

"That was incredible!" Laena's eyes filled with wonder as she helped the girl to her feet.

"Thank you!" the new girl sobbed, hands cupped in front of her mouth.

"My pleasure." Jason waved a hand as he tried to catch his breath. "Laena, take Pi with you guys as you go back and forth escorting the kids."

Laena nodded, huddling the girl close.

"I've got my work cut out for me here." Jason winced as he craned his neck to view the many tiers ahead. "How many of you are there?"

"Two hundred and sixty-four," the new girl said.

Jason stifled a stunned cough.

"I'll be back." Laena giggled as she unslung the packs of robes off Poison Ivy's back, leaving them behind for Jason. Jason watched the three of them leave, then turned to face his objective.

Flustered, Jason only said as he fanned himself, "It's gonna get real hot in here." He pulled off his leather jerkin and shook out his arms. "Here we go."

With a robe on one arm and the crystal chest under the other, Jason tended to the next wyvern…then the next…then five more…ten more.

His shirt dripped with sweat, and he burned feverishly hot. The tingling ravaged his body. Still Jason pressed on. His ailments were worth the shining faces of the children he saved.

Time slipped by, and higher and higher Jason climbed the

spiraling ledge. At one point, Laena returned with a swollen skein of cold water. Jason downed the contents and nearly choked on them in his haste. He splashed the rest on himself. His dark hair was a sticky, tangled mess, and he had cut open his shirt to let his body breathe.

Laena said nothing as she watched him leave. Jason had been in here for hours, sacrificing his own health to save her friends. She hoped the red in his skin was from the light and not something severe like heat fever.

When Jason returned with a robed teen boy, Laena noticed with alarm that Jason was shaking.

"Jason," she said, reaching for him, "perhaps you should rest for a bit."

"No," came his hoarse reply. "I'm almost done. I'm almost done…" He left the boy with Laena and trudged back up the spiral. "…almost done."

His feet felt like they were melting into the ash-carpeted ground. His nose burned with sweat and fumes, and the tingling had rendered his hands numb. *Come on, Jason,* he pleaded with himself. *Ten more. That's it. Just ten more. They need you. Come on.*

Jason dropped to his knees with the chest in front of him and stuck his hand inside. Bare wood. Jason refocused his eyes, rubbed them, and checked the chest again. A small pile—only enough for one wyvern—gathered in the corner.

Breathing heavily in the hot air, Jason tilted the chest and poured every last precious granule into his hands. His wet hair dripped onto the ground as he sat, staring at the crystal in his cupped hands, despair settling in his bones. *What do I do?*

Lifting his head, he met the eyes of his last patients. Anxious. Hopeful. Waiting.

Looking around for anything to inspire him, Jason painfully rose to his feet, the crystal clenched in one hand.

The wyverns penetrated every part of him with expectant eyes.

Jason's mind began to work. *I could divide the crystal among them…supplement the rest with my magic.* Acknowledging at last that it was indeed magic he harnessed fueled Jason with resolve. Instead of his magic providing a helpful boost like before, this time it would do most of the heavy work. Jason would need to use more magic than he ever had before.

"Okay, listen up," Jason instructed as he returned the crystal to the chest. His voice caught in his parched throat. "Follow me to the bottom. There's enough space to form a circle. I have to do this one a little differently, so let's hope it works. Come on."

He grabbed the remaining robes in his other arm and began his descent. Gravity pulled Jason's weary legs into a jog down the spiral, the excited growls of the wyverns bubbling behind him.

Almost too weak to stop, Jason stumbled to his knees, clutching the chest against him.

By the time he swayed to his feet, the wyverns had done as he asked and surrounded him in a ring. "Okay, like the others, I'll administer the Yelnight crystal to each of you. Small incision. No big deal." Jason panted as he made his way around the wyverns, placing a robe in front of each. He prayed this idea would work. It had to. He would *make* it work.

Standing in the middle, he thrust out his arms and gave a sheepish shrug. "Here goes nothing."

The tingling flooded his body, as did the heat. His palms began to glow, and Jason's face contorted as he willed the glow to leave his hands. Ribbons of golden light flowed from his shaking fingers into the wyverns' scars. Breathing like he had run a hundred miles, Jason groaned as he strained to amplify what little crystal he had.

"Come on!" he said through gritted teeth and stinging eyes. He shook the hair out of his face, and fury exploded in his chest. "*Work!*"

Like a dam, something burst in Jason's chest. Golden light lit up his brain like never before, and he saw each wyvern's affliction, ten images overlapping one another. The light from his hands doubled in brightness and thickness, and the ribbons tethering him to the children rippled with sparkles. They rippled faster and faster, like a current from his heart to the wyverns, threatening to drown him in their intensity. Through it all, Jason managed to see the crystal was working. Aided by whatever magic he possessed, it absorbed the poison.

Jason's skin burned like fire, and the ribbons of golden magic began to tug at his insides. He sucked in breaths to keep himself from screaming. Through the light, he saw the wyverns had shrunk to their human forms, and he tried to reel the light back in.

It fought back.

Consumed with terror, Jason felt his grip on reality slipping. He was being unraveled from the inside like yarn. A rising scream was ripped from his soul.

"Jason!" echoed a distant cry.

"Laena!" Jason screamed back. His toes left the ground as his uncontrollable magic suspended him in the air. "I can't stop it! Do something!"

"Get help!" Laena ordered Poison Ivy, who rocketed away without question.

"No time!" Jason tried pulling his arms in, but his magic yanked them back. "Help me, please!"

"How?" Laena ran to him, tears filling her eyes. "Jason, tell me how!"

A frightened roar rolled through the camp, and Melanie's head shot up from her bundle of bed frames. She jogged around outside the tent as Poison Ivy scrambled to stop and tossed her head toward the mountain. Melanie needed no translation and shouted for Scalaed. Jumping onto his back, Melanie wrestled with horrible scenarios rattling her brain. She knew something was wrong with Jason, and she dreaded what she would find.

Scalaed dove into the Maze after Poison Ivy. Heat swirled around them as they descended into the heart of the Arfire Maze.

Pulses of pain pummeled Jason's brain like grievous waves of electricity. Then his Abrielstone began buzzing, a deep sound he had never heard it make before. A message flickered like a warning, but the swirling, blinding lights in his mind obscured most of it: *...doing too much...ask the...for help...* Jason refused to focus on it further. He needed to turn off his magic, turn off his brain. Struck with an idea, he shot open his eyes and latched onto Laena. "Knock me out!"

"What?"

"Knock. Me. Out!" Jason demanded. "Do it, Laena!"

Fighting tears, Laena quickly hefted the wooden chest by her head.

"Laena!" Jason begged. "I...can't..."

Banishing her tears, Laena steeled herself and swung.

The sickening crack of wood against skull flipped her stomach. The golden light vanished, and Jason flopped to the ground. Blood trickled from his forehead.

Laena stumbled back just as Poison Ivy and Scalaed arrived with Melanie.

"Jason!" Melanie collapsed by his side, cradling his head. Jason's blanched face was awash in sweat and ash. His mouth hung open and his eyes, barely open, stared blankly. "No, no! Jason, stay with me." Melanie pulled him close, rocking. "I've got you. You're okay, you're okay. Stay with me. Please." Her lungs refused to breathe, and she couldn't blink. If she did, she feared Jason would die. "Don't you dare leave me, too," she mouthed, the air too stuck in her chest to speak aloud.

"His magic was too much," Laena cried. "I did what I had to..."

A shimmer of amethyst washed over Jason, and his Abrielstone hummed to life. Melanie leaned back and watched the stone blanket him in a purple shield before fading back into the necklace.

She cupped Jason's face. The color slowly returned, and his breathing leveled out.

"He's okay." Her breath rushed from her lungs in a great sigh, and Melanie hugged him tightly, her shoulders shaking.

A relieved sob escaped Laena's chest, and she turned to find the ten children clutching their robes around them and staring in horror at the scene.

A shrill cackle pierced the air. Melanie and Laena paled in recognition.

"Get out of here!" Laena ordered as she spun around trying to find the source of growing laughter. Head on a swivel, she helped the children mount Scalaed.

Ignoring the fact he had become a school bus, the black dragon only had eyes for Melanie, roaring to make her move.

Melanie hoisted her brother's arm around her and dragged him to Poison Ivy. Laena ran to her side and grabbed Jason's other arm. "Hurry!"

The ominous giggling was growing louder.

"Our screams must have alerted it," Melanie said shakily

as they flopped Jason over Poison Ivy's back.

A stream of fireballs spiraled down from a hole in the chamber's ceiling, alighting on the ledge behind the frightened group.

A wall of fire erupted between Melanie and the others.

Poison Ivy shoved Laena onto her back and snapped at Scalaed to leave while they still could.

"Go!" Melanie ordered as she was corralled to the flaming horde. "Get everyone out of here!"

Scalaed wanted nothing more than to rescue Melanie. She didn't even know these kids. He didn't either. Why should he care? Scolding himself at the heartless thought, Scalaed let an angry Poison Ivy shove him once again, and he bounded out of the Maze.

Melanie unsheathed *Ilvir* and planted her feet as anger replaced her fear. She had had enough of this world trying to kill her. She glared at one of the fireballs that crept toward her.

The flame shrunk, and Melanie saw eyes—bright embers of red. Then the mouth opened with a grin. Crimson lips curled back to flash fangs. The head began to appear—fire-breathing, hungry, and close to human. The female face scrunched with fury, and flaming hair spiraled high into the air. Her orange skin sizzled and shimmered like molten glass. She smiled wickedly, and what Melanie had thought was a dress suddenly unraveled into a long pair of sparkling, membranous wings.

"Ours," she hissed. The word sounded unnatural, as if these creatures weren't meant to speak.

Immediately her horde of companions revealed their

true forms, all laughing as they fluttered their wings in anticipation. They held out their arms to Melanie, their fiery fingers crawling with greed.

Melanie gripped her Abrielstone. She would not die today. She would see herself adorned in armor, a victor. She squeezed her sword and jabbed it in their direction. With a snarl, she said, "Let me go."

"Food!" one shrieked, and they buzzed closer to her.

"No!" Melanie snapped, her voice like a whip. "Let me go *now,* or this blade will be the last thing you ever taste, demon."

"We," corrected the leader, "are Fyrads."

"Eat!" Another snaked closer on legs jointed like a bird's and bared her fangs.

"Leave." Melanie's eyes bored into theirs. "My patience is wearing thin."

"Leave?" they taunted. The leader waved to the Arfire Maze. "We fire nymphs. This…our kingdom. You, intruder."

"Eat intruders." Another grinned, and lashed out a hand for Melanie's neck.

"No!" Melanie recoiled, flicking *Ilvir* through the Fyrad's arm, but to no effect. The arm reformed around the blade as it phased through. Regardless, her defense prompted the fire nymphs into action. With loud, twisted laughter, they all jumped for Melanie.

Melanie clamped her eyes shut. In the fraction of a second before she was mauled, she sucked in her arms in defense. With that motion came a wave of cold over her body. Melanie shot open her eyes. She had descended into her own shadow, and the Fyrads and the Maze hovered far above her. Like a whirlpool, the shadows funneled her faster and faster until they shot her out into the daylight. Airborne for mere seconds, Melanie thrust out her arms to catch her landing, *Ilvir* twirling from her grip, and she tumbled down the grass until she stopped. Rising to her hands and knees, she slowly lifted her head, blinking through her disorientation. Everything around her looked to be in a haze. A high ringing descended on her ears, and she shook her head, but the movement felt delayed.

A familiar roar came from somewhere far away.

She sat back on her heels, and the shadows called for her again, seducing her with their coolness. She reflected on her display of power—no, her *magic*—and it filled her with unexpected pride.

Scalaed came into focus as the ringing faded from Melanie's ears. He searched her face, placing a concerned claw on her lap.

"Hi, buddy," Melanie hugged his head. The world settled to normal, and Melanie took in her surroundings as she retrieved her sword. The rocky black mountains overshadowed her, reminding her where she had just come from. Melanie's eyes widened. "Jason!"

CHAPTER 5

The Warning

Empress Elethýna descended into the darkness without fear. Something unnatural kept the sunlight far above at bay. An ocean of shadow blanketed the air, and the only light came from a swirling orange bonfire.

Moist soil clung to the hem of her dress, and the damp air condensed on her porcelain skin. Shadowy figures lurked just beyond the bonfire's light. But her target was the dark shape that twisted at the edge of the light beyond the fire. A slumped figure shifted weakly, arms rigged up into exposed roots.

"I have come to take what is mine," the Empress declared, and startled animalistic shrieks emerged from the shadows. They stalked her on all fours, glowing yellow eyes gleaming from the darkness, studying her.

Elethýna tried to draw out the creatures from the dark with her penetrating stare, daring them to step into the light.

A deep, growling voice broke the crackling sound of the fire. "You own nothing here."

"Show some respect, you accursed savages," said the hoarse voice from the captured figure.

A quick strike from the blackness put the prisoner back in silence.

"Watch your tongue," the deep voice said, "lest I feed you to the crows."

"Do not lay another hand on him," Elethýna ordered, her voice steady like a blade. Light began to bloom around her.

"Oh," the deep voice purred. "You do not frighten me."

Noises rose from beyond the fire like cackling and snapping of teeth.

"She should," the prisoner spat. "Go back to Merrendogith, seeing as you cannot withstand the light!"

A metallic *shing* came from the darkness. "So annoying…"

Elethýna stretched out an arm, freezing the sound of scraping steel. "Merrendogith?"

"It is not a place we know," the prisoner mumbled.

"No one knew until they banished us there." A new voice interrupted, softer than the first speaker, but no less threatening.

"You are wrong." Elethýna faced the darkness, a glimmer in her eyes. "I know of where you speak."

"You should all be dead." The prisoner blinked hard against the sleep that threatened to steal his consciousness. "Enemy of the Hündr."

"Wrongfully convicted!" the voice shouted.

Elethýna narrowed her eyes with recognition.

"Ahh," said the first deep voice from before. "She does know."

"You allied with Helnah…" Elethýna walked closer, putting herself between the shadowy horde and the prisoner. "It is *you* who needs the Pyrium Dragon."

"Yes, for we are trapped," the lead voice snarled. "But the dragon must send itself to Merrendogith to be useful."

"No one will ever free you for what you've done," the prisoner accused. "And Helnah is dead. You'll never get your precious dragon now."

"Don't sound so sure." The whisper sounded aggravated. "She may be dead, but we have you."

"I will never talk!" the prisoner seethed. "Take your questions elsewhere. I'm sure Thendrell would love a visitation in whatever dark cell he dwells in."

There was silence, and a deep, ominous growl reverberated through the small camp. "Thendrell, you say? I know of him. Observing from the shadows, I have seen his fondness for my puppet. Perhaps she shared one of her many secrets with him. I may need to pay him a visit. Thank you for confirming your uselessness."

A ragged growl erupted from beyond the fire, and something emerged from the blackness, bounding toward the captive. Roars and screams from the shadows shattered the silence as they advanced.

"You will not touch him," Elethýna retorted, standing resolute like a pillar between the prisoner and the oncoming horde.

Claws and blades slashed at the Empress but shattered. Silence befell the enemy as the Empress stared them down. Elethýna thrust out her arm, and the bonfire exploded into an inferno. Thick yellow whips of flame lashed out at the enemy, vaporizing the dozen of them.

Snapping the ropes like they were made of paper, she helped the prisoner to his feet.

"Thank you, Your Majesty!" The man fell to his knees, burying his face in the hem of her dress.

"Let me provide some comfort," Elethýna offered, touching her head to his. The bitter cold released its hold, and heat filled his body.

"Thank you," the man said weakly.

"I will be your strength," Elethýna assured. "And I must send you back. Tindoria is in danger, and you must warn them of this threat. Godspeed, Elken."

A voice echoed to Jason, pulling him from the black fog his mind had sunk into.

"Oh, my son," came a tender male voice. "You tried to do too much yourself, when you have yet much more to learn."

"So teach me," Jason begged.

"Your powers are my gift to you," the voice replied. "The time is coming when we will meet. But for now, wake."

One by one, Jason's senses returned: anxious whispers, followed by the soft fur beneath him, then the smell of sweat and tarps. His eyes finally opened to meet dozens of wide-eyed children surrounding his cot.

"Um, hello?" Jason hesitated. His tongue tasted like

sandpaper.

"He's alive!" a child cried, and the tent erupted in cheers and applause.

Jason managed a weak smile to hide his embarrassment from his frailty.

"Let's give him some space." A crystalline chuckle pulled Jason's attention to Laena's sparkling turquoise eyes.

Jason pressed a hand to his head as he sat up. "What happened?"

Melanie appeared from the disbanding crowd of children and sat on the edge of his bed. She placed a hand on his leg. "You saved them, Jason. You saved them all."

"Nearly at the cost of your life," Laena added.

Jason's memories crashed over him like a tidal wave. Then he looked down at himself, half expecting to see his body destroyed beyond repair.

"I think I know how my magic works," he said, checking his arms. "It's a trade."

"What do you mean?" Melanie asked him.

"When I healed Elken, I began to feel what he did. Some percentage, at least. My chest hurt where his wound was, and I felt all the side effects of extreme blood loss. It went away, obviously, but at the time I had no idea what that was."

"That was just one wound on one person." Laena's eyes widened as she realized the implications. "Just now...you suffered... two hundred sixty-four..."

"My body underwent the sensation of turning into a dragon hundreds of times, yeah." Jason nodded.

"You should be dead!" Laena's voice was a horrified whisper.

"He would have been if it weren't for his Abrielstone," Melanie said. She leveled her brother with her stare. "Don't do that again. I thought I lost you!"

"I don't think I have the strength to even heal a paper cut right now," Jason confessed, holding up weak fingers. "Wait, what do you mean 'lose me'? You should have known my Abrielstone would work; it has in the past."

"My faith in them has waned," she said grimly. "Elken's didn't save him."

Jason frowned and, to avoid the awkward silence, changed the subject. "Where's Pi?"

"She left to hunt with Scalaed," Laena said with the faintest discomfort.

"Man, she never does stick around for long," Jason noted. "She seems hungrier lately."

"She shouldn't stay a dragon, Jason." Laena nervously rubbed her arm. "It's not right."

"She hasn't complained," Jason said as Melanie helped him up from the bed.

Beyond the tent, Jason noticed General Lingolm scanning the dispersing children. His knuckles were pressed against his lips in worry. When the children were gone, he entered the tent.

"Jason, I'd like you to talk to Gavlin." Lingolm crossed his arms in concern. "I think he's having a hard time adjusting."

"Gavlin?" Laena straightened in recognition. Her brow

pinched with worry. "He was Helnah's first subject. He's been a dragon the longest."

"Oh, poor boy," Melanie said.

"Where is he?" Jason asked, already exiting the tent with Laena and Melanie on his heels. Lingolm walked briskly through the camp, and Jason's face twisted in concern as they approached a small tent. Lingolm reached to open the flap, and with a nod, bid them follow him inside.

Gavlin, a tall, wiry teen with shaggy blond hair, sat away from them on the edge of a cot farthest from the entrance. He stared intensely into oblivion, his knees tapping anxiously. Melanie thought he looked to be around seventeen.

"Gavlin?" Laena asked softly.

The boy whipped his head in their direction, not even having heard them enter.

"Laena." Gavlin's gravelly voice made him sound older than he was.

"How are you doing?"

"My mind is so quiet now." Gavlin's gray eyes unfocused. "The dragon's voice…that evil voice is gone."

Jason cast a glance at Laena and Melanie before sitting down next to Gavlin. "What did it say?"

"Horrible things." Shuddering, Gavlin released a breath. "It hated me. Hated humans. It wanted me to die."

"Your dragon self said this?" Jason placed a steady hand on the boy's back.

"Yes." Gavlin nodded solemnly. "It fought to take over me completely."

Jason turned to Laena, whose grim expression told Jason she already knew of this. Melanie looked to be just as disturbed. His lips thinning, Jason returned to Gavlin. "But the voices are gone now, right?"

"Yes, but it has been too long since my mind was my own." Gavlin's shoulders sagged. "I will be fine, I think. The silence, as liberating as it is, will take some adjusting to."

Jason nodded understandingly. "Take it slow, rely on your family, and rest often. If you need anything, I'll be there."

"Thank you." Gavlin gave a faint smile and turned to his uncle. "I think I'm ready to go home."

Taking the cue, Lingolm embraced his nephew in a strangling hug. The general looked up once to Jason, eyes wet with gratitude.

Jason returned a smile and slipped away to give them privacy. Melanie and Laena followed, and as the tent closed behind them, Briefur and Fallon whipped around the corner. Briefur gripped the tent to catch his breath, clutching the fabric like he wanted to strangle it.

"Briefur, are you okay?" Melanie asked, startled at his sudden appearance.

"Oh, thank the Celestials you're alright, Jason!" Fallon said breathlessly. "You gave us quite a scare, looking so lifeless after the Maze."

"You'll need your strength," Briefur said flatly. His skin was nearly as pale as his eyes. "You need to come at once."

As the cousins led them all through the compound, Jason asked, "Did I miss one?"

"Briefur, you have to tell us what's wrong," Laena begged.

"We didn't have time to question him," Fallon answered for her cousin. "We just knew we had to get you immediately."

"Who?" Melanie asked.

They arrived at what they assumed was Chief Helmir's tent.

Inside was moderately furnished with a long table and tree stump stools. A map of the realm lay sprawled at one end of the table. Helmir stood at the back of the tent with his arms crossed, conversing silently with his wife. Sat at the table was a disheveled man hungrily clearing the last bit of food from his plate. His armor had been stripped away, leaving only a torn chainmail shirt and mud-caked trousers.

The siblings stopped. Melanie's heart dropped to her stomach.

"Elken?" she breathed.

Melanie's legs threatened to give way. Elken shot to his feet, accidentally knocking the table and sending the plate and fork clattering over the edge. Seeing Melanie sucked the breath from his lungs, and he slowly made his way to her. Watching him approach freed her legs, and Melanie found herself standing inches from him, studying his torn attire. Her hands shook as she touched his arms, hardly believing he was real. She then looked up into his eyes and traced the scar that trailed from the corner of his right eye to his temple. Elken melted into her touch, his body starving for tenderness after enduring such trauma.

"Melanie." Elken held her face and smiled.

Unable to say anything, Melanie sobbed and grabbed hold of him. Elken hugged her closely, comforted by her warmth, and pressed his face into her shoulder. "I'm sorry I wasn't there for you." He squeezed his eyes shut. "I'm so sorry."

Melanie ran her hands through his tattered hair, trying to hold all of him at once. He smelled like smoke and was thinner. She wondered what exactly he had endured. "How?" she choked out. "You fell—I saw Helnah—"

"I promise to tell you, Melanie"—Elken wiped her eyes—"but I was sent to warn you of a greater evil."

"Now that we are all here, I sense this is a discussion best received sitting down," Helmir said. His heavy voice filled the tent.

The rest took their seats, and Melanie scooted her stool closer to Elken. She never took her eyes off him. While Elken gazed back, his smile slowly twisted in embarrassment.

"Have I got something on my face?" he asked, hoping food wasn't left on his chin.

Melanie's laughter came out high and trembling. Her heart raced to catch up with her emotions and left every part of her shaking. Finally, she said, "You're really here."

Elken looked down at himself. "Last I checked."

"Tildain's Chasm is a serious drop. How did you survive that fall?" Jason asked.

"My Abrielstone protected me," Elken answered. "While it covered me with a shield, I was caught in the roots and shrubbery of the lower cliffside and hung there for a time. My arms were inhibited, and I could not cut myself free. But something—some things—were waiting for me."

"Who?" Melanie asked.

"I only saw their eyes." Elken turned grim. "Yellow and piercing. They emerged from the shadows and pulled me down. They spoke in whispers and growls and refused to answer my questions. I was tied to the chasm wall, where they asked me what had become of Helnah. I told them she had been defeated—though at the time I didn't know for sure. The news seemed to distress them greatly. I gathered they must have been allies of some sort."

"What did they want from you?" Jason asked.

"Scalaed's whereabouts," Elken replied. "I assume they're after the same power as Helnah—a secret she took to her grave. They refused to let me eat or sleep unless I gave them what they demanded. I lost sense of time and fought delirium from sleepless nights. The shadows down there distorted the sunlight. Then, one day..." Elken's voice softened. "...I saw a light. Warm, golden, and salvific." One corner of his mouth rose. "And Empress Elethýna saved me. I recall little of what happened, but there was a loud noise and terrifying light. She helped me up and kissed my head, and a new strength surged through me, sending me here."

"He suddenly materialized in front of us," Briefur added.

Melanie placed a hand on Elken's. He held it tightly and looked at her. She wanted to say something but felt silence would say more. She wanted him to know she was sorry he had to endure what he did, and she could be his safe place like he had been for her.

Elken smiled, seeming to know her thoughts, but the expression died as his attention returned to the others.

Helmir hadn't moved a muscle as he listened. He asked, "Who were they, your captors?"

Melanie felt Elken anxiously tighten his hands. "Helnah was in league with a higher power. With her death, her masters have revealed themselves. The…" The words felt heavy in his mouth. "…the Kottrans have returned."

The chieftainess covered her mouth and reached for her husband, who rose to his feet, eyes flaming with rage. Briefur and Fallon also paled.

Helmir's whisper was deadly. "I dearly pray you are mistaken."

"I saw them, my lord," Elken clarified. "I wish I was wrong."

Helmir turned away wearily, hands clasped behind him. His eyes met his wife's as she approached him. "Helmir," she whispered, "if what they say is true, they will come for you."

Helmir grabbed her hand, not caring about the sweat that dampened their grip. "I know." His heartbeat pounded against his lungs.

"I cannot lose you, my love!"

"Vytia—"

Vytia pressed his hand to her abdomen. "*We* cannot lose you."

"Excuse me"—Jason raised his hand meekly from where he and Melanie had been listening with fearful interest— "we're still kind of new here, so could someone tell me what are 'Kottrans'?"

"They were once our allies," Helmir seethed.

CHAPTER
6
Mortal Enemies

6 Years Ago…

"Victory!" Helmir announced breathlessly as he wiped his blade. His voice echoed over the forested slopes of the Diamond Mountains. The rest of his weary troops scattered among the Vahlsap trees cheered. Even the boughs of the purplish trees seemed to heave sighs of relief. The smell of hundreds of sweaty warriors mingled with the syrupy, sappy smell of the coveted trees. The Vahlsap harvest had been preserved.

A great lion bounded up to Helmir and rose to the form of a man. His dark hair flowed loosely like a mane, with only two small beads clasping it away from his face, which grew a well-filled beard. His eyes gleamed with yellow intensity from the battle. He was Klarn, chief of the Kottrans. A circlet of gold wove around his head—a symbol of his chieftain status that had been passed down from his ancestors. Like the Hündr, the Kottrans had animal patrons, but they were feline-kind— lions, panthers, tigers, leopards, and cheetahs.

"For such a large force, they were quite easy to kill," Klarn gloated.

"Is this the same enemy that attacked Yolderain those years ago?" Helmir asked, adjusting his silver chieftain circlet.

Klarn shrugged indifferently and looked through the forest toward the mountain's base. Emaciated figures like skeletal wraiths scrambled in the distance for cover. "They came from the Deplorable Waste, so I call them Wasters. Scavengers with not even rocks to their names and battle tactics so weak they would lose to a graveyard." Klarn scoffed with a smile and clapped Helmir on the shoulder. "Honestly, Helmir, we should pursue and wipe the rest of them out."

Helmir allowed a small smirk at his friend's comments and followed his gaze. Seeing some of the enemy collapse and cease to move, he said, "I don't think that will be necessary. They look too frail to last the night."

"What were they after?" Klarn scanned their surroundings, his lion ears twitching. "The Vahlsap trees are a versatile resource that we use daily—food, clothing, oil, building materials—that could be their motive."

"No," Helmir mused as they joined the resting troops, "they're far too feral for such ingenuity. What are the casualties?"

"I didn't bother to count. The Wasters were slaughtered so easily, one would think they were blind."

"No, Klarn."

"Oh, *my* casualties? My dear Lord Helmir, I'm offended you'd ask. I have the speed of cheetahs, the strength of tigers, and the claws of panthers and leopards in my army. You think I lost a single soldier?"

Helmir laughed. "I appreciate your pride, but best keep it in check."

Klarn smiled and looked beyond Helmir. "Ah, our other allies have returned."

From the base of the mountain came the thundering of thousands of hooves. Shields and spears rattled. Horns blew in triumph. The centaurs were esteemed allies in Hvitrian struggles. As all three tribes dwelled in different regions of the lush mountain valley, they united when their home or resources were at stake.

"Lord Cevian." Helmir and Klarn bowed in greeting as the armored centaur chief split from his troops to join them.

"The last of the enemy have fled the mountains," Cevian stated nonchalantly as he flicked a bit of sticky gray flesh off his spear. His bronzed skin glistened with sweat under his breastplate.

"What a way to end our Vahlsap harvest." Klarn crossed his arms, and the leather of his straps squeaked under the flexing muscle.

"And for such a weak enemy," said Cevian. He swished his black tail annoyance as he buffed black blood from his copper chieftain circlet. "They threw themselves at us without care, as if they valued not even their own lives."

"If you could call them *lives* at all." Klarn curled his lips in disgust. "They smelled like death."

"My lords, I believe the chieftainess has favorable news this evening," Helmir replied with a smile. "This skirmish delayed the announcement, but if you would follow me to the White Village to refresh, we shall reconvene in the Great Hall."

The Flüm Helfar roared in white frothy rapids from the peaks of the Diamond Mountains to each of the three Hvitrian villages. By the time it reached the valley, it had calmed to a great clear ribbon that washed away the blood and grime from the Hvitrian warriors, who cleansed themselves in its waters.

Flicking his wet mane of hair behind him, Klarn took a refreshing breath as he gazed up at the mountains in pride. Thousands of purplish, arrow-like trees blanketed the slopes. And he had protected them.

Klarn and Cevian dismissed their troops to return to their respective villages and entered the White Village an hour's walk away. Vytia, flanked by other Hündr tribal leaders, was already waiting for them at the Great Hall's entrance.

Klarn bowed. "Lady Vytia, always a pleasure and an honor."

"Lord Klarn, Lord Cevian." Vytia smiled warmly and bid them inside. "As my husband may have told you in passing, our duties don't lie with battle, but with the stars and clouds."

It was true. Many times the Hündr women had predicted favorable times and weather for planting and harvesting, as well as strong seasonal storms. They were esteemed and valued by all the tribes.

"My courtiers and I have been studying the weather," Vytia continued, her ivory-white tail swaying behind her, "and believe a strong storm will be upon us in three weeks' time. This storm will bring enough snow and wind to veil our valley from anyone beyond the Diamond Mountains."

"Any enemies will be sealed outside." Cevian nodded in approval.

"But will this storm not also seal us in and curse us with a frozen famine?" Klarn asked.

Vytia gestured to her companion. "No, for Lady Tessyn has discovered something unique about this storm."

Tessyn stepped forward. Her soft brown hair that paired with her coyote features was chopped short on one side. "Common storms sweep like a wave over the land. But this one will not. Rather, it will swirl around itself and create a cloudless hole in the center. This eye of the storm, as we call it, will form over the valley, and we will avoid all the rest of the storm's effects."

The lady of the froxil tribe added, "This storm will be controlled by the mountains and be so great that it will guard us for a decade. Lost to the elements, any enemy will perish."

"Simply brilliant," Klarn marveled. "The language of the air and sky is knowledge I can only hope to understand."

"This news is cause to invite all to Hestur Village for a night of celebration!" Cevian declared as they exited the Great Hall.

Helmir pointed a teasing finger at the centaur. "Better

control your intemperance, Cevian."

"Me?" Cevian took a step back. "You should be looking at Klarn."

The Kottran Chief shrugged innocently. "I can't help that women love me. You're the only married chief, my dear Helmir; you wouldn't understand."

Laughter mingled with the bonfires' crackle as cheers flooded the night. Pipes and flutes, drums and cymbals filled the air with music. The streets of the centaurs' settlement, Hestur Village, thundered with hundreds of dancing feet, and the village square overflowed with the smell of food. Benches lined the streets, and a great table encircled the bonfire in the center of the village.

"A toast!" Cevian raised a goblet from his place at the table. "To a victory defending our rich valley, and to the Hündr women whose wisdom predicts fair fortune."

More cheers erupted around the table, and goblets and mugs clanged against each other, although the majority missed under the influence of ale and wine. Klarn aimed for a toast but poured it all over Brefiüll. The trarewolf's fleeting horror and Klarn's embarrassment soon melted into uncontrollable laughter.

"Bring another ale over here!" Klarn shouted boisterously

from his seat, surrounded by several lounging feline women who toyed with his hair.

Helmir stepped away from the revelries and crowds to an empty bench against a house. He slid close to his wife seated there and slipped a goblet into her hands. "I toast you, my love," he said softly, "and the bright future we may now have."

"To our bright future." Vytia smiled and raised her goblet.

Helmir would later blame the wine, but the next thing he knew his lips were pressed to his wife's.

"Helmir!" Vytia laughed through the kisses.

Her husband smiled and pulled her closer. Her sweet lips tasted like the wine.

"Your staunch reputation is at stake!" Vytia joked.

"I care not." Helmir smiled as Vytia kissed him back. "This is a night of merriment, and I will make merry with you."

The orange glow of the blazing fire continued through the night and into the early morning. It cast shadows and silhouettes around the village. The centaurs played music and danced, the Kottrans started drunken brawls, and the Hündr were caught up in a little bit of everything.

Cevian was laughing loudly at a joke he no longer remembered when he felt a tap on his shoulder.

"Chief, I must speak with you," a young centaur said.

"Ohh," Cevian groaned, "can it wait, Feltzspar? Grab a drink! Dance with a girl!"

"Sir," Feltzspar said grimly. "It's Rake. He is missing."

Hearing the name of his best scout seemed to clear some

fog from Cevian's mind. "Missing?"

"Yes, I saw him leave the village and go into the woods. I went looking for him myself, but it appears he has vanished."

"So go look for him," Cevian ordered.

"I…just did," the young centaur sighed, "but I will try again, sir."

Feltzspar trotted through the quieting crowd. The bonfire had calmed to a soft glowing mound, spewing little orange licks of flame. The same calmness had spread to the Hvitrians. Only a few musicians still played, and the dancing slowed to intimate sways with partners, while sleep took the rest one by one. Feltzspar grabbed the arm of a female centaur.

"Ow!" she cried as she rubbed her head. "Careful, Feltzspar, my head aches."

"That was your arm, Arnis, and I need you. Rake is missing."

"Why would he leave this wonderful party?"

"I don't know. He looked unwell."

"Ah, he's a young centaur." Arnis waved her hand. "His first taste of ale was probably too much."

"Whatever the case, he should at least sleep it off in his own home and not somewhere in the woods."

Arnis threw back her head and groaned. "Very well."

The two stepped through the sleeping village and out of the gates. The trodden ground outside Hestur Village held a congested pattern of hoofprints, but Arnis's expert eyes locked onto a set that trailed away to the forest. "These are his horseshoes." She knelt down and gingerly felt a smudged hoofprint. "He was indeed inhibited to some extent; see his erratic walking pattern? He went this way."

Arnis led Feltzspar through the woods. The early morning chill brushed past them, and the forest swallowed all sound. The silence drew goosebumps on Feltzspar's skin.

"Why would Rake have gone this far?" Arnis asked.

"I know as much as you do. I just need your tracking talent to find him."

"Was it my talent you were after?" Arnis swished her spotted rump. "Or my company?"

"Arnis, be serious. Rake could be hurt."

"Well, his prints have been slowing. We must be close."

Arnis and Feltzspar pushed a Vahlsap branch out of their way, and they saw Rake. He had collapsed, his body slumped against a tree.

"Rake!" Arnis laughed and cantered over to him. "Perhaps drink less next time, eh? We would hate to lose such a prodigious scout."

Pulling him away from the tree, Feltzspar saw blood trickling from Rake's mouth and ears.

Arnis's smile vanished. "Rake? What happened?"

The young centaur coughed weakly.

"He's alive, at least." Feltzspar pulled Rake's arm over his shoulder and told Arnis to do the same.

The journey back was painstaking. Rake was mostly unconscious but would occasionally step once or twice. His limp body weighed on the two centaur's shoulders, and Feltzspar panted from the exertion.

"Are you sure we are heading the right way?" Feltzspar asked.

"I am positive," Arnis snapped, "and, yes, the ale wore off a long time ago."

Feltzspar looked between them. His skin had a gray hue, and the hair of his coat was thinner.

Arnis saw it too and voiced what Feltzspar was thinking. "I don't think wine or ale did this."

"No."

Something cracked. They both felt it through Rake's body. Feltzspar immediately knew it wasn't a branch. Arnis did, too. They stopped walking and warily looked back. Rake's back leg was snapped in a very, very wrong angle.

Arnis gagged. "What did you do?"

"I did nothing!" Feltzspar defended.

Rake's eyes shot open and he jerked his head back, gasping hollowly, "Run."

Feltzspar and Arnis stared wide-eyed.

"Run, you idiots!" Rake gasped again.

Arnis felt Rake's arm slip off her shoulder with a sucking *pop*. Something warm ran down her back, and she looked to find Rake's disconnected hand in her own, her fingers tightly wrapped around the shattered wrist.

Feltzspar and Arnis screamed and dropped Rake. Both centaurs backed up and gaped at the crumpled figure they left. Rake's back was bent at a sharp angle, and his left hoof had been ripped off. After a moment of stillness, Rake shuddered.

Feltzspar and Arnis were frozen. They could only watch in

horror. Rake's top half swung forward with a grinding sound, and he clawed at the grass in front of him. His rear rose up as if it were a separate body. Despite the increasing breaking bones and shedding of his hide, Rake managed to stand.

"Rake?" Feltzspar reached out shakily. He touched the very still Rake, but his fingers sank through his chest like it was rotten fruit. Feltzspar's heart stopped. Recoiling, he almost tripped over his legs while he scrambled away.

Rake's head creaked to his other side, his face wide-eyed and blank. His mouth opened unnaturally wide and moaned—a sound that struck terror in both centaurs and fueled their retreat. The sound of crunching bones followed them as they fled downhill.

Feltzspar and Arnis skidded behind a tree shrouded in bushes and peeked out from behind. Rake stood at the top of the forested hill—a gangly, twitching silhouette against the moonlight. He took another step, his crooked head flopping lifelessly with each movement.

Arnis gripped Feltzspar's hand, her nails digging into his skin. "We have to tell the chief!"

They raced back to Hestur Village and screamed for Cevian through the streets. The ruckus woke the town.

"What happened?" Cevian demanded, scrambling for his nearby spear.

"It's Rake, sire!" Feltzspar gasped. "We don't know what happened, but he is very sick."

"No," Arnis corrected, "he is dead, but something evil still gives his corpse life."

An echoing wail rose from the forest.

"He is here," Arnis whispered.

Sensing a fight, the thousands of Hvitrians pulled out weapons where they stood. Like a wave, the sound of unsheathing metal, leather, and wood rolled through the streets. Klarn impatiently bounced the throwing axes in his hands to feel their weight. Next to him, Helmir flexed his hands bristling with faint white fur as his fingers extended into black claws.

Rake, or what was left of him, dragged himself around the corner of the village gate. Felztspar's fingerprints on his chest had grown to a gaping hole down his side, exposing his rib cage. His tail had thinned to tattered wisps. His jaw limply hung ajar, and he had only one arm. His eyes bubbled out of his head and reflected the moonlight in an unbroken stare. Whatever hair remained was patchy, and massive bruises and wounds marred his hide. Snapped bones stuck out of his joints and ground with every movement. He was awash with blood.

Klarn gasped. "What in the sacred—"

Hearing the Kottran's voice, Rake locked eyes with Klarn and charged with frightening speed on hoof-less legs. Klarn swung his sword, but Rake bent backwards to avoid the blow. Roaring, Rake snagged a Hündr and broke her neck before retreating back into the dark. Helmir cursed loudly in shock as panic flooded the tribes.

Someone shrieked from the edge of the crowd. Rake struck again.

"Cevian!" Klarn bellowed. "Kill it!"

The centaur chief hefted his spear.

Rake roared again and targeted Cevian. The clattering of his decaying legs echoed throughout the village. Cevian gripped his spear as tightly as the horror gripping his heart. He tried not to see Rake as his friend, but a cursed, soulless corpse. With a swift lunge, Cevian skewered Rake through his throat and into his skull. After a horrible moment of twitching, Rake's body hung, motionless. Feltzspar held Arnis as she sobbed.

All was quiet.

"Burn it," Cevian ordered coldly as he removed his spear. It slid out too easily. "And bury the dead." Cevian walked away, but was tailed by the other chiefs.

"Cevian!" Helmir barked. "What was that?"

"If that is infectious, we are all in danger!" Klarn hissed.

"I don't know what killed Rake!" Cevian reeled back. "I know not if this is illness, poison, or curse. I just had to put down one of my own, so leave me be!"

"That was not Rake, Cevian," Klarn said. "He was gone long before he arrived in the village. You killed nothing but a mindless body."

Helmir put a hand on Klarn's shoulder, silencing him. Cevian turned and walked away without another word.

The night's horror haunted the tribes to the following day. Healers from all three villages converged and discussed what had befallen Rake. They tested the wines and drinks and foods from the night but found no evidence of poison. Feltzspar and Arnis worked closely with the healers, as they were the ones to witness Rake's condition. Questioned for hours on end, the two centaurs rarely left the centaur's Great Hall, yet the cause or cure for Rake's condition eluded the tribes.

Then Feltzspar fell ill with extreme fatigue and murderous headaches. Arnis soon followed. Everyone knew what it meant. And there was very little time.

Quarantined in a house on the outskirts of Hestur Village, Feltzspar and Arnis were under close guard and observation.

"So this is how we die," Feltzspar lamented as he lay against a barrel, his lower body curled on the floor.

Arnis didn't respond. Her face was stained with tears, and she squeezed her eyes shut. Forelegs curled in pain and her arms wrapped around herself, she wept silently.

"I dreamed I'd die in battle." Feltzspar winced as he continued, "Die a warrior's death."

"Slain in our wizened years, with a history of astounding victories," Arnis added weakly.

"They would sound horns for us. I would have died defending my land and a wife whom I loved." Feltzspar closed his eyes and smiled.

"Our bodies sent down the Flüm Helfar in burning ships." Arnis coughed and tasted blood. "Our souls…joining our ancestors…our bravery bringing pride to our families."

Arnis shook as she cried. "Feltzspar, I don't want to die!"

Feltzspar reached out and held her hand.

"Our deaths mean nothing now!" Arnis sobbed.

"I have wished you greatness since I've known you, Arnis." Feltzspar squeezed her hand, feeling blood trickle down from his ears. "Perhaps I should have wished for life."

Arnis held onto his hand with both of hers and brought it to her face. "I should have done the same."

"We fought well together, didn't we?" Feltzspar asked softly, his voice fading. "You were a strong warrior, Arnis. You deserved…better."

"Feltzspar?" Arnis shook him, but he had slipped from consciousness. "Feltzspar…" Choking, Arnis crawled to his body and cradled him. "May we meet again…in death." Arnis's vision blurred, and she accepted the blackness.

Their corpses shuddered and scrambled to stand, alerting the centaurs who stood guard. Two healers rushed in and tried to contain the victims to apply potions, but nothing worked. Arnis shrieked and ripped the two centaurs to pieces. Feltzspar crashed through the door and killed the guards.

Cevian, who had been conversing with those guards just mere seconds ago, ducked to barely escape the rampage. Sounding the alarm, he hefted his spear and pursued the corpses through the village.

"Helmir!" Klarn bellowed as he marched into the White Village's Great Hall.

The White Chief looked up from the crowd of Hündr surrounding him at the long table. His people continued their clamorous arguing over plans to defend the villages as Helmir approached the Kottran chief.

"Cevian is under attack by more living dead," Klarn continued. "I don't think there is a cure. By the time they find one, all the centaurs will be afflicted! We must kill them all!"

The Great Hall instantly descended into deathly silence, and horror-filled eyes locked onto Klarn.

"Give us the Hall, please." Helmir did not break eye contact with the Kottran chief as he gave the order. His people quickly funneled toward the exit in silence.

"Klarn!" Helmir approached him after the Great Hall emptied. "Surely you don't mean slaughtering the entire centaur race!"

"I do."

"No!"

"This is highly infectious! We don't know who will be next to turn."

"Klarn—"

"Do you not understand? We must wipe out this infection before it turns to us!"

"How do you know it hasn't already?"

"It works quickly. We would have shown signs by now."

"But engaging in combat will surely spread it to your people, though."

"Not if we burn their village."

Aghast, Helmir stood back, staring at his friend. Klarn stood with fists clenched and jaw set. He was fully committed to his plan, and Helmir feared he wouldn't be able to change his mind.

"I will not join you, my friend." Helmir shook his head, eyes glaring. "This is wrong!"

"If there is no cure, Helmir, what choice do we have?" Klarn roared. "Do you want to slaughter your own while you wait for a cure? Do you want to slay your beloved wife?"

Helmir screamed and transformed into a white wolf, pinning Klarn to the wooden floor with a grating snarl. "Do not speak of my wife." His claws slowly pierced through Klarn's clothes.

"You know we have to do this!" Klarn threw him off and jabbed a finger as they prowled around each other. "Deep down, Helmir, you *know!* You know this is the only way!"

Face knitted in rage, Helmir marched forward to come nose-to-nose with Klarn. "Stop this insanity or I'll kill you."

Klarn shoved him back and straightened. "It's too late, old friend," he said grimly. Gripping the nearest bench, Klarn spun it around into Helmir and sent the Hündr chief crashing into the wall, unconscious.

There were no moons that night, no crickets or owls. The forest knew what was about to take place, and it waited in anticipation.

Yellow eyes in the darkness scanned Hestur Village. The centaurs had lit extra lanterns in hopes to better see the silent reapers, but now not a living soul was in sight—they were hiding, trying to defend themselves from the walking corpses, whose numbers had increased to over two dozen. Like ghosts, the infected wandered the streets.

With every able-bodied Kottran supporting him—a force two hundred strong—Klarn and his troops crept through the grass toward Hestur Village. In their feline forms, their paws absorbed the sound of their approach. When he reached the village gate, Klarn assumed his human form and lifted a lantern off its post. His thick hair ruffled in the night wind. Wind was good. It would spread the flames.

Looking around, he saw his troops in position around the village, in human form, and ready for his command. Klarn tossed the lantern against the nearest dwelling, engulfing it in flames. His troops did the same to other homes around the village.

The swelling inferno drowned out the screams. Ravenous flames consumed wood, thatch, and flesh. The corpses were the last to be affected by the fire as they felt nothing. Only when their muscles were incinerated were they defeated.

Patrolling the perimeter of the village, the Kottrans prevented any escape. Careful to never touch a centaur or set foot in the village itself, they used javelins and bows to bring down any who tried to flee.

An agonizing cry came from Cevian as he crawled from his village, body scorched. Though almost blind, he saw Klarn's form watching him.

"Why?" he managed to scream. "Klarn, *why?*"

Coughing in suffocation, Cevian tried to speak as the Kottran chief approached. Klarn's dark body was a harrowing silhouette with glowing yellow eyes against the flames. Not breaking eye contact, he unsheathed an axe from his back.

Cevian rasped, "My people—"

Klarn threw his axe at Cevian's head, killing him. "Forgive me, my friend, but hearing you speak was too painful."

The thick smoke hung in the air, as if mourning the sacrificial massacre.

A tiger, Klarn's captain named Telfath, emerged from the hazy perimeter and approached his chief. "It is done, my Lord," Telfath said. His striped coat looked even more orange in the firelight.

Having resumed his lion form, Klarn sat on his haunches, only the tip of his tail moving, not bothering to face his captain. He said nothing, and the fire continued to burn its reflection in his eyes. The Kottrans waited until the last flame died, then assumed their human forms to return home.

The Hündr were already waiting. A formation of wolves, foxes, and coyotes lined the rim of the hilltop just before the Kottran Village. Polished leather armor glistened in the dawn light, and wrath stained their faces. Klarn's blood ran cold. Standing next to Helmir in a shining robe towered a statuesque figure holding a swirling orb of colors. At ten feet tall, he bored into Klarn's soul with the penetrative gaze of golden eyes. Great crystal wings rested behind him, and the living sculpture of diamond and light held out the orb.

"You will pay for your treachery, Klarn!" Helmir declared. Old blood streaked the side of his head, tainting his white hair. His steel gray eyes were ringed in red rage. The Hündr army behind him bared their teeth.

Klarn locked eyes on the orb wherein he saw his forces burning Hestur Village.

"*Klarn son of Ekthos,*" came the thunderous voice of the empyrean judge. "*Upon reviewing the past hours in Hvitria, it has been declared that you and those who acted with you are found guilty of genocide. You are hereby condemned to Edgial Execution.*"

"Execution?" Klarn trembled with fury at Helmir. "I *saved* us!"

"You killed an entire *race!*" Helmir spat, voice laden with venom. "There is nothing you can do to remedy your crime."

"*Never before has such a great number of souls been convicted.*" The judge said emotionlessly as he lifted the glittering bugle from his belt. "*Do not resist the Naiads lest they devour you.*" Then he blew. A song of haunting, repeating notes flooded the land.

Klarn roared, took the shape of a lion, and launched himself at Helmir.

Being slightly smaller than the Kottran proved advantageous for Helmir. He slid through Klarn's legs. Taking a stance behind Klarn, he summoned black claws at his fingertips. With fluid precision, Helmir slashed Klarn's arms and shoulders. Klarn was unable to intercept or compete with his opponent's speed and decided to reflect the fighting style. He rolled to the side, using the action to take on his human form. When he stood, he flexed his hands open to flash white, knife-like claws.

They fought like dancers—graceful footwork, swift acrobatics, deadly flexibility, and vicious punches. Combined with their human forms, they summoned claws and teeth and strength of their patrons, adding to the severity of the fight.

Helmir focused all strength into his fist and hurled it into Klarn's throat, which sent him curling to the ground. He stood sadly over Klarn who writhed as he struggled to breathe. "It brings me no joy to see you end this way, Klarn. But justice must be done."

Black fingers clawed the edges of Klarn's vision, slowly shrinking his view of the world. But not before he saw the Flüm Helfar erupt in blue fury. Finned figures with glowing sapphire eyes rode the waves like steeds to shore and over the land.

Ascending to the sky on glowing wings, the judge pointed at Klarn. *"Take him and his guilty tribe."*

Klarn could only see the judge's silhouette before it vanished in a shower of sparkles, and the squeals and chilling laughter of the Naiads stabbed his ears like needles as they descended upon the Kottran ranks.

When Klarn awoke, he was tied to the mast of a crude, unmarked boat of Naiadian make. Kottrans were lined against the rails, all soaking wet, including himself. The Naiads' chuckling—a tinkling sound that made him twitch—bubbled from the water below them. Klarn looked out and saw he was flanked by twenty more boats that carried the entirety of the Kottran tribe.

Struck with horror, he lashed against his restraints and screamed at a pair of blue eyes peering over the boat's railing, "What have you done?"

The Naiad tilted her head blankly, a waterfall of liquid hair pouring over her face. "Judge say take tribe." She shrugged innocently with her broken language. "We took tribe. Eat jumpers."

"You've taken my *whole* tribe, you fools!" Klarn screamed. He gasped for air and looked around. All were in the middle of the ocean, with no land in sight, and only an ominous whooshing of waves ahead. With no sails, the boats were at the mercy of the Naiads.

Filled with rage and betrayal, Klarn roared to the sky. "I will not die like this! Do you hear me, Helmir? I will return. This I swear!"

CHAPTER 7

Whispering Voices

You sent them over the edge of the world," Melanie said. The realization squeezed her lungs to where her voice was no louder than a rushed whisper.

"An execution that, until today, was thought to be effective," Helmir said. "The Naiads subdued his people and devoured any who abandoned the ship—the standard procedure for Edgial Execution. But it appears that one doesn't die beyond the edge and can even return."

"Hang on, the world is flat?" Jason shook his head in surprise. *Never expected I'd believe in a flat world.*

"They said they came from Merrendogith," Elken explained. "Does anyone know where that is?"

"If I was listening correctly, it sounds like somewhere across the ocean," Jason said.

"No." Laena looked up. "Not across." She grabbed the map of the realm and spread it on the table. "Tindoria is flat. If they returned from the Edge, they weren't across the ocean." Laena flipped the map over and pointed to the back of the paper. "They came from beneath."

"Merrendogith is under Tindoria!" Jason gasped. "That's like a whole other *realm!*"

"Anything could be there." Melanie felt uneasy knowing an underworld lay somewhere far below her.

"These are your enemies, sire," Jason addressed Helmir. "Will you be joining us?"

"I must be with my people," Helmir said heavily. "No doubt the Kottrans will look to us for revenge. I will continue protecting my tribe, my family, and"—Helmir quickly exchanged looks with Vytia—"my heir." When he looked at the others again, his steel-gray eyes pierced the siblings. "You *must* decipher the Spire's Scroll. It may be what tells us how to defeat Klarn; it could be our only hope. Please." Helmir's voice cracked. "My world is in your hands."

Melanie and Jason immediately looked at each other, their eyes asking what choice they had.

"We'll do what we can, sire," Jason vowed. "Once I've ensured the children have arrived safely home, we'll visit the Spire's Scroll."

Melanie leaned forward against the table and tried to take deep breaths. Clinging to her vision of the mirror, she lifted a weary gaze at her companions. "We've been through more danger, trauma, and loss than we ever wished to experience, not to mention what torment our inexplicable absence has wrought on my poor parents. I know helping with this Scroll is the right thing to do, but…" Powerless against her emotions, she crumbled. "…I am so exhausted, I don't know if I can go through all that again." Melanie stood, her brow knitted in distress. "I'm sorry, please excuse me." She hastily exited the tent.

Seeing the pinched expressions of Helmir and his wife, Jason said, "I'll talk to her." Then he scrambled off his seat in pursuit.

"Melanie!" He burst out of the tent and ran after his sister, who had retreated to the edge of camp and now stood facing the forest with her back to him. "These people need us!"

Melanie turned around, her face striped with tears. "I know, I'm sorry, but you know as well as I that prophecies are dangerous. I got Elken back, but who's to say I won't lose either of you again somehow? I want to help, I really do, I just need some time to process." Without waiting for an answer, she ran off into the woods.

Elken, Briefur, and Fallon joined Jason at the forest's edge. He sensed them waiting for an explanation. When he turned to face them, all he could give them was a helpless shrug. "She'll come around, but she's right. I sense another quest at hand, and we've barely recovered from the last one."

"That's why you have us," Elken said. "We're all in this together. We have to support each other."

"Especially now. There's something in the air of late." Briefur's nose twitched. "Like a waft of cold decay."

"I could hear it at King Eldrain's celebration." Fallon's golden eyes glimmered. "Faint whispers like scratching in a cage. But it's stronger here."

"Thoughts on what it is?" Jason asked.

"It drifts like a lost soul," Fallon whispered. "Like a consciousness without a body."

"Hmm. So I was mistaken," Briefur added, subtle suspicion

in his voice. "Perhaps it *is* a person. And with a familiar scent, I now realize." He curled his nose in a grimace.

"Familiar?" Jason echoed. "Kottran?"

Briefur didn't respond.

Unnerved, Jason folded his arms to hide his apprehension. "Well, we better be on our guard, then."

Melanie tripped over a root, and her face smashed into the earth. Sucking in a breath as she strangled the dirt in her fist, she felt angry heat flooding her face. It released itself in a scream.

"What do you want with me?" she yelled at Tindoria.

Melting into the moss, she felt her shadow beneath beckon to her. Promises of silence and velvet blackness enveloped Melanie, and she succumbed without a fight. Like loving arms, her shadow bloomed around her and sucked her inside.

Instantly the forest changed to a flickering world of gray, and Melanie floated weightlessly in the intimate quiet. She sighed in relief, wrapping herself in the warm shadows. "Let me just stay here," she said. "It feels so good. So safe." Her voice echoed like in a dream. *Who says I can't?* Melanie thought.

"Melanie!" Elken's voice rippled through the shadows around her as if she were underwater. "Where are you?"

"Elken," Melanie spun around, catching a distant form of

a man running in her direction. *Just…a few more minutes.* She dissolved into the deeper blackness. *Please.*

Elken stopped running and scanned the forest for any sign of Melanie, tensing his jaw.

A shadow moved among the trees, cast upward as if by a light from below the ground. It was the shape of a woman, and it passed from tree trunk to tree trunk.

"Melanie?" he asked slowly. "Is that you?"

The shadow stopped at one tree.

Elken anxiously approached it as Melanie's silhouette turned to face him.

"What happened to you?" he asked, pressing his hand against the tree. "Are you alright? What is this?"

From the shadows, Melanie saw his form flickering like everything else around her, but he was the clearest thing in her gray-painted world.

"Can you come back?" his voice echoed again.

Shadows wrapped around her, luring her back into their embrace. Melanie squeezed her eyes shut to block out their pleas. *Fight it. You can't stay here forever,* she thought. Her mouth tensed as she struggled to finally say, "No." The shadows continued to swallow her, and Melanie shot open her eyes. "You can't control me." She reached out her hand through the shadow to Elken beyond.

He grabbed it.

Like breaking through the surface of water, Melanie emerged from the shadow and fell into Elken's waiting arms.

"I've got you," he whispered. "What was that?"

Melanie met his gaze. "My new ability. Shadow-travel."

"Amazing!" Elken gasped. "Hang on, is this the same magic that helped you escape the fortress that one time?"

"Yeah." Melanie sighed wearily. A tear trickled down her cheek. "Those shadows are my safe space," she confessed, looking up into Elken's face.

Elken trailed a finger down her cheek to under her chin. "I know how it feels when the world seems to crush you. It would be so easy to lie down and let it bury you forever. All your problems would vanish if you ceased to exist."

Melanie's lip trembled as she melted back into his arms. "I almost didn't come back," she whispered, her eyes wide against his chest. She gripped his cloak as words tumbled from her mouth. "I want to do the right thing, but it's so hard to be strong. I'm so scared of what I might lose. And I miss my family so much. I really thought we'd get to go home." She looked back up into Elken's eyes, still a mysterious swirl of colors. "All these worries make me want to disappear. Help me find my courage."

"Oh, my sweet alien," Elken said tenderly. As he thumbed her cheek, he said, "Courageous does not mean fearless. Courage is resisting fear, triumphing over it by doing the terrifying right thing. I hear you. You are scared. But now hear me." Elken cupped her face and held her closer. "Fear does not own you."

Melanie released a trembling breath.

Elken gave her an encouraging smile. "So don't let it. Put your next foot forward. Small steps are still progress. Take one with me."

Elken stepped to her side, his arms steadying her, and together, they took one step back to camp.

"Good girl," Elken kissed her head, and suddenly Melanie felt a little more alive. "Now, for the Spire's Scroll. It prophesizes the arrival of a warrior whom all scribes and scholars agree to be a savior. However, no one knows who it is, but look at what Jason has done and the victory you won. To me, that sounds like the makings of a savior. Will you come to decipher which one of you it is?"

Melanie took a deep breath, looking around her as she tried to steady her heart. Then she straightened her posture and nodded.

"There's that courage." Elken tapped her nose, and Melanie turned to squeeze him in a hug.

"Thank you, Elken," she whispered.

When she looked back up, her gaze dropped from his eyes to his lips. Elken leaned down in the subtlest movement, but Melanie slipped from his embrace. "I should let Helmir know," she said softly, "that I've chosen to embark on this mission."

Mouth hanging open, Elken managed to say, "Uh…I think that would be good."

Melanie clicked her tongue and awkwardly pointed

behind her, then ran back to camp.

Why did I do that? she screamed at herself. *He was right there. So much for courage!* Melanie shook her head to reject the thoughts. *I panicked. Besides, with the tremendous weight the recent news has placed on Helmir, I want to give him some positive news.*

A glint of metal caught her attention as she neared the outer ring of tents. When the trees cleared, she saw Helmir.

He stood still, facing away from her, a long, guard-less blade in his hand. Lifting it up, he closed his eyes and twirled the blade. It spun and sparkled in the light as it floated around and over his arms, flipping in precise movements with his dance. This graceful display entranced Melanie as she watched. The blade flew weightlessly from his arms, over his back, and around his neck, ever lightly touching the tips of his fingers. Helmir's legs carried it all in a waltz, his tail swaying in step. It ended with a final twirl with the blade pointed to the horizon.

"This form is not for combat," he told Melanie without turning around. "It is a relationship of balance with your weapon. This strengthens your bond with it. You know its balance, its weight, how it moves and feels in your hand, and therefore, how to use it in real combat."

"It was beautiful," Melanie said.

"My way to pass the time." Helmir's performance had relaxed his composure. "It has taken me many years to perfect it." He subtly stroked the blade and, from the corner of his eye, noticed Melanie's own sword. "What are your skills with a blade?"

"I'm afraid none, but I hold my own in a fight, somehow."

"'Somehow?'" Helmir raised an eyebrow, amused. "And what do you mean by 'somehow?'"

"In a duel with one of Helnah's minions, I suddenly… knew my sword. *Ilvir* felt like a part of me, and using it became as natural as using any other part of my body."

Helmir tossed his blade to her, and she caught it instinctively. Helmir let out a hum as he circled her. "Does this oneness exist only between you and *Ilvir?*"

Melanie shrugged. "I'm not sure."

"Hold this one. Feel it. Perceive every detail of its make."

Melanie held the blade with two hands and, bringing it up close, scanned its grip all the way down to the tip. It was longer than *Ilvir*. She bounced it lightly in her hands, rolled it over, and gave it a quick spin. She spun it forward, then backward. Almost like she couldn't help herself, she wove it expertly through her hands, twirling and flourishing above her head and behind her back.

"Impressive." Helmir crossed his arms. "You've been bestowed with talent likely to aid your fulfillment of the Spire's Scroll."

Melanie asked, "Do you know what it says?"

"There are few who don't. The essence of the script foretells of a warrior known as the Descendent of Light who will come from afar to save Tindoria from a world-wide war." Helmir clasped his hands behind him, looking thoughtful. "Prophecies are a curious thing. Some things foretell the future, and others are only meant to illuminate the past. Sometimes the meaning is veiled until the era of its time has come, only at last revealing itself when we need it." Helmir put his hand on Melanie's shoulder. "Know that you will not fight alone, Melanie. You will have my aid, should you ever need it."

"Thank you." Melanie bowed her head. "And I'm sorry if I sounded dismissive earlier. I will do my part if that's what the Scroll wants, but I'm so homesick, and I feel like I've run out of bravery despite my efforts to keep it."

Helmir's gray gaze softened. "I accept your apology. I, too, may have been too aggressive with my words, but you've given me hope in knowing you've consented to the will of the Celestials."

"I'm trying to, at least," Melanie said sincerely. "I confess I'm pretty overwhelmed."

"So say we all." Helmir sighed heavily. "Melanie, I see a fire in you. The fire of a fighter."

"Then why do I feel so powerless?"

"Virtues are gifts from the Celestials," Helmir said, eyes raised to the heavens. "But we are flawed. Prideful. Weak. We search for total sufficiency in ourselves and drown when we find our qualities lacking. It is our mortal nature."

Melanie shifted her weight onto one foot. "That about sums me up lately."

Helmir faced her once more, his gray eyes glimmering in wisdom. "But for our every flaw, there is hope. The key, Melanie, is to accept your gifts as just that: gifts. The giver has a design for them and for you, and you are capable of wonders if you are humble enough to ask for guidance. You are not powerless, Melanie of the Separate Realm; you are a sword forged to cleave voices of defeat. Do not forget it."

The White Chief placed a heavy hand on her shoulder as he imparted the words that settled into her very bones. "The Celestials are with you."

Helmir's wisdom fanned the meager flame of courage that had been flickering, fading, and now it ignited Melanie's veins, renewing her weary heart. With a grateful smile, Melanie set her shoulders. "Thank you, Helmir." She returned his weapon. "And congratulations to you and Vytia."

Helmir actually smiled this time. It was a warm sight, and Melanie suspected it didn't occur often. He nodded in thanks as Melanie bowed to take her leave.

Deep in the forest, the distant rumbling of approaching carriages and wagons reached Scalaed's ears. Lifting his head from the deer carcass, he listened further. Poison Ivy, however, had no interest and continued eating her share of the kill. Scalaed ripped off another mouthful of red flesh and mentioned the caravan's arrival to Poison Ivy.

Still tearing away at the deer, the green dragon hmphed.

Scalaed narrowed his red eyes, slowing his chewing to study her. Her green muscles looked more defined today, and he thought her black horns looked longer. Swallowing, he nudged her with his tail, signaling to her they should probably head back.

In response, Poison Ivy lashed out with angry teeth, her fuchsia eyes aflame. Startled, Scalaed froze, and the green dragon slowly returned to the carcass, hissing in annoyance.

Leave me alone.

Scalaed demanded how she was able to have telepathy.

Poison Ivy slid an eye in his direction, eying him up and down. *All dragons do it.*

Scalaed scoffed in denial. He didn't have telepathy.

Poison Ivy snorted dismissively. *You hold back your full potential.*

Scalaed growled in frustration and snaked around to be in front of her. What did she know about full potential? She wasn't even a real dragon, was she?

I was a horse—a dumb beast—until an arrow gifted me with this power. Now, I follow my guide's voice to fulfill my destiny. She cocked her head as she straightened. *It says you're a disgrace.* Snagging one last dripping chunk of venison, she bounded deeper into the forest.

Scalaed did not like this new Poison Ivy. Branches snapped underneath him and the forest trembled as he returned to camp. What was happening to her?

He vowed to tell Jason, but the question was wiped from his mind when he saw Melanie. In conversation with Jason, she was smiling and leaning her head on someone's shoulder. Scalaed widened his eyes in shock, and his core burned with jealousy when he realized it was Elken. The first thought that shoved its way to the front of his mind was: *He's supposed to be dead.*

With a low growl, Scalaed quickened his pace and loomed behind them.

"Hey, buddy!" Melanie craned her neck up to meet his face. Her brown eyes twinkled with a happiness he hadn't seen in her for a few days. His insides twisted at the realization he wasn't the cause.

The dragon cast a glance at Elken, who looked up and smiled. "Scalaed! You look well."

Scalaed couldn't stop the scoff that broke through his throat. This guy did not know him at all. This guy was stealing his Melanie.

"We were just about to help organize the departures," Melanie explained, gesturing to Jason. Feeling the tumultuous rhythm of the heartlink, she pressed a hand to her chest in discomfort and shot Scalaed a glare to cool it down. "We'll be off soon, back to Endlewood."

Scalaed banished his emotions and raised an eyebrow in a follow up question.

"And then," Melanie said, "we meet Baraden to read the Spire's Scroll."

Scalaed frowned. What had he missed while he was gone? What happened to going home? What happened to having Melanie all to himself again in a world where there was no Elken? When was the last time he and Melanie had a moment to themselves to simply talk like they used to?

Melanie caught on, again signaling with her eyes to stop

irritating the heartlink. "We need to stop a genocidal psycho who somehow foiled his execution and has vowed to return. We suspect he was Helnah's boss."

Scalaed tensed his jaw and finally nodded in understanding. He thought Helnah was horrible. Who knows how much worse her boss could be?

General Lingolm and Laena approached the group. "We'll station the carriages and wagons by country. Rhydrah has arrived first, although Lady Laena here has generously lent her personal stagecoach for Endrial children for a head start."

Jason looked at Laena, who shrugged a freckled shoulder. "It's nothing. I'm happy to help, and the stagecoach can carry six."

Heat flooded Jason's face, and he hoped the blush wasn't noticeable. But Laena's attempts at stifling a smile told him otherwise. That made his face hotter.

A blond-haired boy skipped in front of them toward a group of young children. He paused and looked up at Jason as he passed.

"Wren!" Jason waved, and the boy's face lit up in a smile. He giggled as Jason knelt down for a hug. "Hey, buddy, how's it going?" Jason asked as he hoisted Wren onto his hip.

"Good!" he whispered, leaning in. "Mother and I brought sweets." He opened the drawstring of his bag. "I wanted to make my friends happy, so we came here to help them."

"That's so kind of you, Wren," Jason whispered back, his heart melted by the little boy's initiative. "What's your favorite?"

"This one!" Wren pulled out a yellow sugary cube. "It's made of lemon creams. But Mother makes it extra good because she puts her own honey on top. It's a secret."

Jason smiled and touched his finger to his lips. "I won't tell."

Laena watched the exchange with fondness. Jason's effortless charm with children made her smile.

Wren's mother stepped hurriedly from a tent with a basket of wrapped parcels. The brief expression of panic washed away to relief upon seeing her son safe.

Jason nodded politely as Wren wiggled out of his hold to return to her.

"He wasn't getting into mischief, I hope?" Wren's mother asked as she ran her fingers through her son's hair.

"Not at all," Jason replied. "We were having a nice little talk." He winked at Wren. "You should stay close to your mom, now." He addressed his mother again. "I don't think I ever got your name."

"Delia."

"It's good to see you again, Delia. Thank you for volunteering."

"Likewise." She smiled kindly, and held out her hand to Wren, who grabbed it tightly.

Jason winked again at Wren. "Don't eat all the sweets at once."

The boy laughed mischievously as mother and son vanished in the bustling crowds of Hündr and other volunteers.

"What a darling," Laena said.

"Oh yeah, he's a great kid," Jason agreed.

More carriages arrived, and Jason's heart swelled with joy at seeing the teams of horses ready to carry the lost children home. There must have been close to fifty. Volunteers directed traffic and organized the vehicles by banner.

In the meantime, Hündr women and other adult volunteers served stew in a large tent to the waiting children. The smell of spices and warmth permeated the thick fabric walls, and inside hungry children lined the simple benches and tables. Chatter was scarce as each devoured the steaming stew in their bowls. It had been too long since many of them had eaten a proper meal.

"You know, Scalaed can carry some, if we run out of carriages," Melanie offered.

Scalaed blinked at Melanie volunteering him without consent.

"That's a good idea," Elken agreed.

Scalaed stifled a groan.

"Which city?" Jason asked.

"Endlewood," Melanie replied. "If we have a scroll to read, it only makes sense to head back there."

Jason felt a hand clasp him on the shoulder, and he turned to meet Briefur's stern face. A quick flick of the trarewolf's icy blue eyes hinted he had news.

Stepping away into a quieter corner of the tent, much to the curiosity of their companions, Briefur whispered, "I just received word via Avis Messenger from my sister Bareth."

Jason straightened. "What did she say?"

"She plans to infiltrate the fortress."

"Okay"—Jason shifted his weight—"and you're sure she won't be caught?"

Briefur's eyes narrowed. "Do not doubt my sister."

Jason chewed his cheek with an anxious nod. While his curiosity matched Briefur's, he also worried about Bareth's safety. *Why does Thendrell want to stay in that fortress so badly?* Jason wondered with unease. Thendrell may have surrendered several crates of contraband, but who could prove that was all of it?

CHAPTER
8
The Castle of Ascenya

Despite Kyle's prayers, his cousins did not return. The following day came and went without any news. The silence stretched into a week, two weeks, a month. Melanie and Jason had been missing for twenty-nine days—so the detectives estimated—and the case had been picked up by international news stations. Lucy and Ian were bombarded by reporters and law enforcement, and Kyle tried his best to avoid the nightmare. One night he returned from the stables to see his family seated around the kitchen table with two detectives. Overwhelm sucked out his energy for conversation, so he promptly went to his room to sleep.

Edmund stopped by the ranch frequently in eager hopes that the police or detectives had any developments, specifically anything animal-related. He had lost the binder the day he found it. He had kicked himself so many times for leaving it out. The dinner rush that day had lasted two-and-a-half hours, during which the garbage truck had already come and gone. When Edmund had finally returned to the back to revisit the album, he saw the worktables cleared and sanitized, and he exploded. Of course, he couldn't divulge details as to why it was so important, but Gus felt horrible having not known.

Unfortunately, the album was lost forever.

Now, as the Waldens family converged in the kitchen to speak with the head detectives, Edmund sank into the leather sofa and thought of what Conrad had said earlier that month. The tracks could be fake. That prompted Edmund to wonder if the photos were fake as well. Maybe Melanie had an artistic hobby of generative imagery or photo manipulation, perhaps obsessively. Maybe she faked the instant films by taking a picture of her laptop screen displaying the altered image. Maybe believing the dragon had been real was completely unreasonable after all.

Who am I kidding? Edmund rubbed his face. *The dragon was probably the reason she was buying meat in the first place.* He opened his eyes. *Did I just casually acknowledge a dragon's existence? Maybe I should bring this up to the detectives.*

Considering what he knew about dragons, they liked to keep princesses in towers. Maybe the monster was forcing Melanie to be its servant, chaining her to silence and forcing her to retrieve food. That would explain a lot of Melanie's personality.

Once again, acknowledging dragons are real is pretty nuts, man, Edmund thought as he tossed a glance toward the kitchen. *Maybe Jason had come to rescue Mellie, but the dragon found out and...* Edmund froze at the next thought. *What if the dragon killed them?* His stomach twisted in nausea. *I need a professional's opinion, now.*

Launching himself from the sofa, he jogged at the brisk pace of his racing heart to the kitchen, where the other adults sat around the custom oak table.

"What is it, Eddie?" Lucy asked, noticing his concerned state.

All eyes landed on him, and the two detectives narrowed their eyes. Detective Harris, a tall woman with neat black plaits pulled into a bun, leaned forward. "Lost your tongue, sir?"

Edmund took a deep breath. "I found a photo album in a hidden compartment in Melanie's camper."

Conrad frowned. "What? Lewis never mentioned that feature when I bought the camper from him."

"The photos inside were…" Edmund's mouth dried, and he paused to bring back some moisture. "Startling, to say the least."

Ian crunched the napkin in dread until his knuckles popped. Lucy was visibly trembling.

"Son, does this album feature illegal activity?" Harris's partner, Detective Sandoval, raised a cautionary hand to pause Edmund, his face softening with concern.

Realizing how he was presenting the evidence alluded to possibly heinous crimes, Edmund stammered, "No! No, it's just…well, I'm gonna sound crazy, but I saw pictures of Melanie and Jason, and—and a dragon!"

"Oh really?" Harris asked, her penciled brows arching accusingly. "And where is this photo album now?"

"It…was thrown away. Accidentally." Edmund saw the room deflate, and he wanted to melt from embarrassment.

"Oh." Harris leaned back, lowering her false lashes skeptically. "How convenient."

"No, it was real! I swear!"

"We don't appreciate pranks at a time like this," Sandoval said angrily. "A phantom photo album with dragons and fairy tales...I think it's time you left." He scooted his chair back with a grating screech.

"I'm serious!" Edmund protested as Sandoval escorted him out. "Melanie is in danger! There were tracks! Please believe me!"

Ian and Lucy stared at each other in silent conversation, their eyes wild.

"Go home, son." Sandoval pushed Edmund out the door and closed it behind him.

Conrad stood up. "Wait, Detective, let him speak—"

"Mr. Waldens." Harris held up a hand to silence him. "We hear hodgepodge like this all the time. The human brain is capable of incredible fiction to compensate for extreme trauma. Believe me when I say there's no substance to it, and we didn't see any tracks."

"Well, it rained before you two showed—"

"Let's focus on what we know for a fact, which, frankly, isn't much," Harris's dark lips frowned, and she softened her voice, "Mr. and Mrs. Waldens, despite our exhaustive investigation, we haven't been able to find any evidence of your children's whereabouts. I am so sorry, but the more time passes, the less likely we will find your children alive if there was foul play."

Kyle opened his eyes to find himself surrounded by steep mountains. Looking down, he saw he was floating a good distance from the rocky ground.

I'm dreaming, he realized. *Is this a normal dream or another freak dream?*

The answer came as a shove, which directed Kyle deeper into the mountains, immune to his control.

Freak dream. Kyle thinned his lips. *Fantastic.*

A castle was nestled between two peaks. The light of the setting sun glinted off its sandy plaster so it blinked with flecks of gold. Pale green roofs and turret tops capped the towers, and the dramatic golden gates were edged with emeralds.

Kyle widened his eyes as he touched down in the luxurious courtyard. A great fountain blooming with crystal water filled the air with its soft voice. It was flanked by caramel marble griffons who spewed water in impossible currents; the coils of water twirled in spirals midair before joining the pool in the center. The golden stone gleamed in subtle rainbow colors as Kyle passed it. He tried to identify the rock, but his expansive knowledge came up empty.

Then, a distant song soared from the heights of the castle, and Kyle was pushed inside by the same invisible hands. Showers of golden light rained down from the many windows. A grand staircase lined with a glittering green rug led to a massive stained-glass window. The gentle hold over him released, and Kyle fanned out his arms in confusion. He had been given control. The freedom brought an excited smile to his face, and he moved himself closer to the image.

A beautiful woman glimmered in rainbow light. The intricacy of the cut glass, whose colors swirled in marbled shades, breathed vivid life into the picture. Adorned in golden armor, the warrior woman held a white banner of peace and wielded a sword.

Her waves of golden hair and gem-green eyes struck Kyle with a sense of familiarity.

The song returned, echoing from his left. The staircase split, the halves soaring in opposite directions, and Kyle floated up the left one.

The song grew louder as he followed it to an open doorway. He stopped before entering.

The sun spilled into the room in soft rays, the air sparkling in its warmth. A grand terrace lay past the room, opening to the mountain range and horizon beyond. The song filled the air—rich, slow, and aching. Kyle gasped at the beauty of the woman sitting with her side to him. Eyes closed to feel the music, the elegant woman from the stained-glass window filled her castle with melody. Her porcelain fingers stroked the strings of the strange instrument in her arms. The woman played it like a harp, but it sounded rich and full like a cello. Her fingers fluttered over the thick strings—if they *were* strings. Kyle inched closer. The way they pierced the light into prisms told Kyle the strings were fine tubes made of crystal.

That's ridiculous, Kyle humphed. *There's no way something so fragile could work.* The woman continued to play, her fingers delicately stroking the strings like one would the cheek of a loved one. He looked back at the woman's face. Her eyes were still closed, but the purest, softest smile played on her pink lips. Kyle felt warmth spread through his chest. She was gorgeous.

The music had called someone else.

Sensing another presence, Kyle turned to find the Golden Prince standing in the doorway in silence, smiling at the woman. Then it clicked. Kyle looked between them and realized this was the Celestial Empress Tavnir had mentioned in his first dream.

Kyle took a step back, knitting his eyebrows. He had never dreamed up a sequel before. Looking back at the Empress, he watched her hair, electrified by the golden light, flow to the music. Kyle could almost smell the sweetness of the song in the air.

She stopped playing, to Kyle's disappointment, and the last note was whisked away by the breeze. The Empress rose to her feet and held out her arms to the Golden Prince.

"My son," she greeted the man lovingly as she took his hands in hers.

Kyle wanted to melt from her voice.

The Prince smiled in reply. "Mother."

She adjusted his crown unnecessarily and stroked his face. "The darkness has grown. Thornbrill's defeat stirs something in the shadows."

The Prince held her hand to his face and kissed it. "I feel

it, too."

The Empress stepped away, leading them to the terrace. "What do you see, my son?"

Kyle lingered behind them, eager to eavesdrop, as the Prince joined his mother and took a deep breath of the evening air. "I see the darkness of which you speak. Shapeless, like a form of black mist, it haunts our steps. I cannot see into it. The enemy hides beyond my sight."

"An enemy that may bring an evil Tindoria has never known." The Empress folded her hands together in contemplation.

"But the Descendant does not stand alone," her son said.

"You must send the other, for he holds the key to the Adamas Chamber."

"Yes, I intend to do so soon."

The Empress turned to face her son. "Do not interfere heavily," she warned. "If we control every turn of every future, then who can truly find who they are meant to be? The Descendant and the Descendant's allies must bear these events themselves. We, as Guardians, observe and present the beginnings of their paths when the time is right, but only they can take the first steps. They learn and grow by their own independence."

"Yes, Mother." He held her hand then looked off to the side. "I see something else…"

"Is that so?"

"Yes." He closed his eyes as he leaned on the terrace rails. "The boy…" He opened his eyes, confused. "…is here."

Both Celestials turned and looked directly at Kyle.

Feeling like an intruder, Kyle backed away. "I am so sorry. I didn't mean to eavesdrop, but it's kind of not my fault, it's my dream."

The Celestials did not look angry, but amused more than anything.

"I'll just see myself out." Kyle spun on his heel but tripped. He felt his cheek hit the carpet, and he awoke. Half of his body remained tangled in the sheets, suspending him by his waist while his head and arms lay sprawled on the floor.

Disoriented, Kyle managed to free himself and lay panting on the floor. A creeping suspicion told him these dreams were no longer just dreams.

CHAPTER
9
Conversion

The fortress now felt like a tomb—silent, but no less threatening. Bareth hoped Thendrell *was* hiding secrets here. If he were exposed as a liar about his solitude, he would also be sent to prison with the rest of the Thornbrillians. And for Bareth, that was exactly what he deserved.

Scanning the tree line before leaving the forest, the trarewolf caught the whiff of haunting familiarity. Wolf ears upright and eyes alert, she took one step back into the trees. It was a scent unearthed from the corners of her mind. She lay low and crawled into a wild berry bush. Hoping the berries would mask her, she watched anxiously. She could see nothing, but sensed someone, or something, was very close.

Helnah stood in front of the window of her bedroom watching the distant relief compound disperse. She had tried to discern what its purpose was, but her fragile circumstance prevented any investigation. She was a ghost. Invisibility cloaked her with a peace she hadn't known in years. But like a rose, the beauty of her peace was riddled with thorns. She may have inadvertently fooled the world with her death, but she lost her empire. Helnah set her shoulders and closed her eyes. She would not be defeated so easily. Against all odds, she had survived her dragon self's death. She had been given a second chance to save this realm. And one day, she would live in Tindoria, safe and freed.

Thendrell opened the door behind her and placed a tray of food on a table before he slowly approached her side.

"I can feel it, Thendrell," Helnah sighed. Eyes still closed, she slowly opened her hands. "I can feel the warmth again. No longer does the cold stalk my every moment." Helnah allowed a smile as she breathed in. "None will understand the joy I feel in this moment. And over such a simple thing…"

Thendrell smiled, too. "It's good to see you smile, Helnah."

She turned around. Her hair was now combed back behind her ears. Despite the wrinkled scars crossing half her face, Helnah looked stronger for them.

Thendrell gestured to the food, and both sat.

"Thank you, Thendrell," Helnah finally said, "for not abandoning me."

"Helnah, without you we could all perish. I never thought my demands for surrender would be honored, but perhaps someone is still listening to this poor man's prayers."

"Now all believe I am dead." Helnah nodded.

"And I will uphold my end of the treaty to keep it that way. My only desire was to tend to you in secret."

"I can only hope Elken found the Kottrans when I threw him. I knew he had that enchanted necklace to protect him."

"Indeed. It was a risky strategy to reveal the true enemy."

"It's not just Klarn we face, but others he may have recruited. Other corrupted kings. If he was able to avoid Edgial Execution, who's to say others didn't as well? That would expand his plan beyond Hvitria." Helnah's dark eyes pierced the window beyond.

Then a bellowing voice from outside called, "Thendrell of Thornbrill, show yourself!"

Helnah froze, and Thendrell put a finger to his lips. He crept to the window and squinted down at the dark figure below.

A black fur cowl draped the muscular frame of the large man. He wore a long velvet overcoat, black like his hair, tied with a silver belt, from which hung a long sword. Though his skin was gray, devoid of all color, his eyes were sparkling yellow. His long, black tail lay behind him, only the very tip flicking.

Helnah carefully peered through the window. "It's him." She felt her body tightening with hatred. "Thendrell, it's Klarn." She grabbed a sword. "I need to kill him now."

Thendrell took her arm. "He must not know that you live. That would destroy your advantage." Helnah held her penetrative gaze as Thendrell continued, "Should he have allies, his death could expedite whatever plans they made, and we are not prepared. We need to know more."

Helnah's furious grip finally loosened, and the sword slipped into Thendrell's hand.

He opened the window and called down, "What do you want?"

"Just to talk with, as it seems, the last of the Thornbrillians," Klarn replied.

"I have nothing to say or share."

"I don't think that's true." Klarn tilted his head, unblinking. "Where is the Pyrium Dragon?"

"I don't know what you mean."

"Spare me your feigned ignorance. I know your late leader found one. What has she done with it?"

"Alas." Thendrell sighed. "Helnah was slain in battle, and most of her knowledge has died with her."

"Hmm." Klarn looked down at his silver clad boots. "Thendrell, perhaps you know not with whom you speak. Deny me what is mine, and I will haunt the very air you breathe, steal it away into the shadows, and leave you groveling for your life."

Thendrell could not let him know Helnah was alive. He needed him gone before he found out. He needed to divert him. "The dragon is no longer in my possession. It was stolen by a girl who has trained it to be a pet."

Thendrell noticed Klarn breathe deeply through his nose. He seemed either nervous or annoyed.

"Where are they now? By what name does this girl go?" Klarn asked, eagerness in his voice.

"Melanie," Thendrell replied. "Melanie of the Separate Realm."

Klarn's eyes glowed in sudden interest. "Interesting. Thank you." He turned to leave.

"I warn you," Thendrell added, "she and her brother have power. I do not think you will obtain what you seek so easily."

Klarn seemed to ignore him and disappeared into the shadows of the woods.

"Thendrell!" Helnah whacked his arm. "You talk too much."

"I sent him away! He will no longer bother us. I simply redirected him."

Helnah wearily rubbed her forehead.

"What?"

"I cannot believe I am saying this," she mumbled. "We must help Jason."

Thendrell scoffed in disbelief. *Has she gone mad?* "But everyone will see you're alive!"

"Thendrell, listen to me, and listen well." Helnah poked his chest with each sentence. "I knew Jason and his sister had powers. I knew their mysterious arrival was significant. I knew they must be part of the Spire's Scroll. I wanted them on *my* side to help defend Tindoria from Klarn's return." Helnah curled her fingers into a contemplative fist, then dropped it by her side with a sigh. "They are our only hope, Thendrell, do you understand? And since you've sent Klarn to them, we must leave now to protect them. I know more about that monster than they, and they will learn who I really am."

Thendrell stepped closer to her. "They will try to kill you," he warned, his brilliant blue eyes glaring sharply.

Also taking a step closer, Helnah enunciated, "They saved me." She blinked. "I owe it to them."

Thendrell grabbed her arms as concern laced his voice. "But will Klarn's spies not see you?"

"It is a risk I am willing to take." Helnah turned up her nose, now mere inches away from Thendrell's.

Torment and fear—not for himself—rolled in Thendrell's eyes like storm clouds. His grip on Helnah's arms softened as did his voice. "Then I will take it with you."

Slowly, Bareth's legs had gone numb, but she dared not move. Being frozen with fear was a foreign sensation for her. The scent vanished, but she was fighting to convince herself it was safe. Her nose must have been mistaken. She could not have possibly smelled...*that*. Bareth wagged her tail once and scoured her surroundings. Nothing. She sat back on her haunches. Nothing.

The fear melted away, and she sprinted on wolf paws to the foot of the mountain. Keeping close to the mountainside and low to the ground, she snaked up the pathway to the daunting red gate. It was far too heavy and conspicuous to open.

Assuming her human form, she summoned her claws, gripped the fortress's stone walls and scaled to the nearest window, slipping through it like liquid.

Bareth took a steadying breath upon realizing she was in

the throne room. Like the cave of a dragon, it oozed stale evil. The cold chandelier, black and skeletal, hung like a trap poised to kill her, and the red rug stretched to the ominous throne like a trail of blood. But Bareth knew the dragon that lived here had been slain; this room did not threaten her. With a scoff, she lowered herself on all fours to take on her wolf form. She sniffed the ground. So many smells. All human. All before the battle, except one. *Thendrell,* she thought with distaste. Creeping along the floor, she followed the fresh scent out the room to the main hall.

Bareth bolted upright at the approaching sound of footsteps and voices. There was more than one person.

Devious delight fluttered in Bareth's chest at the prospect of throwing Thendrell in prison for lying, and she hid behind one of the empty, cold braziers that lined the otherwise bare hallway.

Two cloaked people rushed into the hall from the room opposite the throne room, and the next smell that hit Bareth's nose filled her with shock and rage.

Helnah was alive.

Her cloak swirled about her as she strode purposefully past Bareth, and the trarewolf lost all sense.

Returning to her human form, Bareth climbed on top of the brazier and unsheathed her knife. Then she leaped with a scream toward Tindoria's ruthless enemy.

Helnah wheeled around and caught her by the throat, ripping the knife effortlessly from Bareth's grip.

"What…" Thendrell stumbled back stunned.

Helnah held Bareth's murderous gaze. "Now, what have we here?"

Bareth, prying at the woman's strong grip, locked eyes on the web of scars that covered half of Helnah's face. "Snake!" she choked.

"Funny, you look more Hündr than snake." A dark, satisfied smile twitched on Helnah's lips, and she let go of Bareth, who crumpled to her knees, gasping.

By the time Bareth composed herself to retaliate, the frigid point of a sword kissed her neck. Her eyes trailed up the weapon's edge to where Helnah's hand held the grip.

"Listen well, Hündr." Helnah's voice was as cold as the blade. "I am not the enemy."

Bareth's nose curled in a canine snarl.

"What is your name?" Thendrell's calm voice interrupted.

"Bareth, daughter of Brefiüll," she said.

"Bareth," Thendrell said levelly. He hoped sounding kind would convince her of the looming danger. "The true enemy is coming for Melanie and Jason. I can see in your eyes you've sensed something amiss."

The trarewolf spat. "I sense a darkness I can only assume is the haunting of your sins."

"Spare me, wolf." Helnah rolled her eyes. "My sins haunt me enough without your mentioning. Almost as much as he who has imposed himself to be my master. You may recognize his name."

Helnah withdrew the blade and knelt to Bareth's level to whisper into her ear. "Klarn."

The walls warped in Bareth's peripheral, and she felt like she was shrinking. Kottrans cloaked in smoke and ash burned in her mind. Yellow eyes void of remorse seared her memories as she heard the screams. "No," the word was barely audible.

"He is trying to escape his banishment," Helnah continued in a whisper, eyeing the darkness around them. "With a Pyrium Dragon, he and his tribe could return to wreak havoc on Tindoria."

Helnah stood up with a changed composure—a somber tilt in her head, a weary sag in her shoulders—and sheathed her sword. "Your friends are in danger, Bareth," she pleaded in a tone that struck Bareth with its genuine desperation. "Please, tell me where they are. I can help them."

Helnah reached out her hand in a truce, vaporizing any logic in Bareth's brain. Bareth lifted her eyes from the hand to Helnah's face, and the woman stared into her soul.

"I know you smelled Klarn," Helnah said. "We must warn Melanie and Jason." She inched her hand closer.

Bareth recalled the smell that had stayed her earlier advance. Helnah was right. Klarn had returned.

Studying every detail of the woman's hand, Bareth could only smell Helnah's truthfulness. And that unnerved her more.

The trarewolf grabbed Helnah's hand. "Endlewood."

CHAPTER
10
Conspiracies

Helnah tossed her hair out of her face as she hurried down the hall, gripping the scrolls and manuscripts that slipped out of her arms. She smiled at the guards in passing.

"Another breakthrough?" one asked in amusement.

"We shall see," Helnah replied with a sparkle in her eye. "Their behavior has calmed since the mating season, and I may yet be able to communicate with them."

"You are a crazy woman, Helnah." The guard shivered playfully. "I could never be so close to dragons."

"I quite agree." Helnah hefted her scrolls. "They'd find you more appetizing."

The guard shooed her away. "Have fun."

"You too, Thendrell."

"I'll try," Thendrell called back. "Standing here…it's riveting."

Helnah smiled to herself. Her three dragon specimens were proving to be a treasure trove of discoveries. And with the support of King Eldrain's Royal Science Society, she had the workshop space and equipment to fulfill her mission of protecting Endlewood. Her happy mood made the palace appear especially beautiful today. The long, tiled hall flanked by ballrooms and libraries shimmered in faint shades of green. The spilling curtains that framed the soaring windows flowed in the breeze. Even the weather agreed with Helnah: today would be a good day.

At the end of the hall, Helnah greeted another set of guards and passed through the doorway. Descending the ornate spiral staircase, she entered the lowest castle level.

Helnah's lab adjoined an arena. Sunk into the earth so the highest tiers of seats were level with the ground above, the arena was empty this time of year. With no fights, jousting, or theater, Helnah took the opportunity to observe the dragons in a large space for flight and social behavior. She had commissioned a chained lattice over the arena to keep her subjects protected and contained. Her lab was technically the backstage of the arena that connected via iron gates. The daylight from the arena shone through them and its accompanying windows, lifting any doubts of feeling like a dungeon.

"Good morning!" She released her cargo on a table as she waved to her dragons.

The dragons stopped pacing in their spacious cells and eyed her through the barred steel divide.

"Did we sleep well last night?" Helnah asked as she rolled up her dress sleeves. She approached the first cell, which housed a male dragon. "You know the routine." Grabbing a fistful of meat, she unlocked the cage. While the dragons were now accustomed to her presence, they still were not fully at ease. Helnah distracted the beast with the treat as she extracted a red scale with a pair of long tweezers. After pocketing it, she unraveled a thin rope and deftly measured the length of the dragon. "Growth is consistent," Helnah noted as she reeled in the rope. "My predictions have been accurate thus far since our beginning three months ago."

Helnah spent nearly a year preparing for the dragons. Clearing the arena, formulating a training program, and collaborating with the top hunters of the city in tracking down dragons before they successfully captured three of them.

Helnah repeated her morning routine with the other two dragons, a blue male and a green female.

"I'm trying again today," she warned her dragons. "I do hope you'll listen to me this time."

In the early stages of her research, this test almost always ended in fiery breath, which cost her some singed clothes and burnt notes. But she was determined to train them to listen to cues and commands. If only she could make them trust her.

She unlocked the female's cage, and the green dragon cautiously emerged. Grabbing her shield as per protocol, Helnah dangled a nice steak to entice her subject.

"Now *sit*. Like this." Helnah sat on the floor, the shield still off to her side.

The dragon shifted her gaze between Helnah and the steak.

"That's right," Helnah nodded. "Pick the steak this time. You should be well aware that trying to roast me doesn't get you what you want."

The dragon took a step closer, penetrating Helnah with her yellow eyes.

Helnah had a revelation. "If you won't do something different, perhaps I will."

She let go of the shield, letting it roll to the wayside.

The dragon froze, analyzing the new situation.

"Sit," Helnah commanded again.

The dragon flicked her tail, settled it around her claws, and sat.

"Yes!" Helnah wanted to cry out, but kept her exclamation to an overjoyed gasp. She tossed the steak at the dragon and snatched a scroll to scribble in her newest success.

King Eldrain had granted her access to this room for her research. Their deal was such: if she could provide improvements to the royal military, she would be given command of it. Over the past fifteen years, each of the other cities had been attacked by an unknown force. Hvitria was the latest, with a harrowing development of animated death arising in the battle's aftermath. Endlewood had been spared so far, but the royal council concluded the Green Capital was well within the warpath. Thus, King Eldrain ordered for stronger defenses. With that motivation, Helnah had devised a program for training dragons as weapons. Unmatched in strength and power, and gifted with fire, dragons would be the perfect opposing force for such an infested enemy. And now, upon discovering a lead in communicating more clearly, the path to domestication seemed all the clearer.

"Well done!" Helnah praised the green dragon and lured

her outside into the arena by wiggling another juicy slab of meat. She watched with pride as the dragon stretched her wings and flew laps around the arena.

When Helnah returned inside, she immediately noticed the other two dragons had lowered their heads, glaring in her direction, still and unblinking.

"What's wrong?" she asked them, recognizing their anxious behavior.

The blue dragon shot fire through the steel bars of his cage, and Helnah spun out of the way, instantly procuring a sword and shield from the table next to her. She knew her dragons well enough to realize it wasn't her they were anxious about.

A sound, like the whisper of a sheet, floated from the darkest corner of the room. Helnah snapped her head in its direction. A mountainous man emerged from the wavering cloud. Gray tendrils poured out of the walls and swirled around him.

Helnah adjusted her grip on her sword and extended it toward the intruder.

Like an illustration abandoned to its gray incompletion, he was devoid of any color, except for his unnerving yellow eyes. They met Helnah's.

She took a few steps closer to the intruder, sword ready to strike. "Do not move."

"Oh, you misunderstand," the stranger said in a deep, rich voice. "I have no quarrel with you."

"Who are you, and what is it you want?" Helnah

interrogated.

Now the man took a step toward her, and in the subtle change of light, Helnah could identify the ink-black ears and lion tail. He was Kottran.

Klarn. The shock stole Helnah's boldness. She took a step back, her face twisting in disbelief. *This is impossible. I heard he was executed a year ago!*

"I need your help." Klarn folded his hands behind his back.

Dread settled in the pit of Helnah's stomach.

"And should you refuse or alert anyone of this, I will kill you. My spies will be watching you from any shadow. Anyone you tell will be murdered in front of you, and your own demise will follow." Klarn's eyes narrowed with a sly grin. "I hope this is quite clear."

Helnah's arm wavered beneath the weight of her sword, and Klarn noticed.

"Let's dispose of the weapons and discuss my demands like civilized people," he said.

Fighting to find something to say, Helnah ultimately kept her silence as she lay down her sword and shield.

"Now..." Klarn walked past her and scanned the two male dragons. "You have been studying dragons for His Royal Highness's army, is that correct?"

"Yes," Helnah said.

Klarn eyed her over his shoulder, and the thick black fur of his cape seemed to bristle. "Have you ever heard of the Pyrium Dragon?"

"I don't know." Helnah gathered her wits and began to calm her nerves. While vaguely tuned to this conversation, she sifted through possibilities of how Klarn had survived and what such a result could forebode. One thing was certain: Helnah would not help this twisted creature. How to avoid that and remain alive was another matter.

"The Pyrium Dragon is a rare beast of legend that harnesses an incredible ability," Klarn said as he approached Helnah. "It does indeed exist, and you will train one for me."

"Why?" Helnah stared him down.

"Don't you see?" Klarn continued, displaying his gray arms. "I cannot be in Tindoria for long. My people are anchored to the realm called Merrendogith: a fallen, decaying reflection of Tindoria. We are chained to the shadows and cannot escape beyond shadow travel, and the oceans that join our worlds are guarded by the Naiads. Only the Pyruim will free us!"

Helnah thinned her lips. So Klarn was still trapped. She intended to keep him that way. Already the looms of her mind began weaving a plan for his destruction.

"This will be such fun." Klarn's eyes twinkled, and the corners of his mouth curled slightly in a smirk. "My spies will help in the search, and you will be the one to capture and train the Pyrium. And in the end"—Klarn's eyes roved over Helnah—"it will be yours to do with what you wish. I'm sure King Eldrain would be most pleased. In the meantime, act as if we never had this conversation. I will return to give more instruction and oversee your progress. Do not fail me." Then he stepped backwards into the corner and dissolved into the shadow, his glowing yellow eyes the last to disappear.

Helnah breathed heavily as she dropped into her chair. Rummaging through her stack of borrowed dragon books on the worktable next to her, she shakily fanned through the pages for any information on the mysterious Pyrium Dragon. There was nothing. Frazzled, Helnah snatched a quill and paper and shuffled through the panicked thoughts in her mind as she scribbled.

The paper was like lead in Helnah's hands as she dropped them in her lap. *There's an uncharted realm about which we know frighteningly little.* She leaned forward on steepled fingers, eyes wide. *Who dwells there? What dwells there? What instruments of war or magic has Klarn harnessed? What is his plan? How do I warn others without risking their lives?*

Weary from the headache and from fear, Helnah leaned down on the table. She was trapped. There was no one to help her. And for all she knew, Klarn's invisible spies were watching her every move.

Two palace guards approached Thendrell and his partner for rotation.

Thendrell's partner nudged him as they left their post. "So?"

"So *what*, Emmid?" Thendrell's thumbs found his belt,

anxious for something to fidget with. Emmid's mischievous smile left little doubt as to what he was thinking.

"It's happening today, isn't it?"

Thendrell smiled. "I think so."

"You *have* to invite her out for a romantic afternoon," Emmid insisted. "The Jade Bridge is a perfect place to get to know her!"

"You act like I don't want to through with it," Thendrell chided him.

Emmid threw up his hands. "I'm simply making sure."

"Demina has already assembled the basket, and I'm going down to the kitchen to fetch it. Then I'll go to Helnah and ask her if she is available this afternoon," Thendrell explained.

"Do tell me tomorrow how it goes," Emmid clapped his friend on his shoulder and parted ways. "She's a lovely catch," Emmid called back. "Aspiring general, intelligent, clever, all you have to find out now is if she can clean and cook."

"You are aware I do such basics myself. My aunt is the head palace cook, after all!" Thendrell retorted.

Smells and warmth wafted through the hall as Thendrell entered the palace kitchen. Teams of servants and footmen bustled in and out with polished platters and pressed linens in preparation for the royal lunch. A tall woman with silver-streaked hair, his Aunt Demina, waved over her staff members to Thendrell.

Demina presented a large basket, which she passed to him. "Fresh, warm bread, a jar of your favorite savory spice spread, a lovely serving of chilled ham, fruit, cheese, and a bottle of wine," she listed proudly.

"Thank you, Aunt Demina." Thendrell kissed her cheek. "You are an angel."

"I know, dear. Now off with you!" She shooed him away playfully. "I have a kitchen to rule."

Thendrell had never been to the arena since Helnah commandeered it for her research. Being so close to multiple wild dragons unnerved him. But his affection for Helnah pushed him forward. He wanted to make his move, so he steeled his nerves and descended the stairs.

"Hello?" Thendrell called cautiously from the winding stairwell. He first saw the three large cages empty, their doors hung ajar. Helnah must have given the dragons their recess, something she had once told him when describing her routine. "Helnah?" he called again as he reached the bottom step and saw the rest of the room.

Startled, Helnah launched herself from her seat at her worktable and quickly flipped over her notes. "Thendrell!" She dumped a stack of books on them. "What are you doing here?"

Now is not a good time, my friend! she thought. Then she noticed the basket.

Thendrell cleared his throat and summoned a steadying breath to keep his voice level. "Would you happen to have some free time in your busy schedule to spend the afternoon with me?" he asked. Noticing her state, he added, "Helnah, what's wrong? You look frazzled."

Helnah nervously combed her hair, "Oh, it's nothing," she lied. "Perhaps a break would do me good. Let me return the dragons to their cages."

"I'll wait for as long as I need to." Thendrell smiled warmly and sat on the table's edge next to his basket.

Helnah's smile looked like a mask, and Thendrell watched in concern as she entered the arena.

What could have happened to her? He glanced once more at the arena gates before slowly pulling out the piece of paper he'd seen her hide. His eyes widened in horror. Klarn was alive. *It can't be!* He rubbed his face and tried to take a breath.

The clang of steel shook Thendrell from the note, and he quickly returned it to its place under the books.

Helnah walked beside the red dragon as she led him inside his cage.

The size of the beast added to Thendrell's alarm. Muscle rippled beneath the dragon's scales as he walked, his tail swayed in step, and his wings bounced from their sheer weight.

Helnah remained with the dragon for a moment, placing a hand on his shoulder. The dragon looked back at her, his eyes searching for a translation of this new attitude. Helnah sighed as her hand glided down his scales, too overwhelmed to notice how easily the dragon had allowed her to touch him.

The other two dragons filed into the room, and Helnah beckoned them into their respective cages followed by the gift of meat-filled buckets. She quickly returned to Thendrell, who stood quite still and looked pale.

Helnah almost smiled in amusement. "You can relax. The dragons have no interest in you."

Thendrell could only give a brittle laugh in response; the

dragons weren't the only things that left him terrified.

Before they left, Thendrell caught Helnah quickly throwing her notes into the fire. He did not pursue the topic.

The Jade Bridge arched over Endlewood's main road, joining the higher levels of the city. Like the palace, the bridge was constructed of green marble, and gold filigree decorated the parapets surrounded by blooming flowers and ivy, which beckoned butterflies and small, colorful birds. A balcony filled with seating ran alongside the bridge for citizens to stop and enjoy the sights of the city. It was here that Thendrell set down his basket and pulled out a chair for Helnah.

She hadn't spoken since they left the arena, and it pained Thendrell not to ask why. He knew the reason.

"My research has taken a different direction," Helnah finally said as Thendrell prepared the snacks.

"Oh?" Thendrell glanced up from his spread knife. He had calmed his nerves for Helnah's sake and intended to give her a pleasant outing. "How so?"

"It's a daunting undertaking, one that I'm very restless about, but it is absolutely necessary in these times."

"I see." Thendrell slid Helnah her plate filled with warm bread slices covered in a green, fragrant spice spread, with plump strawberries on the side. He hoped the fresh food would comfort her. "And your dragons will be a part of this?"

"They are vital." Helnah slowly nodded. Conflict churned in her stomach and threatened to steal her appetite, but she took a bite of strawberry to spite it. Desperate pleas for help clawed up her throat. Helnah clenched her fingers but managed to say, "I fear this is too much for me to do alone."

"I'll help." Thendrell barely let her finish.

"You have no idea what it is I'll ask of you," Helnah said with a tinge of sadness.

"I trust you. Just let me be there for you." Thendrell swelled with resolve. He reached to hold her hand, but Helnah shakily withdrew.

"Thendrell." Helnah's voice was sweeter now, though heavy. "I am aware of the mutual feelings we share, but with this new operation, there will be neither time nor room for romance. We must put aside all personal desires for the greater good."

Thendrell's heart dropped. But he understood. She needed his support, and he would wait for her. "Then let us enjoy this afternoon together as best we can." He raised his wine glass. "To your success, and to patience."

Touching her glass to his, Helnah gave him a smile, though it sliced her heart like a knife. It was all so unfair. She had been waiting for Thendrell's advances, but now that future was shattered. *How is he so understanding?* She had barely divulged any details, yet he had joined her blindly. Now here he sat with those brilliant blue eyes and a warm smile that melted Helnah. The misery made it hard for her to breathe, and her fingers clenched her wine glass so tightly she thought it might break. She vowed to use this newfound rage to destroy Klarn if it was the last thing she did.

"Yes," Helnah agreed in no more than a whisper. "To our success and to patience."

CHAPTER

11

Dinner at Edgestone

Excitement and life infused the relief camp, and the laughter of anxious children bubbled from the fleet of carriages as they boarded.

Melanie watched the scene with a smile from the edge of camp. She was proud of Jason. And with Elken alive, she felt lighter despite the looming mission ahead.

"It will take them more than a day to reach Endlewood," Elken said as he stepped up behind her.

"They're so close to going home." Melanie nodded at a pair of boys laughing and bouncing, their borrowed robes flopping about their little frames. A hand grabbed hers, and Melanie's heart leaped as she was spun into Elken's embrace.

"You have no idea how much I've missed you," he whispered.

She melted into his arms. There was the faintest brokenness in his voice, and Melanie's eyes began to sting as she responded shakily, "I missed you, too."

Elken nuzzled his face into her neck, his thumb stroking her back. Her heartbeat permeated through to his, syncing the two in a calm and steady rhythm. Melanie hooked her arms higher up Elken's back as he combed her hair.

"Don't let go," he breathed. "Let's just stay like this. For a bit."

Melanie smiled as she pressed her face into his tunic and squeezed him. "I'm here."

Suddenly Elken lit up. He released Melanie and grabbed her hand, pulling her along close behind him.

"Where are we going?" Melanie skipped to match his pace and wrapped both of her arms around one of his. Her heart soared at the mystery and excitement ahead.

The two hurried through the forest, following a sloping path to the Flüm Thrae. In this particular spot, the river became a bubbling brook that sparkled like glass. Birdsong flitted from the treetops, which occasionally dropped a leaf to the vibrant, spongy moss below.

"Romantic, isn't it?" Elken said. "Water, waves, rivers… something about its sound is musical and restorative. I could lie here and listen to this woodland symphony for hours."

"Why don't we?" Melanie nudged his shoulder and plopped down on her back in the moss. "Like you said, we have time before the kids arrive in Endlewood."

Elken lay next to her. He opened his hand for her to place hers. Melanie brushed her fingers against his palm, then settled her hand in his. Butterflies fluttered in her stomach as they slowly entwined their fingers. His hand was warm and rough—the hand of a soldier, of a protector.

"Back home, there was a forest kind of like this," Melanie began. "It was years ago, and I had gone to camp in the woods for fun. It's an activity people on Earth do as a way to disconnect from the busyness of cities and people and work. To reconnect with the tranquility of nature and find peace in its beauty."

Elken had turned on his side to listen more closely. He held her hand close to his heart, and his eyes twinkled with delight as she continued.

"So I was on this trail that wound through the forest." Melanie gesticulated with her other hand. "And I saw something sparkle deep in the bushes." Her voice dropped to a dramatic whisper. "It might have been treasure."

Elken leaned in, their noses almost touching. "Was it?"

Melanie smiled as she bit her lip, stretching the suspense. "Nah, it was trash."

"That's not true." Elken squinted playfully as he tapped her nose. "What was it really?"

"You have the most beautiful eyes." Melanie toyed with him. "So many colors. Heterochromia?"

"No, no, don't avoid my question!" Elken poked her side, increasingly amused. "What was in the bush?"

Melanie squealed and squirmed to escape the tickling, but Elken wrapped his arms around her tightly. "Where do you think you're going?" he asked, laughing.

Melanie giggled through his restraints. "I warn you, I will not be at fault if I injure you during this altercation." She managed to slip out from his grasp and landed in the shallow brook, where she swiped water at Elken.

"Oh, now you've done it." Elken jumped into the water and scooped a bigger splash onto Melanie.

Exclaiming in shock from the cold, Melanie recoiled, but soon rebutted by playfully kicking waves into his face as she closed in.

Shielding his face, Elken reached blindly through the attacks and grabbed Melanie, whisking her out of the water. He stumbled, and both fell onto the mossy shore with Melanie landing on his chest.

Wet and breathless, they remained still. His eyes locked with Melanie's in an affectionate gaze, and Elken brushed back a wet coil of Melanie's hair.

"So what was the sparkle?" he whispered.

Settling on top of his chest, Melanie finally divulged the truth. "It was Scalaed's egg."

"So it really *was* treasure," Elken added.

"Yeah." Melanie chuckled softly. "I gained a wonderful friendship, and I don't think Jason and I would be this close if Scalaed hadn't crossed my path. Of course…" Melanie cocked her head and subtly thumbed Elken's goatee, "…it also led me to you."

"My beautiful alien," Elken joked and wrapped his arms around her again. They rolled to their sides, disregarding the moss clinging to their clothes.

A breeze blew over them, carrying the distant sounds of camp. Reality of the world beyond, sobering and unwarranted, slowly returned.

Still in a tight embrace, Melanie reluctantly reminded him, "We should head back."

"No," came Elken's muffled reply, although he released

her shortly after. Picking himself up and briskly dusting off any clinging moss, he offered Melanie his hand.

"Seriously though, what color are your eyes?" she asked as she was raised to her feet.

"I've never had to describe them," Elken confessed.

"Maybe my brother, Mr. Diagnosis, would know," Melanie suggested as she ascended the slope.

Hand in hand, they returned to the disbanding camp.

Scalaed noticed them first. With a judgmental glare, he alerted Jason, who turned around from a conversation with Laena.

"There you are!" Jason exclaimed.

"We weren't gone that long." When she caught Scalaed's snide expression, Melanie rolled her eyes. "We were just talking," she enunciated, specifically to the dragon.

Scalaed snorted, unconvinced.

"About my eyes." Elken stepped in. "Apparently she finds them intriguing."

Jason was instantly interested. "Let me see."

An awkward gaze was held between the two men as Jason studied the colors in Elken's irises.

"Hey, man."

"Hey."

"How are you?"

"The usual. You?"

"Same."

Jason stepped back with a satisfied grin. "Well, dude, I'd say you'd have both sectoral and central heterochromia in both eyes, but I never knew a case could have that many colors."

Melanie pivoted to face Elken with a wide smile. "See? I told you that you've got the most beautiful eyes!"

"I agree; that's super cool," Jason nodded. "How come I haven't seen this until now?"

"We're never in close romantic proximity." Elken smiled and patted him on the back.

Jason smirked. "Touché. Let's keep it that way."

Melanie leaned against Elken's shoulder as she looked around. Horses pawed the ground, impatient to gallop away with their precious passengers.

"That's the last carriage right there." Briefur approached, pointing to Laena's personal coach. Four Vhysper horses struggled against their bridles, snorting in their craving for the road. Painted a pearl green signature to Endlewood, the coach was furnished with gold-leaf trim and luscious seats, each of which held a giddy child. Some had fallen asleep instantly, while others pressed their faces against the windows, anxiously watching for a sign they would begin their return journey.

Two men on horseback finished trotting through the fleet of carriages, having verified all had boarded. With a circular wave, they cleared the fleet for departure. Children yelled their goodbyes and waved as the carriages rumbled past.

Jason waved back. "That's amazing you brought your carriage, Laena."

"It bears the most important passengers it will ever know," Laena said with a final wave. Cries of goodbyes and well wishes from the volunteers sent the carriages off in an ocean of joy.

"I hear you are off to Endlewood soon?" Briefur asked.

Jason nodded. "And you?"

Briefur looked around as he inhaled deeply. "As our chief, Helmir carries a ponderous weight, especially now that Vytia is with child. Fallon and I will do what we can to support him as he reveals the appalling news to the rest of our people. We will return to the White Village once I receive Bareth's update."

"Well, in case I don't see you…" Jason held out his hand.

Briefur clasped it firmly, and Jason brought him in for a reassuring pat on the back. "Thanks for everything, man. It means a lot."

"Don't say it like you'll never see me again." Briefur pulled away with one eyebrow raised. "I sense another entanglement of fate in the near future."

"Safe travels, Briefur." Jason waved the trarewolf off and turned again to the distant fleet of carriages. Their flags soared as high as Jason's spirits.

Laena watched Jason beaming at the scene. "Jason," she began, her heart beating faster.

Jason turned to face her.

She feared she would appear presumptuous, and only managed to say, "Dinner."

Jason's eyebrow popped up. "Sorry?"

"Well," Laena squeezed her hands. "Seeing as your work here is done, my father, Lord Evinsor, wants to invite you to dinner at our home."

"He does?" Jason blinked in surprise.

"Well, I do, too," Laena added quickly. "Please say yes." She bit her lip in apprehension. "It's the least I can do to repay you for all you've done."

"Uh…" Jason laughed awkwardly. The flash of excitement simmered down to anxiety. *I'd have to make a good impression.* "What time again?" he stammered.

Laena smiled nervously. "This evening."

"Oh, of course!" Jason shook his head to clear it. "I'm sorry, my brain is just a little fried right now."

"It's alright. I can only imagine what else is in it, I'd love to know."

"Well…" Jason took a step closer despite the heat reddening in his ears. "Maybe we can talk over a flight?"

"I'd love to." Laena tilted her head, spilling her rose gold locks over her shoulder.

As he led Laena to find Poison Ivy, Jason caught Melanie giving him a sly thumbs-up, her face scrunched in teasing approval. Tossing back an equally teasing expression, Jason mouthed, "Oh, stop."

He cleared his throat and returned his attention to Laena. "You look really good. I mean, you know, healthier. Have you had any issues since coming back?"

Laena shook her head as she strolled closely next to him and fanned out her hands before them. "Not a scale to be seen."

"That's great." Jason walked more slowly to keep in pace with her. "Yeah, very good." Her hands looked so much smaller than his. He wanted to hold them.

Poison Ivy napped under the tree line after having feasted on deer. With a short whistle, Jason instructed her to stand. The dragon stretched with a yawn, her lips curling back to reveal her glistening fangs. Jason hadn't noticed how long they were. *Have they grown?*

Shaking it off, he mounted his steed and held out a hand to Laena. But her gaze roved over Poison Ivy. She gingerly brushed the dragon's green, scaly neck.

"Laena?"

"You don't find it selfish?" she asked softly as her petting gained confidence. She moved her hand to Poison Ivy's nose. "To withhold her original nature when you can so easily cure her?"

Jason shifted in his seat. She had a point, and it dripped guilt into his heart.

"We don't even know what that daft poison does to a creature left untreated!" Laena whispered fearfully as she stepped closer. "You heard about Gavlin's voices. Jason, you are an advocate for the sick. Does that not include the animals in your care?"

"Pi can get me to places far faster than any carriage," Jason countered. "She's saved both valuable time and lives. And with this new mission, now is definitely not the time to sacrifice that. How about this: I'll turn her back when we're done dealing with the Kottrans." He moved his hand closer, a smirk playing on his lips. "In the meantime, I'd hate to be late for dinner."

Lanea softened and returned the smile. She gripped his

arm tightly. Jason's sleeves were thin, and she felt his muscles flex as he pulled her behind him. Laena noticed how strong he was.

Jason prayed he wasn't sweating as Poison Ivy took off into the sky.

"So…" Laena began. "How different is your world?"

"Very." Jason nodded to accentuate. "We have electricity." At Laena's confused expression, he continued with a laugh, "Uh, it's like lightning. We make it and harness it to give light to our houses and power to our transportation. We don't need candles or horses."

"How magical!" Laena beamed in wonder.

"Hah, the buildings where it's made sure don't look magical."

"How do you make it?"

"Oh, I don't; other people do it. I had a different job working as a waiter in a restaurant, so I was kind of like a servant or a butler of sorts that served people food."

"You? In service?" Laena scrunched her brow in surprise. "Surely not, your talents would be wasted!"

"I didn't have magic back then. Actually, magic doesn't even exist in my world. In any case, I'm sure I've been fired at this point for vanishing."

"Fired?"

"It means they no longer want me to work for them."

"Oh dear!" Laena patted his shoulder in sympathy.

"Nah, it's fine. This has been the most eventful my life has ever been. Much better than cleaning tables and balancing plates."

"Now perhaps the purpose of your healing gift lies in the Spire's Scroll," Laena suggested eagerly.

Jason had nearly forgotten about the Scroll. He feared it would have filled him with unease, but instead Laena's enthusiasm invigorated him with excitement. "You're right," he said. "That destiny would be a major upgrade from waitering. What do you think?"

"I think you're wonderful," Laena said without guard. Her arms stiffened as she quickly corrected, "I mean, because you saved me, and saved all the others—I'm sorry, I was too forward."

"Don't be sorry," Jason reassured. "You can say whatever you want to me. I think communication is super important for connection." Jason stammered through his next comment, "That is, of course, if the lady felt the same way the guy did." He realized his arms had lowered closer to rest on hers.

Laena's breath caught in her chest as she blushed.

"And...if he *did* fancy a lass who approved of his intentions?" Laena led on.

"Well," Jason said, shrugging playfully and looking over his shoulder at her, "he should have dinner with her and meet her father for proper introductions."

"It would appear such an occasion has already been arranged." Laena smiled, taking in his gaze. She was lost in Jason's hazel eyes. As Jason returned to facing the horizon, she hugged him a little more tightly. "Thank you for saving my life."

"It was my honor."

"No, truly," Laena insisted. "You restored everything to me—myself, my dignity, my home, and just when I had begun to pray I would die."

"It just seemed like the right thing to do. A calling, if you will."

"How are you so selfless to a people that aren't even yours?" Laena asked.

Jason scrunched his brow. "I am a healer." Saying the words out loud brought a swell of pride in his chest. It was the first time he had officially acknowledged himself as such. "So therefore, those in pain or suffering are my people."

Laena's heart fluttered at Jason's words. She was drawn to his character—nobility, compassion, and loyalty were traits she held at the highest value. She knew her father would approve of him.

"I am so sorry for what Helnah did to you," Jason said, a tinge of hatred in his voice.

"We are defined by those events," Laena replied softly. "But we can choose how. I feel stronger for surviving it. There were times I thought of starving myself till I died so I could escape the misery and agony. But something deep down, a small voice, begged me to push through. It told me that despite the blackness, there was light in the distance. And then you came and visited me, and I dared to hope that voice was right." Laena's arms tightened around Jason a little more. "It was."

Jason couldn't help but smile. "You know, my whole life I've just done the minimum. Not really striving for anything, just living in the moment and getting by. But since I've become this healer and saved lives, it's shown me that I can be better."

"You are a good man, Jason, and Tindoria is indebted to you."

The sun sat low in the sky by the time they reached the Green Capital. Laena directed Poison Ivy to Edgestone, a modest two-story mansion with most of its stucco exterior draped in ivy. Breezeways encircled the upper level, and a tiled courtyard with a fountain stood in the middle. The green roof with its finials shone brightly in the sunlight, and Jason thought he saw a peacock or two perched on the ridges.

"The city harbors many wild peacocks, but most days they don't bother us," Laena explained, catching his stare. "They come and go as they please, and we respect them as Endlewood's symbol."

"Back home, we have these nasty birds called pigeons," Jason grimaced. "Basically rats with wings. One time I was in the city, and I had just bought this delicious burrito—it's like meat and vegetables wrapped in very thin bread—when a pigeon swooped down and stuck its beak in it. It had no fear of me, it only cared about my food."

"Oh no!" Laena tried not to snicker.

"Yeah, then it pooped on the burrito. I'd take peacocks any day."

"Don't be fooled," Laena warned him. "They have quite the temper if you get on their bad side."

"But they're prettier and don't carry diseases." Jason eyed a peacock, who was glaring defiantly at Poison Ivy's approach.

"Probably."

Lord Evinsor awaited their arrival in the grand entry. His broad frame filled nearly the whole doorway, but Jason couldn't determine what was him and what was his fur cape.

Poison Ivy landed gracefully, fluttering her multicolored wings upon landing. Jason dismounted and held out his hand to Laena. Her skin was so soft, and he wanted to hold her hand longer. As soon as they stepped away from Poison Ivy, the dragon shook her head and flew off without ever looking back.

Jason narrowed his eyes in suspicion at her shrinking green form in the distance. Poison Ivy seemed more and more eager to be by herself, and it left him with a faint unnerving feeling in his gut.

Laena slipped her hand out of Jason's and took to her father's side. "Father, this is Jason of the Separate Realm."

Mentally, Jason thanked his mom's British TV drama addiction for teaching him how to address ranks of nobility. He bowed. "It's an honor, Your Lordship. Thank you for the generous invitation."

"The pleasure is all mine." The baron smiled, his lilting brogue like his daughter's. "Please, come in."

"I must ready myself for dinner." Laena bowed to excuse herself. She glanced at her dirty clothes before adding, "This is not appropriate attire for this evening." Then she disappeared into the mansion.

Lord Evinsor escorted Jason into a hall decorated with banners, weapons, and paintings that Jason assumed had been passed down through the generations. Lord Evinsor answered his questions with eagerness, delving into the collection's history with pride. Trophies of the hunt popped up occasionally as well, though Jason couldn't identify half of the animals.

One particular set of antlers astonished him. The expansive rack filled nearly half the wall, five feet long from tip to tip. The pearling shimmered like moonstone, but what stood out to Jason above all was the color of the set—the antlers were a soft blue.

"One of my grandfather's trophies," Lord Evinsor said with pride. "Even King Eldrain himself has never acquired such a rack."

"They're blue," Jason stated obviously.

"Aye, the Blue Elk. A rare beast to be sure, and highly coveted for its colorful antlers. King Eldrain's grandfather Nordian offered to pay handsomely, but my grandfather would not part with them. He did sell His Majesty the hide. The only blue there is along the spine, but still a beautiful piece."

The baron directed Jason to the dining room. Lined with glistening candelabras and matching dinnerware, the table sat before a large terrace. Though the table had yet to bear food, the smell of dinner soaked the air.

As he entered the terrace and looked at the city beyond, Lord Evinsor leaned against the ivied archway and sighed. "I can finally enjoy this view in peace. Laena's screams haunted my dreams for so long. I pray you never experience the horror, my lad."

Jason turned his head as he listened.

"I had feared the worst of my girl's returned condition after her abduction. Would all her light have been snuffed out? Would she be subjected to the horrors of memory like so many soldiers after war?"

Jason caught the baron's voice hitch.

"Yet…" Evinsor smiled as his eyes stared into the sky. "In the Celestials' infinite wisdom, Laena is now happier than she has ever been. I'm eternally grateful for you, Jason."

"We both are," Laena said from behind.

Jason's heart skipped at her voice, and he turned around. His eyes widened, and he quickly shut his stunned mouth.

Laena had dressed into a satin gown that matched her eyes, and it shimmered like a tropical ocean. Her arms were draped in ivory bell sleeves, and oval cutouts exposed her freckled shoulders. A glittering string corseted the front of the gown, matched the shining gold trim of her skirt. Her hair had been cleaned, though Jason suspected in haste, because she had tossed it up in a high ponytail that left wavy strands of rose gold free about her face. He thought she looked perfect.

When he realized he had been staring, he searched for words but could only say, "Wow."

Laena fanned out her skirt for his opinion. "Better than dragon scales?"

Having lost his vocabulary entirely, Jason nodded his head with a nervous laugh.

Blushing, Laena fiddled with the back of an ornamental chair.

A team of three men in deep-green livery entered and

assisted them to their seats. Lord Evinsor sat at the head with Jason and Laena flanking his sides. As the butlers departed to another room to fetch food, Jason began to wonder how rich Lord Evinsor really was.

The butlers returned balancing platters with engraved cloches concealing the food within. In perfect synchronization, they lowered the plates and revealed the dish beneath. Jason's mouth watered as the intensely fragrant cloud of steam mushroomed past Jason's face.

A hefty crimson rib chop dripping in golden gravy rested on a swirling scoop of speckled mash, all wreathed in vibrant greens and vegetables Jason couldn't identify.

"This looks beautiful," Jason said, hoping his expression didn't look too wild.

Laena's turquoise eyes twinkled. "It tastes even better."

Lessons from his high school's dinner etiquette workshop resurfaced, and Jason sighed in gratitude. It was a single evening class, but his mom had insisted he attend, saying no son of hers would lack mealtime grace. He just hoped American dinner etiquette would be acceptable enough for Lord Evinsor.

Stop overthinking it, dude, he told himself, *As long as you hold your utensils properly and don't smack, this will be a breeze. Just remember to begin after the host does.*

Lord Evinsor and Laena bowed their heads, and Jason quickly did the same. The baron thanked the Celestials for all their blessings, then he slipped his knife into the chop. The meat melted off the bone with barely a touch. Laena then followed suit, and Jason copied them.

Jason had no idea what animal he was eating, but it reminded him of the bacon he had for breakfast back at the Verdant Suite. Whatever it was, he nearly cried knowing it probably wasn't on Earth, because it was the best meat he had ever had. It melted in his mouth with salty juiciness, and the gravy brought a hint of sweet amber syrup. The mash was definitely a tuber of some kind, fluffy and buttery and full of spice. After patting his mouth respectfully, Jason complimented Evinsor again on the dinner's divine tastiness and asked what it was.

"Truffen pig from my acres," Lord Evinsor replied. "I raise the best pigs in the kingdom just outside the city. King Eldrain himself is partial to those ruddy beasts." Jason nodded as the baron continued, "And what about you, lad, what is your trade?"

The butlers returned to take wine preferences as Jason thought before answering. He had to make the best impression he could. "Well, my path has changed since arriving here, Your Lordship," he answered. "Lae—Lady Laena may have told you that I am from the Separate Realm where my life was vastly different."

"Aye, she mentioned the rumors."

"And they're true. I was what you might call a butler, but here I've found a much nobler purpose. I've been given magic that allows me to instantly heal the sick and injured with knowledge of the precise procedure needed. It was how I rescued Lady Laena." He took a sip of wine.

Lord Evinsor listened with twinkling eyes. "You are

a beacon of hope, lad. Many sons and daughters have been snatched from us. Laena had been missing for nearly six months, and I'm sure countless others had been imprisoned for longer." The baron stood, raising his glass. "Let me toast to you, Jason."

Laena happily mirrored her father's action.

"To your success and prosperity. May you continue to heal those in need. I cannot thank you enough for saving my darling girl. Ask for anything, and I shall do my best to grant it."

Oh boy, Jason thought. *What do you do when a ranking noble owes you? What do you ask for? Oh, who am I kidding?* There *was* one thing he wanted. He just didn't know how to ask for it. But it was now or never. Locking eyes with Laena to give him confidence, he faced the baron and spoke up, "Actually, Your Lordship, there is one thing."

Lord Evinsor smirked knowingly and bid him continue.

"With your approval, I would like to get to know your daughter better. She is an impervious flame of bravery and beauty"—Jason looked at Laena as he said these things and watched her cheeks and nose blush—"and I know I'm not of noble birth or anything, but I'd love the opportunity to talk to her more."

"Jason, noble birth is of no value to me," Lord Evinsor said sincerely. "I've gained insight into your character this evening and determined you are indeed noble of heart. Nothing would make me prouder nor Laena happier than to give you my blessing to court her. I grant you your request."

The soft trickle of the fountain blended with Jason's and Laena's leisurely footsteps. Laena had slipped her hand into the crook of Jason's arm as they paced the courtyard behind the manor. Scents of flowers and dancing butterflies filled the evening air.

"So," Jason began, resting his other hand on Laena's. "Any ideas you could give me for our next outing?"

Laena tilted her head toward him in thought.

"What's something you've always wanted to do?" Jason asked.

Laena perked up and gave a subtle squeeze of excitement. "I do have a secret dream."

"Oh, do you?"

Laena beamed as she lowered her voice. "For as long as I can remember, I've dreamed of seeing a unicorn. Legend says they are the steeds of the Celestials. Alas, in my eighteen years I have never found a single trace of one." She whipped her head to face Jason, her coral locks flying behind her. "Have you ever seen one?"

Jason shook his head. "Nah, the closest thing I've seen are horses. My uncle has a ranch."

"Do you like horses?"

"Oh, yeah, they're amazing, beautiful animals. I love and respect them."

"But Poison Ivy?"

Jason stopped walking and sighed.

"You are a good man, Jason." Laena stepped in front of him, moving her hand down to his. "Blessed by the Celestials even! With your gift, should you not also be a steward of all creation?"

"Laena, even if I wanted to, my magic is drained." Jason dropped his shoulders. "Since the Maze, I don't have the energy and besides, I don't have any Yelnight crystal."

"I have connections." Lanea shrugged a freckled shoulder. "Acquiring a handful of expensive crystal will be no problem." When Jason said nothing, Laena's tone sharpened. "Jason, you heard Gavlin. There are phases to the poison that we don't understand. And your horse appears to adapt much more quickly than humans. We cannot trust anything from Helnah."

Jason thinned his lips as he looked away.

"You know it's the right thing to do." Laena gently slipped a hand to his cheek and returned his hazel gaze to hers. "She has no voice, Jason, so as someone who has experienced the same pain and torture of a poisoned existence, I am her only advocate."

Her delicate hand on his cheek softened Jason like magic. She was as noble and strong-willed as he. He admired her vouching for Poison Ivy. While he would miss having a dragon of his own, Laena was right.

He sighed and gripped her hand in his. "When you get the crystal, let me know. I'll be staying at the palace in the Verdant Suite."

Laena smiled, and her eyes twinkled with gratitude. "Thank you."

CHAPTER 12

Hall of Records

The Endlewood carriages arrived the next day, and their return sent the Green Capital into another kingdom-wide celebration. Children squealed out the windows at the crowds as they were driven through the streets, escorted by the city guard to the Royal Square, which burst with anxious families and friends. A green tent had been constructed atop a stage to receive the children. The carriages rolled around behind it, and the guards helped the children off and up the stage steps into the tent. The reunion began with some difficulty, as the crowds were understandably impatient and loud.

Melanie, Scalaed, Jason, Elken, and Laena stood on the far end of the stage to watch. One by one, the city guards asked for the children's names and shouted them to the crowd, which were met with happy cries and screams of recognition from their families.

Finally, the children were home. Jason had completed his mission, and he beamed with pride as he looked over the crowds to see joyous faces and happy tears.

Unable to contain her joy, Laena wrapped Jason in a hug. "King Eldrain is here," she whispered with a smile.

Jason looked up and saw a royal entourage cutting through

the crowds. Twenty soldiers in royal armor marched in pairs. Long ribboning banners twirled from spears, and the bugler at the helm silenced the crowds with his song. The rhythm of marching armor ceased as they drew to a halt. Each guard pivoted to face their partner, then took a step back to open a path to the stage.

King Eldrain, his fur cape trailing behind him and his golden crown gleaming in the sun, approached the stage. "Jason Waldens of the Separate Realm."

Stunned, Jason quickly bowed. "Your Majesty."

"Jason," the king began, "you have unwavering determination and loyalty to the noblest of causes—unyielding love for not only my people, but for the people of our neighboring kingdoms. Kneel."

A cushioned stool was placed before Jason, who looked at Laena for an explanation. She simply squeezed her hands together in excitement and nodded in approval.

Jason obeyed and lowered his head.

King Eldrain continued, "In the name of chivalry, of honor, and of loyalty, I raise you to the rank of knight."

Jason's head shot up. He glanced at Laena and Melanie, who were all smiles.

"Never again shall an armed hand touch you or innocents without response." King Eldrain unsheathed his sword and tapped each of Jason's shoulders with the flat of the blade. "Arise. A knight is born."

Jason, hardly believing his ears, slowly rose with a newfound pride.

King Eldrain smiled and produced *Clavnir*. He presented it to Jason. "And now, for you, this is the sword of the greatest princes. Use it in justice and righteousness."

Jason respectfully received the sword and buckled it to his waist.

"I present," King Eldrain announced to the masses, "Sir Jason the Mender! Knight of Endrial!"

The crowd erupted in cheers, and many threw flowers toward Jason. Elken clapped proudly, and Melanie and Laena cheered more loudly than anyone. Scalaed roared happily.

Melanie tackled her brother with a hug. "Congratulations!" she whispered.

"Thank you!" Jason said, laughing through his shock.

"Helmir had recovered *Clavnir* from the battlefield and returned it to me," Elken said. "But it should be yours, my friend."

"You all knew about this?"

"Well…" Melanie shrugged at Laena, "…Laena requested it."

Laena curtsied, and Jason smiled. "This was your doing?"

"Don't act so surprised!" Laena laughed. "My father has a seat in the royal court, and the decision was quite unanimous. After all, you saved some of the courtiers' children, including me. It was the least Endlewood could do in repayment."

Jason hefted *Clavnir,* which glinted flecks of light around the square. "Sir Jason the Mender. Doesn't sound too bad, does it?"

Through the hugs and congratulations, Jason's eyes once

again met the anticipating blue stare of Baraden in the crowds. The old scribe and *Clavnir's* former owner tilted his chin up with a smile to convey he had been waiting.

Melanie and the others noticed Jason's gaze, and followed it to Baraden.

"I believe congratulations are in order!" Baraden said jovially as he approached. "With your mission successfully concluded, the Spire's Scroll awaits."

Jason and Melanie looked at each other, then to Scalaed. The dragon shrugged as he eyed the city around them. It appeared they would not be sent home today after all.

Melanie took a steadying breath. From what she knew, prophetic scripts rarely foretold paths of leisure and fun.

"You have things to discuss." Laena stepped back. "So I will excuse myself."

Jason whipped his head to face her. He wanted to plead with her to stay.

"I do have my own duties," Laena reminded him with a sad smile. "But I know I'll see you soon…Sir Jason." She said the name in a playful tone, then vanished into the crowd. Jason's heart sank.

Elken, on the other hand, was paying little attention. His eyes scanned the crowd, darting to find something.

"Melanie," he put a hand on her shoulder, still searching the royal square, "forgive me, but I must tend to something as well."

"What, why?" Melanie grabbed his hand.

Elken faced her, but his demeanor was distracted. "I

cannot say," he stammered and quickly brushed a finger against her chin. "But I must go now. I'll come back, I promise."

"Elken, wait!" Melanie reached out for him as he left. Her hand caught his, and he looked back one last time. Then like the kiss of a breeze, that soft voice whispered in her heart, *"Do not be anxious."*

Something then uncoiled around her chest, allowing her to breathe. Untying her tongue, she gave Elken's hand one last squeeze and locked eyes with him. "We'll be at the palace in the Verdant Suite. I'll let the maidservant know to expect you."

Elken's eyes, a marbled galaxy of colors, shone as he said, "I'll be there." Then he left, focused on something Melanie couldn't see. Whatever it was, Elken cut through the crowds like a knife before disappearing down a street corner.

"Well, let's not tarry!" Baraden held out a white object hanging from a leather cord. Made of porcelain, the shell-like object was revealed to be a whistle. With a crackled glaze accentuated by rose-gold ink, it was large enough to fill the palm of his hand.

"Jason, you might find this a more convenient means of summoning your dragon." Baraden winked as he gave it to Jason. "It's called a sibulus. It's mostly used as a musical instrument, but it is a shrill little thing that should work for your needs just as well."

"Oh, wow, thank you, Baraden," Jason turned the glossy whistle in his hands before looping it over his head.

"Give it a try." Baraden's sky blue eyes sparkled.

Jason put the sibulus to his lips. A high, vibratory tone

soared through the air, clear and melodic. Scalaed nodded in approval.

"I'll explain this to Pi next time I see her," Jason said excitedly.

"Very good. Now come with me. It is glorious weather for walking, and we'll talk along the way," Baraden invited. He led them out of the royal square into the bustle and noise of the vast city. "The Spire's Scroll is a prophetic document written by the first and only Seer of Tindoria, Tavnir."

"Seer?" Jason asked.

"Tavnir had the gift of prophecy and the task to recount Tindoria's most notable events, to give them to scribes and historians. She dwelt in a solitary tower of stone built for her in the very center of the world: the Spire of Tavnir. At its pinnacle lies the Adamas Chamber, where all her work was recorded. Every battle, every monarch and lineage, every turn of the age, she documented it all with startling detail. But the most important of her works was the Scroll."

"So, Tavnir was like the ultimate scribe," Melanie said.

"Indeed," Baraden said, "but the Scroll was different. While most of her documents were observations of current or past events, the Spire's Scroll foretold the future. Tavnir therefore took great care and inscribed what she had foreseen of the Scroll on a crystal obelisk with an Indomitable Glass stylus. It was her only prophecy. The copy we are about to see was written in parchment and given to the First King here in Endlewood."

As they walked down the increasingly busy streets of the

Green Capital, passersby shouted to the siblings in excited recognition. Melanie and Jason smiled and waved in response.

"Now, the security is heavy," Baraden continued. "Very few have access to the Scroll—only scribes and scholars and the like. Luckily for us"—he smiled—"I was once a scribe."

Melanie, Jason, and Scalaed followed Baraden down through streets and vendors who, after recognizing the siblings, swarmed and begged to give them free items as gratitude. Not wanting to appear rude by refusing, Melanie and Jason obliged. Unfortunately, they soon learned there were far more vendors than they anticipated, and they quickly ran out of arms to hold, while Scalaed was in seemingly too sour a mood to offer his help.

Through his pile of new clothes, food, and knickknacks, Jason managed to see a basket weaver and acquired two baskets to collect their items. As they left, the little old woman began bragging excitedly to her neighboring vendors how the heroes of Tindoria owned her best baskets.

The market streets cleared, and they neared the neighborhood region. Tidy buildings of wood beams and plaster walls lined the roads in a range of beiges and greens. With their own little cobblestone walkways, they differed greatly from the pillared, cuboid houses of Lakéthion.

Baraden whistled, signaling an approaching coach to stop.

"Cool," Melanie whispered to Jason as they boarded. "Endlewood has a taxi service."

Scalaed whined after they closed the door.

"Just follow us from above, buddy," Melanie said.

With no other choice, Scalaed reluctantly flapped his wings and took off. He was not happy to be left out. Ever since Elken came back, he felt like Melanie had been shoving him aside. Jealousy reignited in his chest, and he breathed black smoke from his nostrils in agitation.

As the carriage began to move, Jason started to sort through his baskets. "I don't even know what I was given, exactly. There were so many hands throwing stuff at me!"

"Maybe we can have the coachman drop all this stuff back at the castle to be taken to our rooms," Melanie said.

The coach ride took them to what Melanie guessed was the equivalent of downtown. The buildings grew larger and the crowds appeared thicker. Inns and hotels flagged their presence with banners and signs. Lampposts waned with signage and advertisements. Roads bustled with traffic, and the smells of kitchens and shops floated by them. Their ride stopped in front of a particularly large building.

"Welcome to the Hall of Records," Baraden announced as he opened the coach door.

A grand flight of steps rose to the towering black doors, which were framed by polished pillars. Built of beige stone with faint green speckling, the architecture spoke of the building's importance.

"It looks like a museum from back home," Melanie marveled, and her heart sank at the homesickness that threatened to overwhelm her. She shoved it down and quickly entered the front doors. She was needed here, and she would try her best to fill that need.

Inside were shelves beyond shelves full of scrolls, maps, and books. Statues and busts of important historical figures lined the walls, which were painted with large reliefs of pivotal past events. An entire mural of the Tindoria atlas filled the back wall. Groups of men and women in identical beige robes dispersed into little rooms along the edges of the Hall, holding rolls of parchment and pots of ink.

In the center of the building stood a single room. All the shelves seemed to lead toward it. Almost a separate, smaller building itself, it had a single entrance with two guards flanking its frame. The doorway, barred with intricate metalwork, hinted at its importance.

"The Spire's Scroll lies beyond that door," Baraden explained, but Jason and Melanie had already guessed.

"Proof of clearance, sir?" a guard asked Baraden.

Baraden held out his hand and flashed a ring signifying his scribe status. "These are my pupils." He gestured to the Waldens siblings.

The guards nodded and unlocked the door.

"I thought you were banished as a scribe," Melanie whispered once they passed.

Baraden smirked. "That was in Lakéthion, and I surrendered a decoy ring when I left."

Illuminated by a skylight, with four more guards in each corner, was the Spire's Scroll. Displayed on an elegant pedestal, it beckoned them to come closer.

At first, Jason couldn't read the runes, but then they blurred into letters he recognized.

FROM KINGDOMS AND COUNTRIES AFAR

NO KING NOR SCHOLAR CAN PLACE,

A HERO HAS ANSWERED THE CALL

TO BE TINDORIA'S GRACE.

THE RISE OF THIS WARRIOR'S FATE

BEGINS WITH SINS OF THE BEAST.

THE EXILED IN BANISHMENT WAIT

FOR WAR ON MORTALS UNLEASHED.

THE SHADOW THAT TRAVELS UNSEEN

AND LIFE IN THE HANDS TO HEAL

A DREAMER OF YOUTH HOLDS THE KEY.

THE DESCENDANT OF LIGHT IS REVEALED.

Jason fished a stylus and crumpled wrapping paper from his basket and started scribbling the prophecy down. Finally reading the Scroll everyone had been talking about made his heart race. He had another opportunity to be a hero—Laena's hero.

He hadn't realized he was smiling until he thought of the Lady of Edgestone. Her sparkling turquoise eyes made his cheeks burn. He wished she was here. Remembering his surroundings, he quickly composed himself and finished writing the last sentence.

Melanie read the Scroll again. Her nerves flared through her body as she stared at the seemingly harmless paper. But the words hammered stakes of anxiety into her bones. Something deep down told her she was reading her own fate. *Be brave, Melanie,* she thought to herself. *You were chosen for this. Own it.*

"I got it." Jason folded his copy. "Now we just have to decipher it, I guess."

"Not quite," Baraden said heavily.

"Why not?" Melanie did not like the way he said it.

"Once the Scroll was delivered to the kingdoms, everything changed."

"What happened?" Jason asked, sensing a dark turn to the tale.

"Mankind," Baraden answered sadly. "Once mankind realized that the Seer's post had the power of prophecy, they lusted after that position with a fierce, selfish vengeance. On a journey to Endlewood, Tavnir was murdered, and her post at the Spire sat vacant. Quests to overtake the Spire for men to write their own futures were made, but all failed. Tales say those who returned were stricken with madness. Thus the quests ceased after a month." Baraden cast a quick glance at the guards in the room. "Now, what I say next is highly secret knowledge," he lowered his voice. "This Scroll is incomplete."

Jason and Melanie exchanged looks, not knowing if this was good or bad news.

Baraden continued, "Right before my banishment, I was on an archeological expedition in the Trellin Forest where I found a letter of correspondence from the palace to Tavnir. Out of spite for my peers, I kept it secret from them and took it with me into exile. The sender, a palace representative, mentions his anticipation for a *second* scroll that Tavnir had written and was to deliver—the final verse of the Spire's Scroll. The date of the letter implies she would have been carrying this scroll when she died. It never made it to Endlewood, nor was it ever found."

"So what do we need to do?" Jason asked.

"You must journey to the Spire of Tavnir wherein lies the original script inscribed in its entirety on the crystal obelisk," Baraden answered. "You cannot fulfill the Scroll without it."

CHAPTER
13
Intercepted

Groaning, Kyle rubbed his face with his hands in the aftermath of yet another dream.

The castle was gone. He was back in his room. The clock read four twenty-three in the morning. Kyle released another angry grumble as he crawled back in bed, praying he could get back to sleep. But the itching restlessness returned to his fingers. He balled his fists, then tucked them under his stomach as he rolled over. *Nope, that makes it worse.*

With an exaggerated moan, Kyle dragged himself out of bed, smacked his dream notebook onto his pillow, and scribbled the details of what he'd just seen. With every sentence written, the aggravation in his fingers was pulled out, as if laying the ink unraveled it like thread. Once finished, he threw the book on the ground and flopped back in bed.

Half asleep, his mind wandered between reality and the nonsensical images that made up his dreams. Through the slimming vision of his eyelids, Kyle saw an orb of piercing yellow light floating just outside his window. He slowly sat up, eyes now wide and unblinking. The orb phased through the glass and hovered into his bedroom, sending a lump into Kyle's throat. This light suddenly became much more foreboding and threatening than he first thought. *Is this another dream?*

Kyle grabbed the baseball bat next to his bed. It was not a great weapon, but it would have to do. After all, this floating light was no bigger than a baseball. Holding the bat defensively in front of him, Kyle yelled, "Leave me alone!"

The orb continued to creep in.

"I'll whack you into oblivion!" Kyle warned. "I did *not* invite an alien abduction, and I'm not taking you to my leader, so go away before I make a home run out of you."

His rant faded when the orb began to shift. It grew larger and longer, forming the shape of a man.

Okay, I died. Now here's my escort to judgment dropping by to pick up my soul.

Formed of golden light, the man grew more detailed. His long hair was brushed and neat with not a hair of his trimmed beard out of place, and he wore a shimmering cape draped over glistening armor.

The Golden Prince? Kyle thought. *Okay, so am I dreaming?*

"Hello, Kyle," the Prince said.

"Wait, you can see me..." Kyle narrowed his eyes and lowered the bat in confusion. "Am I dreaming or not? How do you even know me? Who are you?"

The Prince smiled. "I come from Tindoria, a realm beyond your own. There is little time to waste, and I am in need of your assistance."

Kyle was still stuck at the "different realm" thing. "Are... are you from Heaven?" he asked in disbelief. "Wait...are you an angel? Why would you ever need my help?"

"Your visits have revealed the role you must play."

Kyle dropped the bat. "That was *real?*"

"A new enemy threatens my world, and you will be a vital instrument in our victory," the Prince continued. "What do you make of this?" He held out his hand, and a long, angular gemstone appeared. The ruby facets sparkled as it hovered in his hand. "Look at it. Study its details."

Kyle grinned, and his hands reached out to it. "Oh, yes please." His fingers went through it like it was made of air, and he groaned. "Oh."

"This is a mere projection; a guide for you to use when you remake it."

"Wait, how am I gonna make *this?*" Kyle squinted his eyes. "And what is it again?"

"Look closely."

Kyle leaned forward toward the ruby, squinting as he examined it. "Umm, it might be around a thousand carats... octagonal cut, five inches long, maybe fifteen millimeters in diameter...ditetragonal prism...beautiful table and crown..." Kyle's eyes trailed down to the bottom. The ruby seemed to dissolve into strips of puzzle-like cuts. "Are these some kind of bits? Hold on, this is a key."

The Prince raised an eyebrow, pleased. "You know your gems."

"I'm an aspiring gemologist." Kyle smirked proudly. "I read a lot of books, know a lot of random things." Then he paused. "The gorgeous Empress mentioned a key."

"Yes, my mother and I believe you are ready to join your

cousins' mission."

"You mean Melanie and Jason?" Kyle paled. "You know them? Wait, are they with you? They disappeared, and the news is all over the story. My poor aunt and uncle are losing their minds—"

"No one will return alive if you fail. This foe is unlike any other. I will take you to Tindoria, where you will join your cousins."

"Excuse me?" Kyle squeaked. "No can do. This is impossible. This is—it's just a wild dream. It has to be. My brain is short-circuiting from the stress and compensating with insanity. My cousins are *not* in another world, *you're* trespassing, and *what* are you doing with that key?"

The Prince was reaching out to Kyle's head, directing the floating key toward it. "This is how you'll remember it." The Prince placed the projection into Kyle's forehead, where it vanished into his mind.

Kyle waved his arms, smacking the air around him. "No! I don't *want* to remember *any* of this! I am going back to bed. I'd say it was nice talking with you, but it wasn't. You're crazy, good night."

The Prince draped a hood over his face, saying through a faint smirk, "You won't escape this so easily."

"Watch me," Kyle retorted, and flung open his bedroom door. The dead silence of the house drew goosebumps on his skin, but he continued down the stairs. The light of the Prince appeared in his peripheral vision, and Kyle ran to the kitchen and struggled to open the back door. As soon as the glass panes opened wide enough for him to fit through, Kyle sprinted out into the morning darkness. Panting in the wild air, he ran straight to the stables. He could hide there.

The silhouette of the stables neared, and when Kyle arrived at the doors, he slid open one side. Sleeping horses stirred at the sound, and he shut the door behind him more quietly. Leaning against the wood, Kyle closed his eyes and heaved a sigh to steady his breathing. The smell of hay, feed, and horse wrapped around him like a comforting hug, and it drowned out the anxious thoughts and fears that knocked around in his brain. He crept down the stable breezeway, passing the sleeping horses toward Babe's stall.

He froze when he saw the glowing figure leaning against the opposite doorway at the end of the stables.

Kyle paled as his mouth dropped open, and his mental alarm wailed.

"You—you—how…!" he stammered.

"Are you ready?" the Golden Prince said, looking around as if it was the most beautiful night ever. "Let's go."

"Nope!" Kyle turned on his heel only to find the Prince had materialized in front of him.

"Your destiny awaits." The Prince guided Kyle by his arm and pulled him away, kicking and screaming.

The Prince pointed to the stable doors, and the wood swirled into a rainbow vortex. Kyle stopped fussing and suddenly lost feeling in his legs.

"Tindoria depends on you," the Prince said, and with a wave of his hand, transformed Kyle's pajamas to jeans, a white t-shirt, and his orange hoodie.

Kyle shook his head adamantly, panicking before the swirling gateway to the unknown. "This can't be happening!"

"Off you go, then," the Prince said and gently pushed Kyle into the vortex.

CHAPTER 14

Another One

Melanie and Jason's presence had not gone unnoticed in the Hall of Records. Shortly after leaving the Spire's Scroll exhibit, scribes descended upon them, begging for an audience. Baraden appointed himself the siblings' representative and insisted the scribes not disturb Melanie and Jason on their vital mission. He ushered the crowds away to answer any of their questions himself.

Freed, Melanie and Jason strolled through the aisles of archives, occasionally picking up a scroll or book. Surrounded by knowledge of everything Tindorian, Melanie could not pass up the opportunity to learn a few things. She saw Jason through a slot in the shelf from the next aisle over.

"So," she asked slyly, "how was your date?"

Jason's eyes widened as his face reddened. He smiled. "Laena is a wonder."

"She is really pretty."

"Oh, she's more than that," Jason shook his head wistfully. "She's brave and selfless and kind. For a girl with riches, she has the most generous heart. It makes her…" Jason's bashful smile spread. "It makes her glow."

"Well, Sir Jason could do far worse than crush on a

noblewoman," Melanie teased, still leafing through a book.

"So you can read the books, too?" Jason asked.

Melanie nodded. "It first happened when I got *Ilvir*."

"I mean, it makes sense." Jason shrugged. "Why would a foreign realm write in English? But since we seem pretty important, we're able to read it."

"Important meaning we *are* who the Scroll is talking about?" Melanie slid her eyes up from her book.

"Come on, Mel, you read that first part." Jason tilted his head. "Kingdoms and countries no one can place. Sounds a lot like the Separate Realm to me. Aka Earth. Who else could it possibly mean?"

Melanie nodded and returned to her book. She turned the page and saw a gilded illustration of Empress Elethýna adorned in golden armor, standing tall as she waved a banner. In her hand was *Ilvir*.

"No way." The words escaped Jason's mouth with a gasp. He had sneaked up and was peering over her shoulder. "Your sword…it's Elethýna's."

Melanie looked back and forth from the book to her sword. Somehow, it didn't come as a shock.

"I think…" Melanie rubbed the glass-rose pommel by her side. Deep down I had already figured that out. Maybe I knew it was a gift from the Empress that night."

Jason nodded thoughtfully, then held up his own book. "I found something else, Mel." He tapped a page.

"What is it?"

"Well, Tavnir wasn't the only one in her story." Jason

plopped the book on a desk and sat down. "Apparently, there was the Golden Prince."

Melanie read where Jason's finger pointed:

The alleged son of the Empress Elethýna, the Golden Prince's existence has become a topic of debate. Throughout the course of time, his reported appearances were few and far between—unlike those of his prominent mother—until they ceased altogether following the murder of Tavnir. According to Tavnir, this Prince of Allendia personally chose her to be the Seer of Tindoria. Elevated from her humble upbringing, she was led to a Spire in the middle of the world and was there taught by the Prince. Tavnir asserted he gifted her with prophecy and long life and prepared her for her ultimate purpose, that of recording and guarding the Spire's Scroll. Such an important script was etched on a crystal obelisk in the Adamas Chamber to prevent any desecration or alteration of fate. Eventually, the Golden Prince entrusted the entirety of the Spire to Tavnir alone and bequeathed to her the only key to the Adamas Chamber. After the murder of Tavnir, a vast barrier of fog enveloped the Spire, forever severing it from discovery, and the Golden Prince was never seen again. Belief in his existence dwindled until the majority of Tindoria began to think he was a fictional figure and nothing more. If the Prince had a name, it had long since been forgotten.

Jason put his hands on his hips. "You'd think Baraden would mention a guy like *that*."

"But you read it." Melanie gestured to the text. "Maybe he doesn't actually believe this Golden Prince is real."

"Pfft, as a scribe you'd think he wouldn't be biased."

"Well, then let's ask him." Melanie smiled dutifully and closed the book. "After all, there's no getting to this Scroll without that key."

Scouring the aisles and people of the Hall, the two finally found Baraden tucked away in a corner conversing with aspiring scribes. Being from Lakéthion, Baraden and his banishment remained unknown to the scribes of Endlewood.

"Baraden," Jason interrupted rather brashly, but he justified it with his mission of saving the world. "Have a second?"

Excusing himself, Baraden led the siblings out of earshot.

"Hey, so according to this"—Melanie held up the book—"you need a key to unlock the Adamas Chamber."

"And since Tavnir's key is lost to the world," Jason added, "the only person who could replace it would be the Golden Prince, who gave the key to Tavnir in the first place."

Baraden smiled and chuckled. "This Golden Prince might also never have existed."

Jason eyed him skeptically.

"Jason"—Baraden wrapped an arm around him—"if Empress Elethýna had a son, why would he hide? If he is as powerful as his mother, our world could have used his aid on many occasions. Could he not be bothered with Tindoria's troubles? If he does exist, he is the most selfish of all, and no help would you receive from a man like that."

"Well, after all I've been through, it's not hard for me to believe in the Golden Prince," Melanie explained. Then a thought sparked in the back of her mind. *Is that who the voice in my heart is?*

Jason held up his hand to interrupt her. "Okay then, Baraden, so if there is no Prince and evidently no key, how do you propose we get inside the Adamas Chamber?"

"If there is no key," Baradan replied blandly, almost mockingly, "there is evidently no lock, so you shouldn't have a problem. Begin your journey and all your answers will be revealed." With a dismissive wave, he turned to the scribes. "Now if you will excuse me, I'm needed elsewhere." Then Baraden was engulfed in a clamor of questions from the scribes.

"Dude, that's so unhelpful," Jason whispered.

"Yeah, I think we hit a nerve there," Melanie observed. "We can probably count him out on being helpful on our little quest."

Jason scoffed. "You think?" He rolled his eyes and caught a glimpse of the massive atlas of Tindoria. Curiosity swelled in him, and he approached the wall that stretched nearly fifteen feet high.

The Tindorian continent was almost a perfect circle with a single bay cutting into the southeastern region of Rhydrah. Tindoria was divided into five countries, using the landscape as natural borders. The countries converged in the center of Tindoria, where the mural depicted a twisting spire.

"The Spire of Tavnir," Melanie said softly as she approached from behind.

Jason was still looking at the halo of the ocean, which the painting depicted as a blue fading to the edge of the mural into nothingness.

"Dang," Jason sighed. "What a way to die."

"No kidding." Melanie crossed her arms. "Except, Klarn didn't die."

"Yeah, might want to keep your voice down when talking about that," Jason whispered.

Melanie scanned the different flags painted below the atlas, matching them to each country. Except one. South of the Spire of Tavnir and below the Trellin Forest and Great River lay a barren wasteland. No markers, no flags, no forests or rivers—nothing.

"There's the Deplorable Waste." Melanie stepped closer to the atlas. "Didn't Helmir say the creatures they fought came from there?"

"I think so. Excuse me." Jason waved to whom he hoped was a member of the Hall's staff.

The woman looked startled that he would speak to her. "Sir Jason!" she exclaimed and quickly bowed. "What an honor, sir," she rose again with a blushing smile. "How can I serve you?"

"What can you tell us about the Deplorable Waste?"

Instantly, the woman's smile and blush vanished. "It is nothing but pure sand. A deadly landscape that has claimed many explorers. No country wanted it, hence the name. It stands alone and ungoverned, where nothing lives save for the savage beings."

"What are these beings, exactly?"

"Oh…" The woman made a grave face. "Beings of darkness and death, they are. Nearly destroyed Hvitria." She clutched her chest with a pitying sigh. "Oh, such a *tragedy*. You know that frightful animated death wasn't around when they attacked Yolderain and Lakéthion years prior."

Melanie held up her hand. "Wait, there were other attacks?" she asked, surprised.

"Yes." The woman nodded seriously, her eyes wide. "And mark my words, Endlewood is next, but there's no telling when they'll strike." Then she hustled off.

Jason crossed his arms and stepped in front of Melanie. "This just got a lot bigger." His hazel eyes glanced around warily.

Melanie nodded. "But Helmir said they wiped them out, right?"

"It's been six years and no sightings."

"Well, then"—Melanie raised her eyebrows—"let's just stay clear of the Deplorable Waste, shall we?"

"Agreed," Jason said.

A scream from outside stole their attention. Melanie gripped Jason's arm as everyone popped up their heads and looked to the doors. Her voice shook. "Jason, didn't that sound like…?"

"Yeah." Jason's eyes were still locked on the Hall's entrance. While the other visitors murmured among themselves, both siblings ran to see the commotion. Something about that scream was horribly familiar.

Two carriages jostled in the street in front of the Hall of Records as the spooked horses brayed and bucked. The drivers were yelling and pointing at something in the road between them.

Leaping into action, Jason jumped in with the intention of calming the steeds. When he arrived at the scene, Melanie on his heels, his heart stopped.

A disheveled figure with watering blue eyes shook straw from his orange hoodie, stammering hysterically.

"*Kyle?*" Melanie and Jason cried.

The fifteen-year-old locked eyes with his cousins, and the blood drained from his face. Raising a violently trembling finger at them, he then dropped backward in a dead faint.

CHAPTER

15

Meetings

"Where are you taking me?" Elken hissed to the voice in his head as he walked deeper down the alleyway. "You do not even need secrecy if you have telepathy."

Oh darling, it's not my cover I'm worried about, the Avis Messenger replied, her voice dripping with its signature pomp. *But Bareth claims this news to be horrifying beyond speech! I simply cannot have you react unreasonably in such a public space, and in my presence. Very unbecoming. Such as talking to yourself aloud like you're doing now. Silence!*

Am I a child to you, Varsie? Elken thought.

You're human, the blue jay replied flatly. *You're all unreasonable to a degree. Here is good.*

Elken stopped walking upon reaching the darkest part of the alley. A flutter of feathers brought his attention to Varsie perched atop the building. Her plumage shimmered in a deep blue, matching the immaculately preened crest of feathers on her head.

Elken son of Elkarim, Varsie began, her telepathic voice level with seriousness, *I have been instructed by Bareth, sister of Briefur, to direct you to a meeting she has arranged. Given your connection to this subject, Bareth figured it best to meet with you before it is revealed to anyone else.*

Just tell me where. Elken crossed his arms, disbelieving this could be the grave news Varsie warned of.

There will be someone with her, though she did not say whom, which honestly offends me, for I am most trustworthy, Varsie continued. *And much to my confoundment, Bareth says to come unarmed.*

Now Elken narrowed his eyes as he tilted his head. *Unarmed?*

It was not my *order!* Varsie threw up her wings. *But you are to meet outside the city at dusk, at the southern fruit orchard under the orange trees.*

It's nearly dusk now! Elken thought in exasperation.

Oh, so it is, Varsie blinked, as she had been oblivious to the fact before that moment. *You best be off, then. And I shall repeat: come unarmed. There is a reason for it, and I can only hope it's a good one.*

Elken nodded, then turned to leave, wondering what in Tindoria this meeting could be about.

The noises of carriages and crowds faded behind as Elken exited Endlewood. A trail of beige gravel wound to the manicured grounds of the orchards. Citruses in every color of sunset glistened among the tree branches in the setting sun's light. Fruit smells wafted in the air as Elken walked through the orchard to the orange trees at the end, his boots crunching in the gravel.

"Bareth?" Elken called when he saw the trarewolf girl standing among the trees with her arms crossed. She turned to him, her expression tense. "What have you to tell me?" Elken asked her as he continued his approach, but a different voice responded from behind the tree between them.

"The truth." Thendrell emerged into view, and Elken's eyes bored into him. Outrage boiled in his chest as he pointed at his enemy.

"Who let you out of prison?" He looked at Bareth for an explanation, but she only appeared the stiffer.

"He never saw prison." Helnah's voice stopped Elken's heart, and he slowly turned to face the woman. He shook from constrained wrath.

"You..." Red wreathed his vision as he said in a deadly tone, "You should be dead. You tried to kill me." The rage in his voice intensified. "You tried to kill Melanie!"

Helnah held up pleading hands. "Elken, calm yourself."

"Calm myself?" Elken repeated. His anger rose into his throat until it exploded. "You killed my parents!" he screamed. "Your dragon fire froze my father's face in a blackened contortion of agony. Do you know the smell of smoldering flesh? It will haunt me forever. My mother's tears seared the wounds of her raw skin. Unable to speak, she died in my arms." Elken's eyes stung as the traumatic memories resurfaced. "And now you have evaded your fate and have the *audacity* to show your face? Do not *dare* tell me to calm myself!"

Helnah hadn't moved. Her brow was pinched as if in pain, and she finally said in a soft voice, "Elken, I didn't know—"

"Of course not! I spent every moment in that cesspit of a fortress concealing my past until the day I could see you destroyed."

"I'm sorry," Helnah whispered. "Truly."

"Does she really expect my forgiveness?" Elken asked Bareth with an incredulous smile. "After everything you've done, Helnah? The people you've murdered? The children you've tortured?"

Helnah's eyes sharpened, and she shot back, "I had no choice!"

Elken jabbed a finger in her face. "*Everyone* has a choice."

"Not me!" Helnah gritted out. She stepped close to Elken. "When a demon of the past enslaves you to do his bidding, when he binds you to an oath of silence that prevents you from warning your kingdom, when he threatens to kill whomever you told in front of you, you have *no choice*." Elken's chest heaved as she continued. "I threw you to the Kottrans so you would see the truth—the real enemy I've been trying to save us all from. If I had breathed a word of their existence, he would have killed me."

Elken maintained his scowl.

"Even now, his invisible spies could find me alive and kill me for exposing them, but it's a risk I must take." Helnah wearily shook her head, breathless. "And if Klarn isn't alone... if he's a part of a larger plan, serving a higher power...it could be the end of Tindoria should he escape. Elken," she pleaded, "we have to warn the others. They must know what I know about him."

Elken's nostrils flared, and he glared at Bareth who finally said, "She speaks the truth, Elken, and I must tell my brother the same. Like it or not, she is valuable."

"Please," Helnah whispered. "Where are Melanie and Jason?"

Sharp prickles of red grew in every corner of Kyle's dream. Shards of ruby constantly reminded him of the key the Golden Prince had placed in his memory. They popped up from the ground he walked on until a sea of crinkling red glass swallowed Kyle completely. He tried to call for help, but he had no voice nor air to breathe. Suffocation came for him, and the torrents of adrenaline heightened his terror. Waking with a start, Kyle fumbled around in his sheets as if he would find red shards. Sleep instantly fled his mind, and his eyes widened. *Wait, where am I?* Kyle dared not move. He cautiously took in his surroundings, only hearing his panicking heart. He was reclining on a large bed in a lavish suite surrounded by a ridiculous number of pillows. A coffered ceiling rose fifteen feet above him, and a glass door flanked by floor-to-ceiling windows filled the wall to his left. It was night. The green walls in the yellow candlelight made him feel more nauseous, and everything smelled foreign.

"Hello?" he shouted.

A simple door across the room groaned open, and Melanie and Jason entered in a rush from the adjoining suite.

"Kyle!" Melanie sat down and wrapped her arms around him. "Oh, my gosh, are you okay?"

Jason felt Kyle's forehead. "You good, dude? Hope you didn't sweat through my sheets."

Hearing his cousins' voices was the final blow to convince Kyle they were, in fact, *not* dead. Shock melted to relief, and his shoulders relaxed, until he remembered the trauma their disappearance had brought upon him. Kyle immediately straightened and screamed, "How dare you!"

Jason shot his head at his sister as they exchanged embarrassed looks.

"Do you have any idea what you've put us through?" Kyle shot out of bed, more hot tears threatening to blur his vision. "You two have driven our families insane! We've had detectives at our house for weeks! We sent out search parties! Not to mention the sleepless nights and my panic attacks. You…you…" Kyle shook with rage as he stammered for words. "You malodorous imbeciles!"

Jason raised an eyebrow, trying to stifle a laugh.

"You're gonna explain yourselves right now, or I swear I'm gonna die of a heart attack!" Kyle demanded, his voice rising in pitch.

"I guess we should start from the beginning," Jason

suggested as he crossed his arms.

"Okay." Melanie folded her hands and took a deep breath. "I raised a dragon when I was fifteen," Melanie started, and pointed to the balcony where Scalaed slept. "That's him. Scalaed." His black form nearly rendered him invisible in the night.

Kyle turned, blinked, and his mouth dropped open. "That's... that's a real dragon?"

Melanie nodded, a smile toying with the corner of her mouth.

"Ah..." Kyle accepted in a daze. "Okay." Now he knew whatever he learned next would only get weirder.

Melanie continued on how for five years they'd kept Scalaed a secret for everyone's safety, until they were sucked into Tindoria where Helnah captured them, and how she escaped thanks to Briefur, Fallon, and Elken.

Jason stepped in. "Meanwhile, at Helnah's fortress, Scalaed and I got separated. I assumed the identity of Elvis—yes, Kyle, stop laughing—and found out Helnah poisons and mutates kids into dragons—don't worry, we cured them. I busted out and stole a horse who was accidentally injected with said poison, and now she's my dragon Poison Ivy. Pun intended. Then I met up with Melanie in a village of shapeshifters. From there we pretty much battled Thornbrill and rescued Scalaed, and in so doing, killed Helnah and restored balance to the Force." Jason punctuated his tale with a smile.

"We also got these protective necklaces from the Empress Elethýna," Melanie added.

Kyle gasped in recognition. "Now *her* I know."

"What?" Melanie and Jason froze.

"She and her son have been monopolizing my dreams lately. Then the Golden Prince trespassed into my room and *yeeted* me into a freakin' vortex, which sent me here."

"Hah!" Jason bumped Melanie. "The Prince *does* exist! Just wait till we tell Baraden."

"Why did the Prince send you?" Melanie asked.

Kyle shrugged forlornly. "Explanations are a thing of the past now. Logic and reason have abandoned us."

Kyle's head swam, and pressing his hand against it to clear the fog, the ruby key surfaced in his memories, watermarking his every thought. He groaned.

"You okay?" Jason noticed.

"I'm on another planet who knows how many lightyears away from Earth with my cousins who were presumed dead," Kyle said flatly. "I'm fantastic."

Jason cleared his throat awkwardly as the cousins eyed each other in the silence.

"We also have powers," Melanie said, lingering on the last syllable.

Kyle flung up his hands. "Oh wow, why does that not shock me?"

"Jason can heal anyone from pretty much anything," Melanie said. "He turned all of Helnah's prisoners back into humans and sent them home."

"I'm still kind of a dead battery in that regard, but yeah," Jason said. "Melanie can walk through shadows, though."

Kyle slowly turned to face his eldest cousin with wide eyes. "Oh really? Care to demonstrate, Miss Magical?"

Melanie smiled at the thought of returning to her shadow haven. "Don't freak out."

"It's impossible at this rate, but whatever." Kyle crossed his arms, waiting.

Standing up, Melanie took a breath and fanned out her fingers down by her side. Whispers filled her head, and wisps of darkness tickled her fingertips. Latching onto them, Melanie melted into the floor.

Tumbling freely in the silent void, Melanie descended deeper than she ever had before, and the relaxation intensified. She closed her eyes and sighed softly at the sensation. *What's the rush in returning so soon?*

Then her Abrielstone began buzzing, a deep sound Melanie had never heard it make before. Her chest tightened. This felt like a warning. *But of what?*

She couldn't stay, as much as she craved the idea. *We need to know why Kyle is here.* Ascending to the surface, Melanie rose from the floor, and the cold of the room settled on her skin. She groaned internally at the change. Her Abrielstone instantly silenced.

"There you are!" Kyle gasped. "We were beginning to think you got lost."

"I'm fine," Melanie said distractedly.

Scalaed awoke at Kyle's outcry and stuck his head in the room, warbling in concern.

"Wow." Kyle's jaw hung limply as he looked upon the

dragon. "Hey, hi." He approached Scalaed as he fished out his phone. "So, this is, like, super cool. As Melanie's cousin, can I take a selfie with you?"

Scalaed raised an amused eyebrow, asking Melanie who this kid was as he lowered his head into the camera's view.

With a stunned chortle, Kyle held out his phone and posed for the bright flash of the picture. He excitedly showed Scalaed the result. "Dude, we look sick!" The dragon nodded in agreement.

"Being a camera is all your phone is good for, by the way," Melanie said. "No cell service or Wi-Fi here."

"Yeah, I figured as much." Kyle nodded as he pocketed his device. "Better conserve my battery. Good thing I charged it last night. Sorry, I got distracted there. Back to the magic." Kyle waved his hands to refocus. "Jason's ability sounds super useful in helping others," he continued. "What is *yours* good for, Melanie?"

Melanie opened her mouth to speak, but she couldn't find the words.

"He's kind of got a point, Mel." Jason smirked.

"I don't know what it's for," Melanie finally confessed. "Right now it's kind of my comfort place."

Kyle clicked his tongue, unimpressed. "Wow. *Real* useful."

"Maybe the prophecy will tell you," Jason said, nudging his sister with his elbow.

Kyle perked up. "You guys are in a *prophecy?*"

"More or less." Melanie shrugged with a sheepish smile.

"No way. You gotta let me see!" Kyle begged.

Jason pulled out the folded parchment from inside his vest and handed it to his cousin.

"So"—Kyle stared at the Scroll—"we have 'from cities and countries afar, no king nor scholar can place, a hero has answered the call to be Tindoria's grace.'"

"Yeah."

"Of course it rhymes," Kyle joked. "It's clearly referring to Earth in that first part."

"Except which of us is the Descendant of Light?" Melanie asked.

Scalaed shrugged his wings.

"Yeah, and there appear to be three candidates now," Jason added.

"It's probably me," Melanie said pensively. "Scalaed is my dragon, I was chosen to raise him, and he's the reason this whole thing started."

"But I was just knighted," Jason interjected. "If that's not a sign of 'a hero has answered the call', I don't know what is."

"Shut up!" Kyle shot his head up with a look of wonder. "How cool is that? I can honestly say my cousin is a freakin' knight!"

Melanie nudged Jason teasingly. "Thanks to his girlfriend."

"Girlfriend?" Kyle's jaw dropped. "So how does it feel to be the guy who has everything?"

Jason's heart fluttered as he thought of Laena, and he didn't restrain the smile that played on his lips.

"But in all seriousness..." Kyle turned up his nose. "Elethýna's son personally escorted me to Tindoria. I think

I'm the Chosen One."

"But you missed the whole first part of the adventure."

"Pfft, does that matter? All good things to those who wait." Kyle looked back at the scroll. "Next part says, 'The rise of this warrior's fate begins with sins of the beast.'" Kyle's eyes flew through the rest of the verses, his eyes widening. "You really couldn't figure this out?"

"I mean, we haven't had a lot of time with it," Melanie excused.

Kyle started reading again from the top, and Jason's handwriting began to glow. Like a curtain parting, the true meaning of the words unveiled itself in Kyle's eyes. Flashes of images filled his mind, and Kyle gasped, waving the paper in his cousins' faces. "Do you see this?"

Jason and Melanie quickly cast each other a confused glance and shook their heads.

"You don't see that the prophecy is glowing?" Kyle asked, dumbfounded.

"No..." Melanie said. She looked to Scalaed, who shook his head cluelessly.

"I guess I'm the only one who can see it," Kyle realized with wonder, and looked back at the paper. He furrowed his brow. "This can't be all of it, right?"

"What makes you say that?" Melanie asked, stepping behind to look over his shoulder.

"Well, it tells me everything but how to defeat the lion."

"Whoa, stop," Jason flapped his hands. "You can understand the Spire's Scroll?"

Kyle shrugged. "Seems pretty clear to me."

A soft twinkling came from the corner of the room, stealing their attention. A golden light bloomed into existence like an unraveling flower, and Empress Elethýna stepped out from the brightness.

Melanie gasped in wonder. "Empress Elethýna." *Finally, someone who can tell us what to do,* she thought elatedly.

"Hello, my dear ones." The Empress smiled as she glided across the floor. Her smile brightened as she greeted Scalaed. "How you've grown."

Scalaed sniffed her, shocked he was finally meeting her in person.

Empress Elethýna tilted her head in reflection. "Those long years ago I sent you away, and now you're home again."

Scalaed gently pressed his head into her hand, thanking her for saving his life those years ago.

"You are not safe yet," Elethýna warned him. "The enemy is after your power."

Scalaed leaned back. What power was she talking about?

"There is another who knows of your abilities and will help train you. Your paths will cross."

Scalaed bowed, still trying to understand.

Elethýna smiled, but Scalaed saw a glimmer of sorrow in her eyes. When the Empress turned back to face the rest, she smiled.

Jason bowed. "Your Majesty."

Kyle copied Jason but couldn't formulate his own words. In person, he now felt unworthy in her presence.

Elethýna raised a finger. "Do not leave for the Spire of Tavnir without your companions. There are others who have yet to join your quest."

"Who?" asked Melanie.

"Every person you meet serves a purpose." Elethýna's tone was now serious. "Some of those people will play important roles in your story, but you *must* control your emotions."

"Yes, Your Majesty," Melanie replied, and quickly made eye contact with Scalaed, who shrugged his wings.

"Be ready for whatever comes." Focusing on Jason, Elethýna said, "Even a great gift cannot change destiny."

The Empress looked upon each of them with tenderness. "Harness your own powers, for they will truly be tested. Your powers are greater than you know. And remember: those who fight for the good of the world are my soldiers." With a twirl of her hand, the Empress produced an Abrielstone from the air and bestowed it on Kyle. "And my soldiers never stand alone."

"Cool, citrine!" Kyle flipped his new necklace in his hands. His Abrielstone's gem glowed orange as Elethýna spoke, and when he looked back up, the Empress had left once again. Scalaed looked around and leaned out the balcony, trying to find where she had gone.

"She's gone, Scalaed." Melanie patted the dragon's back. "But don't worry." She leaned against him in reassurance. "We'll see her again."

CHAPTER
16

Behind the Veil

Blades of light lit up the walls of the Castle of Endlewood, illuminating the three anxious faces gazing upon its gates.

"They *had* to stay at the castle," Thendrell frowned.

"How do you plan to smuggle us in?" Helnah slid her eyes to Elken between them.

"Melanie's maidservant is already expecting me." Elken loosened his shoulders to calm the nerves. "Keep your hoods up, mouths shut, and follow my lead, and we should be fine. It's all candlelight at this hour, so the dimness should shield your faces."

Elken approached the gatehouse and cleared his throat before knocking. The square window panel slid open to reveal the vigilant face of the castle sentry.

"The hour is late," the sentry said gruffly. "What could you possibly want?"

"I'm a companion of Melanie Waldens," Elken said. "She is expecting me at the Verdant Suite. Her maidservant has also been made aware."

The sentry's dark eyes moved past Elken and narrowed at the two hooded figures behind him. "Who are they?"

"Ah, they..." Elken followed his gaze and gathered his wits

as he stared at Thendrell and Helnah. "... they are counselors. To provide Melanie and Jason wisdom for their new mission, yes."

He turned confidently back to the gates, where after a pregnant pause, the sentry hmphed. "Wait here." Then the window shut.

"Wait?" Thendrell whispered. "For how long?"

The gatehouse's silence was broken with the high ringing of a bell.

Elken flinched at the noise, to which Helnah said, "It's a bell push for summoning servants, Elken. Compose yourself."

Elken nodded and steadied his breathing.

The castle gate opened slowly with a rumble, and the sentry gestured to the neatly dressed young woman holding a bright candlestick next to him. "I've confirmed your identity with Eliva. She will take you to the Verdant Suite."

Elken's heart raced as he and the others passed under the castle sentry's watchful eyes. Even as they entered the castle itself Elken could still feel him staring. It wasn't until they began ascending a spiral stairwell that his heart rate slowed.

"I confess you arrived later than I anticipated, sir," Eliva said, her arm holding her candlestick high ahead of them as they wound up the stairs. She led them out of the stairwell into a wide, quiet hallway. "Madam Melanie did not tell me when to expect you, but I assumed it would have been before dark." If Eliva was sleepy, her brisk steps didn't show it.

The end of the hallway dropped them into a comfortably lit common room, where Eliva turned to face her guests. "Allow me to confirm Melanie is even still awake."

A knock at the Verdant Suite's door was followed by a young woman's voice, "Elken of Yolderain is here, my lady."

Melanie brightened. "Oh, yes!"

"Wonder where he's been off to," Jason said.

After Eliva dismissed herself, Elken entered the room, his expression stiff. "Don't kill him," he said, half-heartedly.

Then Thendrell came through the doorway.

"Thendrell." Jason's voice dripped with venom, and he immediately unsheathed *Clavnir*. Scalaed arched his shoulders and loosed a loud snarl that rumbled through the floor.

"Please, listen!" Thendrell raised his arms as the glass blade hovered inches from his face. "Please!"

Disgusted, Jason nudged the sword closer. "Why should we?" His voice was like gravel. "It's taking all the strength I have to not drive this blade into your skull and split it open." Jason doubted he could actually do such a thing, but he wanted Thendrell to fear him.

"I'm trying to save your life, Jason!" Thendrell sounded more frustrated than afraid. "I come unarmed."

Melanie wanted to grab her own sword. "Why would you want to save our lives after you were trying to kill us this past month?"

"We will tell you, but—"

"Hold on, what do you mean, 'we'?" Jason lowered his sword.

"You *must* promise not to do *anything*," Thendrell added. "Your lives depend on it."

Melanie looked to Elken, who only nodded in confirmation.

Kyle's hand shot up. "We promise! Now spit it out, guy, I'm dying from suspense over here!"

"Who is this?" Thendrell asked.

"You heard him," Melanie said. "Explain."

Thendrell stepped back into the doorway and held out his hand to someone outside. Helnah slowly stepped into view.

Melanie could barely speak. "It can't be."

"Helnah," Jason breathed.

Helnah, hands raised, cautiously entered the suite.

The first thing the others noticed was her hair. It was combed back, revealing the scars it hid that were once dragon scales. Her deep-purple dress had a wide boat neck and lavender sleeves with floral embroidery—a shocking contrast to her previous look.

Taking advantage of the stunned silence, Helnah spoke haltingly. "I...understand that you may not accept this." She continued to approach them, and her chest tightened in awkwardness. "And I know too well the thoughts running through your mind. But let me first say..." Helnah lowered her arms. "Thank you."

"*What?*" Melanie blurted as she unsheathed her sword.

Thendrell snagged *Clavnir* from the stunned Jason and swung it to block *Ilvir* as Melanie slashed toward Helnah's neck. A crystal ringing reverberated throughout the room. Helnah flinched at the sword that nearly decapitated her.

Scalaed stomped toward Helnah, growling murderously with eyes and throat aglow with brimming fire.

"Scalaed, don't!" Elken said.

Mouth still open and heaving rippling air, Scalaed's display dared Elken to speak one more time and be added to his terminate list.

Thendrell carefully lowered *Clavnir* and said, "I don't want to fight you. Just let Helnah speak."

Gently pulling Melanie away, Elken guided her sword back to its sheath. In turn, Melanie reluctantly motioned for Scalaed to stand down. With a frustrated snap of his jaws, Scalaed huffed a cloud of stifled smoke at Helnah and slunk into the shadowy corner. He did not vanish completely; he breathed a constant low bellow to remind everyone who was the most powerful weapon in the room should they continue to aggravate him.

Kyle waved for attention. "Excuse me, hi, new guy here. Perhaps I should mediate. Why don't we all just take a seat and listen to what she has to say, huh? I mean, heck, you guys could just leave the room and they can talk to me."

"No." Jason crossed his arms irritably. "Be quick, Helnah."

"I say thank you because you freed me," Helnah explained. "For years, I suffered from the dragon form until you killed it. Slowly, I recovered, and I stand before you now because I owe you the truth. The Kottrans are planning their return," Helnah willed her voice to be steady, "and Tindoria is in danger."

"Yeah, we already know this." Melanie shook off Elken. "Care to share what your boss's plan is?"

"I...don't know. He's done very well veiling that from me," Helnah confessed with a frown. "But it is not just Klarn," she explained, clasping her hands in front of her. "Who and what else lies in Merrendogith? Has anyone else survived execution? What foul magic dwells there?"

Jason turned up his nose as realization settled in. "Klarn gave you the dragon poison, didn't he?"

"Yes." Helnah sighed, averting her eyes while wringing her hands. "What evil lies in Merrendogith to spawn such horror? That is why I'm afraid."

Scalaed's thoughts immediately went to Poison Ivy. Glancing at Jason, he saw Melanie's brother was thinking the same. This couldn't bode well for the green dragon.

"How come you were never banished?" Kyle asked. "From what I've heard, you were no saint."

Scalaed scoffed.

Helnah stood stiffly. "None could get to me with my dragon army."

"And why'd you want an army?" Kyle probed.

Helnah moistened her lips as she scanned the shadows of the room. Tensing her shoulders, she replied in a quieter tone, "I wanted an unstoppable force to defeat Klarn before he ever stepped foot in Tindoria. I avoided his suspicion because collecting dragons was part of my process in finding his real prize, the Pyrium Dragon. I could tell no one of the danger, and my paranoia worsened in the eyes of Eldrain's Royal Scientific council. They saw me unfit for my position and cut my funding. When I realized I was on my own, I abandoned Endlewood for Thornbrill. But I soon ran out of time. Hunting and training dragons was not as efficient as I needed, and Klarn in his impatience suggested I make a Pyrium with the poison he gave me. I refused to test it on children like he advised and subjected myself to it first in hopes I could become my own weapon against him—to use the Pyrium's power to stop him before he could escape." Helnah's voice caught on the next words. "It failed. My mind was shared between two hosts, and I dissolved into illness and madness. Elthar made me a potion to keep most of the effects at bay, but I fought with visions and headaches for years after, slowly succumbing to my dragon-self."

"That's no excuse for abducting and poisoning children!" Jason spat.

"I lived in pain, fear, and insanity!" Helnah retorted shakily. "The dragon half of me was an abomination whose evil I battled daily. I needed a Pyrium before Klarn did, so in desperation, I committed atrocities: burning down cities, kidnapping and poisoning innocent children. They are sins that will haunt me forever. By the time Klarn's spies told me they found an abandoned Pyrium nest, Empress Elethýna had already taken possession of the egg. It vanished, and I never saw another Pyrium until you two arrived. Desperate for your dragon's power, I captured you. Then when you tried to stop me, I had to stop you."

"Wrap it up, Helnah." Jason spun his hand.

"Ultimately, I needed help, but I couldn't tell anyone." Helnah tossed another nervous glance at the shadows around the room, praying they held nothing but cobwebs. "The Kottrans gathered in Tildain's Chasm because its shadowy abyss extended their stay in Tindoria. So, in the Battle of Thornbrill, I sent Elken over so he would see the true enemy. Killing him was not my intention. I knew his necklace would protect him, as I have seen with you, Jason, but I apologize for any inconvenience that may have caused the rest of you."

Melanie balled her fists when Elken said, "Well, you succeeded."

"And my plan remained a secret," Helnah concluded. "My death was certainly unplanned, but now I can speak of Klarn without arousing suspicion. But he is coming for you." Helnah's dark eyes bored into the Waldens siblings. "Your dragon is the heart of his plan, Melanie."

"Everyone keeps talking about this power Scalaed has," Melanie said, tossing a look to her dragon. "Perhaps you'd like to finally share it with us?"

"I am...quite stunned you never figured it out." Helnah put a hand on her hip, her brow furrowed. "Have you never wondered how you arrived in Tindoria?"

"Baraden said it was Elethýna," Jason replied, though his tone voiced his doubt. He looked at his sister and saw her face tense. She flicked eyes over to meet Jason's, revealing they shared the same thought: they would finally discover how they arrived in Tindoria.

Helnah shook her head. "The Pyrium Dragon can create portals."

CHAPTER 17

The Adamas Chamber

Portals?" Melanie echoed.

All eyes landed on Scalaed, who now fell into silence. Revelation dawned on him as he recalled the pink flowers, his vibrations, and the shimmering ring they flew through. It all made sense.

"Yes," Helnah confirmed. A wildness filled her eyes as she spilled more secrets. "Klarn's appearances here are merely from shadow travel. Being in Tindoria physically drains him. He claims Merrendogith has cursed them and slowly turned them into shadows within the first year. To escape properly and regain his mortal body, he must do so through a portal."

"And he needs Scalaed to do it," Jason said heavily in realization and leaned back in his seat. "That's been Klarn's mission all along."

"*I* wanted a Pyrium to create a portal to Merrendogith and set my dragon forces upon everything in that realm," Helnah revealed. "I would annihilate Klarn and anyone else before they could ever escape."

Kyle was confused. "So, you were the good guy this whole time?"

"Hardly!" Jason wrinkled his nose. "How could you ever

think we would trust you, Helnah? How could you possibly think we would *forgive* you?"

Helnah opened her mouth, her brows pinched in hurt. Composing herself, she finally said, "I suppose you can't." When Jason's eyes narrowed, Helnah scoffed in irritation; she was getting nowhere with them. "I need you to save Tindoria, which happens to be my home, and I'd prefer it not to be destroyed."

"Jason," Kyle whispered, "remember what Elethýna said."

Melanie folded her arms. "There's no way we can trust her to come with us."

Both siblings drilled their gazes into Helnah. Her posture had lost its ruthless rigidity. Now she stood with tense shoulders and her hands close together. Anxious glances at the shadows exposed her vulnerability.

How can this even be the same person who tried to take over Tindoria? Jason curled his lip and looked at his sister, who shook her head.

"How can you tell us all this without Klarn making good on his threat?" Elken asked, narrowing his eyes.

"Seems to me he's sparing you because you're still allies," Melanie added.

Helnah shot another look around before continuing. "He has no reason to search for me, but the more you say his name, the higher chance nearby spies will overhear and find you." She took a shaky breath. "Then he will see me, and he can still easily kill us; he's not a spirit. Elken would know."

"Oh, good grief, ya bunch of toddlers!" Kyle threw up his

arms. "Just say we're all going to the Spire and call it a night."

Helnah tilted her head in curiosity, checking the faces of those around her. "Is that your mission?"

"Part of it," Melanie said reluctantly.

"I have been honest with you at the risk of my life. For any of this to work, you should try to be honest with me."

Jason scowled. "You entitled—"

"The cryptic Scroll is missing the last part, so we gotta go to its birthplace and find it," Kyle interrupted. "Just a couple of fancy words to send kitty-boy to his doom."

Helnah raised her eyebrows in hopeful shock and directed her gaze back at Melanie. "There is another way to stop him? I must go, too."

Melanie approached Helnah slowly. "I really don't want to trust you," she said heavily, "and I will certainly never forgive you. But Elethýna must have been referring to you as our new companion." She stood tall in Helnah's face, mouth pinched in disgust. "I hate this. You're coming."

Scalaed choked in shock from the corner.

Helnah's dark lips smiled. "Wonderful."

"Um, I think we've surpassed our max capacity on passengers," Kyle winced as he tried counting possible seats on Scalaed's back.

"I'll stay," Thendrell said from his seat.

"Fine, nobody cares about you anyway." Jason waved his hand dismissively. "I'll bring Pi, so we'll have room for everyone else. We leave in the morning."

The pink sky of the early morning blended seamlessly with a pale blue. After a quick breakfast, Elken, Helnah, and Thendrell convened on Jason's suite balcony after spending the night in another one of the castle guestrooms.

While Poison Ivy acted indifferent toward Helnah, Scalaed did not. Every time Helnah looked in his direction, he made a point to bare teeth and growl, his pupils slimming to slits. He was not happy she would be joining them. And even less so when Melanie reluctantly convinced Scalaed to let Helnah ride him.

Melanie sat with Elken behind her and Helnah in the back. Jason mounted Poison Ivy with Kyle in front.

"Let's go," Jason announced.

A whoosh of unfurling wings blew through the balcony. Scalaed gave a gusty test flap, while Poison Ivy fluttered her vibrant wings to feel the wind. With a huff and a jolt, the dragons launched into the early morning sky.

Kyle made a strangled whine as he sat rigidly in front, fearing any movement would send him falling off the dragon's back.

He was an experienced horse rider, but horses stayed on the ground. Flying on a dragon was nothing like the movies he saw. Nothing could prepare him for sitting unsecured with the open ground hundreds of feet below his dangling legs.

He was completely exposed with no plane cabin or parachute to protect him. While Jason insisted he would be safe, Kyle wished he had straps, especially since dragons shifted—unlike planes, they bobbed up and down like a carousel as they beat their wings. If he was ever to get used to flying, it would take a lot of time and even more trust.

Awkward silence befell the early morning flight as everyone tried ignoring the elephant onboard. Everyone but Kyle, who was craving a distraction.

"So, Helnah…is that Thendrell guy your bodyguard, or…?" He trailed off, hoping someone would fill in the blanks for him.

"No," Helnah was quick to say. "There is a mutual affection between us, but these are not the times for such a thing."

"How does Scalaed's power work?"

"There is magic in the core of the dragon's heart. It opens portals to wherever the dragon wishes—from neighboring towns to other realms. If the dragon concentrates enough, he can feel this magic and utilize it."

"Cool. How'd you get your scars?"

"A remnant from my dragon form."

"How old are you?"

"Let me ask you a question," Helnah redirected, hoping to have a more useful conversation with the only person who didn't seem to mind talking to her. "You understand the meaning behind the Scroll. Is that true?"

Kyle shrugged. "More or less." He pulled out the parchment, feeling the other's curious gazes on him, and cleared his throat. "The first part says the hero comes from Earth. Pretty easy. The next part…" Suddenly images like a movie flashed in Kyle's mind as he read the next stanza. A great lion murdering and setting fire to a village. Screams and falling figures. "I see a lion," he said, his wide eyes staring into oblivion.

"That's Klarn," Helnah explained.

"He killed everyone!" Kyle cried. "And his crime has set the prophecy into motion. The beginning of the Descendant's fate begins with the lion's sin."

"How are you doing this?" Jason asked in shock.

"Zip it." Kyle drew his hand across in a hush motion. "I'm seeing something else. This is so cool!"

"What is it?" Melanie asked.

Kyle slowly cocked his head, still unblinking. "Klarn was aboard a ship, being tossed like a toy in enormous waves…I see glowing eyes and teeth glittering in the water…mermaids? No, Naiads. Oh, they're *creepy*. The ship ran aground on a beach… He's marooned. His coat turned as black as his crime. Figures dart in the shadows, whispers, waiting for revenge."

"Against whom?" Elken asked.

"What is his plan?" Helnah asked.

"I…I…" Kyle blinked rapidly as the vision faded. "I'm losing it, I can't tell." He tried reaching for the deteriorating rags of images, but they dissolved into the air, and Tindoria's sky came back into view. "I lost it. I'm sorry. I think I need practice."

"It's okay, Kyle," Melanie said. "That was still really cool."

Jason shuffled his cousin's hair. "You'll be super useful when we find the last verse."

"I hope so," Kyle sighed. "Speaking of, anyone wanna place bets on who's the Descendant?"

Melanie rolled her eyes. "No."

Kyle slumped in his seat. He wanted everyone to be in a good mood. He reasoned if everyone was happy, they were more likely to get along. So he came up with another idea to promote comradery. Kyle held high his phone to fit both dragons in the shot. "Let's take a selfie!"

"Selfie?" Helnah scrunched her face in confusion.

"A picture," Kyle clarified, waving an encouraging hand. "Come on, everyone just smile and say cheese."

Jason groaned. "Kyle…"

"What does cheese have to do with anything?" Elken asked.

"Let's go, people! Three, two, one, cheese!"

A white flash lit up the group, and Kyle settled back in his seat to examine the photo. He frowned. "Helnah, you weren't smiling."

"Because she can't," Melanie grumbled.

Silence befell them once again, and Kyle groaned and leaned back against Jason. "This ride is getting so awkward. Too bad your dragon doesn't have Bluetooth."

The dragons cut through the Emerald Mountains to the green fields beyond. They had been flying for over two hours, so Elken checked their progress with the map they brought. He looked back up and pointed at the horizon blooming with mountainous clouds.

After another thirty minutes of flying, everyone realized not all of them were clouds, which brought the dragons to a hovering stop.

"What is that?" Kyle pointed.

A white wall of dense fog churned before them. Starting from the plains far below, it spread to the sky high above them and for many miles left and right. The monolithic scale dwarfed them.

Melanie had seen photos of sandstorms and wall clouds before, but to hover before something so large in real life filled her with nausea. She felt so small and wanted to wrap her arms around herself in protection. The cloud's height was veiled in the distant pink sky, perhaps too high to even breathe.

"This must be the Fog of Tordin," Elken revealed as he scanned the map again.

"What's Tordin?" Melanie asked.

"An archaic word meaning 'punishment'," Helnah replied.

The word settled like a weight over the group. The dragons hovered before the fog while everyone silently considered whether to proceed.

Kyle, unblinking, lifted his phone and snapped a picture.

"So, remember when Baraden said people searching for the Spire were stricken with madness?" Jason reminded them.

"Maybe we should land and think this through."

Immediately Scalaed lurched forward as he began his descent, causing Elken to squeeze Melanie.

Melanie looked back at him and chuckled. "Are you okay?"

Elken grimaced with discomfort. "My stomach and heart switched places."

Scalaed tried to ignore Elken's voice. How he ended up with the people he hated most was a cruel twist of fate. Hate was the perfect word for Helnah, though it was too strong for Elken. Or was it? He shook his head, his patience running out, and he mentally begged over and over for his riders to just get off his back.

We won't serve these humans forever, came Poison Ivy's voice as she descended next to him. Noticing Scalaed's irritation, she had moved a little closer. *I play my role until my guide tells me otherwise.*

Scalaed furrowed his brow. What did she mean, otherwise?

Poison Ivy shook her head. *You* are *a disappointment.* The green dragon distanced herself and descended faster.

They landed in a field of wild yellow grasses and flowers. As soon as Scalaed's claws touched, he bucked his passengers off.

"Hey!" Melanie reprimanded as Elken picked her off the ground. "That was rude."

Scalaed growled. A new feeling intruded on his heart. Pride. He loved the power he wielded, the fear he evoked. He quickly tried to repress that feeling.

Looking like she had expected the mistreatment, Helnah

wordlessly brushed herself off before standing the farthest away from the group, unfazed by Scalaed's antics.

The wall of fog now sat twenty feet away, dense and white and softly whooshing.

As the others gathered in a circle to discuss their next move, Kyle noticed Helnah by herself, and he slipped away.

"You like being by yourself?" he asked.

Helnah shrugged with folded arms. "I've been alone for years."

"That didn't answer my question."

"It doesn't matter what I like." Helnah's voice softened. "I deserve any misery coming my way. They'll never forgive me for what I've done. I suppose they shouldn't."

"That's ridiculous!" Kyle shook his head. "It can't be that unforgivable."

"The lives I destroyed…" Helnah pinched her mouth and her voice faded. "At the time, I had no remorse. What kind of monster am I?"

Kyle thought for a moment as he looked at Helnah. She was fighting tears as she looked at the rest of the group.

"You do know Jason saved them all, right?" Kyle asked.

Helnah looked back, her brow less furrowed.

"Yeah, his magic turned every dragon back into a kid. Brought them all back to their cities and he even got knighted."

Helnah's lips parted in a gasp of disbelief.

"They'll come around, eventually. Grudges can gnaw away at you until you're a miserable skeleton. My cousins won't let it get to that point." Kyle patted Helnah's arm in reassurance.

"Be patient. I'll work on them, too." He returned to the rest of the group, leaving Helnah with welling eyes.

As Kyle reinserted himself into the group's circle, he noticed Jason had approached the cloud with an outstretched hand.

"What's he doing?" Kyle asked Melanie.

"Testing a theory," Melanie replied apprehensively.

Jason craned his neck up to view the remarkably smooth wall of fog. Looking straight ahead again, he inserted his hand into the white cloud. Cold dampness wrapped around his skin. While condensation seemed innocent enough, Jason's gut warned him of something unnatural floating in the fog. Jason withdrew his hand, verified it was still normal looking, then returned to the group.

"Got an unnerving sense when I touched the fog just now."

His remark was met with crossed arms and glares of discontent.

"And we *must* fly through it?" Elken asked.

"There's really no other option," Jason scoffed. "That fog must be close to tens of thousands of feet high; there might not even be any oxygen."

"Does anyone want to prove that?" Melanie suggested.

"You all seem to forget the Empress gave us her protection," Kyle reminded them as he flashed his Abrielstone. "What's the worst that could happen?"

"Scalaed and Poison Ivy don't have necklaces," Elken said.

Kyle frowned. "True, neither does Helnah."

"Pfft, she can go crazy for all I care," Melanie mumbled under her breath.

Kyle scowled and shoved her arm. "She's trying to be good, you know. She didn't have to warn us about the bad guy."

Melanie looked down at her cousin with a grimace. "You never had to deal with her when she was evil. You'd never be this nice if you had."

"You don't know that, McGrudgeson," Kyle retorted confidently.

"Kyle," Melanie snarled, "shut up."

"I suppose the only way is through, then." Elken craned his neck up at the wall of fog.

"Is walking an option?" Kyle asked.

"That could take forever," Melanie argued. "The map says the fog is twenty-something miles across, but can we even maintain a straight path if we're blind? I do not want to be stuck in there when night falls."

"So we fly through it then?" Kyle asked.

Tension settled like dew over them all.

"I guess so." Jason sighed, voicing the sentiment of the whole group.

"Right then," Kyle rubbed his hands. "Anyone got a compass?"

"This is a flat world, Kyle," Jason said flatly. "I doubt Tindoria has a magnetic field."

"Seriously?" Kyle dropped his arms limply. "I should have known nothing would be easy. What have you been using to navigate the map then, Elken?"

"An asterguide," Elken said and held out a silver octagonal disc with a needle.

Kyle held it, examined it, then stared blankly at Elken, unimpressed. "This is literally a compass. What makes it different?"

"The needle always points north."

"That's a compass, dude!" Kyle scoffed incredulously. "It detects and responds to a planet's magnetic field which exerts a force on the compass needle, causing it to rotate—"

"It points to Toreus," Helnah interrupted. "The Great North Star."

Kyle paused, his mouth still open mid-sentence. "Ah." After a moment of processing, he shrugged, "Well, that works. I'll sit in front of Jason on Poison Ivy, and everyone else flies close behind to keep us in sight. The map says we are northwest of the spire. With the *asterguide*"—he said the word with a sarcastic flair— "we should get there no problem."

"Provided we stay sane," Elken added.

"We'll be fine." Kyle waved a hand. "Let's go, time's a-wastin'!"

While Kyle immediately took off for Poison Ivy, Melanie mounted Scalaed and noticed his low growl when Elken settled behind her. Taking a deep breath, she gritted her teeth and said, "Come on, Helnah."

"Everyone ready?" Kyle looked around. "Here we go."

The dragons beat their wings and lifted off the ground. After a moment's hesitation of wondering what lay beyond, they delved into the cloud. The whiteout swallowed them with an ominous whoosh.

"Just take it slow, Scalaed," Melanie told him.

"Can you guys see us okay?" Kyle called back to Melanie and Scalaed.

"Yeah, keep this steady pace. We don't know where we'll end up."

Sound slowly became more muffled the deeper they flew. Kyle flexed his jaws to pop his ears, thinking it was just his own hearing failing him. But the fog only swallowed the noise more. The whiteness grew thicker, and the dragons flew closer to each other. Kyle kept his eyes locked on the asterguide to maintain their path southeast. Encased in silver and covered with a crystal glass, the sapphire needle was a steady beacon. Kyle wanted to ask how it worked but didn't want to risk being distracted.

Jason looked around at the white nothingness, feeling more uneasy with each passing moment. A glance at his sister told him she was feeling the same. The fog began to soak their clothes, and the temperature was dropping. Kyle turned away from the wind to wipe the condensation off the asterguide with his sleeve. He froze. The glass had fogged from the *inside*. Dread seeped more deeply into him than the foggy chill as Kyle realized they were flying blind.

Jason popped his head over his cousin's shoulder. "Everything okay, Kyle?" His voice reverberated strangely in the fog, like a lost memory coming in and out of focus.

Kyle quickly slapped a hand over the asterguide. "Um, sure! Just keep flying this direction, as best as you possibly can, as if there wasn't a compass to guide you."

"Kyle…" Jason narrowed his eyes and grabbed his cousin's wrist to discover the faulty instrument. "Ugh, this fog. Now what?"

"Your dragon is a flying animal," Kyle whispered back. "Shouldn't she have built-in navigation to direct her?"

"Can you keep us straight, Pi?" Jason leaned forward to stroke his dragon's damp green scales.

Poison Ivy looked around, and gave a somewhat convincing nod.

"I really don't like this," Elken said. "We should have tried to fly above."

Scalaed couldn't see a thing. Nothing but white surrounded him, and he began to fear he wasn't flying up anymore, but down…or maybe to the right. His head began to swim, and disorientation blurred his senses. He lost his bearings. He began to panic.

"Uh, Melanie, are you okay?" Jason asked from his position on Poison Ivy. "You're kind of creeping me out."

Melanie was tilting her head and staring at her brother wide-eyed. "Did you always look like that?"

"Like what?" Jason looked at himself then patted his face. "What's wrong with my face?"

"Your head is squishy."

"*Excuse* me?"

"Ugh." Elken leaned all the way back into Helnah. "We never should have come here!"

"Pull yourself together, Elken!" Helnah smacked the back

of his head.

"Hey," Elken whined. "Don't hit me."

"What's wrong with you?" Jason demanded.

Kyle giggled in front of him. "This air tastes like cupcakes."

"*Oh, no.*" Jason felt his heart stop. "The madness."

"I told you, no fog!" Elken wailed. "This is *baaaaad*."

"Oh my *gosh!*" Melanie sobbed. "Why is your face melting?"

Jason seemed to suddenly lose his ability to speak and just barked.

Helnah rubbed her forehead. "I'm surrounded by idiots."

Scalaed panted heavily and resolved to go back the way they came, so he wheeled around.

"No, dragon!" Helnah screamed as she braced herself.

Elken's arms flung up above his head. "Whooo!"

Poison Ivy flapped desperately to intercept Scalaed, cutting in front of him to prevent his escape.

"I can't breathe," Melanie gasped. "I want Mom."

Scalaed roared, ordering Poison Ivy to back off. The green dragon shook her head and insisted they must press on. Scalaed lurched forward, jaws snapping, trying to save his riders. Furious, Poison Ivy fought back.

Riders screamed and gasped for clearer minds as the world around them spun. Melanie was sobbing hysterically, Kyle's tongue was hanging out to taste the air, Jason's eyes were rolled back, and Elken was hollering excitedly.

Helnah looked around at her incapacitated companions and wondered why she was only mildly affected. The dragons appeared to be sane so far as well. *Is there a connection?* Taking advantage of this, she squeezed out from behind Elken and Melanie and crawled up to the front of Scalaed. Her vision began to blur, but she had to take control of the situation.

"Scalaed!" Helnah yelled.

The dragon reared back from the duel with Poison Ivy to stare angrily at Helnah.

"You must create a portal to the Spire or we will be lost here forever, do you understand?"

Scalaed's anger melted away, and he begged for clearer instructions.

"Think of how you arrived in Tindoria." Helnah rubbed her eyes. "How did you feel when the portal opened? Your heart's core. What did you do?"

Scalaed squeezed his eyes shut and tried to focus. But he didn't know what the Spire looked like. Maybe if he could just get above the fog…to the clear blue sky…

Suddenly, he felt it deep within himself, a hot pulse that expanded throughout his whole body. As it rumbled, he was filled with a buzzing vibration. At once a huge, shimmering ring expanded in the air to show an open sky of deep blue beyond. Electrified by the sight, Scalaed snatched Poison Ivy's foreleg with one claw and flung them through the portal.

Gravity switched. Forward was now up, and the vicious pull yanked the dragons backward. The portal vanished, and the dragons tried to right themselves. Flapping in desperation, they managed to slow before seeing stone and crashing.

Jason came to by gagging on a vaporous tendril that leaked from his mouth. Rolling over with blurred vision, he clawed his way out from under bodies and wings as his Abrielstone's amethyst aura dissipated. He gasped in the air and squinted at the brilliantly shining sun. Feeling his body steady itself, he walked out onto a ledge. The sky was a rich blue—a much darker shade than what could be seen from the ground far below. The air was crisp, clean, and cold, and Jason could only guess how high they were. An endless sea of cloud and fog spanned to every horizon. All was held in a silence Jason had never experienced.

Everyone else coughed the last of the fog from their lungs and managed to stand.

"That was rough," Melanie groaned as she stretched her neck.

They had landed on a long strip of stone with small gardens wildly overgrown with bright green grass and flowers. Behind them towered a pinnacle that twisted to a sharp point well over a hundred feet high with a massive, relieved doorway at the bottom—the entrance to the Adamas Chamber.

"The Spire of Tavnir," he breathed. Exhilaration rushed through Jason and fueled his steps closer to the door.

Melanie appeared next to him, looking at the Spire in awe. "We made it!"

"And we can breathe up here!" Kyle exclaimed in relief. "But how? And how *did* we get here, anyway?"

Scalaed nodded to Helnah as he helped Poison Ivy to her feet, explaining she helped him make the portal.

"I told you I'm on your side." Helnah crossed her arms. "And also, I refused to die."

"Thank you," Kyle said, though no one else echoed him.

Helnah sized up the pinnacle. Wonder gave way to skepticism when her eyes landed on the doorway. *A place this sacred would undoubtedly be difficult to enter.* "I suppose one of you has the means to open these doors."

"If there really is a lock, we're screwed," Jason said.

"Why, you need a key?" Kyle's eyes widened.

"There was only one ever made, and it was lost with Tavnir's murder," Melanie explained. "We have no idea what it looks like."

Kyle's Abrielstone lit up in a brilliant orange, and he was struck with realization.

"I have it!" He raised his hand then ran to the doorway.

"What?" Jason cried.

"All this time you guys needed a key and didn't tell me?" Kyle's finger tapped the keyhole. "I think I know what my power is." He closed his eyes, and the blueprints of the key appeared as clear as day in his mind. Now intentionally scanning every detail, Kyle felt the key forming in his hand. When he opened it, a perfect replica lay in his palm.

"You can just make anything you think of?" Jason sputtered.

"Sure, if my Abrielstone tells me," Kyle said as he slipped the key into the hole. He slid it all the way in until a loud *chlunk* vibrated through the door. It slowly opened to reveal a grand nave—a long, towering room soaring a hundred feet high with an arched ceiling supported by pearlescent vaults. Prismatic light filtered through the crystal ceiling in showers of rainbow rays.

"Wow," Melanie breathed.

"Yeah, wow!" Kyle jumped, the reality hitting him. "Did you see that? I created something with my mind! Oh, you meant...ohhhh. Wow!"

Twelve shimmering pillars that seemed to glow with every color pulsed down the length of the cathedralesque room. Scrolls wrapped around golden rollers neatly filled the multitude of dark stone shelves that covered the walls, each scroll appearing to give off its own light. Near the far end of the chamber stood a glittering stairwell that descended to the base of the Spire.

"The Adamas Chamber," Jason awed.

At the far end of the nave the ceiling rose higher in a chancel, and great windows poured light into the chamber. The air in its heights sparkled. Below, reflecting the rainbow, stood the crystal Obelisk, upon which was inscribed the original Spire's Scroll.

Suddenly, a loud rumble rocked the place. Two towering sentinels at least twenty feet tall appeared inside the doorway from either side of the entrance. Their bodies—masculine and humanoid—shimmered like they were formed of pale blue gemstone, and their robes sparkled like the pillars. From behind rested a massive pair of crystal wings.

Crossing their double-bladed swords, they asked in thunderous, unison voices, *"How have you entered this sacred place?"*

Their intimidating display caused hesitation before anyone responded.

The Sentinels' glowing eyes intensified. *"Speak or be destroyed!"*

Helnah stepped forward. "We wish to read the final words of the Spire's Scroll, for it is imperative we understand its meaning to save this realm."

"None shall have access to the Obelisk, for it was for Tavnir's use alone."

"Yes, but you see, she's dead," Helnah stated flatly. "She intended to share the last of that work with Tindoria, so what is the issue, pray tell?"

The Sentinels' wings slowly spread, filling the doorway completely. *"How have you gained access to the door?"* They slammed their weapons against the ground with a clang like church bells.

Kyle and the others flinched at the vibration.

"I made the key," Kyle finally said, his voice a pitch higher.

There was a pause as the Sentinels exchanged looks. *"'A dreamer of youth holds the key,'"* they quoted. They retracted their swords and receded to their posts inside the Adamas Chamber.

Cautiously, Kyle and the others walked further into the

Chamber.

The Sentinels then crossed their weapons before Scalaed or Poison Ivy could enter. *"Dragons are forbidden from entering the sacred Adamas Chamber."*

Melanie and Jason turned and met the offended eyes of their dragons. Poison Ivy huffed, snout turned up haughtily, and walked away with a quick lash of her tail.

"Scalaed…" Melanie didn't know what to say as she tossed a hapless shrug at the Sentinels. "I'm sorry, we'll try to be fast." Then she and Jason turned their backs on the dragon.

Heat seared Scalaed's heart, and his smoky breathing elevated. Little by little, he was being shoved aside. He longed for the spacious ponderosa forests, Melanie's camper, and their private corner of Earth where they had been all each other had. Growling murderously at the unfazed Sentinels, Scalaed slunk away to sulk in the gardens.

In the Adamas Chamber, while Jason and the others made their way to the Obelisk, Helnah wandered to a shelf and picked up the nearest book and began reading. Kyle snapped pictures left and right as he walked, mumbling something about no one believing him otherwise. He even managed to sneak a selfie with the Sentinels and ask how they could breathe there. The Sentinels revealed the Celestials placed an enchantment over the Spire, granting air at such a height.

Footsteps echoed in the still air as they all gathered around the Obelisk, which stood waist-high.

"That's the clearest white quartz I've ever seen!" Kyle marveled as he snapped another picture.

The top was sheared smooth at an angle for inscribing, and on the crystal was etched the Spire's Scroll.

Tavnir's flawless, calligraphic script filled the Obelisk's surface. Most of the text Jason and Melanie recognized as the first part of the prophecy. But even the beauty of the script wasn't enough to mask the ominous dread of the final stanza:

BEHOLD THE SPILT BLOOD OF THE DARK
THE SELFLESS MAGIC IS SHED
THE MORTAL CRIMSON CLEAVES THE HEART
THE END OF LIFE, DEFEATED

CHAPTER
18
Release the Panther

Klarn sat splay-legged in his throne, and he heaved a deep sigh, fingers pinching his lips in thought. His eyes wandered around the dilapidated hall. The walls had long since crumbled in disrepair, and the roof had yielded to the dark gray sky. How he *burned* to leave this place.

Nothing in Merrendogith lasted. It was as if even the stones had lost the will to stand. There was no life, no wind, no color. It was a stagnant world, a dead reflection of Tindoria, a cursed realm of unknown origin or purpose. Even the sun refused to grant any warmth, floating across the sky in cold, white light.

The cruelest trick of all was the Kottrans' inability to die. The irony. Some sinister force lay the rules of this realm, where Klarn and his people suffered the pangs of starvation yet could not die. They could only steal from Tindoria, but whatever scraps they hoarded quickly rotted after returning to Merrendogith. Weakness would not overtake them, so they were fueled by a vicious desperation for escape. Oh, how Klarn despised this place.

His eyes trailed upward above his throne where a dragon skull bored into him with empty eye sockets. He had been led by a mysterious voice to the Valley of Ossium. Where above in Tindoria glittered Sungold Lake, in Merrendogith lay a dry bed of bones. There, at the foot of a Pyrium Dragon skeleton, the voice revealed the secret of the beast's magic, and how Klarn could find one and harness a portal to escape. Yet in the years since its discovery, their efforts had been useless. He glared at the skull. Oh, how he envied its peace in death.

The echoing of footsteps drew Klarn from his thoughts.

"Telfath, did you find the Pyrium?" Klarn stared down his approaching captain.

Telfath replied, "We lost it when it left Tharretill. It will take time to locate it again since it can fly and we cannot."

The mention of his former puppet's country caused Klarn's ear to twitch. "It was that close? Why was it in Tharretill?"

Telfath scrunched his mouth in uncertainty. "Perhaps the Thornbrillian we captured warned the encampment there. They must know we exist."

"Explain to me"—Klarn rose and walked to Telfath, his voice rising—"how you and your warriors failed to kill him when he escaped!"

"He disappeared by magic; we didn't know where he was sent, and in our search for him we missed the Pyrium Dragon."

"Elethýna and her interventions." Klarn's voice dripped with venom. "Now our secret is known, and we must move swiftly."

"We need a plan, Klarn. All we've done is follow it around the realm. Are you sure we can't capture it and bring it to us through shadow travel?"

"Tindorian beings are not meant to shadow travel like us, so they might be killed in the process. We cannot risk it. The dragon must enter Merrendogith as we have or create a portal. However..." Klarn twisted the hairs of his beard in thought. "If we were to capture one of the dragon's friends, it would go to any lengths to rescue them."

"The prisoner might not survive the transfer," Telfath reminded.

"Ah"—Klarn smiled, his fangs glittering. "It will not matter. If they die, it is of no loss to us. If they live, we'll have information. There will be no way for the dragon to know. Regardless, it will journey here to save one of its own, and we will have what we need."

"Brilliant, sir." Telfath nodded. "So who is the target?"

Klarn waved a hand. "Either of the Separate Realm siblings."

Telfath nodded and turned to leave.

"Telfath, have someone you trust carry out this simple task. I will need your assistance in preparing for the dragon's arrival."

Telfath cast a glance over his shoulder and gave a single nod of acknowledgment before departing.

Alone once more, Klarn reached behind his cracked throne and pulled out a sword. The blade tapered with jagged edges like a bolt of lightning. The crossguard was twisted purple glass, and a heavy pommel stuck out from the hilt. Inscribed in the Indomitable Glass blade was *Dacvir.*

"'Hopeful Beacon'," Klarn translated softly as he

recounted the day he found the sword of legend. It was one of the rare days he eagerly anticipated journeying through Merrendogith. Guided by a voice promising he would reclaim the priceless weapon, he was led to the House of the Dead—the fallen reflection of the Castle of Endlewood. Klarn twisted a smile at the memory of slaughtering the undead horde that dwelled there. He sought his vengeance through their utter destruction, and amidst the carnage that filled the fetid throne room, he found *Dacvir*. It had been two years since then, and the sword truly had become his beacon of hope. Fate had chosen him to be its new bearer, and Klarn believed that to be a positive omen for his future as chief and his people's savior. Before sheathing the Indomitable Glass sword, he brought it to his lips and said, almost like a prayer, "May you lead us back to the light."

"Klarn." Telfath returned with a young Kottran woman in tow.

Quickly regaining his composure, Klarn sized up Telfath's candidate. "Caito," he greeted as he descended the dais.

Caito's shiny black hair was short and curled inward just above toned shoulders. A white blaze in her sleek, black tunic matched the white strands that framed her face. Her clothing revealed her bare back which, despite her petite frame, was sculpted in muscle.

"What is my mission?" she asked.

"You must find the Pyrium Dragon and its company. Abduct Melanie or Jason Waldens, which will entice the dragon and its companions here to mount a rescue," Klarn ordered. "Make your respites short. I do understand the pain of crossing over."

"Yes, my lord."

"One last thing." Klarn crossed his arms. "Should the prisoner struggle during the return crossing, kill them instead. Revenge is a strong motivator."

The fire in the Great Hall crackled and swirled in a myriad of colors. Chief Helmir and Vytia sat rigidly in their thrones, dreading the news they were about to share with their people. The Hündr that filled the seats murmured quietly among themselves. Briefur and Fallon sat close to each other. The anxiety was thicker than the smoke. Fallon met Vytia's distraught gaze, and her heart ached for her and her unborn child. Vytia looked away to compose herself and wrapped her arms around her stomach like a shield. Melting into her seat, Fallon desperately wished she could comfort her.

Helmir finally rose and thumped his staff against the ground. "My fellow Hündr, what I am about to tell you is most disturbing. I must ask you to not panic, but to steel yourselves and make preparations."

Worried eyes met all around the hall.

Taking a slow, heavy breath, Helmir spoke. "The Kottrans have returned."

Briefur felt like the air had been sucked from the hall with the collective gasp of horror that echoed around him. Shocked chatter elevated to fearful cries, and Helmir quickly restored silence and order with three swift thumps of his staff.

"No doubt Klarn will set his vengeful eyes on Hvitria for our hand in his execution. The Kottrans are alive but trapped in a realm below Tindoria. We have no clue when he will find his escape, or what dark magic he may bring with him, so we must arm ourselves to the teeth. Sharpen your blades, fit your armor, and prepare your minds. We cannot spare a single moment."

Many Hündr tried to make their way to the chief, but his personal guards blocked them. As the stunned crowds began to funnel out of the Great Hall, Briefur and Fallon stayed behind until the place had emptied. The guards were the last to depart, leaving Helmir and Vytia the only other two who remained. Helmir stood by the fire pit, gazing intently at the fire, and Vytia sat with her hands pressed to her lips in distant thought.

The cousins approached, and Vytia lifted her face to them, trying to smile bravely as Helmir eyed the young Hündr.

"We suspect Klarn is somehow observing us beyond from this realm," Briefur began.

"We first noticed it at King Eldrain's celebration," Fallon continued. "A darkness only our senses could detect. And again at Thornbrill. For reasons unknown, we fear it is targeting Melanie and Jason." She cast a quick glance at Vytia, who stood with a hand over her chest in worry, and the inkling of an idea formed in Fallon's mind.

"We wish to go to their aid," Breifur said. "We must know why the Kottrans want the siblings, and why they appear to have little interest in *us*."

"Very well," Helmir sighed. "Do be careful, you two." He dismissed them.

"Wait." Fallon slipped off her Abrielstone. Approaching Vytia, she pressed the necklace into her hand. "You need it more than I. It will protect you and the baby."

Vytia pursed her lips as emotions swelled. "Thank you, Fallon," she whispered barely audibly.

Helmir felt a hand clasp him on the back as Briefur surrendered his Abrielstone to him. "You need to live to see your child." Briefur smiled softly.

Helmir was never one to publicly show much affection, but in his state, he did not refrain from hugging Briefur.

Jason wrote down the final stanza on his copy of parchment as the others reread in silence. Kyle instead just took a picture of it, and Jason gave him the side-eye.

"What, lost your phone?" Kyle shook his own device as a tease. "Much more convenient."

"Thendrell dumped pee on it," Jason grumbled.

Kyle froze. "Aha...anyway, this verse. It's good news,

right?" He looked around for affirmation. "It sounds like the bad guys are gonna die."

"You can't understand it?" Melanie asked him.

"I don't know how to turn on my magic." Kyle folded his arms defensively against the disappointed gazes of his companions. "Heck, I didn't even know I *had* magic until yesterday! Cut me some slack."

"The verse sounds really morbid to me," Melanie said as she stole another glance at the final verse.

The Sentinels bellowed from the entrance, "*Your time here has ended, for this Spire belongs only to the Seer of Tindoria. You have had privileged access to only read the Spire's Scroll. Take with you that which you sought and leave.*"

Jason double-checked the Scroll and stowed it away in his vest.

Melanie ran a mental head count as she looked around. All were gathered except for Helnah, who stood off to the side with her nose buried in a thick, dusty tome. As tempted as she was to leave Helnah here, Melanie wasn't one to leave a member of their team behind.

"Come on, Helnah," she said reluctantly. "We're leaving."

"Oh...yes, of course," Helnah stammered uncharacteristically and replaced the book, trying to read the last of the page.

Once everyone had exited the Adamas Chamber, Jason asked, "What now, Melanie?"

Scalaed instantly appeared at Melanie's side, but she only gave him a quick neck scratch as she responded to her brother.

"We need to solve this Scroll. We're going back to Endlewood."

Scalaed snorted hot breath into her hair, dissatisfied with the lack of proper affection. Poison Ivy passed him on her way to Jason, and she gave him a knowing look. *Humans will always disappoint you eventually. It's what they do.*

Scooting closer to Melanie in denial, Scalaed told the green dragon to shut up.

"This time, let's fly *over* the fog," Kyle begged the group. "If I smell a cupcake again, I *will* throw up."

"Or Scalaed can conjure another portal." Helnah put her hands on her hips. "It would be faster, would it not? If we intend to use his ability, I strongly suggest he learns to harness it."

"Helnah's right," Elken said. "Scalaed?"

Scalaed set his jaw. Once again, he had been reduced to a tool of convenience. All interactions were simply asking for favors. But he knew they had to leave, and he agreed he should learn to control his own power. Trying to ignore the festering resentment, Scalaed scanned everyone's faces and gave Melanie a look which she translated as *Well, here goes nothing.*

Scalaed shook out his wings as he walked to the edge of the Spire. Closing his eyes, he tried to tap into his power. What exactly was he feeling for? Helnah had said his heart contained the magic. Maybe focusing on his heartbeat would be a good start. Scalaed tried to ignore everyone staring at him—especially Helnah and Elken—as he concentrated on his pulse. With every beat, his vision of Endlewood became clearer.

Out of the darkness, the capital city came into focus. It brightened, and Scalaed could smell the stone and shops and hear the bustle of life. Endlewood was so close he could touch it. He moved through the city and brought the palace into view…fifth floor…the Verdant Suite. It was then Scalaed realized his eyes had been open, and he was now looking at their suite through a shimmering portal.

"Amazing!" Melanie was at his side and hugged his neck. "Well done!"

Scalaed looked down at her beaming face. Her words should have made him happy, but she was only pleased by what he did, and not who he was. Nevertheless, Scalaed smiled back. Then he caught Poison Ivy's gaze. A wildness glowed in her eyes as she looked between Scalaed and his portal.

You've succeeded in something. She sounded surprised. *This is most pleasing to my guide.*

Scalaed responded with a disturbed frown and turned to be the first to walk through the portal. His companions followed close behind as they crossed seamlessly from the Spire into the Verdant Suite.

When everyone had passed through, Scalaed let the portal close, but not before Kyle stole a picture of it.

"Okay, can we agree that's the coolest thing we've ever seen besides my powers?" Kyle looked around excitedly.

"It took quite a while," Helnah said coolly. "If we are to use this as a battle tactic, he must learn to summon a location at the drop of a coin."

Scalaed knew better than to have hoped for a thank you

from Helnah. He needed to get away from her. Scalaed leaned toward Melanie, begging to be excused.

"You get fifteen minutes," Melanie granted. "Take some deep breaths and then come back, okay?"

She had barely finished speaking before Scalaed soared off the balcony, Poison Ivy following suit.

Outside Endlewood, the two dragons touched down in a field spotted with fruit trees. Scalaed helped himself to the snacks, but Poison Ivy didn't even approach.

Scalaed tried to convince her of the deliciousness, but she shook her head. Rolling his eyes, he pushed a few with his nose into her direction, enticing her to at least smell it.

Poison Ivy stamped her foot.

Scalaed insisted by pushing the fruit even closer.

That must have annoyed her to the point of anger, because Poison Ivy's pupils narrowed to a shape Scalaed had never seen in her eyes before, and she roared with a voice much deeper than normal.

Scalaed jumped back, raising his wings in surrender, and cautiously put the tree between them.

Poison Ivy's shoulders arched above her neck, and her tail slashed the grass like a whip. Her eyes beamed with a soulless glare.

Giving an unsettled growl, Scalaed demanded she stop. What was her problem?

Just as quickly as it had come, Poison Ivy's mood reverted. Looking at Scalaed, then the tree, she huffed, tossed her rump, and flew off.

Scalaed sat on his haunches in bewilderment. Something very wrong was happening to his only dragon friend, and he knew Helnah's poison was to blame. He grabbed another mouthful of fruit and flew back to the city. Jason needed to know about Poison Ivy's development.

"Any ideas on the meaning of the final verse?" Helnah addressed the room from her seat on a settee. Melanie and Elken sat on the bed, with Kyle and Jason at the dining table.

"Someone dies," Kyle announced confidently.

"Obvious, but correct." Helnah motioned with her hand for Jason to give her the paper.

Hesitating for a moment, Jason gave it to her.

"What of the third stanza—do you know the meaning of *that?*" Helnah looked around, one eyebrow raised.

"Well, those archangel dudes quoted the third line when they saw me," Kyle answered. "I must be the dreamer of youth with the key. Makes total sense."

"So that means..." Helnah hoped the siblings were intelligent enough to make the connection.

Realization flashed over Melanie and Jason's faces.

"'Life in the hands to heal' is about me," Jason said. "I'm a healer; I save lives."

"Yes, good." Helnah actually smiled, her expression like

that teacher who finally drew the right answer from a student. "Melanie?"

Melanie nodded. "I've got the shadow travel."

"Precisely."

"So that leaves us with the final stanza," Elken spoke up.

"Klarn must be defeated, but how?" Jason slid his hands through his hair and leaned back in his chair.

"Do not say his name so insouciantly," Helnah snapped. "His spies could be around us at this very moment. We do not see them because they stay in the shadows. Interesting that they share Melanie's power. Surely there is some significance."

Thendrell walked in the suite followed by a young kitchen servant pushing a cart of food. "Oh!" Thendrell exclaimed and quickly stepped in front of the servant boy, blocking his view of Helnah. "You've returned…so soon." He took possession of the cart and ushered the kitchen servant out the door, which he promptly closed. Thendrell turned around and squinted in confusion. "How did you get—"

"Just the man I wanted to see!" Helnah cut him off as she snagged an open bottle of wine from his cart. "My dear Thendrell, thank you," she gasped in relief as she guzzled from the bottle.

"That was mine—"

"I need this," Helnah said sharply.

"It's yours, I insist." Thendrell raised his hands and backed away. "I'm thankful the younger servants don't recognize me; I was able to acquire plenty of food for everyone. I just didn't expect your impeccable timing."

While the others gravitated toward the food, Melanie remained seated on the bed, twisting her ring around and around her finger in concentration. She sifted through the Scroll's words in her head and tried different combinations and synonyms in hopes of a revelation. But every time she came up empty, and depression soaked through her bones even more.

"Are you alright?" Elken placed his hand over hers, stilling her anxious fidgeting.

"If I am the Descendant, I have to figure out what that last verse wants of me. It doesn't sound cheery. Blood, shed magic, end of life, defeat."

"Melanie." Elken turned her chin to face him. The softest smirk played on his lips. "We will solve this. I think you will feel better if you eat something. I spy some delectable pastries calling your name."

Melanie smiled, and Elken gave her hands a final squeeze.

Something in her ring went *click*.

And Melanie disappeared.

CHAPTER 19

So Small a Thing

The Verdant Suite instantly vanished.

Horrified, Melanie stumbled forward onto a road surrounded by familiar desert. Breathing heavily and heart pounding, she spun in circles with shock and confusion.

There's no way, Melanie thought, her fingers grappling her hair.

HONNNNNNNK!

Melanie hadn't seen the oncoming car, and she scrambled to safety before it could collide with her. The 4Runner screeched to a halt, sliding into the other lane.

The terrified driver exited the vehicle and ripped off his sunglasses. Their eyes locked in a moment of stunned silence.

"*Melanie?*" Edmund ran over and hugged her. "I can't believe it—what happened to you? Where were you? What on Earth are you wearing?"

"Edmund," Melanie stammered, her arms too frozen to return the hug. "Hi…"

The scent of Edmund's cologne and his car's exhaust hit her with an intensity she didn't expect. Her old life flashed before her eyes, and her breathing shortened. It felt like it had been years since she lived in her camper.

She tentatively patted Edmund's back. "It's…great to see you."

"You're telling me! Is Jason okay?"

"Uh, yes, yeah, we're all fine," Melanie replied anxiously as she stepped out of his arms. She looked at the vast landscape around her. Arizona had never felt so big. The world sounded different, too, but Melanie couldn't explain how. She held up a hand to shield her eyes as she squinted in the bright sun that appeared to mock her.

"Oh gosh, we have to take you to your parents!" Edmund gripped her arms tightly, startling Melanie and sending her heart in another frenzied rhythm. "They'll be overjoyed. The whole country is looking for you guys. I'll take you there. Hop in, we're only five minutes away."

"Uh," Melanie could barely think as Edmund shoved her in the front seat. "I shouldn't stay," she finally stammered.

"What are you talking about?" Edmund froze for a second before putting the car in gear. "What *happened*, Mellie? Is that a freakin' *sword?*"

Melanie heaved a sigh and leaned her head against her arm on the window. The warm window eased the tremor in her arm, but not in her voice. "Ed…um…" She knew she had to tell him. He had to know everything. "You've deserved the truth from the very beginning when I met you, but I was so scared." Melanie's heartbeat flooded her ears. Her secret would finally be shared after all these years, and it rattled her to the bone.

"Oh no…" Edmund's voice cracked. "You're part of a cult."

"What? No! *Gosh* no." Melanie nearly smiled at that.

"Nothing like that. To tell you everything, I have to go back five years…"

Edmund anxiously searched her face as he put the gear in drive.

"I found a dragon." Melanie winced, the old habit of clenching her hands returning to her fingers.

Edmund pounded the steering wheel. "I knew it!"

Melanie leaned away at his outburst. "How?"

"I found your photo album during the investigation."

Melanie's mouth dropped open. "But…I hid it so well!"

"Well, I'm going into forensic science, so…" Edmund clicked his tongue as he stuck a proud thumb at himself. "Gotta do better if you want to hide stuff from me."

His humor tempted Melanie back toward the present. If it wasn't for *Ilvir* sitting against the dashboard, she may have let it. The steady rumble of tires on asphalt made Melanie uneasy. It felt wrong. She shouldn't be here.

"There is so much you don't know," Melanie said, her gaze distant. "I've been to another world. I defeated a dragon army. The same world my dragon came from, and where he accidentally sent us through a portal." With every word, the locks around her secrets shattered, and her heart lightened.

"The dragon is your friend?" Edmund cast a confused glance at Melanie before looking back at the road.

"His name is Scalaed," Melanie replied with a warm smile. The words came more easily now. "I found his egg in Kaibab Forest and raised him in secret for five years."

"He didn't have you enslaved to his will?"

"Not all dragons are evil princess-stealers, Edmund." Melanie shook her head. "But he did have to eat, and luckily there was a local butcher boy willing to help me out."

"Except you lied." Edmund adjusted his grip on the wheel. The sting of her betrayal settled in his chest. "You could have told me, Mellie."

Melanie scoffed, tossing him a look with her mouth hanging open. "Do you know how hard it's been to keep Scalaed a secret? In a town bordering one of the world's biggest tourist and photographer attractions, Scalaed could have been discovered—and believe me, there have been many close calls—and government agencies would track him back to me and possibly arrest anyone else who knew for harboring a bio-weapon or some nonsense! Besides, there's no way you would have believed me."

"I would have," Edmund snapped back.

Melanie stared at him, not sure what to say.

"Oh, come on, Mellie." Edmund tossed his hand. "When has it ever ended well for the guy in the movies who *didn't* believe the girl's crazy story?" Edmund cracked a sly smile, but Melanie could still see the hurt he masked beneath. She should have seen an old friend, but instead she saw her own deception, her mistrust, her solitude. She wasn't that girl anymore.

They said nothing else until the 4Runner creaked to a stop in the bleached-white driveway. Melanie didn't exit immediately. It felt like it had been decades since she had last been here. Her parents' house with its gray stucco walls and orange tiled roof pummeled Melanie with memories. She really was back home. But she felt like a stranger.

"Up till yesterday, your parents had been staying with your aunt and uncle," Edmund explained as he observed Melanie's hesitation. Her wide eyes danced all over the house, as if she had never seen it before. "Your dad's been at the ranger base trying to see if there was anything there to help with yours and Jason's search."

"Oh." Melanie's voice was small as she finally stepped out. The sharp smell of fertilizer and hot asphalt assaulted her nose, and the sound of cicadas and a passing car's blaring radio made her jump.

The front door swung open, and Mrs. Waldens froze in the entryway, hand clamped over her mouth.

Melanie's heart thundered upon seeing her mother, and a gasp stole her oxygen.

Breathing shakily as she lowered her hand, Mrs. Waldens took a step closer and blanched at Melanie's outfit. Her face contorted in confusion, her lips trembling for words.

Fearing she would break, Melanie said in a small voice, "Hi, Mom."

Mrs. Waldens's stiff posture crumbled, and she sobbed. "Oh, Melanie!" She ran to her daughter and inspected her. "You're alive! Oh, you're alive! Where have you been, sweetheart?" Mrs. Waldens wailed and wouldn't let go. "Where's Jason?"

"We're okay, Mom, I promise." Melanie spoke tenderly and gently rocked her poor hysterical mother, willing herself to recognize she was real. "I'm here. I'm okay."

After a few minutes, Mrs. Waldens composed herself. She again examined her daughter, then turned to Edmund. "Where was she?" she asked him.

Edmund shrugged. "Standing in the middle of the road, all disoriented."

"Come inside." Mrs. Waldens sniffed and wiped her eyes. "Um, are you hungry? Thirsty? I have lemonade, coffee—"

"Lemonade sounds wonderful!" Melanie gasped excitedly at the prospect of a cold, properly refreshing drink. All the water she'd had in the last month had come from skeins or city pipe systems of unknown sanitation levels. Triggered at the thought of water, Melanie shook her head. "But I have to use the bathroom first." She hurried past her mom. "A real one."

"Oh?" Mrs. Waldens frowned in confusion as Melanie disappeared into the house.

Never before had Melanie been so grateful for modern toilets and toilet paper. She thought for a moment about smuggling some back to Tindoria. If she *could* get back... The thought struck her like lightning. The sink continued to run water as she stared at herself in the mirror.

"Where am I needed?" she asked.

The memory of her warrior reflection came to the forefront of her mind. Gripping the sides of the sink, Melanie weighed her options. While one world missed her terribly, they were not in danger of being destroyed by a murderous maniac. She shut off the sink, sealing her decision to find a way to return to Tindoria.

Once finished and on her way back to the kitchen, Melanie was passing the master bedroom when her ring vibrated. Melanie froze outside the room, thinking she had imagined it, but then her ring vibrated again. Looking up from her hand, Melanie saw the master closet light flicker on.

She narrowed her eyes. Her parents could never get that light to work. She cautiously entered the bedroom toward the closet and saw a wooden chest peeking out under the hanging clothes.

"Huh." Melanie knelt before it. The box looked to be older than her. *Why would Mom have this filthy thing?* Something buzzed inside the chest. Fingers trembling at the possibilities within, she opened it.

The smell of old wood varnish rose from the contents. Inside was embroidered fabric—stained, torn, and speckled with burns.

Melanie pulled it out and heard a light *thunk* hit the chest's bottom; a tiny wooden box had fallen out of the fabric's folds. Melanie's heart began to race as she unfolded the fabric. It was a flag. Melanie had seen it before, but where? Her ring vibrated once more, but with a new intensity, and the tiny box appeared to buzz in response. Shakily, she opened the box. Inside was a ring—identical to hers save for a pearl center stone.

That was when the memory hit Melanie like a truck.

Mrs. Waldens shakily pulled glasses from the kitchen cabinet. "Edmund, honey, what was she doing in the middle of the road?"

"I'm sure she'll explain it all when she gets back," Ed reassured her as he set a pitcher of lemonade on the table.

"Mom," Melanie said rather seriously behind them.

Mrs. Waldens turned around to see her daughter standing at the kitchen entry and inhaled sharply.

Melanie let the purple flag unravel to reveal its crystal emblem, and she held up the ring. "I don't think you've been completely honest with me."

Mrs. Waldens melted into her chair. "What do you mean?" she asked quickly, her voice trembling.

"This is Tindorian, Mom. *How* did you get this?"

Mrs. Waldens's voice was barely audible as she folded her hands in front of her mouth. "So you *were* there…" Eventually she gestured for Melanie to sit.

"Wait, what is happening right now?" Edmund asked. When neither Melanie nor Mrs. Waldens answered, he receded into the background, listening intently from the end of the adjoining dining room.

Melanie couldn't sort through all the assumptions and theories that were bombarding her head. *Am I hallucinating all this? Is this a prank? Maybe Earth never existed and is only a dream!* Nothing made sense. She almost couldn't focus. She couldn't breathe.

Her mom held her hand, and the words she spoke came out haltered. "I am not from Earth."

Melanie's wide brown eyes darted back and forth in hers.

"Melanie, I am Tindorian-born. I lived in a city called Yolderain all my life."

"Did this bring you here?" Melanie placed her mother's ring on the table.

"Yes," Mrs. Waldens replied. She gingerly picked up the ring and sadly rolled it in her fingers. "My best friend Nyvelle and I had identical rings as tokens of our friendship when we were young."

Melanie looked up in sudden realization. *Elken's story,* she thought.

Mrs. Waldens lifted her eyes to Melanie's clenched hands and saw the other ring. She gasped softly. "You have Nyvelle's ring."

"Her son Elken gave it to me in Lakéthion," Melanie explained.

Mrs. Waldens gasped with a hand over her heart. "You *know* him? They survived?"

"Only Elken did." The words dried Melanie's tongue.

Mrs. Waldens pressed a hand over her mouth. When she lowered it to speak, her chin trembled. "Does Yolderain still stand?"

"I think so. Mom, what happened?"

Mrs. Waldens's mouth pinched in a trembling frown

before she took a deep breath. "I suppose I should tell you what happened to me." She wiped her eyes and continued in a steadier voice, "Nyvelle and I had gone to the market together and were drawn to this very old woman's stand. She swore these rings carried great magic that would lead us to another world. We were not to tell anyone of this nor practice the magic they possessed unless at the greatest need. We thought they were the coolest things ever, so we bought them, but we were also too scared to figure out how they worked. The most they ever did was buzz when we brought them close to each other. We figured it was prank-magic of some sort. Eventually we just assumed that we'd been scammed."

Melanie leaned forward on her elbows as she listened. Hearing her mother speak of Tindoria in such a casual manner left her speechless. It felt like a dream, and Melanie latched onto every word so she wouldn't miss a single detail.

Mrs. Waldens smiled at her memories as she continued, "Time passed, and Nyvelle was the first to get married. Her husband was a great man with a wonderful sense of humor. They eventually had a son, Elken. Then I married the following year and soon became pregnant with you."

Melanie's heart dropped to her toes. "Wait, I'm also Tindorian?" Her breathing quickened, and she gripped the edge of the table to steady herself against the swirling sensation in her stomach.

"Yes, sweetheart." Mrs. Waldens reached out and placed a hand on her daughter's.

"Hang on, that..." Melanie rubbed her legs that had gone

numb. "That doesn't make sense because Elken told me...that would mean...my dad...died."

Mrs Waldens squeezed Melanie's hand, and they met each other's eyes. "I was eight months pregnant when the invasion came. I don't quite remember what caused it, but somehow these...*things* had made their way across Rhydrah's borders. They began burning Yolderain, spreading a scent of death so strong it was worse than the smoke. Rhowen, your father, told me to flee the city and save our unborn child as he went to fight. To protect myself against the flames, I wrapped myself in a fallen flag damp from the city runoff.

"When I reached the city gates, I turned around and saw a horrible creature twitching in a sickening way. I couldn't look away as it flung Rhowen from the parapets."

The words stabbed Melanie in the heart. Elken had told her the story, but now that man was her biological father. And he was dead. Tears sprang to her eyes. Mrs. Waldens grabbed Melanie's other hand and stroked them, her own eyes filling with tears.

"My world died with the city that day," Mrs. Waldens said in a choked whisper. She tenderly wiped the pouring tears from Melanie's cheek. "I ran and ran, smoke burning my eyes. Then I remembered the ring. Praying that maybe that old woman had been right, I put it on, switched hands, flipped it around, but nothing happened. I started smacking it, cursing and crying, and then the center stone clicked. I was immediately transported to Earth, to a beach in San Diego.

"Oh, the shock was immense. Electricity, cars, the noise,

the smells. I wept for what seemed like hours, wandering up and down the coastline. The ocean and palm trees reminded me of home, but I couldn't go back there. Rhowen was dead, my city was at war, it was just not safe for us.

"Exhausted and probably delirious, I was lying by the rocks when a man approached me, a Marine from the nearby base. It was your dad, Ian. He was undoubtedly concerned and knelt by me and asked what happened." Mrs. Waldens scoffed anxiously with a slight smirk. "Well, I told him, and at first, he thought I had escaped from a mental hospital. Thank goodness he didn't call the cops, but instead took pity on me and bought us food. While we ate, that's when he began to suspect I might not actually be insane. Perhaps it was the flag or my clothes or my accent at the time or my utter ignorance of anything earthly. That night he let me stay with him in his apartment—I don't think he believed an asylum would be a good idea for a foreign pregnant girl. I wanted to show my gratitude for his immense kindness as well as earn my keep at his place by cleaning it. In turn, he taught me about this crazy new world. Then you were born. Ian fell head over heels for you. Your big brown eyes and curls…he started calling you his little brownie. Ian and I fell in love and eventually got married, and Jason was born two years later. I never looked back."

Melanie pondered the news for a long time. Her fingers drummed lightly on her glass, but her eyes stared through it, unfocused.

"This means," Melanie said, "that Jason is my half-brother."

"Yes." Mrs. Waldens nodded. "I never told you of my past in Tindoria because it all happened before you were born. And after starting a new life, it no longer seemed necessary to share."

Melanie nodded in understanding. "I mean, yeah, I guess that makes sense." She sipped her lemonade. It tasted even more sour than before. "What happened next?"

"Well, we had to become American citizens, because you and I didn't exist in the eyes of the government. So during that fun process, I shortened my name from Luciana to Lucy, and Ian suggested your name Melanie. He liked it because it means 'dark,' like a brownie."

Melanie slowly straightened in her chair, a chill creeping up her back. "Did you say my name means 'dark?'"

Concerned, Lucy hesitated. "Yes, and mine means 'light.' What are you getting at?"

Melanie threw up her hands in revelation. "*You're* the light!" She laughed in shock. "*I'm* the Descendant. Mom, we just cracked the Spire's Scroll! We gotta go back." Melanie jumped to her feet.

"What do you mean, 'we?'"

"Don't you want to see Jason and the others?"

"Of course, but, Melanie, no!" Lucy laughed uncomfortably. "I cannot leave the *planet*. I have to tell your dad what happened and let him know you're safe."

"An hour or two tops. Just to explain what we're doing and meet the team and read the Scroll. You'll be back before anyone misses you, I promise. Besides, you've got your own ring to leave whenever you need to."

Lucy threw her head back and sighed. Stepping close to Melanie, she wagged a finger in her daughter's face. "No more than an hour."

"Yes!" Melanie pumped her arms. "Let's go."

"We're not leaving without some supplies. For heaven's sake, pack some snacks, first aid, flashlights, whatever you want."

Melanie grinned. "And toilet paper?"

"Take as many rolls as you want," Lucy chuckled. She anxiously held up her phone. "I'm going to call your dad."

As Lucy stepped away, a hand alighted on Melanie's shoulder, startling her. "You're going back there?" Edmund asked in disbelief.

Melanie turned to face Edmund, her determination settling in her features. "I have to, Ed."

"But you just got here!" He grabbed her hands. "This is your home. Why would you go back?"

Melanie sensed he wanted to add more to his statement. She gently wriggled her hands free. "I belong to both worlds, and right now, Tindoria is in danger. They need me. I'm not the girl you remember, Ed."

Edmund's eyebrows wilted in sadness as he looked over her buckled vest and sword hanging from her side. "Clearly." A hollowness filled his chest when he realized he really had fallen in love with an alien.

"I'm sorry," Melanie whispered.

"Just..." Edmund inhaled deeply, his shoulders rising

with the effort. "Just be safe, okay, Mellie?"

Melanie nodded. "I'll do my best."

CHAPTER 20

Fly on the Wall

Merrendogith had claimed the Kottrans. After being there for so long, they had eventually become a part of it; they were enslaved to it. If anyone or anything crossed over into Tindoria, they would be colorless. Maybe it was a way for Merrendogith to mark them—a sign the realm owned them. Above that, it seemed to work against them—to keep them trapped there at all costs. When the Kottrans had arrived there and tried to turn their ships back whence they came, the gray waves and current trapped them by command of the Naiads— the only creatures who could travel unscathed between the realms' oceans.

Caito stood in a barren field of cold, gray rock with jagged mountains of stone to her right. There was no grass or birdsong, no trees or rivers. Caito sometimes thought they *were* dead, and this was the underworld. She'd once tried to make sure. The blade had left an empty hole, but it didn't kill her. It had only left her with pain.

Overall, the pain of her existence fueled her rage and envy for everything: Tindorians, the Hündr, the dead, Klarn. She was one of those who had opposed his mission for the centaur genocide, but it had made no difference; all had been overtaken by the Naiads. The water nymphs had engulfed every Kottran that day, not bothering to differentiate guilty from innocent, and dragged them all to their boats. Sweeping through the Kottran ranks and as far as her whole village, the Naiads had been a tidal wave that left no one behind. This was all Klarn's fault. This was the Hündr's fault. This was the centaurs' fault. Everything held blame. Except her. She was innocent. She didn't deserve this.

Caito festered in the heat within her chest; it was the only thing warm in this cursed place, so she loved her hate. Then her shadow opened up, swallowing her.

Merrendogith flattened around her as she slipped from the dimension. As she phased from the world around her, Tindoria expanded from the darkness. Rising to her feet, Caito stepped from her shadow and took a deep breath. Already it was much harder to breathe. She didn't belong to this realm, and Merrendogith knew it; it was an accursed place that fought for control over her. She hated it.

The only reason she had accepted Klarn's mission was to find a means to escape Merrendogith. Once she was free, she and others who agreed with her would kill Klarn for all the suffering he had imparted on their race. She was determined to find a way to make Klarn mortal again—killable again.

Scanning her surroundings, Caito ascertained her location. A mountain range rose on her left. She recognized the green peaks as the Emerald Mountains, which meant Endlewood lay beyond. Caito grabbed her chest as a sharp pain struck her lungs. Sinking into her shadow again, she recovered her breath.

Merrendogith never let anyone stray for long. She stilled and listened to the shadows' whispers. A tangled nest of distant voices flooded her panther ears, but she knew which word she was listening for. Then she caught it—an echo of conversation.

Klarn must be defeated, but how?

Do not say his name so insouciantly!

The ghost of conversation zipped past her from the north, and using the flickering shadows around her, Caito traveled to Endlewood with terrific speed. She stayed in the shadows of the city walls and buildings. As a shadow, she was weightless. Climbing buildings and sinking into crevices was simple. Despite its efficiency, shadow travel left her feeling like she was being crushed.

It will all be worth it if I can find a way to kill Klarn, she told herself.

Briefur and Fallon walked down Endlewood's main city highway. Carriages rolled past with the loud clopping of hooves, but Fallon barely registered the noise.

"The darkness is back." Fallon's large ears twitched as they tried to latch onto the source of the darkness.

"Yes, I smell it, too. Stay close to me."

"Briefur, I'm not a child," Fallon continued, her golden eyes reflecting the sun. She didn't turn when she spoke to him.

"I am grown enough to—"

"Fallon." Briefur crossed his arms. "The Kottrans are a threat we do not take lightly. It is my duty, as your kin, to look out for you and see your safe return to your family." Fallon opened her mouth to speak, but Briefur continued, "Anything could happen, so I will only be that much closer to you."

"I'm not afraid!" Fallon raised her voice. "I can do whatever it takes to protect others."

Briefur said nothing but gave her a sideways glance.

Fallon huffed angrily and quickened her pace to put distance between them. She kept that gap until they reached the Castle of Endlewood.

Briefur approached the castle sentry who stood in deep green leather armor at the gatehouse. "Excuse me, sir. We are looking for Melanie and Jason Waldens? Can you tell them we've arrived?"

"It's vital we meet with them immediately," Fallon added.

The sentry nodded and motioned for a servant girl passing behind him in the green courtyard.

While the sentry gave the girl instructions, Fallon whispered to her cousin, "The darkness has settled here, too." Her fox ears twitched left and right.

Briefur merely let out a low "hmm," but Fallon noticed his tail flicking with anxiety.

The heartlink vanished, and its sudden absence shocked Scalaed like a wave of cold water. His fear intensified when he returned to the Verdant Suite and saw the chaos. Jason and the others were clamoring and asking what happened to Melanie. Preparing to blast anyone who had harmed his best friend, Scalaed thundered into the room, demanding what happened. He hoped Elken or Helnah were at fault.

"Scalaed, Melanie vanished," Jason explained breathlessly. "Elken said her ring clicked and then she disappeared. We don't know where she went or how to get her back."

Smoke coiled from his nostrils as he zeroed in on Elken. Heaving threatening black puffs, Scalaed reveled in the moments before he incinerated this man.

"Scalaed!" Jason shouted. "Stop it! He didn't do it on purpose, and you know it."

Squeezing his eyes shut to block out Elken's face, Scalaed stifled the restless fire within. Jason was right. Melanie would never forgive him if he killed Elken. Finally, he cleared his throat, choking down the remaining flames.

"She's been gone maybe twenty, thirty minutes." Jason rubbed his face in worry.

"Your sister has survived worse," Helnah reminded them blandly as she rolled an apple in her hand.

Twitching, Scalaed sent her a warning growl and murderous eyes.

Jason glared alongside him. "You're not helping."

"I'm sure everything will be fine." Thendrell tried calming the room. "She has her special necklace, does she not?"

Helnah nodded through a mouthful of fruit.

Thendrell nodded, satisfied. "Then I'm sure there is nothing to fear—"

As suddenly as she had vanished, Melanie appeared in the room with a shower of sparkles, her mother in tow.

Helnah choked on her apple.

"*Mom?*" Jason's mouth hung open.

"Aunt Lucy?" Kyle squeaked.

"Oh, boys!" Lucy ran to hug them.

Elken rushed to squeeze Melanie in a hug. "Oh, you scared me!" he whispered. His hand cradled the back of her head and pressed her even closer.

"I know, I'm sorry, I didn't mean to," Melanie replied, muffled.

"Never do that again."

"I won't." Melanie pulled back to stroke his cheek. "I promise."

"What the heck are *you* doing here, Mom?" Jason asked after embracing his mother. "Don't get me wrong, I've really missed you, but…"

Lucy kissed Jason and Kyle on the head. "It looks like my secret is out—" Then she saw Scalaed and stepped back, jaw gaping. "…and that's a dragon."

Scalaed had lost all hatred and instead sat in utter bewilderment.

"Introductions are far overdue." Melanie laughed as she motioned for Scalaed to come. "Mom, this is my good friend Scalaed. I raised him from an egg, and he's the one who brought us here in the first place."

Scalaed could only nod his head in greeting.

Lucy laughed nervously. "Ah."

"Mom, why are you here?" Jason asked again. "I don't understand!"

"I was born in Tindoria," Lucy said, "and we came back with these realm rings."

Helnah raised her eyebrow in amusement. "Oh, this just got interesting." She took another bite of apple.

Jason stepped back. "What?"

"Well, that's freakin' awesome!" Kyle clapped. "My cousin is a knight and my aunt is from another world! Can this day get any better?"

"Yes, if perhaps your mother can crack the Spire's Scroll." Helnah tossed her core out the window, at which Melanie scowled.

"Actually, I think we already did." Lucy raised her hand.

"I am the Descendant of Light," Melanie announced soberly.

"Aww, since when?" Kyle sounded betrayed.

"Since I am also a full-blood Tindorian."

"Excuse me?" Jason crossed his arms.

Scalaed also leaned back in shock.

"Mom is the light. That's what her name means."

Kyle pointed excitedly at Jason. "Oh my gosh, and Jason's name means 'healer!'"

"How do you even know?" Jason asked.

"Dude, I read hundreds of random books a year."

"But Jason is also her son," Elken said.

Melanie wrung her hands. "He's actually my half-brother."

Kyle's mouth dropped open and shot his head in Jason's direction.

Jason slouched forward in his seat and exhaled his shock through folded hands. "That's...I mean, it's shocking, but..." He stood up. "It won't change anything for me. Melanie will always be my sister, regardless of how much DNA we share. But still..."

The door knocked, snapping Kyle out of his trance, and he ran to open it. He cracked it open lest he reveal the apparent archnemesis of Tindoria, and asked the servant girl what he could help with. She mentioned the Hündr, and Kyle shrugged happily. "Send 'em up! The more the merrier, I say."

"Hang on, who?" Melanie stood to her feet.

"Excuse you!" Kyle was shoved to the side as the snarling Hündr bounded inside in their canid forms, teeth bared.

"Briefur," Jason asked, raising his hands, "what's going—"

Briefur leapt for Helnah and pinned her to the ground, glaring murderously into her dark eyes. *No. This is not who I expected.* "I didn't want to believe it," he growled, his hot breath blasting Helnah's face. "Bareth was right."

Fallon shouted what Jason assumed was a Hvitrian profanity.

Elken approached Briefur and placed a firm hand on his back. The fur started to lie flat, and Briefur slowly let Helnah go with a quick snap of his jaws.

Helnah smoothed her dress nonchalantly. "I don't believe

I've made your acquaintance."

"Guys, can we please just try to be nice to Helnah?" Kyle pleaded.

Scalaed rolled his eyes as Fallon changed form and stepped close to Jason. The darkness had settled near him. She would make sure nothing could happen to him.

"Hey, Fallon, are you okay?" Jason asked softly in concern. He couldn't place it, but looking into her golden eyes felt different. "What is it?"

Fallon's eyes seemed to look into his deepest parts. There was worry in them. "I don't know," Fallon finally said in a small voice and looked back at the room. She met her cousin's gaze in an unspoken conversation. It wasn't Helnah they had smelled.

Caito had slipped into the suite and had been observing from the shadows of the corner for nearly a half hour. The realm rings opened a whole new door of possibilities. Those would be much easier to steal than a dragon. They could send Klarn to Tindoria with a realm ring, and then kill him.

Then the two Hündr had entered, and panic had set in. There was no way she could evade their detection. So she remained frozen.

The humans and Hündr spoke of fabulous mysteries—the

Spire of Tavnir, travel from yet another realm, and the survival of none other than Helnah, Klarn's puppet. It appeared that her strings had been cut. Caito absorbed all the information from her invisible post, biding her time until she could make her move.

"How has Klarn not seen you?" Briefur jabbed a finger at Helnah, his nails looking longer than usual.

"Oh, for crying—not this again," Kyle groaned. Clapping his hands for attention he said loudly. "Listen up, we need to all be—"

"Kyle, just stop!" Jason snapped. "Who made you the peacemaker?"

"Hey, I'm just trying to find my purpose here and figure out why the Golden Prince chose me," Kyle shot back. "I assume we're supposed to be heroes, and heroes don't hold grudges—"

"You don't know anything, okay?" Jason snapped. "You're just a kid! We had to go to battle against this witch, Kyle, a *real battle*. I've seen things so horrible that I don't want to sleep anymore because they haunt me every night! Helnah has destroyed so much, so shut up about being nice to her." Jason's voice shook with rage as he took a step closer to his shrinking cousin. "Because I *never* will." Jason's hazel eyes burned into Kyle, ensuring he understood. "Let's just get back to the Scroll."

"Jason…" Lucy scolded sadly.

Kyle instinctively removed himself from the crowd and slid toward the door. "I was just trying to help." His small voice went unheard. *How do I help now?*

The room froze. The sounds stilled. The people in the room stood like statues, frozen in time. Only Kyle remained unaffected. *Great,* now *what's going on?* He looked around anxiously, not daring to move himself.

"Your heart is in the right place, Kyle," the Golden Prince said from behind the boy.

Kyle spun on his heels to see the Celestial seated on a lush sofa. The suite had vanished, replaced by the Adamas Chamber. The Prince gestured for Kyle to sit next to him.

"What did I do?" Kyle asked as he melted into the red cushions.

"You are trying to rush forgiveness." The Prince smiled in understanding. "And force happiness. Your cousins have been through much pain, and your manner, while well-meaning, invalidates them."

"So make me understand!" Kyle begged. "We're not going to make any progress with grudges festering in our company. If I need to meet them where they're at, I want to relate to them."

"You don't need to experience their trauma to support them, my son." The Prince shook his head. "All you can offer is to be an ear that listens and not a mouth that speaks. There is a reason you were created with two ears and one mouth."

Kyle smirked. "Funny, I saw that on a bumper sticker the other day."

The Prince winked. "You cannot force them to change, Kyle. That is *their* mission." The Prince laid a gentle hand on his shoulder.

"So what am I supposed to do?"

"Your destiny lies elsewhere," the Prince said. "There is a reason Tavnir and I saw you in your dream that night. I commend your striving for virtue; continue that course, and you will pass the tests."

"Tests?" Kyle blinked, and the Prince and vision were gone. He had returned to the Verdant Suite, where Melanie, Jason and the others gathered in a circle discussing the Spire's Scroll.

Melanie held the paper this time. While everyone else conversed among themselves about their theories, she read in silence. With her recent revelation from home, she read to herself the Scroll in its entirety with a new perspective.

From kingdoms and countries afar

no King nor Scholar can place

a hero has answered the call

to be Tindoria's grace

The rise of this warrior's fate

begins with sins of the beast.

The exiled in banishment wait

for war on mortals unleashed.

THE SHADOW THAT TRAVELS UNSEEN
AND LIFE IN THE HANDS TO HEAL
A DREAMER OF YOUTH HOLDS THE KEY.
THE DESCENDANT OF LIGHT IS REVEALED.

BEHOLD THE SPILT BLOOD OF THE DARK
THE SELFLESS MAGIC IS SHED
THE MORTAL CRIMSON CLEAVES THE HEART
THE END OF LIFE, DEFEATED

She subtly mouthed the final four lines. She knew she had heard 'dark' in the Scroll. "The blood of the dark," followed by "selfless magic" being shed. Melanie felt a pit settle in her stomach as she read the final verse over and over.

Blood of the dark. Shed magic. Mortal crimson. Defeated. The blood of the dark is shed.

I have to die, she realized in terror. *To defeat Klarn, I have to die.*

CHAPTER 21

Stolen

Caito's eyes hadn't left the Hündr. She feared if she looked away for even a second, they would see her. They knew something was wrong; she could smell it. The way they exchanged looks, their subtle movements, their still tails. She hoped her Kottran scent was old and unfamiliar enough to remain a mystery. Part of her wanted to flee, but she knew the information being divulged was too vastly important. She was so close to the answer to kill Klarn. And she, more than anyone else, deserved to be the one to do it. She would kill him slowly. Burn him from the inside out, perhaps. A fitting end considering his heinous crimes.

Melanie hadn't realized she had stopped breathing until her lungs ached. It was so clear now. The hero's selfless sacrifice was hers to make.

She couldn't tell anyone; they would try to stop her, and the enemy would win.

Scalaed felt her rapid heartbeat through the heartlink and warbled softly.

Melanie quickly pasted on a smile. "Don't worry about it."

"So Klarn and his Kottrans killed all the centaurs," Lucy said, drawing all eyes to herself. "That's appalling, of course, but *why* did he do it?"

"Zombie centaurs," Kyle said dramatically as he took the Scroll from Melanie's limp hands.

"It sounds like a severe escalated case of septicemic plague," Jason explained. "Skin and other tissues can turn black and die. Internal organs bleed, then fail completely. You can catch the bacteria from handling or being bitten by an infected animal. Obviously, that doesn't explain how they still moved around after it killed them."

"Does anyone know what caused the, uh, zombies?" Lucy asked.

"Animated death, some called it," Elken clarified.

"I'm sorry, did you say animated death?" Lucy held up a finger.

"Welcome to Tindoria." Kyle leaned back as he read the Scroll.

"Someone screamed those words the day Yolderain was attacked twenty years ago," Lucy gasped. "Animalistic, no tactics, oh, and the *smell*...nothing will ever come close to that stench."

Fallon nodded grimly. "Yes, we called them Wasters."

"They attacked Lakéthion ten years after Yolderain," Breifur added. "Then Hvitria five years later. It was the first time the animated death became contagious."

"So the Wasters caused the plague?" Lucy asked. "The plague that Klarn wiped out that got him sentenced to death?"

"Everyone, quiet!" Kyle shouted. He stood atop the bed, the parchment clutched in his hands with his eyes wide as a vision unfolded. A black wave rose from the horizon, stretching into the sky until it blocked out the sun. It was a swarm of animalistic figures that crashed upon the cities, engulfing the land in blood and fire. No structure remained. Kyle's eyes refocused as he looked around the room in horror. "Klarn's target is *everyone*. The whole world. He's got a massive army. A war against mortals unleashed."

Jason's thoughts immediately honed in on Laena. A nauseous cocktail of fear and anger welled up in him at the thought of Klarn killing her. *I'll kill him before he touches a single hair of her head.*

Briefur's head snapped to his left. His icy eyes locked onto a black shadow warping in the corner. Fallon looked, too.

Caito mouthed a curse. She had tried adjusting her position to relieve her numb legs. She had to make her move now.

"There!" Briefur shouted and dove at Caito as she emerged from the darkness.

Swords were drawn, and everyone leaped to their feet. Kyle quickly grabbed his aunt and fled to the adjoining suite, slamming the door behind them. Scalaed snapped at Caito, but she nimbly slipped through his attack and reached for Jason's arm.

Lips curled back, Fallon chomped down on the Kottran's arm and dragged Caito away from Jason. With an angered cry of pain, Caito unsheathed a knife and drove it into Fallon's chest. The froxil crumpled with a loud yelp.

Jason roared and threw one of his knives at Caito, but she somersaulted toward Melanie and Elken. Scalaed stepped in front of her, shooting a hot, thin stream of fire, but Caito slipped into his shadow. Scalaed's bulk inhibited his nimbleness, and he bellowed in wrath, hurling the settee at the wall with his tail. Emerging behind him, Caito morphed into a large black panther and tackled Melanie to the ground, skidding toward the balcony.

"Melanie!" Helnah screamed, and despite having no weapon, charged Caito and yanked Melanie out of Caito's clutches. "You won't take her," Helnah snarled.

Caito twitched a smile across her feline muzzle, her eyes glowing, and launched herself into the women. Then she, Melanie, and Helnah melted into the ground.

"Helnah!" Thendrell scrambled to the site, scratching at the floor in vain.

Scalaed whimpered and pushed Thendrell aside. Melanie was indeed gone. And the heartlink was dead.

Elken panted and grabbed his hair in disbelief. "No." He trembled. "Not again. Not again!" he said breathlessly. "Don't do this to me, Melanie..." Then Elken heard faint cries.

Fallon lay curled on the floor in a growing pool of blood, silent. Jason knelt at her side.

Cradling her head, Briefur brushed aside her hair, but

couldn't bring himself to say it would all be okay. His face contorted in pain as he sobbed.

Jason had exposed the wound and was pressing a cloth napkin into it, but the blood flow was profuse. The red warmth soaked the napkin and coated his hands. He muttered fearfully to himself, "I can't fix it…my magic…why isn't it back yet? No, no, I must be doing something wrong, I can save you, just give me a second…"

Fallon didn't respond. Her golden eyes stared tiredly at her friends.

"Wait, where's her Abrielstone?" Jason yelled. *If she doesn't have her necklace and I don't have my magic…* He began to hyperventilate.

"She"—Briefur stammered—"she gave it away. Use yours!"

"Briefur!" Jason's eyes widened in horror, and his arms fell limp. "They aren't transferable!"

The dread almost crushed Briefur's lungs.

"Now what do we do?" Jason panicked. Though he clawed at the barren well within himself, no magic remained.

"Fallon, *please* fight." Briefur knew he asked for the impossible. *Can she even hear me?*

Her eyes looked different now. They slowly lost focus, her pupils dilating, and Briefur and Jason saw the sparkle vanish. The faintest breath left her lungs, taking all her life with it.

"*No!*" Jason threw his other knife at the wall in rage and buried his head in his hands.

Briefur hugged Fallon tightly and gently rocked her, ending with a broken, "Forgive me for failing you." He held her cheeks and kissed her on her forehead.

"*Why?*" Jason pounded the floor, cursing repeatedly. His hands failed him. He slammed his fists into the wooden floor again and again and again and again, punishing them. His magic failed him. Larger and larger splotches of blood stained the floor as Jason's knuckles burst. He needed to feel pain. *I could have saved her. I failed her. I failed!* Heat strangled Jason's chest, squeezing choked sobs from his lungs. Tears splashed onto the bloody floor and Jason's hammering slowed as desolate weakness overtook him.

Then Elken's arms wrapped around him and helped Jason to his feet.

"It happened too fast, way too fast." Jason shook his head, his voice violently trembling. "She needed her Abrielstone! Because obviously I couldn't do *anything!*"

"She was stabbed through her heart, Jason," Elken said. "That is beyond any skill to save without magic."

"Exactly." Jason flung out his hands. "I'm the healer. 'Life in the hands to heal,' right? So why didn't my powers work?"

The roaring in Jason's ears faded, and he heard pounding against the suite's shared doorway. Blocked by the settee, it struggled to open. With each pummel, the door jerked open a crack until Kyle and Lucy could squeeze through and around the piece of furniture.

"Is it over?" Kyle asked.

Realizing Melanie was nowhere in sight, Lucy asked, "Where's Melanie?"

"The Kottran took her and Helnah into the shadows,"

Thendrell replied shakily, still on his knees at Helnah's last seen location.

"Melanie is gone, too?" Jason stumbled back into Elken, who braced him with steady arms. Jason's legs wilted, and he sank to the ground as he tried to suck in oxygen. "They're gone, Elken, they're both gone!" Jason wheezed as he clutched his chest.

"Say that again?" Kyle was sure he misheard. "You mean they're in Merrendogith right now?" he panicked.

"Undoubtedly," Thendrell replied. "We have to rescue them. Helnah doesn't have an Abrielstone to protect her from death, and we need to get her before Klarn does. The things he could do to her when he sees she's alive..."

"Unless Helnah gets to Klarn before we do," Kyle pointed out. "She is a pretty powerful woman."

"What are we gonna do?" Jason's eyes burned as tears painted his cheeks. He stammered anxiously, "Melanie... Scalaed, what does the heartlink say?"

The dragon finally tore his eyes from the floor that had swallowed Melanie and looked at Jason with hopeless sorrow. Just like when Melanie's ring had taken her to Earth, she was far beyond the heartlink. There was no way to tell if she was alive.

"Come on, dragon, summon a portal!" Thendrell ordered Scalaed. "Take us to Merrendogith."

Scalaed sniffed anxiously and tried to explain he had no idea what the place looked like, and therefore couldn't envision a destination. Without the heartlink to speak to others, he could only shake his head.

In anger, Thendrell swung his hand at a stack of plates on the tray he'd brought in earlier, sending them flying to shatter against the wall.

"Hey, chill out!" Jason said as he retrieved his knives. "My sister is gone, too! Let's figure out another way."

Everyone looked at the floor, their minds blank.

"Um, I have an idea," Kyle said, "and it'll work because it obviously did for Klarn. We take a ship over the edge of the world."

A cacophony of protests attacked Kyle.

"Have you lost your mind?"

"We could die!"

"No one knows what happens."

"There's got to be another way."

"You're insane!"

"Alright, alright!" Kyle stepped back. "Geez, just trying to be helpful. Anyone have a better idea?"

"Mom, your ring transports people between realms," Jason said. "We'll use that."

Lucy wrung her hands nervously. "It doesn't work that way. The ring can only be used by one person at a time. Besides, Merrendogith might not be even in the ring's itinerary."

"Need more rings? Maybe I can make some," Kyle offered excitedly. "Problem solved!"

He asked for Lucy's ring and, cupping it in his hands, stared at it intently. Suddenly, he felt as if the stones and metals were speaking to him. The pearl pulsed with an airiness like the ocean, and the diamonds flanking it tinkled like ice. But the metal emitted a low vibrato that rattled Kyle's bones when he honed in on it. He could not identify what material Lucy's ring was. One thing his Abrielstone did tell him was that the ring was enchanted with a very strong, possibly dangerous magic. When his Abrielstone turned quiet once more, Kyle returned his aunt's ring, "My Abrielstone says I can't recreate enchantments, and that ring is made from who-knows-what. Plus, if I'm being honest, I didn't like the way it talked to me."

Jason blinked and told himself to not even ask.

"So, magic clearly won't help us." Thendrell shot another glare at Scalaed. "Then we make the dragons fly us over the Edge."

Scalaed leaned back in shock and shook his head adamantly.

"We have no idea how long of a flight that would be, Thendrell," Elken countered. "Do you really suggest that Scalaed and Poison Ivy carry multiple passengers over an unknown distance with no places to land until the destination? Not to mention how much farther it might be to Merrendogith once we cross over."

"I'm sorry, but didn't going over the Edge kill Klarn?" Lucy stepped in. "I was under the impression that the underworld is where dead people go, and he's trying to escape. Wouldn't we die, too, if we crossed the Edge?"

"Klarn is not dead." Elken shook his head while scuffing his boot. "They are very much alive but tied to Merrendogith."

"Won't going turn us into shadows?" Kyle realized.

"If we do turn into shadows," Elken replied, "Helnah also said the only way to fix that is by going out with a portal, which Scalaed will be able to summon by that point because he can envision Tindoria."

Jason pinched the bridge of his nose. "Say we do somehow come up with a way to get into Merrendogith. We have zero clue what's down there!"

Scalaed snorted, reminding them of his fire breath.

"True," Jason agreed, "and we also have our Abrielstones."

Thendrell crossed his arms and glanced at Lucy. "*Some* of us."

Elken sighed. "Then Melanie may be safe for now."

"Sounds like my plan is the only one we've got." Kyle shrugged. "Nobody thank me or anything…"

The room fell into contemplative silence. Anxious gazes met all around as a cloud of unease settled over them.

"This is insane," Lucy finally said. "But if this is the only way, I know just the ship."

"Really?" Jason looked quizzically at his mother.

"My old home Yolderain is a coastal city. Melanie's father had a boat we could use."

"Is it still there after twenty years?" Elken asked.

"It's worth a look. If not, I can bribe someone to lend us one," Lucy said. "This won't be the first time I bribed a ship owner."

Jason leaned back in bafflement, his faintly amused eyes prodding Lucy for an explanation.

She rolled her eyes. "I had a crush I wanted to impress

with my sailing skills."

Jason's eyebrow popped up, even more amused.

Lucy dismissed him with a wave of her hand. "My point is, when my daughter's life is on the line, you bet I'm pulling out all the stops to get her back. I'll get that ship. You should fly Fallon's body back to Hvitria on the way to best preserve her."

"Thendrell is not coming to the White Village," Briefur said.

Jason almost jumped. He'd nearly forgotten Briefur was in the room, the trarewolf had been so quiet.

"Very well." Jason turned to face the Thornbrillian. "You go with my mom and protect her." Jason unsheathed one of his knives and pressed its tip under Thendrell's chin. "Heaven help you if you fail."

Thendrell's nose crinkled subtly with his sarcasm. "Glad to be of service, Sir Jason."

The moment Fallon's life left her body haunted Jason. When it abandoned her eyes, released her muscles, and departed with her final exhale, it crushed his spirit in a way he had never known. While her body was still there, Fallon felt like a stranger. Despite the familiar face, without the very soul that animated her, she seemed like a shell of herself.

These were the thoughts Jason pondered as he and Briefur wrapped Fallon's body in a bedsheet.

"You tried, Jason," Briefur said softly as he stroked Fallon's covered shoulder.

"Doesn't matter," Jason said, gritting his teeth. "I failed."

"I failed her, too!" Briefur beat his chest. "I promised her parents I would stay by her the whole time. Look where that led me."

"You know deep down this wasn't either of your faults," Elken said. "Fallon saw the danger before most of us and took action. She sacrificed her own life to save Jason."

"She was always compassionate," Briefur agreed. "That's why she gave her Abrielstone to Vytia, to protect her and her baby. If only we had known her selflessness would be her demise." His chin scrunched. "Now, when I return to my village, it will be with Fallon's body. And I must inform the chief and chieftainess that the stones are useless to them."

CHAPTER 22

Let the Flowers...

No one was tired that night, even during the two hour flight to Hvitria. Elken rode on Scalaed with Briefur, who tightly held Fallon's body, while Jason and Kyle rode Poison Ivy. The green dragon was none too pleased to be summoned by the sibulus during her nap, but she obeyed nonetheless. The clouds hid much of the moons' light, which left the world feeling even more sullen.

No one spoke, either. There was nothing to say.

Briefur trembled at the thought of returning to his home with his fallen cousin. He dreaded her parents' reaction, and that of her little brothers. *You smelled the Kottran before you even entered the room,* he conversed with himself. *Why did you let her in with you? She could still be alive if only you had used your head.*

In the darkness, Briefur stared at the dark-red spot that stained the sheet. Fallon couldn't be dead. He gently unwrapped the top hem and looked at the corpse's face. It looked like Fallon. The same dark lashes, soft blonde hair, large ears. But it couldn't be her. This didn't *feel* like Fallon.

No, this must be a nightmare, Briefur reasoned. *I will wake up soon.*

"Briefur," Elken said softly as he turned around to face him. "We've crossed into Lethios and are flying over the Sea of Starlight."

Briefur nodded, barely acknowledging Elken's presence.

Elken opened his mouth to say more but decided against it. His own emotions wreaked havoc in his mind: pleas to scream, urges to break something, whispers to give up. But Elken knew he had to be the rock for his companions, the resolute mast to keep their ship on course. So he stifled the emotions, painfully swallowing them back with the rising lump in his throat. He would not break. He could not.

Kyle did not speak either. He sat behind his cousin, whose muscles felt like stone.

Jason never looked anywhere but forward, and his hands gripped the hem of his tunic. He only moved to hold on to the bridle reins when the dragons began their descent. His knuckles whitened in rage. His face grew hot to the point where he could feel his heartbeat in his cheeks. He had failed Fallon and lost Melanie in a matter of minutes, and the double blow had hollowed him out.

The hundreds of torches illuminating the White Village directed their nighttime arrival. With the sound of a horn, the Hündr were made aware of their visitors. Chief Helmir bounded through the growing crowd and assumed his human form. He knew something grave was amiss since the dragons and their passengers entered the village at such a late hour

Brefiüll approached the dragons with his daughter Bareth following close behind. Then he saw the bundled sheet. Briefur dismounted, carrying the shrouded body, and met the worried gaze of his father and sister. Briefur couldn't move, and the sudden swell of sorrow escaped through his tears that shone in the torchlight.

Immediately, Brefiüll knew it was Fallon's body. He returned to the crowd, and his passing expression revealed to Helmir the tragedy behind their arrival.

Having dismounted the other side of Scalaed, Elken checked in with Jason for the first time since takeoff.

"How are you doing?" he asked.

"Not great, Elken," Jason replied as he watched Brefiüll approach Briefur with Fallon's father Freign and his wife Viexa. Fallon's mother crumbled to her knees as horror stole her breath. Briefur also knelt down and lay Fallon's body in the arms of her father, who rocked his child as his shoulders shook violently in grief. As the cries rose, Helmir signaled the bystanders to leave them in peace and prepare the funeral arrangements.

Overtaken with emotion, Kyle stepped closer to Jason. His older cousin glanced down, saw Kyle's glistening eyes, and wrapped an arm around him, pulling him closer.

Jason inhaled with difficulty as the corners of his mouth turned into a sharp, pained frown.

After giving them their moment, Elken pulled the young men close and hugged them tightly. Scalaed stepped in front, his wing providing privacy for their sobs. In the darkness, he saw Poison Ivy's eyes glimmering as she receded from the crowds.

Pathetic. You will know what a true dragon's potential looks like.

Scalaed gave a short huff. What was wrong with her? Now was clearly not the time for such a stupid comment. He blocked her out with his wings.

"We'll make it through this, alright?" Elken rubbed Jason's back as their tears lessened. "This kind of pain is unlike any other. We will mourn, we will remember, and we will honor Fallon's life. We'll be alright."

Fallon's body lay on a simple thatched stretcher that was processed by her froxil relatives to the outskirts of the village. Drums beat slowly, and woodwind instruments haunted the midnight air with heartbreak. The path, barely worn, led to a field blooming with a multitude of flowers. The rainbow of colors was subdued by the burning oranges and yellows of the lit procession. Any floral fragrance was lost in the smell of the smoke and incense. Rising above the flowers were wood-burned markers of deceased loved ones, and a new one stood above a freshly dug hole of soft black soil.

The stretcher was suspended over the grave, and Briefur thought the number of torches increased, causing the whole field to glow with light. In this, Briefur saw it was as if the fire returned a warmth to Fallon's skin. But it was also in this moment, as she was slowly lowered into the earth, dressed in white with her knives on her bosom, that he knew Fallon was indeed dead. The realization struck him like lightning, and Briefur fell to the ground and screamed in anguish.

As he wailed, Vytia bid Fallon farewell. "Let the flowers that grow on your grave blossom with the memory of your legacy and spread the story of your life on the wings of the breeze. For the body that lies in death recalls your continued spiritual presence among us, and will do so until the end of all ages."

Fallon's parents draped a final white cloth over her body just before she was blanketed by the black earth, forever laid to rest.

The majority of the Hündr dispersed, leaving Fallon's family to mourn at her new grave.

Though Kyle had barely known Fallon, he felt dissatisfied at seeing the simple grave marker. He felt compelled to give Fallon a prettier one. She had saved Jason. She was a hero. He slipped away from the torches and knelt in the flowers.

"Is it okay to do this?" he asked his Abrielstone. The citrine gem glowed softly in reply. Closing his eyes, Kyle sorted through his mind's library of favorite rocks and stones. *Marble is overused. At least on Earth. Opal? Agate? Esquel Meteorite would be nice, too.* Kyle decided he would go with the flow and make whatever came to his mind. Taking a deep breath, he placed his hands on the grassy ground and watched his creation grow and rise under his touch.

It was a freeform shape—round with a soft curve and

slope to a subtle point. Almost like a simple candle flame. Kyle made it from a warm agate. The outside rings were subdued warm browns that lightened to vibrant oranges near the top. Above the text that he copied from the wooden marker, Kyle had put in a small citrine geode. The headstone was no bigger than the others, so Kyle carried it to Fallon's grave.

"Excuse me?" Kyle said softly.

Freign and his wife turned bleary-eyed, their small twin boys bundled in their arms.

"I knew Fallon the least out of everyone here, but she's a hero. So I, um, I made this for her. I can't read what this text says, but I hope I got it right." He put the stone on the ground and turned it to face her family. The remaining torchlight made the geode glow the exact shade of Fallon's coat, and more tears rushed down her family's faces. "It's my gift to you for her. I'm so sorry for your loss." Not wanting to impose any longer, Kyle bowed stiffly then shuffled off before he embarrassed himself.

But a weight had been lifted, and Kyle felt peace fill its place.

Jason and Elken had watched the whole thing, and while Jason said nothing, Kyle could see the approval in his eyes. They returned to the village, where black iron torches of mourning burned in a sorrowful red outside the tree homes and Great Hall. Helmir noticed their passing through the village gates and approached. "So I do not burden her family with questions, will you tell me the cause of Fallon's death?"

"She was killed protecting me from a Kottran attack," Jason answered.

Helmir's steel eyes glimmered evilly at the mention of his enemy.

"It happened so fast, and—"

"Fallon's Abrielstone would have saved her," Briefur interrupted.

Jason nearly flinched; Briefur had materialized out of nowhere.

"It was a grave mistake on our part, my Lord." Briefur's voice shook with dismay. "We did not know the Empress's gift to be untransferable. I'm afraid…" He hesitated. "I must ask for their return; they will not aid you like they did us."

The White Chief's shoulders dropped. Slowly, he removed the Abrielstone. "I understand. Your selfless act will not be forgotten." Helmir slipped the necklace into Briefur's halfheartedly open hand. "I will relay this to Vytia."

Briefur parted with his final words to Jason. "Continue without me, Jason. A grieving soul will be of no use on your quest."

As the trarewolf departed, Jason observed Briefur's tail tucked motionlessly between his legs as the night wrapped around him. He, too, felt like his motivation had been sapped away, but he could never abandon Melanie.

"What is this quest he speaks of?" Helmir asked once Briefur vanished from sight.

"The Kottran that murdered Fallon took Melanie in its escape," Elken continued. "They melted into the shadows, and we assume that they're in Merrendogith. We sail for the Edge immediately."

Helmir crossed his arms in thought. "Surely you will stay here for the night and rest before such a dangerous journey?"

"My sister needs us," Jason insisted, though the thought of sleep seduced him. He didn't know what time it was, but the funeral had taken a lot out of him. "We'll sleep on the ship."

Looking concerned, Helmir opened his mouth to speak, but then closed it. He softened his expression and simply said before departing, "May the Celestials be with you."

"Thank you," Elken replied.

"Hey, has anyone seen Pi? Why does she always leave?" Jason groaned in exasperation and fished out his sibulus. "What does she even do?" He blew the whistle.

Scalaed moved his head in front of Jason's face, trying to convey that Poison Ivy might not be the dragon pet he thought she was. And something told him she wouldn't listen to the whistle.

"What is it?" Jason asked. "Do you know where she went?"

Scalaed tossed his head in the direction she had gone. A moonlit trail, nearly invisible from abandonment, wove through the drooping black woods.

"Why there?"

Scalaed winced. Nothing good, the expression implied.

"Chief Helmir?" Jason called after him, an unsettling feeling creeping on him. "Where was Hestur Village?"

Helmir's white tail stopped. When he turned around to Jason, his face beheld worry and fear. "Why do you ask?"

"I think my dragon went—"

Helmir was suddenly in Jason's face. "You listen to me,

and listen well," he whispered coldly. Jason thought he saw the trarewolf's fangs growing. "That graveyard should be left in peace in respect for the dead there. We will not risk the resurrection of the curse that befell my allies, so I forbid you from setting foot in that village. Am I clear, Jason?"

The shiver that shot up Jason's spine had dissolved into goosebumps, and he nodded silently. Helmir growled lowly and marched off.

"Scalaed, maybe Poison Ivy went somewhere else?" Kyle asked.

Scalaed shook his head. It was the exact place she would go given her recent sinister behavior. He tried to talk to Jason, begging him to help her. But his communication was in vain without the heartlink.

"Well, we have to get her. I need her."

"We had best hurry," Elken said as he, Jason, and Kyle walked through the outskirts of the village toward the gate. "We have a ship to catch."

"I can't go anywhere without my dragon," Jason shot back.

The village firelight quickly faded as they stepped through the woven gate. The night beyond breathed a chill over them, but Scalaed pressed his way to the front, undeterred and guided by his nose.

Descending deep into the thick woods, Jason questioned Scalaed further about Poison Ivy, but without a heartlink or Melanie's bond, conversations with the dragon were difficult. Scalaed wished he had telepathy like Poison Ivy. She had claimed he was supposed to but failed to explain how he could attain it.

Well, you certainly took your time.

Scalaed froze to a halt, and his companions bumped into him in the dark. The forest had cleared to an overgrown field. From the center, two foreboding lights glowed fuchsia. Though the overgrowth veiled her body, her unblinking eyes paced in the shadows.

"Pi?" Jason called. "You okay, girl?" He approached the field.

Before he could take a step further, Scalaed's tail lashed out and blocked him.

"What's wrong?" Elken asked.

Jason looked from Scalaed's fearful expression to the field.

"It's Hestur Village," he realized. He could now see through the grasses the charred ruins of the village. The years had brought anything still standing to its knees and smothered most of the evidence with long wild grasses and scraggly bushes.

"Why would Poison Ivy come here?" Kyle scrunched his brow in confusion. "How did she know where it was?"

"Not sure." Jason tried unsuccessfully to slip past Scalaed's tail.

Scalaed's better eyesight and instincts told him this was not a good place to be. A dormant evil slept there, and Poison Ivy was sitting in the middle of it all.

Behold the power of my master, Poison Ivy said, a prideful flair in her voice.

Scalaed saw the others flinch with expressions of horror.

They could hear her now, too.

"Poison Ivy?" Jason gasped.

The eyes snaked through the ruins as Poison Ivy began her approach to the group. *That is no longer my name, Jason.* She hissed his name with disgust. *I am Oléthra, servant of Merrendogith, and I welcome you to this birthplace of curses.*

"What happened to you?" Elken asked, hand floating slowly toward his bow. Poison Ivy was still far off, but his aim was accurate, day or night.

What is meant to happen to those who live with Master's gift. Alas, I am now the only one who remains.

"It's the poison," Jason gasped. "Laena was right. I have to fix this."

"Dude." Kyle rubbed his eyes in exasperation. "Look, I love you, but you're being really stupid right now. You're telling us that you want to enter ground zero of the zombie apocalypse and face off with your demon horse? This is a hazard zone! We have no idea what foreign contaminants and whatnot are still there."

"She's getting closer," Elken warned.

Jason paused, patting his trousers and vest. "I don't have any Yelnight crystal." Doubt descended upon him. "And I don't even know if my magic is back."

Weakling, Oléthra taunted him.

Jason looked back, breathing more heavily. "Shut up," he said. He took cautious steps toward the field and cast a glance at the rubble.

An incomplete centaur skeleton peeked through the pale

waving grass. The jaw was gone, as were half the limbs and most of the ribs. The skull resembled a human's quite closely, though Jason noticed how the nasal bone was taller, squarish, and more pronounced from the brow. It was almost helmet-like—Spartan.

Their deaths were a necessary sacrifice to bring about a host for Master, Oléthra purred, now uncomfortably close.

Quickly shooting his head in her direction, Jason sucked in a breath. She had grown twice her size. All semblance of her horse shape had disappeared to be replaced by a draconic form bulked with muscle. Her black horns stretched behind her in evil twists, and as she raised her long neck, she dwarfed Jason.

See now Master's design. I am reborn in black magic to be his weapon of annihilation. I am your bane, and you will fall victim to his reign.

"I don't think so," Jason growled, unsheathing his knife.

You inferior creature! Oléthra snarled as the scales of her chest began to glow.

Jason pointed the knife in her direction, the blade held steady with confidence. He sneered. "You caught me on a really bad day. So this doesn't look good for you, because I'm not scared."

Then a loud, proud voice Jason never thought he'd be so happy to hear echoed in his head.

Your savior has arrived!

Azeur fluttered in front of Jason's face dangling a green velvet pouch from his claws. Seeing Jason's hand on his knife, the bird slowly turned toward the ruins. *Is this a bad time?*

Oléthra licked her lips with a forked tongue. *It's been a long time, pest.*

Azeur yelped in fright upon seeing her and let go of the pouch, which Jason caught by reflex.

"Azeur, I never thought I'd be so happy to see you," Jason said. "Your timing is perfect."

Really? Azeur's voice wobbled, but he composed himself quickly as he used Jason's head as a shield. *I mean, of course my timing is perfect! This is no mere coincidence; this is providence!* His voice trilled with his usual pompous tone. *Lady Laena sends you her most heartfelt—*

Shut up, bird, Oléthra growled and reared on her hind legs, spreading her elongated wings to accentuate her size.

All yours, my good human! Azeur told Jason and retreated, leaving behind a puff of feathers.

Light bloomed from under the scales of Oléthra's neck and chest, and it traveled to her open mouth and eyes. Another arrow from Elken's bow ricocheted off her armored head.

Scalaed pawed the ground with his foreleg, snarling. Whatever this Oléthra creature was, he would dominate her. He would show everyone who the real dragon was. He bounded forward, leaping over a startled Kyle and knocking Jason over with his rush of speed and tackled Oléthra to the ground with a thunderous crash. Still larger than the poisoned horse, Scalaed caught her neck in his jaws, applying enough pressure to squeeze out the flames, but not enough to kill her. He wanted her fixed, not dead. He pinned her, crushing her wings with his weight.

Thrashing like the possessed creature she was, Oléthra's telepathy screamed in their heads. *You cannot stop me!*

Jason ignored the pounding headache her voice caused and hefted his knife. Scrambling to his feet, he screamed back, "I can!" And he charged. *Celestials be with me,* he prayed. *Give me enough magic.*

Realizing his intention, Oléthra shrieked and clawed at Scalaed's legs. Scalaed squirmed at the pain, and the subtle loosening of his jaw was enough for Oléthra to scramble free and roar in violent opposition to the human charging her. Two more arrows from Elken glanced harmlessly off her hide.

She reared with a rapid inhale. Jason planted himself mere feet from her. As fire churned in her throat, Jason lunged with his knife.

With a choking sound, the fire left Oléthra's eyes. Jason slipped his knife out of her chest scar while his other hand pressed Yelnight crystal into the wound. His hand glowed brightly.

No! Oléthra cried.

Jason's magic rushed to fill him like a golden well, and with it came that distant male voice in his heart. *"You shall do wonders if only you ask for my help."* Golden healing exploded through Oléthra's veins and ignited her every cell. Then Jason removed his hand.

Gasping, the green dragon crumbled to her knees. Her telepathic screams faded like a voice lost in a storm, and her panting lost its carnivorous snarl. Her claws receded into hooves, and like a flower scorched by the sun, her wings wilted to black shreds that fell to the ground. Thick sheets of green scales slipped off, trailing blood and mucous. A silver mane glistened beneath the slime, and a neck of midnight fur shook off the remaining scales.

Exhausted and barely conscious, Ivy dropped her head and lay on her side, chest heaving and sounding very horse-like.

Jason, too, dropped to his knees, and the aftereffects of his magic quickly lost their hold on him.

No one dared break the deafening silence that now smothered the field, except Kyle.

"You good, Jay?" he called, wringing his hands. "Need something to drink?"

With a sigh of effort, Jason climbed to his feet. "I wouldn't say no to a Vitamin Water."

As he stroked the damp black fur of his horse, who now slept peacefully, Jason heard Kyle ask, "What's your favorite flavor?"

Jason chuckled. "Kiwi-strawberry, but I don't—" When he had turned to face the others, Kyle proudly held out a pink bottle, and the orange glow of his Abrielstone faded.

"Oh, you're amazing, dude," Jason laughed and took the drink.

"Thanks. No one seems to say it enough, to be honest."

Jason cast him a sideways glance behind the bottle as he downed the cold contents.

"That was eventful," Elken said as he returned his weapons. "Well done, Jason."

Kyle nodded in approval. "You were epically glowing,"

Scalaed nudged the sleeping horse, unable to recognize his feelings. He should be glad Jason restored her to her natural form. No doubt she would be at peace now. But another part of him resented Jason for taking away his only dragon friend. Poison Ivy could have shown him the secrets of telepathy. Maybe he could have saved her from herself, and she wouldn't have had to go back to being a horse at all. Should haves and what ifs clouded his mind with gloom, and he abandoned the little horse in the field.

"I'll leave her in the care of the Hündr," Jason said as he returned the cap to the now-empty bottle. "Guess I'll be riding with you guys from now on."

"Don't sound so disgusted." Kyle swatted his heart.

"I'm not." Jason rolled his eyes with a smirk. "It'll just be—"

"Look," Elken pointed to the middle of the field, his eyes wide.

A warm light sparkled into existence, and Empress Elethýna appeared. She wore a black cloak with intricate goldwork blooming from the hem. Elken had never seen her wear any color other than her vibrant green, and this change was quite foreboding. She appeared to be floating—even she would not touch this cursed land.

"Your Majesty," Kyle said as the team bowed.

Elethýna approached them with a sad smile on her face, as if the weight of the dead affected her.

"You should not be here," she said. "I sense ancient

depravity on this ground. Why have you come?"

"Poison Ivy was drawn here, and I had to stop her before she got any more evil," Jason replied.

"And with all due respect, my fair woman," Kyle said hesitantly, "six years isn't exactly ancient."

Elethýna moved her gaze to Kyle, amusement and endearment flickering in her green eyes. Her pink lips almost smiled. "Indeed," she continued, "but something far older than genocide lies here, though that crime bears much weight and haunts this place. Voices outside of time call to me from these bones."

"Can you tell us what caused this?" Jason asked.

"An evil that has been trying to escape its prison for some time, possessing the dead to ravage the realm. These forces are hungrier than Klarn. To combat this enemy, you will need the assistance of my son," Elethýna said. "He will be your teacher. You have already begun hearing his lessons." While the three young men looked at each other questioningly, she continued, "I also promise you, my dear warriors"—she smiled lovingly and touched their shoulders—"that I will draw swords alongside you when the hour is dire."

She then waved gracefully over them, and ribbons of white light swirled around Jason and his companions. When they rippled away and faded, he saw they had all been returned to the outskirts of the White Village. Ivy had also been returned with them, still sleeping, and tethered to the gates with a shimmering white rope. Jason went to her side, and the horse opened one weary brown eye.

"Hey, girl," Jason whispered as he brushed away the mane on her forehead. "I have to go now, but you'll be safe here. Eat lots of hay and grain, okay?"

Ivy snuffed lightly in response.

"We had a good run together, didn't we?" Jason smiled, though sadness threatened to pull it into a frown. "I'll miss our flights, but this is the real you. I'll see you soon." He gave her one last scratch behind the ears, which lulled her back into sleep.

Scalaed sighed when Jason finally returned to the group. Eager to move on and for a distraction from his dark thoughts, Scalaed knelt down and ordered them aboard. They had to return to Yolderain. They had to get Melanie back.

CHAPTER 23

Begin the Next Phase

Klarn massaged his temples in pain. *What a malicious trick to be surrounded by an undrinkable ocean.* Not to drink the water meant a perpetual migraine and dehydration, but to drink meant vomiting and dehydration. There were no lakes or rivers, just the desiccated beds they had left behind.

Yet, through all his morbid sufferings, Klarn had hoped they would survive. He had more than hope; he had help.

Klarn once more unsheathed *Dacvir* and gazed upon it as if in a trance.

"We are almost free." Klarn felt the words spill from his mouth.

He shook his head. "We still have to force the dragon to open a portal."

His voice lowered as if speaking only to *Dacvir*. *"That is what I am here for."*

Klarn's faint, gaunt reflection in the blade stared back at him.

"Shut up!" Klarn writhed away from the sword and let it clatter down the dais. "Did I permit you to enter my mind?"

The migraine intensified and pulled Klarn to the floor.

"Chief Klarn?" a hesitant voice came from the archway.

Heaving deeply as discreetly as possible, Klarn retrieved *Dacvir*, rose to his feet, and met the visitor. The migraine reduced to a faint throb.

"Caito," he said breathlessly. "Was your mission a success? I see you are alone."

"The girl doesn't matter anymore," Caito replied coldly as she approached, her sleek black tail whipping behind her. "I have found a way to escape."

Klarn's yellow eyes widened in interest. "You have the Pyrium Dragon?"

"No," Caito gleamed. "Something better. Something easier." Holding up Melanie's ring, she continued, "I removed it from the girl using it. We don't need the dragon, just this ring, and it's yours now, sir."

Klarn opened his hand to receive the ring and looked cautiously at Caito. "And if it fails?"

"I still captured Melanie as you commanded." Caito shrugged nonchalantly. "The dragon and its companions are likely mounting a rescue as we speak. Should the ring fail, the dragon will arrive in Merrendogith nonetheless. But this"— she gestured to the ring—"is an immediate solution."

Klarn gripped her shoulder and nodded. "You have saved our people." He examined the ring more closely. "Caito? How—"

Anxious, Caito explained, "I confess, I arrived at the scene after Melanie had left. I only witnessed her return, so I missed the ring's mechanics."

Klarn's eyes narrowed and didn't leave Caito as he held

the ring in her face. "That is not the only issue. This ring is far too small. Explain how I am meant to wield it."

"Oh." Caito only managed to sound half of the single syllable as she tried to think of a solution.

Klarn flicked the ring into her hands. "Does it fit you?"

Caito's yellow eyes widened as an idea struck her with anticipation. "Perhaps, why?"

"You will put on the ring and, joining hands, take us both back to Tindoria. If successful, you will lead our people back in waves."

"Yes." Caito eagerly clung to the prospect of returning Klarn to his mortal state. "Yes, that could work." She fumbled with the ring and tried to see every detail, mentally checking if her knife was still at her side.

The seconds crawled by, and Klarn's penetrative stare did little to ease the pressure.

Caito's thumb finally compressed on the stone with a click. "I think I found it!" She put the ring on and held out her arm to her prey. Klarn grasped it without hesitation, and Caito pushed the stone.

Torrents of warmth flooded Caito's body, and fresh air rushed to her lungs. When she opened her eyes, she stood on a mountaintop from which she could see endless miles of the mighty range strewn with valleys and narrow rivers. Her renewed lungs gulped in the clear air, and, overcome with emotion, Caito dropped to her knees in tears.

The southern Diamond Mountains. The sun. Oh, the glorious sun embraced her with its warm rays. The breeze welcomed her and wrapped her in the smells of nature: grasses, wildflowers, the mountain air, and the rivers. Faint color began creeping into her fingertips. Caito knew it would all eventually return just as it had disappeared. She laughed because she felt the change. She was warm. She was *alive.*

Spinning around, she looked for Klarn. He wasn't there. *What happened? Where did he go? Did he not make it?*

"Klarn?" she called, noting the strength in her voice. "Hello?"

There was no answer.

The ring only takes its bearer, she realized. Defeat swelled in her heart. She needed to devise a new plan. But first she wanted to bask in this life a little longer. Maybe even hunt for food.

Excitement pumped through her veins at the thought, and she assumed her black panther form. This terrain was not in her coat's favor, but she didn't care. It had been too long since she tasted the thrill of a hunt. Caito weaved down the mountainside, her ears open to the fresh world's sounds, her yellow eyes soaking in the wonders, and her nose on a mission for prey.

A smear of dusky fur crossed her vision. *Rabbit,* she thought hungrily. Filled with an energy she hadn't known in years, she flew across the grass, passing trees and rocks. Caito had forgotten the joy in the chase. Her white claws extended and sank into the plump rabbit, pinning it into the dirt.

In a hungry frenzy, Caito tore into her meal and cried. There were no words to describe her gratitude.

The carcass licked clean, Caito purred on her side, debating whether she had time for a nap.

But the Pyrium Dragon was on its way. Klarn would escape eventually. *No, he needs to die.* She stood to her feet in human form and pushed the ruby, but not before taking in every detail of Tindoria.

Klarn froze when Caito vanished, and he was left holding the air where her arm had been.

"No," he said dejectedly. "The ring only takes its bearer." He pressed his face into his hands. Doubt encircled his thoughts as he feared Caito would abandon him. If she tasted the world of the living, there was nothing he could do to bring her back.

Minutes felt like an eternity as Klarn paced in step to his throbbing head. Then soft ribbons of light shimmered for an instant, and Caito returned.

"It works!" Caito gasped. "I've been to Tindoria, and I was truly alive again. But—"

"Yes, I'm aware only one person can use the ring," Klarn finished for her.

As the despair of Merrendogith crept back into her soul, weighing down her shoulders, Caito tried to ignore it and asked, "So what are we going to do?"

Klarn outstretched his hand. "Let me see the ring."

Fear made Caito's heart skip a beat. She brought her clasped hands closer to her chest. "How will I know you won't abandon us, Klarn?" She did not want the ring in his possession, regardless of whether it fit him.

Klarn's eyes glimmered at her accusation. "Caito," he said, tone smooth like marble, "everything I have done since our banishment has been for our people!" He raised his voice as he stepped closer. "For *years,* I have been striving for our escape. I am your chief, and I took an oath, a vow, when bequeathed this diadem." He pointed to the once-golden woven circlet on his head. "I was *wed* to my tribe to be a faithful protector. I live this oath, Caito, even to this day. Never doubt my loyalty again."

"You're the reason we're in this hellscape!" Caito shouted. Strength from the living world filled her muscles once more, and she couldn't contain it.

"I saved our people and Helmir's by eliminating an existential threat!" Klarn said.

"It still resulted in this horrific existence!" Caito shot back.

"Do you think I wanted this?" Klarn roared. The stones of the hall rattled. "I should have been hailed a hero for sparing both our tribe and the Hündr's. I never dreamed of failing so titanically. But since then, I have fought and suffered for a way to give back the lives stolen from us. And now, we are so close! You've tasted it on your tongue! Caito"—he calmed—"remain loyal and help me save our people once again."

Moved by his zeal, Caito was almost convinced. But the only way her people would be free was to be rid of Klarn and start again with a fresh beginning and a new chief. Maintaining his trust was paramount.

"I stand with you to the ends of this world," she said.

Klarn smiled and tilted his head. "Thank you." He held out his hand for the ring once again. "Now this must be examined to understand its properties. I will find a way to bend it to our will."

Caito tensed her jaw, surrendered the realm ring, and departed.

"If only I could see what she saw." Klarn closed his eyes and brought the ring to his lips. "Now," he breathed as he held the ring up to the pale light, "what are you made of?"

"*The answer is fascinating,*" replied a close voice.

Dacvir suddenly in hand, Klarn whipped around for the source. There was no one in the hall, but the voice had been right in his ear. "What do you want now?"

"*Don't sound so jaded,*" the voice said again, just as close as before.

"Do not come uninvited into my mind," Klarn growled.

"Oh, Klarn." The voice sighed. "*Don't tell me what to do in my own realm. I've only ever guided you all these years. Don't tell me you are ungrateful.*"

Klarn scowled.

"*Or have you forgotten all I've done for you?*"

Klarn rolled his eyes. "I haven't forgotten. But you have never told me how this benefits you."

The voice sounded confused that Klarn even had to ask. "*Once you return to Tindoria, I will be restored to my former state, and you will be whole again in the realm of the living.*"

"Your former state?" Klarn scanned the crumbling walls. The voice had never been this candid.

"*My quarrel is not with your people, I assure you,*" the voice cooed.

"Forgive me if I don't sound convinced."

"*You have no one else to trust for your salvation, Klarn. You will be quite safe during my conquest against the Celestials.*"

Klarn scoffed incredulously. "The Celestials! You strive for the impossible. What have they ever done to you?"

The voice hesitated. "*Let me tell you about the ring.*"

Klarn's nose curled in disgruntlement at the voice avoiding his question. He cast a glance at his fist closed around the ring as the voice continued, "*The core of a Pyrium Dragon's heart was fused into the band. That core is what grants the dragon its portal powers. We will construct an archway, powered by the magic in the ring, and be free from the ring's constraints. It would be as simple for your people as walking through a door. But this door would lead back to Tindoria.*"

"Would that work?" Klarn asked anxiously.

"*I have resources,*" the voice said comfortingly. "*It is time we begin the next phase.*"

CHAPTER 24

Greenfields Road

Lucy and Thendrell caught the last stagecoach leaving Endlewood. Their ride's destination was Lakéthion by way of Greenfields Road, a major highway that ran north to south between the two cities. Their coachman said the transit should be around eight hours with a halfway stop at the Drian Forest Staging Post to swap horses. With a well-traveled, well-maintained road, the smooth transit would aid in their speed.

Nonetheless, when Lucy heard "eight hours," her heart sank. She had promised her husband she would be back at a reasonable hour. She replayed the phone call she had with Ian, which, needless to say, was an interesting conversation.

"Ian, Babe, they're alive!" she had told him. "Melanie and Jason are alive!"

"What?" Ian's voice dissolved into happy sobs of relief on the other line. "Where are they?" he finally managed to ask.

"Ian, they're..." Lucy took a steadying breath. "They've somehow landed in Tindoria."

Then the phone went quiet. Eventually came Ian's very short, "Okay."

"Honey, I'm going to go see them, to make sure they're alright and try to get them back—"

"You will do no such thing!" Ian said adamantly. "Not without me."

"This might be our only chance. I promise to be back by tonight. Kyle's with them, too."

She heard Ian's deflated sigh. He was an hour away from home if traffic was good. "You'll bring them home?" he asked hopefully.

"I will do my utmost."

"Promise you'll be safe."

"You do know I spent half of my life there." Lucy gave an anxious chuckle. "I know what I'm doing, and I promise I will be safe."

"I love you so much, Starlight," Ian finally said.

"I love you, too, Babe," Lucy had replied, dwelling on every word.

Thendrell noticed how she twisted her wedding ring. She sat opposite him, looking out the small window.

"Has it changed much?" Thendrell asked.

Lucy eyed him without turning her head. "Tindoria's advancements are definitely slower than Earth's. I lived in Eastern Tindoria, so I rarely made the trip to Endrial, but it's mostly the same."

Thendrell nodded thoughtfully.

"The city is bigger than I remember." Lucy smiled weakly and looked back out the window.

Out of the city, Greenfields Road cut through grassy plains and rolling hills with hardly a tree in sight. It was a cloudless night, and the two moons lit up the road.

"I've forgotten about that," Lucy chuckled, embarrassed. "I can't remember which one's which."

"Targen is the large silver moon that travels east to west," Thendrell said. "Taura is the small golden moon that travels around Tindoria at the horizon."

"That's right." Lucy leaned back and plopped her hands into her lap. "Thank you."

Thendrell bowed his head courteously with a soft smile. "We still have a long journey ahead of us, and this coach goes far into the night. I advise trying to sleep before the dragon flight from Lakéthion to Yolderain."

"Yeah," Lucy agreed. "I don't see myself sleeping at all in that situation."

She slipped off her cardigan, bunched it up, and lay on her makeshift pillow. Despite the friendly conversation, her thoughts still swarmed around Melanie, praying she was safe. They knew nothing about Merrendogith or if Melanie had even survived the manner in which she crossed. Squeezing her eyes more tightly, Lucy tried to let the rhythm of the coach lull her to sleep.

With a lurch and a bounce, the stagecoach came to a stop, waking its two passengers. Thendrell swam out from under his cloak and blinked groggily in confusion for a moment before rubbing the sleep from his eyes.

Lucy also sat up with a groan. "Ugh, my back."

"We've arrived at the Drian Forest Staging Post," announced the coachman. The cabin rocked as Lucy felt him dismount to open the door for them. "You'll find accommodations inside." He smiled as he helped them out. "Make yourselves at home while we attend to the horses."

The post was a large timber-framed building. The aged plaster had taken on the pollens from the surrounding woods which deepened its gold shade. Windows glowed with diamond-patterned panes. Two men exited the thick wooden door and began untethering the team of horses, tipping their hats politely in passing.

Thendrell opened the post's door for Lucy. The chilly night air was left behind as the warmth of a well-tended fire welcomed them. A small kitchen with a stove and pantry was opposite the grand fireplace that heated the space evenly. Fresh cots were made in a loft above as well as the far side of the main room.

Meandering over to the kitchen counter, Lucy smiled sweetly at the maid. The woman returned a beaming smile of her own, though Lucy had the inkling she had been sleeping before their arrival. Her curly hair was slightly messy and hastily pulled back.

"What can I get you?" the woman asked.

Lucy pointed to a small keg. "Is that Ladyberry Malt?"

"Yes, indeed." The woman smirked. "And never mind the hour; would you like a pint?"

"Half, please." Lucy nodded.

Thendrell approached and tilted his head as Lucy sipped the beer. He watched with amusement as she closed her eyes and sighed. She opened them when she sensed Thendrell next to her.

"You know, this is just as good as I remember." Lucy smiled as she looked at the mug. "I really missed it."

"It's a popular choice among the ladies." Thendrell leaned on his arm against the bar.

"Oh, I know." Lucy laughed after another sip. "There's nothing on Earth that tastes like this. It's probably brewed with a special Tindorian grain or something."

"I could never enjoy it," Thendrell said. "It's far too sweet."

Lucy wagged her head. "The only drinks I like."

Their coachman returned and said it was time to depart. That was when Lucy realized she only had dollars. Thendrell slipped a coin to the maid and bid her goodnight.

"Thank you," Lucy said apologetically.

"It's what Jason would have wanted," Thendrell said as he helped her into the stagecoach. "I may not be fond of him, nor he of me, but I abide by my word."

The coach door closed with a squeak, and the next four hours began.

CHAPTER 25

Horizon's Signal

J ason had no idea what time it was, but his eyes burned, and his neck had given up on supporting his head. He must have fallen asleep at some point, however, because Scalaed shook him rather roughly, and he nearly fell onto the cobblestone. *Cobblestone? We reached Lakéthion?* The moonlight glittered off the sea behind the city buildings, which glowed with warm lanternlight.

"What time is it?" Jason asked the others as he melted off Scalaed.

"Well"—Kyle yawned loudly—"I don't know if Tindoria is in sync with Arizona, but my watch says three twenty-seven a.m."

"Let's find the coaching inn your mother and Thendrell arrived at," Elken suggested, his voice froggy from sleep.

"Mm-hm," Jason agreed. He realized his eyes were closed again.

Scalaed was also exhausted. He said nothing as his wings dragged behind him on their approach to the city's gates. Elken stumbled close to him, trying to lean on him when he could, though Scalaed rebuffed, shooting a sharp glare in his direction.

"Someone's cranky," Kyle scoffed sleepily.

Scalaed eyed him irritably and puffed glowing warning smoke from his nostrils.

"Kyle, don't push buttons," Jason groaned. "None of us have the energy."

The city was hushed in sleep with not a soul in sight except for the apathetic gatekeepers who granted them entrance. They directed them to the coaching inn, an inviting building known as The Sleepy Gelding.

Elken opened the door of the inn, and the cousins stumbled behind. Scalaed once again was left to himself to find a field to sleep in.

Inside The Sleepy Gelding, the plump innkeeper recognized Jason and led them by lanternlight to their room.

"Here you are. Enjoy your stay!" she said in a tone too cheery for such a late hour. She handed them a candlestick and hustled off into the darkness.

Jason knocked and slowly opened the door.

Lucy was still awake, sitting on the edge of her bed, but ran to her son and hugged him tightly.

"So happy you got here!" she whispered. "Oh, you look exhausted."

Jason swayed as he mumbled something incoherent.

"Oh, I can only imagine," Lucy agreed supportively despite not understanding what he said.

"Aunt Lucy?" Kyle leaned into the doorway. "Are we staying in here?"

"Yes." She refocused and pointed to the other three small

beds. "Thendrell has his own room, so take your pick."

Kyle face-planted into the pillow before she even finished.

Elken tried to sleep. Fear for Melanie was drowning his thoughts. He worried that her Abrielstone wouldn't work in Merrendogith. What if she didn't survive the journey? He prayed she was still alive, but there was no way to know. He flopped to his side and took a deep breath.

"I'm worried about her, too," Jason whispered from the darkness.

"There's been too much to process." Elken covered his face with his hands. "Melanie and Helnah's disappearance, Fallon's death and funeral, and no proof Melanie is still alive."

"That's exactly how I've been feeling. How are you coping so well?"

"I'm not," Elken said very softly. "But someone has to be sane in emotional circumstances. Suppressing my own grief was a talent I found shortly after joining Thornbrill."

"Dude." Jason sat up. "That's not healthy. I appreciate you being the glue that has kept this…squad together, I really do, but I need you to take care of yourself, too. You can't be an oak tree if you don't water yourself." Jason was too exhausted to understand what he meant by his own metaphor, and Elken seemed too tired to process it. "We need to try to sleep," he finished.

"Yes." Elken pulled the blanket over himself.

"I'm here for you, Elken," Jason said as the Tindorian turned away. "That's how a team works. You don't just look out for all of us, we all look out for each other."

"Thank you."

"You're welcome."

Elken smirked. "'Squad' is a funny word."

"Goodnight, man." Jason shut him down with a dismissive wave.

"Goodnight, Jason." Elken shifted under the sheets, then added, "I think it's a good name."

"The morning coach to Endlewood is leaving in an hour!" announced the chipper voice of the plump innkeeper as she walked down the hall. She repeated the itinerary as she rang her bell.

"We're not even taking a carriage!" In his displeasure, Kyle's voice rattled phlegmatically. Growling like a gremlin, he buried his head underneath the pillow.

Lucy was the first to rise and took charge immediately. She corralled the others together with their belongings and rushed them downstairs to grab breakfast. To arrive at Port Rholdir in a timely manner, Lucy wanted to depart as soon as possible.

An early riser by habit, Thendrell was already finishing his food when the rest of the team joined.

Breakfast was uneventful and bland, but necessary for their voyage. While they ate, Lucy took the time to showcase what her backpack contained from home: energy bars, a few plastic water bottles, the first aid kit from her car, a roll of toilet paper, flashlights, flares, Lucy's multitool, and Ian's big bag of beef jerky.

"We might want to buy food in Yolderain." She passed the backpack to Jason. "Maybe some stuff to make sandwiches."

"Listen…" Jason leaned toward his mother as he placed the backpack on the ground. "I've been thinking. I know you really want to help, but, Mom…you can't come."

Lucy scoffed nervously. "What do you mean? I'm going with you."

"No, it's too dangerous," Jason said. "You need to go home where you'll be safe."

"Absolutely not," Lucy said sternly. "I am your mother, and my daughter is in danger!"

"Mom, you don't have an Abrielstone to protect you like we do. You'll be too vulnerable."

Lucy's open mouth trembled. "My baby girl is all alone in the Underworld. I dare anything or anyone to try and stop me from getting her back."

Standing, Jason chewed his cheek as he pulled her in for a hug. "Mom, I love you so much, you know that."

"I know, Baby." Lucy rubbed his back as she sniffed.

"I can't bear to lose Melanie *and* you. I don't want to worry about your safety on top of worrying about the mission. I'm sure Dad could use an update, anyway."

Jason's logic made sense, but Lucy struggled to find peace with it. Jason was right. Misty-eyed, she pulled away from the hug and held her son's chin. "I'll go with you as far as the port. And if I don't hear from you somehow in forty-eight hours, I'm using this." She held up her realm ring.

Thendrell raised his mug in approval. "A wise decision, Lucy."

Elken agreed. "Knowing you're safe lessens the worry in our efforts to rescue Melanie."

"And Helnah," Kyle added, much to Thendrell's gratitude.

"We better get going." Lucy wiped her eyes. "The harbor will be at its busiest once we arrive, so that might be advantageous in finding someone who knows where that ship is."

Elken paid the innkeeper, who offered them a cheery farewell. "Does this ship have a name?" he asked as they stepped outside.

Lucy winced. "A lot could have happened in two decades, but the last I knew, it was christened *Horizon's Signal.*"

Yolderain was much different than the other cities Jason had visited in Tindoria. For one, it was smaller, and the climate was much warmer with a bounty of tropical trees. Buildings were painted with vibrant colors, and banners and drapes rippled over alleys. Houses and stores were multi-floored with terraces and flat roofs, and each was styled to the uniqueness of its owner.

The ocean air swirled through the streets, tinkling through shell chimes and rustling through the townspeople's flowy clothes. The Bay of Rholdir's harbors were lined with docks and many ships of all sizes, from tiny fishing boats to extravagant galleons. A rainbow of sails fluttered with the wind, swaying the boats in port.

Seeing the iconic black dragon and the Knight of Endrial approach, Yolderain flocked in crowds below as they flew overhead.

Kyle welcomed his celebrity status and waved victoriously at the onlookers as Jason scoffed from the front. "Dude, you realize they don't even know who you are? Besides, we have a mission to focus on."

"Well, if we look excited to see them, they might help us faster," Kyle retorted through his smiles.

Scalaed floated above the streets and touched down in the docks, uncharacteristically quiet. After dropping off Jason and the others in Lakéthion the night before, he'd crashed in the golden fields outside the city having fallen asleep mid-flight. His dreams had swirled in violent imagery. In them, Elken had stolen Melanie away in various scenarios, and Scalaed killed him in response in as many ways. Jason was no better. He had erased Scalaed's only dragon friend, so he was not in Scalaed's good graces either. Power he had never felt before had heated every muscle, and he had used his voice and fire to make them all submit. Before long, all would kneel before him in fear. None would cross him again.

Alas, it had only been a dream. But Scalaed kept the images of Elken dying in the forefront of his mind. All he needed was an excuse. And humans had a tendency to make mistakes.

"You didn't happen to spot the *Horizon's Signal* during our descent, did you?" Elken asked Lucy.

His voice grated on Scalaed's ears, but he would no longer let it show. He would keep his wrath invisible.

"I did not," Lucy replied. Her eyes still searched the sails as she dismounted. "There are so many more ships than I remember, and I can't recall the colors of the sails. Were they blue with white, or blue and yellow?"

The crowds spilled down toward the harbor, hoping to catch a glimpse of Tindoria's heroes. Most murmured amongst themselves about Scalaed, who took notice of their shock and awe. Some were afraid. The dragon's maw twisted in a smirk, and he puffed black smoke to make them flinch. This was power. And he loved it.

"Kyle"—Elken grabbed his shoulder—"why don't you keep the crowds busy while we try to find our ship?"

"But I'm a nobody to them." Kyle folded his arms. "Why would they listen to me?"

"Oh, just do it." Jason patted his back a little too hard. "Just tell them you're my royal spokesperson or something."

"Okay, sweet." Kyle hopped off Scalaed and jogged to meet his new fans.

"Where do we start, Mom?" Jason ran his fingers through his hair in creeping stress.

"Excuse me," Thendrell piped up and waved amiably at a fisherman passing. "Do you know if the *Horizon's Signal* is still in service?"

"Ho, that is a name I haven't heard in many a year." The man chuckled, his silver scraggly mustache flipping up at the ends with his smile. "I don't know whatever became of her after the…well…you know." He shrugged haplessly. "That beautiful cog lost both her captains that day, and I wouldn't know her fate."

"Thank you, friend." Thendrell nodded, and the fisherman hoisted his fish basket and bid them good day.

Jason noticed a small fisherman's pub, the Whale's Keg, and suggested a visit. "Maybe someone there knows something. Pubs always spawn gossip."

Meanwhile, Kyle had quickly become overwhelmed at his rally. Locals bombarded him with questions pertaining to events at which he wasn't present, and civilians pestered him for an audience with either of his cousins; requests neither of which Kyle was able to fulfill. Meanwhile, Scalaed stood behind, looking down at the civilians with a judgmental gaze.

"Listen, hear ye!" Kyle frantically tried to be heard. "As the cousin to the Knight of Endrial, I have a, uh, request. Whoever can help us can get a hug from Sir Jason or something."

That subdued the crowd.

"We're looking for a ship, the *Horizon's Signal*. Its last owner was a guy named Rhowen. Does anybody know if it's still around?"

When people began screaming replies, Kyle recognized

the uselessness of his plan. He groaned with distress and clenched his fists at a loss while Scalaed rolled his eyes at the people's incompetence. Something Poison Ivy had said came unbidden to his mind: *Humans will always disappoint you eventually.*

Then a man with a sun-bleached ponytail approached Kyle and Scalaed.

"Oh," Kyle begged, "*please* tell me you know something, I'm losing the crowd here."

"How do you know about Rhowen?" the man asked. "You're far too young and not from here."

"You can say that again," Kyle scoffed. "He was my aunt's first husband. We're hoping to get the ship back."

The man paled. "Is she here?"

Kyle tried to read the man's reaction but to no avail.

"Please, tell me!" The man sounded desperate.

Kyle looked at Scalaed. "Hey, where are Aunt Lucy and the others?"

Scalaed tossed his head in the direction of the pub.

"You picking up fishy vibes from this dude?" Kyle asked through the side of his mouth.

Scalaed zoomed his head in front of the man. He smelled like the sea and some sort of smoke. The man stiffened as the dragon carefully nudged his salt-encrusted tunic and sniffed down to his sandals.

Scalaed returned his attention to Kyle and shrugged. He smelled of no threat. Perhaps this man would actually be of help.

"Come with me." Kyle motioned and left the crowd. They tried to follow, but Scalaed made his own intentions clear with a growl and show of smoke. The people awkwardly dispersed, and Scalaed stared them down until the docks emptied. When he turned to follow Kyle and the mystery man, they were entering the pub, at which point Scalaed knew he would have to wait outside…again. His pupils narrowed in irritation, and more smoke trailed from his nose.

Meanwhile, Lucy was somewhat cheered to find the Whale's Keg served Ladyberry Malt. She ordered a pint at Elken's insistence.

"It's been twenty years, I know," she said to the bartender, "but I just need to know."

"There are plenty of ships in the harbor, ma'am," the man said.

"I'm aware," Lucy agreed. "But the *Horizon's Signal* is very close to my—"

"Luciana?" cried a voice from the doorway.

Lucy whipped around, almost splashing her beer on Thendrell. She met the wide eyes of a man standing at the pub's doorway.

"Who's asking?" she asked cautiously.

"You don't remember me?"

Lucy stood up while Jason's eyes grilled Kyle into telling him who this stranger was.

"It's me," he sighed shakily, "Brohd."

Lucy's blue eyes widened in recognition. "Goodness," she said, breathing heavily with her hand over her chest. "I didn't recognize you with the long hair!"

"Me? Look at you!" Brohd gestured. "Your hair has never been cut above your shoulders nor would you dare be caught outside in trousers! What happened to you all these years?"

"Too much to recount. But I've returned to save my daughter."

Brohd's face darkened and he glanced at Jason and Kyle. "What has happened to my niece?"

"Niece?" Jason and Kyle repeated.

"That's why we wanted the *Horizon's Signal*," Lucy explained.

"Mom, who is this?" Jason asked.

"Rhowen's younger brother." Lucy stepped back.

"So, Melanie's uncle," Jason clarified, clearly startled.

"A son." Brohd raised an eyebrow. "A bastard?"

"*Excuse* me?" Jason was highly offended.

"No, I remarried!" Lucy pushed Brohd's shoulder with shocked laughter. "And while Ian is no sailor, he's a warrior like Rhowen was."

"You always liked a man in armor," Brohd teased. "I can't believe you're here! What's more, I now own my brother's ship." His voice was saddened. "The *Horizon's Signal* was all I had left of him, so I couldn't let her go."

"Rhowen would be glad to know you've taken care of his ship," Lucy said fondly. "Can you take us to her? We must leave immediately."

"Certainly, though I must confess, I'm harboring so many questions I think I'll burst."

Brohd led them down to the docks, which quelled Scalaed's impatience, and pointed proudly at a cog ship bobbing on the blue water. "Here she is! The *Horizon's Signal*. I think you'll like the paint job."

The *Horizon's Signal* was a single-masted galleon with a spacious main deck. Her sail, large and square, was dyed a brilliant blue with golden-yellow scrolls. Matching paint decorated both her castles but left her hull a natural wood. Flying from the aftercastle and mast were Yolderainian flags

Lucy's breath was stolen as memories resurfaced. It was out at sea, at sunset, when Rhowen had proposed to her. He had then taught her how to captain the ship. It was also at the bow, standing on the small forecastle nearly a year later, that she had announced she was pregnant.

"Are you alright?" Brohd asked gently.

"She's beautiful," Lucy whispered. "There's no other ship I'd trust to take them to the Edge."

"The Edge?" Brohd turned Lucy to face him. "Are you *demented?*"

"Melanie has been captured and taken to what is essentially the underworld," Lucy said. "Turns out Edgial Execution doesn't actually execute, so we have to go there and save her."

"By the stars' creator!" Brohd leaned back. "This could be a voyage to your death!"

"She's not coming with us." Jason stepped in. "She's going back home to be with my dad where she's safe."

"Pardon me, but what in Tindoria has possessed you

to contrive such an outrageous journey?" Brohd asked incredulously. "Surely there are other ways to rescue your daughter."

"No," came the unanimous reply.

"Actually, she's not the only one who got abducted," Kyle said. "There's another chick with her who says we won't die. At least not immediately..."

Brohd looked at Kyle blankly. "Her companion is...a talking chicken?"

"Nevermind," Kyle grumbled.

"Believe me," Lucy insisted, "we thought of every other alternative, but this is the only way."

Brohd assessed the would-be crew. "Is he going with you?" Brohd pointed to Scalaed.

"Yes."

"Well," Brohd paused for a moment, "I thought I lost everyone in that battle twenty years ago, yet here you are. I don't believe in coincidences, and despite the madness of this mission, it has renewed in me a sense of purpose. Thus I feel it is my duty to step in as your captain."

"Thank you!" Lucy hugged him. "I know Jason and Kyle will be safe under your watch."

"Fate has smiled on us, because I was going to take the *Horizon's Signal* out overmorrow. Supplies have already been prepared at my house."

Lunch had passed by the time the *Horizon's Signal* was prepared for departure. Kyle munched on an energy bar while looking back at the dock as the final crate was loaded on board. Brohd claimed it would have taken twice as long were it not for Scalaed's help.

As Jason walked off the ramp, he saw a young woman sprinting down the docks. Her turquoise dress was bunched in her tight grip lest she trip, and her rose-gold hair whipped behind her.

"Laena?" Jason ran to her as she grappled him in a hug. "What on earth are you doing here? How did you get here?"

Laena panted through her answer, "When I visited the palace to see you, a maidservant told me you had left for the Bay of Rholdir. I galloped by horseback with my father's footman the whole way here, praying I wouldn't miss you. Jason, please, tell me you don't mean to sail over the Edge?" She pulled away, her bright eyes misting with worry.

"Laena, I have to. The Kottrans took Melanie, and this is the only way to get her back."

Laena's eyebrows scrunched in pain as she bit her lip. "None who go there ever return!"

"I will." Jason stroked her arms.

"No, you don't know that!" Laena's face burned hotly. "The Naiads guard the uncharted oceans, and they know never to let anyone turn back."

"If all goes well, we won't have to sail back at all." Jason found his hand had ventured to her cheek. "Scalaed will portal us home."

"But you've done so much for us, Jason," Laena cried. "You've brought me back to life! You gave me happiness I'd never thought I'd have again."

Jason's heart ached as his eyes misted over.

"I don't know what I'd do without you." She dropped her head into his chest. "Please don't leave me."

"Laena, I have to. My sister needs me."

"I know," she whispered into his shirt.

"I'll come back, I promise. I have good friends to protect me." He smiled. "Plus a dragon."

"Just one?" Laena lifted her head quizzically.

"Poison Ivy is now just Ivy. She's with the Hündr, probably doing all the horse things."

Laena held his cheek. "I knew you'd help her."

"Well, she didn't give me much choice when she went into villain mode. It would have ended much worse had you not sent Azeur when you did. So, thank you."

Laena smiled, but it faded when the bells of the dock rang. Reality had poisoned the moment. When she turned her head, her nose almost touched Jason's.

"I will see you again, Laena," he whispered, his eyes jumping between her sparkling eyes and her lips. *I cannot sail to the unknown without...*

He cupped her freckled face and kissed her. He was aware

of every little thing in that magic moment: her lips tasted like vanilla, her arms embraced his neck, she rose to her toes to be even closer, her breath hitched as his other hand pulled her waist in. If only he could relive this forever.

When he finally released her, Laena's eyes were dry but appeared to sparkle even more. She tried to stifle her nervous giggles.

An idea popped into Jason's head, and he unsheathed his knife. Holding a corner of his green leather jerkin taut, he cut off a square and carved in his initials.

"It's not much to remember me by," Jason said in a shaky pitch that embarrassed him, "but I'll be needing this back when I return." He pressed the leather into her hands. "My jerkin will be needing it, too."

Laena clutched it to her heart like a gift from the Empress herself and kissed him on the cheek. Filled with a renewed confidence in his safety, Laena took a step back and prepared to watch them set sail.

Jason really wanted to kiss Laena once more, but he told himself to save it for when he returned. *If I return.*

When Jason turned to Lucy, she was smiling behind her folded hands.

"Now you really have to return so you can introduce me," Lucy teased.

Jason couldn't help but beam a smile. It still lingered even after the long hug goodbye.

"We'll be safe," he promised her. "Besides, I'm the son of the bravest Tindorian I know."

"I love you." Lucy rubbed his back and kissed his head. "I'll see you later."

"I love you too, Mom. We'll send an update after we return."

"Bye, Aunt Lucy!" Kyle waved from the deck.

Brohd was the last to board the ship, but he paused before the loading plank. He turned to see Lucy procrastinating with her ring, and their eyes met.

"I'll keep them safe, Luciana," Brohd vowed.

Lucy's smile warped with emotion. "I know you will."

"It was a joy to see you again. I pray it won't be the last time."

"It won't." Lucy said. With an anxious inhale, she showed Brohd her realm ring. "Don't panic." She clicked her realm ring and disappeared.

Brohd jumped back as the shower of sparkles faded. Blinking to process his shock, he returned to the ship, looking back more than once in case he'd imagined Lucy's magical vanishing. *This is a strange day, indeed.*

"Alright," Brohd rolled up his sleeves and detached the *Horizon's Signal* from the dock. "All aboard for a voyage to the unknown!"

Scalaed had already nested around the mast, ready to go. He occasionally glared at Elken, letting dark fantasies play in his imagination. On a journey to cross the edge of the world, accidents could happen...

Jason passed the dragon, smiling to himself and oblivious to Scalaed's ominous smile.

"Nice." Kyle nudged Jason mischievously in approval of his cousin's performance.

"Oh, stop." Jason shoved him playfully. "But thanks."

"Off we go!" Brohd announced from behind the wheel. "Based on current maps, I wager a seventy-eight nautical mile voyage. Be warned, the Edge may be even farther, so we should expect to sail for the next ten hours or more if the wind is consistent."

"That will have been nearly a full day since Melanie was taken," Elken told Jason worriedly.

"I know." Jason itched with impatience at the thought of where Melanie was and what she was going through. He turned toward the mainland one last time, hoping that seeing Laena would give him some comfort.

She stood at the very edge of the dock, her dress rippling like an ocean of its own. Waving her patch of leather, she blew him a kiss in farewell.

"We'll get Melanie back." Jason smiled, looking back at Elken. "I'm not the only guy who owes a girl a kiss."

Brohd had been relatively accurate with his predictions. The *Horizon's Signal* sailed on smoothly into the evening, and the moons looked even larger out at sea. Brohd taught Jason how to keep the ship straight so they could sail through the night on shifts, and he needed another captain to rotate with. Jason, in turn, showed Elken, who then offered to show Thendrell. Wanting to prove useful yet again and further dispel any stains his past wrought on his reputation, Thendrell accepted.

Scalaed also found a use aboard the *Horizon's Signal*. He found himself to be a perfect alternative to wind when there was none. He wished he could take credit for the idea, but he remembered it from a book Melanie read him some time ago. Normally he would complain about being used like a tool once again, but saving Melanie drove his motivation.

The hours ticked by, and Taura slowly slid across the *Horizon's Signal's* view in a golden glow until the sky began to change colors from a dusty purple to an orangey red, and then a golden pink.

Manning the wheel at the eleventh hour of the voyage, Brohd gasped loudly. He sounded a bell to wake the rest of the crew.

Already sensing what this could mean, they all rushed to the forecastle. What they saw stole their breath and instilled fear.

"I didn't notice it until now," Brohd explained through bated breath.

Less than three hundred feet from the *Horizon's Signal*, the ocean rippled away to pink nothingness. Elken thought he could reach out and touch the very sky itself. It was impossible to tell the actual distance between the terrifying end of the ocean and the sky. It could be an arm's length or twenty miles.

The pink void yawned before them, stretching into a golden yellow above, as the Edge crept ever closer.

"What exactly happens now?" Thendrell asked as he held tightly to the rails.

"I think we flip over the edge like it were a table," Elken said, knowing that would provide little comfort.

Kyle panicked. "Whoa, hang on, how is gravity going to work?"

"Excellent question." Hooking his arms through the rails behind him, Jason pasted himself next to Thendrell.

Scalaed growled anxiously and tightened himself around the mast.

Brohd returned to his post and gripped the wheel. "Gentlemen," he announced to the increasingly worried faces of his passengers, "hold on tight."

Acknowledgments

Firstly, I'd love to thank you, reader, for continuing this adventure in Tindoria.

I huge thank you goes to my mom. Mom, you've been my rock and plothole-solver extraordinaire. Thank you for hanging out with me for countless brainstorm sessions. Your enthusiasm and creativity has been invaluable, and I'm forever grateful for your devotion to watch my children, allowing me time to work and finish this book in time. I cannot wait to bring you along for book 3!

Thank you to my favorite teacher of all time, Andrew Pudewa, who taught creative writing with such passion it spurred my own efforts to write and complete a novel; I miss being your student! I always think of you whenever I write participle phrase sentence openers. "The thing after the comma is the thing doing the -inging" will forever be ingrained in my brain!

To my fellow indie authors I've met on Instagram, thank you all for your advice and inspiration. Keep writing your incredible books! There are sequels I anxiously wait for.

Thank you to my team of beta readers. Shylee, Gloria, Heather, Danitza, and Jess, I can't thank you enough for your time and insight, and inspiring me to expand on many of the subplots. Poison Ivy's story would not have happened otherwise. You all are amazing!

And Victoria, you are a light in the indie author community, and I thank you for your prayers and editorial assessment of this wild ride of a sequel. You are a joy to talk to!

Another *huge* thank you to Addison! I have never been more excited while reading an editor's notes. Every comment and recommendation inflamed my love for my story even more. You asked the right questions, pressed for more details, and showed me the importance of setting the scene, character motivation, and character emotional reactions. With every suggestion, I felt my story growing stronger. I devoured your edits and knowledge with hungry obsession!

Renee, you blew through this book so fast, which stunned me! Thank you for your final set of eyes and speedy turnaround time. You're an absolute rockstar, and I couldn't have published on time without you.

Of course, I thank my Lord God for creating me with this fantasy-driven imagination of mine. This story is His as much as it is mine. Dear Holy Spirit, thank you for infusing me with perseverance on days I wanted to give up. I also thank Jesus my Savior for being by my side and talking about what direction to take my book. May It Happen Press is a tribute to You and your holy mother's words of submission to the Divine Will. Heavenly Father, may Your Will always be done in my life and works. May I strive to be who You made me to be. All praise and glory are Yours, forever and ever.

Kickstarter Acknowledgments

Thank you to every single person who backed my Kickstarter campaign! It is because of these generous people that *Spire of Tavnir* was brought to life.

<table>
<tr><td>Maggie Andrews</td><td>Abigail Hathaway</td></tr>
<tr><td>Kayla Ann</td><td>David Holzborn</td></tr>
<tr><td>Carpenter Family</td><td>Addison Horner</td></tr>
<tr><td>Cortney Babcock</td><td>Bill Howard</td></tr>
<tr><td>Amanda Balter</td><td>Charity A. Land</td></tr>
<tr><td>Seth Billings</td><td>Katherine Malloy</td></tr>
<tr><td>Kayla Chitwood</td><td>Cameron Michaels</td></tr>
<tr><td>Alexandra Corrsin</td><td>Angela Morse</td></tr>
<tr><td>Jamie Dockendorff</td><td>Felicitas Odemer</td></tr>
<tr><td>Taylor Fleming</td><td>Howard Pennington</td></tr>
<tr><td>Sara Francis</td><td>Sarah Pennington</td></tr>
<tr><td>Morgan G.</td><td>Zackary Rhodes</td></tr>
<tr><td>Brandt Gibson</td><td>Red Robot</td></tr>
<tr><td>Jessica Gwyn</td><td>Caia, Leon, and</td></tr>
<tr><td>Chanel H.</td><td>Ezekiel Rogers</td></tr>
<tr><td>Danielle Harrington</td><td>Adrian Whitaker</td></tr>
</table>

About the Author

Hannah has been writing stories since she was seven. From stapling together hand-written and illustrated stories to give her siblings on Christmas, to a fantasy collab with her best friend where they alternated writing chapters and put them in each other's mailboxes, to Star Wars: Clone Wars fanfiction, which featured her first original character: a bug-eyed alien named Chihuahua Huffus.

When Hannah was eleven, the beginning foundations of what would later become The Tindoria Chronicles began to form in her imagination. Thus began the very first draft. At first, it was simply a pastime she enjoyed, and she was mainly writing for herself. As her world and story grew, however, she realized she had something really special and dreamed of sharing it with the world. So she began to tackle her writing journey with a new end goal in mind of being a real author. While it took her over ten years to finish Prisoners of Thornbrill (book 1), it was all in God's perfect timing, and Hannah couldn't be happier than where she is now.

She is a proud support of the #ProtectCleanFiction movement, and strives to spread awareness alongside other like-minded authors of the psychological effects from reading explicit sensual content. Visit www.protectcleanfiction.com for more information.

To follow Hannah on her author journey and receive exclusive news and content about upcoming projects, be sure to subscribe to her free monthly email newsletter: www.hannahpenningtonauthor.com/subscribe

Instagram: @hannahpennington.author
Facebook: @hannahpennington.author
www.hannahpenningtonauthor.com